Mason's
Jar

Mason's Jar

A Novel

JOHN JANTUNEN

Published by ECW Press
665 Gerrard Street East
Toronto, Ontario, Canada M4M 1Y2
416-694-3348 / info@ecwpress.com

Cover design: Michel Vrana

This is a work of fiction. Names, characters,
places, and incidents either are the product of the
author's imagination or are used fictitiously, and
any resemblance to actual persons, living or dead,
business establishments, events, or locales is entirely
coincidental.

LIBRARY AND ARCHIVES CANADA CATALOGUING
IN PUBLICATION

Title: Mason's jar : a novel / John Jantunen.

Names: Jantunen, John, 1971- author.

Identifiers: Canadiana (print) 2023014635X |
Canadiana (ebook) 20230146376

ISBN 978-1-77041-701-4 (softcover)
ISBN 978-1-77852-117-1 (ePub)
ISBN 978-1-77852-118-8 (PDF)
ISBN 978-1-77852-119-5 (Kindle)

Classification: LCC PS8619.A6783 M37 2023 | DDC
C813/.6—dc23

This book is funded in part by the Government of Canada. *Ce livre est financé en partie par le gouvernement du Canada.*
We acknowledge the support of the Canada Council for the Arts. *Nous remercions le Conseil des arts du Canada de son
soutien.* We acknowledge the funding support of the Ontario Arts Council (OAC), an agency of the Government of
Ontario. We also acknowledge the support of the Government of Ontario through the Ontario Book Publishing Tax
Credit, and through Ontario Creates.

ONTARIO
CREATES

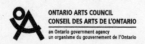

ONTARIO ARTS COUNCIL
CONSEIL DES ARTS DE L'ONTARIO
an Ontario government agency
un organisme du gouvernement de l'Ontario

Canada Council   Conseil des arts
for the Arts   du Canada

Canada

PRINTED AND BOUND IN CANADA

PRINTING: MARQUIS   5   4   3   2   1

For Ron & Dale

*To accept one's past — one's history — is not the same
thing as drowning in it;
it is learning how to use it. An invented past can never
be used;
it cracks and crumbles under the pressures of life like
clay in a season of drought.*

James Baldwin,
The Fire Next Time

They came towards the prison riding two by two under a clear blue sky. All were astride Harleys with an apple tree cast against a hazy diffusion of reds and oranges emblazoned on their fuel tanks, a standard they also wore on the backs of their black leather jackets, to a one freshly oiled and shimmering under the noonday sun. Their numbers were almost beyond reckoning, for even the guard stationed in the tower at the easternmost corner of the prison's frontside wall could not see the end of their reach and watched with muted apprehension as the gathering horde turned off Bath Road, two of their kind mounted in the middle of the oncoming lanes, stemming the flow of traffic, as heedless to the chorus of horns agitating in protest as they were to the guard now glassing them through the sight of his C7 rifle with his finger teasing on the trigger, as if he'd been told to prepare for an all-out attack.

Onward they came trailing after the six pairs of lead riders circling the lot and pulling to a stop at the foot of the prison's main building, its limestone facade and red roofed cornices and dormer windows lending it the appearance of a nation's parliament, or perhaps the country chateau of some long-ago deposed king. Of The Twelve, eleven wore a patch designating them president between their insignias and their chapter names, the list of those a veritable catalogue of the cities and towns located above the province's forty-fifth parallel, the twelfth rider alone wearing a VP patch above the demarcation North Bay. Behind The Twelve the parking lot filled with their brothers, the bikes pressing into the spaces between the prison staff's cars and trucks and joining their brethren in revving their engines, lending their voices to a thunderous din as if the Collins Bay correctional facility was a modern-day Jericho and their aim was to unleash sufficient bombast to bring its walls crumbling to the ground.

Only when the prison's main door opened and a solitary man appeared at its gate did they cease in their sonic assault, the engine rumble all at once stilled and the ensuing quiet a no less foreboding sign of enduring brotherhood. The man was a white male in his mid-forties of an average height and build and was dressed in a pair of black jeans and a plain black T-shirt and wore his head shaven, as was their custom. As he stalked past his fellow presidents he nodded to each in turn, their countenance grim and his grimmer still, devoid of even the trace of a smile to express the jubilation he surely must have felt on this, the day of his release.

Finally he came to the last man in the row. He was dressed the same as the others and bore a similar expression. The only thing which differentiated him in any way, shape or form other than his rank was the tattooed coils of a snake wrapping itself around his neck with the head of a diamondback rattler rearing on his chin, its tongue forking between the two fangs inked on either side of the cleft. The flicker of a smile did then eke its way out from the corners of the man's lips, though it was not directed at his VP, even then dismounting the bike, but at the sight of the motorcycle itself.

It was a vintage 1996 Dyna Wide Glide Classic painted ghost purple. He approached it as he would a prized steed, running a lone hand in a delicate caress over the insignia embossed on the fuel tank and then both hands seeking out the handlebars with the firm assurance of a desperado taking up the reins. He mounted the bike then and once he'd settled onto its seat his VP passed him a lit joint the size of a cigarillo. That seemed to be some sort of a cue. The motorcycles' engines all rumbled forth again, the bikes surging back to life and driving past the man, their riders offering him a deferential nod, welcoming him back into their fold. He returned the gesture with steely eyes peering out through the ever-thickening haze of weed smoke, its billow all of a sudden harried as if by a stiff breeze.

But it wasn't that.

It was a news drone now hovering a few scant feet above the departing horde. Its camera lens angled lower yet, zeroing in on the man and his VP as the latter cinched a black leather jacket over his president's arms and onto his back with the tender grace of a royal valet.

I guess you's the man of the hour there, boss, the VP offered. You got somethin' you wanna say?

His president gazing up at the drone with a dismissive frown, like that was the last thing on his mind, seeming then to reconsider. Exhaling smoke in twin streams through his nose with the patient deliberation of someone who'd been locked away these past ten years, his eyes narrowed to slits and took on the malevolent squint of a dragon about to unleash its hellfire upon some unsuspecting knight who'd dared trespass upon its domain.

Yeah, he said at last, I guess I do got somethin' I wanna say.

M otherfucker!
    Mason hadn't realized he'd spoken aloud until Hélène
was setting a bowl of chocolate pudding in his lap and chastising,
If you're going to talk like you're at the station, then you can
sleep there too.

It's what she'd always said to him when the kids were young
and he'd used a profanity, as if the schoolyard was any better than
a police station when it came to the dissemination of words such
as those. That the youngest of their children was forty-three now
made the remark seem all the more disingenuous. Had Mason
been less occupied by what he was watching on TV he might've
felt inclined to answer his wife's scowl with one of his own. As
it stood, though, he couldn't muster anything beyond a look of
seething hatred seeing the man who'd just appeared on screen,
none other than Clarence Boothe.

He was straddling a breed of motorcycle that Mason knew all
too well, having been party to the destruction of the exact same

make, model and colour some ten years previous. He himself had brought the sledgehammer that had done most of the damage and had also taken the first three swings. At the time, Clarence had been locked in the back of a cruiser in the driveway of the farm he owned outside of Bonfield — his face like it had been run through a pummelling machine and in place of his four front teeth a gaping hole oozing blood over mangled lips. All the while he watched the destruction of his prized Harley through the cruiser's window he'd worn an expression akin to the one he wore on the TV now as the camera zoomed in, his face filling the screen and revealing eyes narrowed to slits over lips curling into the vague impression of a smile, as if he was already revelling in thoughts of his revenge.

Clarence hadn't spoken but two sentences during the arrest, and not a single word over the twelve hours he'd spent hand-cuffed in the interview room back at the station, and Mason didn't expect him to say anything now. He was thus both surprised and alarmed in equal measure when the biker did speak. Through the TV's speakers, he raised his voice above the receding tide of motorcycles rumbling past in the prison's parking lot, calling out above the din:

You all are going to rue the day you ever put *me* in prison!

If there was one *you* he'd be speaking to above all others, it'd have to be the man who'd put him away. Being that man, Clarence's pronouncement felt to Mason like a pin pricking at his skin, the flesh and bones beneath all at once seeming to carry no more weight than helium so that it felt like the very air was leaking out of him.

You haven't touched your pudding!

Hélène was standing at his side, glowering down at him with the same goading reproach she might have used if one of their kids had refused to eat their greens. There was the taste of bile in Mason's mouth. To relieve himself of that more than his wife's scorn, he picked up the spoon, noticing only then that she'd given him the metal bowl she'd used to mix the pudding, rather than one of the smaller ceramic bowls into which she'd have usually doled it out before putting them in the fridge to set.

It seemed a little odd, as did the fact that the bowl was half-full, meaning she'd given him the entire batch, saving none for herself, when chocolate pudding garnished with banana slices and coconut sprinkles was one of her oft-avowed guilty pleasures. Still, he didn't give it any undue significance. She'd been acting plenty odd of late on account of the rapid onset dementia she'd been diagnosed with not four months ago, the name of which Mason could never recall, having always had difficulty remembering names, and foreign-sounding ones in particular. On her bad days it could reduce her to a babbling fool or turn her all of a sudden into a quivering statue standing at the sink in the kitchen or at the top of the porch steps, her body no longer receiving any instructions of merit from her brain, sometimes turning her violent at the drop of a hat.

Mason himself had endured his fair share of scratches, mostly on his arms as he tried to bring Hélène back under control when she was having one of her fits, but the last time she'd raked her fingernails over his face too. Today had been one of her better days, which might have spelled a certain relief except her good days, invariably, ended up spiralling into one of her worst and so they were always the hardest on Mason. The specialist to whom Dr. Ballard had referred them had made it clear that regardless of what she said or did, her sudden mood swings had nothing to do with him, and everything to do with the disease.

Moments of intense anger, the geriatrician had assured Mason, create the most vivid, and lasting, memories, and regrettably for people with your wife's condition, these tend to be the ones which resurface with the most force.

Still it was hard not to blame himself, especially for her worst night ever, five evenings past. It had begun with him coming back inside from mowing the lawn and hearing his phone ringing from where it was charging on the kitchen counter. It was their daughter, Jill, calling from Calgary and she'd dispensed with any pretence of a greeting in favour of, What the hell's going on, Dad?

Mason had feigned ignorance, answering with a forced joviality, Going on? Well, the tractor's about to give up the ghost, other than that —

Jill believing him or not and cutting him off regardless.

I just got a call from Mom. She sounded . . . upset.

Upset?

More than upset.

She was in a good mood, last time I saw her.

That much was true.

It's not her mood I'm worried about. It's —

He could then well imagine his daughter biting her bottom lip and shaking her head, her eyes all of a sudden taking on the vacant sheen of a marble. She was by nature a mousy woman and such was how she often looked when trying to steel herself against the possibility of a confrontation shortly to come.

What is it, honey? Mason prompted when her silence had stretched beyond a second breath. What'd she say that's got you so riled up?

It's not so much what she said, his daughter answered, as it was the call itself.

I — I don't follow.

She made the same call — and I mean the exact same call — ten years ago.

That's strange.

It was more than strange.

It'd help if I knew why she'd called.

15

You mean, ten years ago?

That'd be as good a place to start as any.

A pause then, Jill taking a breath.

It was nothing really.

You said she was upset. Your mother rarely gets upset over nothin'.

That much was true as well.

It was just a . . . an argument she'd had with someone at church.

At church, you say? She usually gets along with everyone at church.

He felt his voice slipping into the all-too-familiar condescension he'd have adopted when speaking to a suspected perp, knowing she was lying and trying to trip her up. For this very reason, Jill had often complained that dinners at their house more resembled interrogations than a family meal and he could tell from what she said next that his daughter was rapidly losing patience with his tone.

What does it matter what it was about? she asked, her voice harried. Will you just listen to me for a second. Taking another breath, calming herself. A couple of minutes ago mom called me upset about something that happened ten years ago, except she didn't seem to realize that it had happened ten years ago. The way she was talking . . . I mean . . . She sounded like she thought it had just happened, like, yesterday.

That is strange.

And you haven't noticed anything else strange about her lately?

She's a little more forgetful than she used to be. But then I'm hardly one to talk.

The call had ended with Jill ordering him to take Hélène to Dr. Ballard for a checkup and a vague promise that she'd come visit them over the summer. Mason had then tracked Hélène to their bedroom on the second floor. He'd found her sitting on the edge of the bed with her head lowered and her hands clasped in her lap as they so often were when Reverend Williams was preaching an especially passionate sermon. Except at church she'd have had her eyes closed too and her face would bear an expression of rapturous serenity and here she was sitting with her eyes downcast yet open, looking utterly defeated.

I can't do this anymore, she'd said as he took his first step into the room.

It was the exact same thing she'd said to him when he'd come home from work one evening ten years ago to find Hélène sitting at the kitchen table, looking similarly defeated, the very day she'd threatened to leave him for letting one of his constables get away with what she'd called *cold-blooded* murder. Could have been she'd just got off the phone with their daughter then too and that was the call Jill meant.

What are you talking about? he'd asked those ten years ago, though he'd known exactly what she was talking about.

Dawson, she'd answered, her voice trembling over the name, like she was speaking of a devil incarnate and not a man at all.

Only then had she raised her head slightly, looking up at him with imploring eyes and Mason seeing a glint of something in their glassy twinkle beyond the acrimony he expected. Maybe it was just a nascent tear refracting the overhead light but to Mason it had seemed like that something could very well have been hope, as if she really did believe he was still capable of doing the right thing. He knew there was nothing he could say to assure her that he was. That words in themselves couldn't offer anything beyond a false hope. But he did know that living without Hélène wasn't much of a life at all. He'd done what he'd had to, to keep her from leaving him. Later — when he'd faced the scorn of his entire police force for turning over to the RCMP what he'd discovered about the intimate nature of the relationship Officer Dawson had been having with the girl he'd shot while conducting a supposed wellness check — he'd only had to remember how she'd looked then to give him the strength to carry on.

F ive days ago, he'd taken that single step into their bedroom, hoping against hope for her to reward him with the same look. But when she did raise her eyes, there was nothing at all hopeful about the pointed glare she'd levelled at him.

In fact, it looked downright mean.

You should have just given me the pills, she spat at him with more venom than he'd heard from her in years. But no, you've always got to do things the hard way!

She was raising her hand from her lap and that's when Mason saw it was holding his Glock. The sudden incongruity checked his step and seemed to freeze the very blood in his veins, Mason knowing then that she wasn't having one of her fits but one of her increasingly rare bouts of clarity, just like she'd had yesterday when she'd begged him to give her the bottle of anxiety meds she'd been prescribed, so she could use them to end her suffering once and for all.

Hél—, Mason choked but before he managed to get out the rest of her name she was already placing the muzzle of the gun under her jaw with the fluid motion of a much younger woman and pulling the trigger. She'd neglected to flip off the safety so there was a breathless moment of silence instead of a *Bang!* and Mason had stormed across the room, slapping the gun out of her hands.

Goddammit Hél— he raged but again he hadn't managed to make it through her name before she was flailing off the bed, her hands clawing for his eyes, screaming, I told you I can't do this anymore! I can't! I can't! I can't! I can't!

He'd grappled her onto the bed and lain on top of her, holding her tight and coaxing, Shhh. It's okay, we'll get through this. We will, I promise. Hush now, everything is going to be all right.

She'd thrashed for a while and had managed to bite his arm but he'd never let her go. She'd fallen asleep a half-hour later, and he shortly afterwards. The next morning she seemed to have forgotten all about it, or at least was pretending she had.

His right arm still bore the evidence of her wrath — four scabbed-over gouges from his elbow to his wrist — and in the meantime he'd let his beard grow in a futile attempt to hide the matching ones on his face. He'd always been clean-shaven and after five days the new whiskers were itching him something fierce. As he spooned pudding into his mouth, watching Clarence Boothe's Harley trailing the others out of the prison's parking lot, Mason scratched absent-mindedly at his cheek, thinking that if Clarence really was plotting revenge then maybe it would have been better if he'd let Hélène shoot herself, if only to spare her any more grief.

The local news anchor had come back on the screen and was saying, That was the scene at the Collins Bay Institution in Kingston when former Bonfield resident Clarence Boothe was released six hours ago.

The *six hours ago* leapt out at him.

It was only a five-hour drive from Kingston to Bonfield and only a fifteen-minute drive from there to Mason's farm on the outskirts of Corbeil. The idea that Clarence might already be out there somewhere, seeking vengeance, had him scanning towards the living room window. It looked down their driveway and would have provided him with a clear view down the road too, as the former served as both a slight extension and also a terminus for the latter. But with the dusk closing in, all he could see through the window's glass was a pale reflection of the room itself.

We caught up with North Bay police chief Howard Brimsby moments ago at the city's annual Spring Fling Rib Fest, the news announcer was then saying. When we asked him what he thought about Clarence Boothe's apparent threat, he had this to say.

Howard then appeared on screen. He was sitting at a picnic table in Thompson Park, wiping barbecue sauce off his mouth with a napkin. He must have been off duty because he was wearing a plain blue button-down short-sleeved shirt and the only thing that marked him as a cop at all was the ball cap bearing the North Bay Police Service crest. He'd gained, best guess, fifty pounds since replacing Mason as chief ten years ago. Pearls of sweat dotted his forehead and a single bead of it was draining down the dough-white of one of his cheeks, though they now more resembled the jowls of an overfed bulldog. Probably it was just the heat making him sweat — the temperature that day had peaked at thirty-eight, including the humidex — and when he spoke his voice betrayed only minor irritation, likely the result of having his dinner interrupted by a news drone, for he'd often made his opinions clear regarding the rapid proliferation of those.

Clarence Boothe is a petty dope pusher, plain and simple, Brimsby declared. I'd put about as much stock in anything that came out of his mouth as I would in a dog turd I just scraped off the bottom of my shoe. Now if you'll excuse me, I'd like to finish my dinner in peace.

Mason shaking his head in utter disbelief over what he'd just heard.

A petty dope pusher, my ass, he growled at his former deputy chief on the television. There weren't nothing petty about his operation, and you ought to know that better than anyone, *Howard*.

Brimsby had, after all, been at Mason's side when they'd raided Clarence Boothe's farm. At the time of his arrest, even low-level street dealers could make twenty thousand dollars a week plying their wares in North Bay. Clarence was at the top of that particular food chain and Mason's suspicion that he was making ten times that was well confirmed by the shade over three million dollars they'd found secreted in three duffel bags under the floorboards in his barn, along with a cache of drugs and weapons worth an estimated two million dollars on top.

T he bust had made the national news and had earned Mason a commendation from the mayor and also a visit from Francis Montagne, an inspector with the RCMP. Ostensibly, Inspector Montagne had come to secure the release of one of his officers who, Mason would shortly learn, had infiltrated Clarence Boothe's inner circle and had subsequently been arrested along with two others at the farm. During the hour they'd spent talking in Mason's office, Montagne had also informed Mason that his, quote, "little bust" had set his own investigation back two or three years, at least. In a rare moment of candour — for Mason had never found the RCMP to be much forthcoming about anything — he'd then confided that he was heading up a national task force looking into a drug called Euphoral.

Mason had, of course, already heard of it.

It was the latest escalation in the opioid pandemic which was sweeping the planet. Mason had watched in rapt horror, along with the rest of the civilized world, the footage of the so-called

"Euphie Riots" which had originated in China. Hordes of ordinary people in withdrawal and driven by an atavistic rage to commit unspeakable acts of violence upon their families, their neighbours and even themselves. The Chinese government had been quick to blame the drug's rapid proliferation among its citizenry on a suicide cult of religious extremists whose numbers had swelled into the millions in recent years, though the general perception elsewhere was that the government itself had developed the drug in a secret lab so they could use the ensuing madness as an excuse to cull their population, then nearing the two billion mark.

Whatever its origins, the drug didn't stay confined to China for long.

Dozens of Euphie Riots had been documented over the past few years, mostly in Third World slums and refugee camps, and during his own research into the matter Mason had read a brief from a DEA agent out of the Houston office which concluded that it posed as much, or more, of a threat to global security than any of the myriad of doomsday scenarios involving climate change. Montagne's own prognostications on the subject also veered towards the apocalyptic and centred on a criminal organization he called The Sons Of Adam who, he said, were stockpiling the drug for reasons yet unknown.

Mason had never heard of them and when he told Montagne the same, the inspector had remarked, I'm not overly surprised at that. At first Mason thought it was meant as another dig regarding his proficiency as an officer of the law but then Montagne had added, They've been keeping a pretty low profile so far.

Two hundred plus of their members showing up at Collins Bay to welcome one of their presidents back into the fold on the day of his release hardly seemed low profile. Thinking about that, Mason was reminded of what Montagne had said next:

But we know they're planning something big.

When Mason had asked him what that was, Montagne had shrugged before answering, From what I know of The Sons, I doubt they'll be overly subtle about it, whatever it is.

That had signalled the end of the conversation and in the ten years since, the only thing Mason knew for certain about whatever it was they were planning — if they were planning anything at all — was that it was still a mystery, at least to him.

The local news had ended while he was ruminating on that and *The National News At Six* had come on. The announcer, a rather large-boned Black woman named Nellie Campbell who'd made her name as the former captain of the women's Olympic hockey team, was reporting that Hurricane Ezra was causing mass evacuations on the west coast and its record three-hundred-eighty-kilometre-per-hour winds were further fanning the flames of the hundred-plus fires burning out of control between San Francisco in the south and Alaska in the north. Over ten million residents had already been evacuated into makeshift refugee camps and their numbers were expected to increase exponentially over the weekend.

Mason watched surveillance camera footage of waves from a storm surge lapping against an apartment building in Vancouver's evacuated West End while running an index finger along the inside of the bowl and telling himself, *The way things are going, maybe it'd be best if you just gave her that bottle of pills like she'd asked and then eat a bullet yourself. There ain't nothing left for us here anyway.*

Further goading himself as he clicked off the TV with, *You ought to do it tonight, get it over with.* Nodding to himself as if it was a done deal, helpless then but to imagine himself sitting beside her on the bed as she fell asleep, waiting for her to rasp her last breath and her hand to go limp in his, certain that the moment she was dead he'd have no compunction about sticking his Glock in his mouth. Seeing his brains splattered in a Rorschach blot all over their bedroom wall and hearing a voice crying out, Oh Mason, what have you done?!

It might as well have been his own calling out in alarm from some distant recess, for the sudden pang he felt imagining killing his wife and then himself, knowing that he'd never be able to more than contemplate that. But it wasn't his voice, it was Hélène's, and she wasn't calling out from some distant corner of his mind but from right beside him.

Looking up and seeing her scowling down at him again.

Huh? he asked. It was all he could muster.

You're bleeding all over your shirt.

Bleeding?

From your cheek.

Mason touched a hand to the left side of his face then pulled it back, looking at the red smear over the pads of two of his fingers. He could also see blood under his middle finger's nail and knew he'd torn off part of the scab on his cheek, itching at his beard.

You must have scratched yourself, Hélène was saying, seemingly oblivious to the fact that it was she who'd scratched him first.

She must have detected a hint of reproach in his gaze for she was then pursing her lips.

Well, don't look at me, she said. I've been telling you to clip your nails for days now.

Plucking then the empty metal bowl from his lap, she peered down at the smudges of pudding his finger had missed with a misplaced sort of intensity, like a fortune teller reading the future in the dregs at the bottom of a tea cup. If she saw anything in there, she made no sign but when, a moment later, she looked back to Mason, her expression had softened. There was even the wisp of a smile curling her lips and, even more than Clarence Boothe's leering grin, that filled Mason with a creeping sense of dread, though he couldn't exactly say why.

Watching her turning back towards the kitchen, already knowing that she wasn't done with him quite yet, and waiting with a petulant sort of impatience for her to say the same thing she'd said to him practically every damned time he'd bled on his clothes these past fifty-seven years.

And she didn't disappoint this time either.

Mind you use cold water when you rinse out your shirt, she called back over her shoulder upon reaching the kitchen door, or else you'll never be able to get the blood out!

When Ron came back out of the house, after taking a leak and grabbing himself and his housemate a fresh beer each from the fridge, the announcer on the portable radio sitting on the patio's table was saying something about a tornado warning.

Is that for here? he asked, his voice shading towards alarm at the memory of how they'd barely survived the last, one of a family of eleven tornados spawned by the supercell thunderstorm which had devastated great swaths of Northern Ontario that past October.

Dale was sitting in his chair at the patio's table, thumbing on his phone. He must have still been texting with his daughter, as he had been for the past half-hour, and looked up at Ron, irritated.

Is what for here?

The tornado warning.

What tornado warning?

The one the guy on the radio was just talking about.

First I'm hearing about it.

Ron set Dale's beer on the table in front of him and cracked his own, looking up at the sky. It had been a half-hour since the sun had set behind the fringe of trees across from the twenty or so acres of overgrown field behind the three-bedroom bungalow they rented from Mason and Hélène Lowry, the elderly couple who lived in an old farmhouse right next door. The last of its light had been swallowed up by a mass of charcoal-grey clouds billowing in from the south. They were moving at a fair clip, though the air at ground level bore not even the trace of a breeze to relieve them of its sticky heat.

Seems a little early in the season for a tornado, Ron said, sitting down and taking a healthy swig from his beer before picking up his phone.

If there was a tornado warning for the area he'd have got a text from NEAT — the Nipissing Emergency Alert System. There were no new messages and he clicked on the weather app, taking another swig from his beer and draining half the can as he thumbed the Special Weather Alerts banner at the top of the screen.

Says it's only for Parry Sound and Sudbury, he informed Dale.

What?

The tornado warning.

Well that's a relief, Dale offered, still texting, as if he couldn't have cared either way.

Damned early in the season for a tornado, Ron repeated, even though he himself had often commented that they seemed to be happening earlier and earlier with every passing year. But it sure is hot enough for one.

Hard to argue with that.

They'd only been sitting there for a half-hour since they'd come home from work and both their shirts were already soaked through with sweat. As he took another sip from his can he told himself he ought to just go in and grab a cold shower, head down to the basement, watch a movie or play a few vids, anything to give himself a break from the all-consuming heat. But first he'd finish his beer and have a couple more chutes. With the latter in mind, he picked up the two-litre pop bottle from the ground beside his chair. He'd cut the bottom off of it and fed a clear plastic bread bag up through the spout, securing that with the bowl from a pipe he'd screwed into the bottle top's threads. It was a design an ex-girlfriend's teenage son had introduced him to when he was in his early thirties and in the fifteen or so years since he'd never found a more efficient way for smoking weed than what he called a "chute."

He kept his daily allotment in a prescription pill bottle. He took a pinch of the ground-up bud from it now, packing the bowl and lighting the herb, pulling the bottom of the bag slowly down, watching it fill with smoke. When it had, he unscrewed the bowl and inhaled deeply from the bottle. He held the weed in for a few seconds and then expelled it in parcelled wisps through his nose.

Trooper's "General Hand Grenade" was playing on the radio and as he packed the bowl again, he sang along with the chorus, feeling plenty high himself. He was just touching flame to bud when he caught a flash of headlights streaking through the string of six weeping willows separating their yard from the Lowrys'. At the exact same moment, a slight gust of wind arose, rustling the leaves and casting its branches aloft, making their sinew appear as a ruffled mess of hair dishevelled by a stiff breeze. Drawing the smoke into the bag, he watched the Lowrys' pickup truck speeding towards the road at a faster clip than he'd ever seen the chief drive before.

The Lowrys' driveway was a hundred feet long, about twice the size of theirs. By the time the truck had reached the end of the willows, bringing it into clear view, it was already accelerating, best guess, towards sixty kilometres per hour. He could hear its chassis rattling violently against the potholed dirt and gravel, its flatbed bucking back and forth as if the chief was having a devil of a time just keeping it on the road.

I wonder what's got into the chief, Ron said, expelling the smoke. He's driving like a donkey stung in the ass by a bee.

The clamour of its departure had alerted Dale too. He'd set aside his phone and picked up the Remington .303 he always kept propped against his chair on the odd chance that a moose or a deer might wander into range. He sighted through its scope, as he often did when Mason drove past, usually adding *Pow!* when the truck had come even with their driveway, as if he'd actually been considering taking a shot.

It ain't the chief, he said. It's Mrs. Chief.

Hélène? You sure?

Maybe she's finally come to her senses, Dale said, lowering the rifle, and left that miserable old coot once and for all.

Dale went back to texting and Ron watched after the truck until it disappeared behind the treeline.

You think we ought to tell the chief? he asked, standing to do just that.

Knock yourself out.

Just then Whisper, their husky cross, let out a whimper from the other side of the table where she'd been lying down ever since they'd let her out after coming home from work. It was accompanied by the frantic rattle of her chain. That told Ron the chain had become caught in the gaps between the boards in what they called their patio, though really it wasn't much of one, as patios go. It was more like a wooden swim raft, big enough for a small table and four chairs, which the previous owner had half-buried, probably because the ground around the back door was hard-packed dirt that turned to mud every time it rained.

A sharp pain shot through Ron's knee when he took his first step towards the dog. It was a holdover from an old baseball injury which always bothered him after standing for so long on the cement floor at Harvesters, the fur auction house where he and Dale spent eight hours a day, nine months a year, drumming a variety of pelts, mainly for export to China. He paused a moment, letting it subside and lighting a smoke before hobbling around the table. Sticking the cigarette in his mouth, he bent to Whisper's chain and gave it a hard tug to yank it loose.

Personally, he'd have preferred letting Whisper run free, but then it wasn't his dog. Point of fact, it belonged to Dale's twelve-year-old daughter, whom Dale only ever called Babygirl. When they'd first moved out to the bungalow after the tornado had wrecked their place in North Bay, she'd made her father promise to keep Whisper on the lead on account she was part husky.

Huskies will run if they're not tied up, Babygirl had said, and mostly they like to run in a straight line. Some will run for over a hundred kilometres before they stop so whatever you do, keep her tied up.

So they'd kept her on the chain even though the half-dozen or so times she'd managed to get free she'd only run as far as the neighbour's front porch before they'd caught up with her.

Freed from her captivity now, Whisper showed her appreciation by picking up her Frisbee and trailing after Ron as he limped towards the willows, begging for a throw. He'd made it about halfway there when a virulent, Goddammit! Son of a bitch!, sounded through the trees that couldn't have come from anyone but the chief himself.

He came stumbling out from beneath the willows, fighting his way through their sinewy drape like it was made of cobwebs and not branches. Whisper let out a sharp bark and a growl and the latter seemed to give the old man pause, for he stopped right where he was.

Clete, he called out. You over there?

Clete was how Ron introduced himself to Mason when they'd first met, a couple of weeks after they'd moved in. He'd quickly amended that to Clete Torres, an alias he often used tongue firmly in cheek whenever he was introduced to someone he'd rather not have met in the first place. But Mason obviously hadn't got the joke, for he'd been calling Ron Clete ever since.

They'd only had occasion to speak seven or eight times since, most often when Mason had come to fetch Hélène after she'd gone over to gift the house's previous owner a jar of homemade strawberry jam, which she'd done five times over the past six months. Each time she'd seemed confused that she'd found a rather portly, shaven-headed, middle-aged Ojibwe man answering the back door or sitting at the table beside it, and would invariably say, I'm looking for Jesse. Is he around?

Jesse was Hélène's late son. Before they'd moved out to Voyer Road, Ron and Dale had heard about him from Val, the woman who owned the boarding house on Hardy Street where Ron had stayed for a year before moving into the place on John after Dale's previous housemate had skipped out on the rent. The boarding house and their old backyard were separated only by a gravel alleyway, and while the former had miraculously been spared any real damage by the tornado, their house had been pretty near levelled along with eight of their neighbours'. It was only a few moments after Ron and Dale had forced their way out from under the wreckage that Val'd told them that one of her cousins owned an empty house, out Corbeil way. She'd said that the house had originally been built for her cousin Hélène's son and his wife. She then went on to tell a story so full of misery and woe that when she'd ended the tale by telling them her whole family was certain that the property upon which the house was built must have been cursed, Ron had felt inclined to agree.

Dale, though, had taken a more philosophical outlook.

I don't doubt it's cursed, he'd said, but then that's what happens when you steal our land.

Val had been affronted by the very idea. Never one to mince words, she'd countered, That land's been in my family for over a hundred and fifty years. Nobody stole it from anyone.

Well, my People've been on this land for over ten thousand years, he'd said, and we ain't yet ceded a damned square inch of it far as I know. So somebody must have stolen it.

Look, Val had then said, sidestepping an argument, do you want to rent the place or not?

Ron had his misgivings, mostly on account that it was so far out of town, but Dale hadn't had any.

I've been thinking of moving back to the country anyway, he'd said. Nice to be able to hunt right out the back door. And maybe having a couple of Ojibwe living there again will break the curse once and for all. Sure as hell beats living in the camps anyway.

There was no denying that.

Anything was better than living in one of the so-called "Transitional Housing Centres" the province had built after the Northern Ontario Repopulation Act had given southern municipalities sweeping powers to round up the ever-increasing masses of poor and destitute for immediate transport north. North Bay's motto had long been "Gateway to the North," so it was only natural that they'd built the first of these "temporary" facilities there. That had been five years ago and in the meantime its razor-wire fencing and armed guards had lent it more the appearance of a concentration camp than anyone's reasonable definition of housing.

With rentals all but non-existent in the city ever since they'd passed NORA, Ron had finally conceded, I guess it couldn't hurt to give it a try.

What Val had neglected to mention was that North Bay's former chief of police would be their landlord and also lived next door with his wife, their only neighbours within a kilometre. Val had arranged for them to pay rent through a direct deposit account at the bank and they wouldn't meet either Mason Lowry or his wife until three weeks after moving in, the first time Hélène had come over to give her dead son a jar of jam.

While Ron could tell right away something was off about her, she was friendly enough, and when she'd realized her error she had been more than happy to offer them the jam instead. She'd then sat awhile and told them a fair approximation of the story they'd already heard from Val before Mason tracked Hélène down.

He'd been gruff to the point of being rude. He hadn't said a word to Ron or Dale, hadn't even had the common courtesy to look either of them in the eye. After the old man had practically dragged Hélène out of her chair and back through the willow trees, Dale had asked, Do you know who that was?

Well whoever it is, Ron had answered, he sure as hell wasn't being very neighbourly.

What do you expect from the damned chief of police.

He's the chief of police?

Was. He's the ex-chief now, I guess. He retired, oh, ten years ago. Adding then: Went a little batshit there towards the end, way I heard it.

Every time thereafter when Mason came to fetch his wife, Ron would greet him with a jovial, Hey Chief. He'd then hold up his resin-stained pop bottle and add, Chute? just to see the crumpled frown appear on the ex-police chief's face.

As the chief approached them now through the willows, Ron greeted him with the same, but Mason obviously had other worries on his mind. In place of a frown he was wearing a smile, though a decidedly pinched one. He was also holding his pants up with one hand and his zipper was open and his belt was hanging loose. Could have been he was on the toilet when he'd heard his truck tearing down the driveway and hadn't found a moment to do them up.

I, er —, he said, as if he'd forgotten what had brought him over, or needed a favour and couldn't quite bring himself to ask for one from someone like Ron.

What's on your mind there, Chief? Ron asked.

I, uh — I need to borrow your car.

You'll have to talk to Dale about that, Ron answered, since it was Dale's car even though Ron was usually the one behind the wheel.

Where's he at?

Ron glanced back at the table but Dale was gone.

He was just here a second ago. He must have gone inside.

It made sense. If Dale was sitting on their patio when the chief came over he'd invariably retreat into the house on account, or so he said, of the rough treatment Mason, then Deputy Chief Lowry, had visited upon him after he'd pulled him over for supposedly making an illegal U-turn, some twenty years previous.

Well can you go ask him? Mason asked, the desperation clearly wrought on his face.

I could, Ron answered. Doubt it'd do much good, though. Dale's real particular about who he lets drive his car.

That was true and Ron laid even odds that he'd lend it to someone who'd once knelt on his neck after zip-tying his hands behind his back on some dark and lonely stretch of highway as he would that one day Dale might actually pull the trigger while he sighted his rifle on the same man driving past in his truck.

He didn't have more than a moment to consider that, though. The back door was even then swinging open. Dale came out twirling his key chain lackadaisically around the index finger on his right hand. He'd taken a moment to tie his long black hair back into a ponytail and had also exchanged his T-shirt for another, one of Ron's point of fact, which he'd fished out of the basket of clean laundry sitting on the kitchen table. It had on it a picture of Geronimo above the caption *All Lives Matter*, and if there was any doubt in Ron's mind about why he'd chosen that particular shirt, it was quickly dispelled by the mischievous grin curling out from beneath the greying bush of Dale's moustache.

Well, what are you all waitin' on? Dale said, walking between the two men, all casual, as if there was nothing he'd have liked better than to do his neighbour a good turn.

Best go fetch the old gal before she gets herself into trouble.

Ron and Dale called the half-kilometre stretch of potholed gravel at the end of which they lived a "road," though it didn't have a name on any map and was really more of a pioneer trail.

On one of her visits Hélène had told Ron that her great-great-great-grandfather had carved it out of the bush some one hundred and fifty years earlier. He'd built the first barn out of wood felled in its trespass and spent a good many years after that burning out the stumps and bolstering the low-lying areas with fill. He'd then laid down slats of wood oiled with creosote and dug ditches on either side as a buffer against the melt which every spring would turn the trail into a tributary of the creek traversing the property from north to south, making it all but impassable for a month or two after the original settlers had exchanged their horse-drawn sleds for wagons.

The municipality had deemed it "private." They refused to either plow or grade it and after the winter its surface had come to resemble corrugated tin. For that reason and because he never drove faster than ten klicks over the speed limit — rarely in fact drove at all since he'd lost his licence for the second time fifteen years ago and had never bothered trying to get it back — Dale usually took it real easy, not wanting to put any undue strain on his antiquated black VW Jetta. But on this night he'd come out of their driveway like a racehorse out of the gate, his haste not so much because he was trying to catch up with Hélène as because of who was sitting in the back seat.

The seat belts' buckles had long since disappeared between the cushions. Dale hadn't given the chief a moment to fish them out before he'd hit the gas, swerving out of their driveway and onto the longer one they shared with the Lowrys, causing him to grab at the hand loop strung over the driver's side door and exclaim, Whoa now, take it easy there! I ain't in that much of a hurry!

Whisper was in the back seat with him. Dale had brought her along because of how excited she always got when going for a car ride, bouncing around in her fevered happy-dance, more like an overgrown squirrel than a dog. Having someone in the back seat with her only increased her zeal. She was spinning around and around in tight spiralling loops, barking up a storm. The dog's tail lashed against the chief's face with every pass and Dale watched with unbridled amuse through the rear-view mirror, trying not to snicker too hard as he coaxed, Settle down there, Whisper, you're liable to take out one of his eyes!

Ron, in the front passenger seat, had wised to Dale's game. He was playing along by packing the bowl in the pop bottle in his lap with weed then lighting it and drawing the smoke down into the bag.

Chute there, Chief? he asked, offering the bottle to Mason and the old man staring past him with grim set eyes. Not to be deterred, Ron pressed, Go on, Chief, have a chute. This here's the good stuff.

The chief ignored him still and Ron held the bottle out to Dale. Chute?

Don't mind if I do, Dale replied, though truth be told he'd have much preferred taking a hit off the vape pen clipped to the collar of his T-shirt. He sucked back the smoke and blew it into the car, the heady musk of its haze quickly filling up its interior as Ron packed another bowl.

You sure you don't want a chute there, Chief? he asked, lighting the fresh herb.

But the chief was then too busy trying to open his window to pay any attention to such foolishness. When pressing the button on the armrest didn't work, he asked, Would you mind rolling down the window?

His frustration was clearly reaching the boiling point but he was trying his best to be all polite about it, as if appealing to Dale's better nature would have got him anywhere.

Windows in the back are broken, Dale lied, having just clicked on the window locks.

Then would you mind rolling down the ones in the front?

Windows in the front are broke too.

The chief opened his mouth, maybe to protest, but they'd come to the end of the driveway. Dale was spinning the wheel with the casual grace of a NASCAR driver, pitching the Jetta a hard left, its tires skidding across the two lanes of asphalt as it came onto Voyer Road. For a split second it seemed like it'd swerve right into the far ditch. The car's back end fishtailed in a flurry of gravel and its tires raked against the shoulder before finding their groove and pushing the Jetta back onto the road.

Voyer would lead them on a straight shot to Corbeil, the closest town, though it really wasn't much of that — just a gas station, a golf and country club, a Foodland grocery store, an LCBO and a community centre. From there it was a five-minute drive north to

Highway 17 and then ten minutes west to North Bay, the direction in which the GPS tracker on the chief's phone had informed him his truck was headed. There were only three houses along the two-kilometre stretch and Dale used that as an excuse to pick up some real speed. The speedometer was passing a hundred in defiance of the 60 KM/H sign just then flashing by and Dale had exchanged both hands on the wheel for one outstretched arm rested on top, like he was out for a leisurely country drive even as he pushed the car faster yet.

Oh god! the chief groaned from the back seat.

It sounded to Ron like he was having a heart attack but when he turned around the chief wasn't clutching his chest as he most surely would have if it had been that. He was holding his breath, though. His expression was pained and there was a trace of fear in his eyes so on second thought it did kind of look to Ron like maybe he was having a heart attack after all.

What's the matter, Chief? he asked.

I need you to pull over, he choked out.

Don't you worry there, Chief, Dale answered, thinking it was the rough ride that had alarmed him so. We'll get you there in one piece. You just sit back and relax.

I need you to pull over, he repeated. Goddammit, *pullthefuckovernow!*

His voice was veering towards all-out panic and Dale finally relented.

You're the chief, he said and jammed on the brakes hard enough that he felt the chief's head *Thwack!* against the back of his seat.

The car hadn't even reached a full stop before the old man was throwing open his door. He stumbled out onto the road with his fingers tearing at his belt buckle and yanking down his pants as he disappeared into the dark enshrouding everything beyond the headlights except a spot of yellow winking through the trees from the light over the door of their closest neighbour's barn.

Whisper slipped out after him and Dale cursed, Shit!, throwing open his own door and pulling himself out, calling, Whisper! Get back here! Whisper!

A sound like a water balloon farting wet air through its lip halted him in his pursuit. Ron had stepped out of the passenger seat. He was lighting a cigarette as he peered over at Whisper standing on the side of the road, pounding her paws on the asphalt and barking, trying to entice them into a game of catch-me-if-you-can. Beyond her, another, less definite figure: the chief squatting in the ditch.

Another wet fart then, this one longer than the last and punctuated by the chief groaning, Oh god, Jesus, Mary!

You okay there, Chief?

This from Ron, his voice tentative, like he didn't really expect, or even want, an answer but getting one nonetheless.

Son of a bitch, the chief cursed. She dosed my damned pudding!

What's that you say? Ron asked, unsure if he'd heard him right.

I said she dosed my goddamned pudding.

Dosed your pudding? With what?

Dulcolax, I'd guess. Must have used half the damned bottle.

What's Dulcolax? Ron asked.

It's a laxative. This from Dale, who quickly added: A powerful one too. My mom gave me a teaspoon of it one time. I was shitting non-stop for three days. And you say she dosed you with a half-bottle?

Sure feels like it.

Well then you're in for a rough ride.

The upward lilt to his voice made it sound like nothing could have pleased him more.

Why would Hélène dose your pudding with laxative? Ron asked, as if the answer wasn't already obvious.

I'm guess'n, the chief replied, it was so she could steal my truck.

Another wet fart, this one coming in undulating waves and the old man moaning like he was shitting out his guts.

There something we can do for you there chief? Ron asked when the moaning had subsided, his voice this time tempered with genuine concern.

Not unless you got a roll of toilet paper handy.

That sent Ron scurrying back to the car. Activating the torch on his phone, he scoured over the front passenger's side floor. Finding nothing of worth there except a dirty sock with a hole in it, he turned the light on the back.

I got some napkins, he said a moment later, holding up a stack of five or six he'd fished from the Tim Hortons takeout bag he'd found crumpled under the seat. He was stalking around the front of the car, stopping when he'd come into its headlights, reluctant to move beyond their glow.

Another fart, this one sounding like a flag flapping against a gale-force wind.

Give me a minute there, will ya, the chief called back. I'm a ways from being done just yet.

It had all seemed so clear in Hélène's mind only a moment ago. Now, though, as she approached the end of Highway 17, she couldn't recall why it had been so urgent that she drive into North Bay at all. The pickup truck was passing under the first of the street lights which announced the turnoff onto Highway 11 and its glow flashed over the yellow stick-it note she'd pasted to the steering wheel. The notes had been Dr. Ballard's idea so that when she got it in mind to do something, she could write her plan out in stages, and if she forgot what she was doing halfway through, she'd have it handy as a reminder.

All she could read of what she'd written in the fleeting illumination was *Dulcolax* and below that *553 Hardy Street*, both written with a permanent black marker in her arthritic scrawl. That didn't speak to her much beyond the vague memory of dosing her husband's pudding with the former and punching the latter into the truck's GPS before she'd set off. The woman's voice chiming through the speakers had been a constant companion throughout the drive and now with the street light dimming behind her it chimed again.

Turn north onto Highway 11 in five hundred metres, it said and she signalled right.

As the off-ramp drew nigh she could see a host of flashing red-and-white lights ahead from three firetrucks racing down the highway's oncoming lane, heading south. These were shortly followed by the blue-and-reds of two ambulances, Hélène watching them pass as she slowed onto the off-ramp and thinking, *There must have been an accident on the 11. And a real doozy too, from the looks of it.*

For most of her adult life she'd been an emergency room nurse at the North Bay Regional Health Centre and had lost count of the number of times she'd been called in early for a shift, or on her day off, after a pile-up on the 11 or the 17 or the 63 had flooded the ER with casualties. Though it had been fifteen years since she'd worked there, the flashing lights had planted the idea in her head that maybe she'd been called in again.

But why then the stick-it note?

She couldn't answer that and as she merged onto the 11 heading north, three police cruisers went screaming past in the southbound lanes. Those only reinforced the notion that she was heading for the hospital to lend a hand. Except that the health centre was another five kilometres down the highway and, as the truck approached the first set of traffic lights on the outskirts of the city, the GPS woman chimed, Turn left on Seymour Street in three hundred metres.

Such confidence in its tone that Hélène was helpless but to activate the turn signal, check the rear-view mirror and, finding the road clear, ease into the left-hand lane. The street lights here provided plenty of light for her to read the rest of the note, if she'd felt so inclined. But the advanced turn signal had just appeared on the intersection's traffic light and she was too busy

43

accelerating after the other vehicle turning left onto Seymour to sneak so much as a peek at that.

Turn right on Franklin, the GPS told her before she'd made it halfway through the intersection, and she activated the corresponding signal.

The car in front of her was a red compact with the familiar bubble on its roof demarcating it as the self-driving variety, the rapid proliferation of which she'd often railed against, accusing their owners of being one step removed from robots themselves. It was turning onto Franklin too. A half-block later it slowed to join the line snaking out of the Tim Hortons drive-thru. She'd often stopped there on her way to work and was even then thinking of how a cup of tea and an apple fritter sure would hit the spot right now. But the lineup was eight or nine cars long — meaning it'd be a five- or ten-minute wait — and the GPS was advising, Turn right at Laurier Avenue in three hundred metres.

She swerved into the oncoming lane to avoid the red compact's rear end jutting into the road, telling herself, *Maybe I'll pick something up on my way back.*

Something about that thought gave her reason to pause and her eyes again trailed down to the address stuck to the steering wheel, seeking some sort of clue as to why exactly she might be driving there. The street light she was passing under winked off at that exact moment, casting the interior of the vehicle into utter black. Peering up through the windshield, she saw it was all dark out there too except for the truck's headlights and the tail lights of a car disappearing around the bend where Franklin curved towards Laurier.

It had been years since she'd driven down Franklin, the route she'd have taken if she was going to the Serenity Hospice on John Street. It was where she'd spent her last five years as an RN, the relentless onslaught of often violent junkies and mental cases in crisis that made up the bulk of her patients in the ER finally becoming too much for her to handle in her advancing years. After she'd retired, she'd taken to volunteering at the hospice as well, spending hours reading to the terminally ill or, if they were too far gone for that, merely sitting with them so they wouldn't be alone in their dying moments. As she drove past the rows of darkened houses on either side of the street she'd begun to think maybe that's where she was headed now, though it had been years since she'd volunteered there.

Why else would she be driving down Franklin?

For as long as she could remember it was the main thoroughfare into the seediest of the city's neighbourhoods. A few of the nicer houses were two-storey brick with bars over their windows and *This House Protected by ADT Security* stickers pasted prominently on front doors beside signs warning, *Beware of Dog*. But these were in the minority. Most of the others were shabby bungalows, their windows as likely to be festering with cracked glass as they were to be boarded up altogether. Their lawns were overwhelmed by weeds and timothy grass gone to seed and their residents — as many as ten or fifteen cramped into a single house — were no better off. If the stories she'd heard from a fellow nurse at the hospice were true, they mainly spent their days scavenging the richer neighbourhoods to the north, south, east and west, pillaging anything that wasn't tied down, and their nights blissed out on their couches or on the floor, too doped up to care even if one of their housemates had accidentally, or on purpose, set the house on fire.

And there had been plenty of houses that had burned down with ten or fifteen people inside while she'd been working in Emerg. Their charred remains had filled the morgue with such regularity that the hospital had purchased a refrigerator truck to house the overflow, though more often than not it was already filled to capacity with the bodies of those who had overdosed, a tender sort of mercy, perhaps, compared to being burned alive.

Driving down Franklin on her way to Serenity, she'd often thought that the cancer infecting the neighbourhood was even then spreading its blight and it'd only be a matter of time before the whole city became one vast and malignant tumour. So it seemed strange to her now, as she came around the bend, that the houses on either side of the street had all been rejuvenated with new metal or wood siding and trimmed with immaculately cut lawns and lavish flower gardens and had two and three vehicles in every driveway or parked on the road to make room for extravagant camper trailers or motor homes.

People were emerging en masse from front doors. Those coming from the unlit houses were guiding their way with the torches on upraised phones and several were carrying young children or babies. One such woman, cradling an infant, was crossing twenty or so paces ahead of her and Hélène lifted her foot from the gas, slowing the truck and letting her pass. She was heading for the house directly across the street and there was another woman stepping out of the front door of it. She was also carrying a baby, though hers was strapped into one of those carriers that snapped into an infant's car seat. The first woman called out something to the other which Hélène couldn't hear and the other responded by calling back something equally unclear.

Could have merely been two neighbours commiserating about yet another power outage, a far from infrequent occurrence these days, what with all the bad weather they'd been having. Except that when the truck had pulled even with the second woman's front yard, Hélène could clearly see she wore a strained expression. Or rather, not so much strained as it was plainly terrified.

Must be on account of the tornado, Hélène thought, for hadn't she heard the weather man say something about a tornado warning when she was watching the news with Mason only a few moments ago?

If there was a tornado heading their way it'd make sense that a woman with a baby would be scared, especially since the one that had torn through North Bay last fall had killed a baby no older than the ones the women were carrying now. But it made a little less sense that the second baby's father would then be hurrying out of his house carrying a military-style assault rifle and wearing what appeared to be one of those high-tech tactical helmets Mason was so enamored with. The man was dressed in a uniform that also called to mind the outfit Mason had worn every year during the force's annual tactical training exercises except the black Kevlar vest Mason wore had *POLICE* stencilled on its front and back in bold white letters while the man's read *SECURITY*.

He was shouting something at his wife, sounded to Hélène like, Get in the truck goddammit, like I toldya!

Not waiting for his wife to answer, he grabbed her by the arm, dragging her and the baby towards the Chevy Blazer parked in their driveway, the scene then relegated to the rear-view mirror as Hélène drove past.

She was nearing the end of the block.

Franklin dead-ended at Laurier, a short street that ran between Fisher Street and the ninety-seven hectares of preserved wetlands and forest that made up the Laurier Woods Conservation Area. The GPS was advising her to turn right in twenty metres but it had nothing at all to say about how she might do that with the hulking figure of a man appearing at the far reaches of her headlights, standing in the middle of the intersection, blocking her way. If she'd have had to wager a guess, he'd have been six-foot-six and pushing three hundred and fifty pounds. He was bald-headed and clean-shaven and naked except for a pair of orange swim shorts that were all but invisible under the flap of skin hanging loose from his belly. His whole body, minus his head, was covered with a thick fur of dark hair and he appeared to be doing an impression of a professional wrestler, stooped over and clenching his hands at his sides like he was showing off his muscles. He was bellowing like a moose on the rut and every one of the people milling about their front yards was standing as stiff as a statue, watching him. Hélène slowed the truck as she approached, edging it towards the curb to give him plenty of room and thinking, *Maybe the neighbourhood hasn't changed that much after all.*

The man was only ten metres away when he went all of a sudden rigid, his body shocked upright the same as the dozen or so unruly patients in the ER whom she'd seen a security guard, or a constable, zap with a taser. His hands were quivering at his sides and his belly was flouncing in rippling waves. A bloody froth was bubbling at his mouth and streaming down his chin as if he'd just bit his tongue clean off.

The sight of the man convulsing and the bloody froth at his mouth spurred a sudden memory of something she'd seen once before, the recollection coming back to her in fragments and her trying to piece them together into something halfway coherent. A drone video of a massacre in China. Something Mason had shown her, years ago. A bit of research he'd been conducting on his own time. She couldn't remember exactly what it was about, couldn't really remember anything about it at all except one image seared into her brain as if with a red-hot cattle brand, infecting her dreams and startling her awake every night for two weeks after she'd seen it.

A teenage girl in the clip, she mustn't have been older than fifteen, was standing in the middle of a four-lane street, could have been in downtown Hong Kong or Beijing. There was smoke everywhere, from fires or tear gas, Hélène couldn't say. And there were bodies all around the girl, a cemetery's worth of them sprawled, interlocking and maze-like, over the entire four lanes, their span concealed by the mist wafting around the girl. It had seemed to Hélène at the time that they might conceivably stretch for miles. The girl was staring straight up at the drone's camera, hovering maybe five feet above her. She had a broken shard of glass in her hand about the breadth of a paring knife and was using its point to carve a jagged line across her forehead. Blood was draining in drips over her almond eyes and her button nose, over her ruby lips, slightly ajar, her mouth and chin also plastered with it like she was some sort of undead fiend who'd just finished making a meal out of one of the bodies.

But what Hélène remembered most about her was the look of startled bewilderment on the girl's face, like she herself couldn't quite believe she was carving a line across her forehead with a shard of glass, her hand then slashing downwards over her cheek, as if her intention was to cut her face off.

Repulsed at once by the sight and yet unable to tear her eyes away from the expression on the girl's face.

See that blood around her mouth? Mason had asked, pointing to the Chinese girl on his laptop's screen. In the early stages of withdrawal Euphies will often self-harm. Sometimes they'll even bite off their own tongues.

He'd spoken with the casual assurance of an amateur entomologist talking about his prized ant farm. That had repulsed Hélène almost as much as the sight of the fiend the girl had become and she'd fled outside, fuming, How could he be so damned callous!

Jarred then from the relentless fret of her reminiscence by the truck's front tire shimmying against the right side curb and seeing, through the driver's side window, the fat man passing by. He was shaking so hard it seemed like his flesh was about to be flung in rippling chunks right off his skeleton. His mouth was a welter of blood, bubbling over his chin, and that brought her right back to where she'd begun.

Sometimes they'll even bite off their own tongues.

Fumbling to recall what Mason had been talking about, and that about as fruitful as fumbling after a nickel grasping at the last flicks of light as it sunk, twinkling, into the increasingly dark depths of some lake.

The GPS woman was saying, Turn left on Maher Street in twenty metres.

The calm and measured direction pierced the apprehension she felt at seeing the fat man in the throes of such a violent seizure and again she was powerless but to activate her signal.

Hearing then a stifled *Pop! Pop! Pop!Pop!Pop!* from behind her and glancing into the rear-view mirror as she turned. The fat man was pitching backwards onto the asphalt, five holes in his chest and his belly blossoming red. He struck the ground with such force that he might as well have been a balloon filled with blood for the spatter of it erupting from the holes torn through his skin.

A horn blaring then, even more alarming.

Turning back to the windshield and seeing a set of headlights veering away from a collision course. Jerking her own steering wheel as it swerved onto the sidewalk, she brought herself back into her lane, breathing hard and her hands shaking on the wheel, all thoughts of where she might be going and why now subsumed by another, equally dire.

That man's been shot!

There was a person running towards her on Maher. When she came into range of the truck's headlights, Hélène could see it was a police constable — a young Black woman with the braided weave of a ponytail trailing out from beneath her cap. Her right hand was lowered at her side, clenching her sidearm, and the other was raised to her collar, apparently activating her radio. She was speaking into that as Hélène stopped the truck, pressing a button on her armrest, scrolling down the passenger side window.

Excuse me officer, she called to the woman as she approached, I think someone's been shot!

The woman didn't slow down or even glance her way and, as she passed by, Hélène could hear a man's voice calling out through the officer's radio, Stay safe!

The roar of an engine and the squeal of tires turned Hélène towards the rear window, watching as the Chevy Blazer raced past along Laurier heading for Fisher. The GPS was chiming, You are two hundred metres from Five-Five-Three Hardy Street. Parking has been detected on Maher Street ten metres from your destination and on Hardy Street five metres from your destination.

Turning back towards the front, she peered through the windshield, seeking any sign of where she might be going, and was blinded by the headlights of a car speeding her way. Squinting and waiting for it to pass and applying the gas again, driving forward, hearing another sharp succession of *Pop!*s sounding just like firecrackers, though it could just as well have been gunfire too. She couldn't tell where they were coming from but it must have been Hardy, since everyone in the groups of people lining either side of the road were looking that way. Passing them by, she heard two more *Pop!*s, louder than the others. Those caused ripples to shudder throughout the clusters, breaking them apart, a few people fleeing back into their houses but most towards their vehicles.

A green minivan was backing, heedless, out of the last driveway on the block. Hélène slammed on the brakes to avoid T-boning it as it veered into the left lane. Laying then into her horn, to express her sudden fright, she muttered, It's like the whole city's gone crazy!

The words were barely out of her mouth when a black SUV came careening around the corner, tires squealing. The green minivan was already surging forward but hardly fast enough for the SUV. It smashed into the back of the van with a horrific crunch of buckling steel and shattering fibreglass. The sudden *Poof!* of the van's airbags filled its windshield as the vehicle was catapulted forward, its rear crumpled, accordion-like, and its front end thrust across Hélène's lane not two feet in front of the truck's bumper. Hélène gasping in horror as the minivan slammed into the metal post elevating a darkened streetlamp. The airbag had already deflated by then and two blotches of red flowered over the inside of the windshield's spiderweb of cracked glass from the driver's and passenger's heads slamming into it.

Stunned out of all recourse to words, or even thought. Gaping in mortal dread and her world suddenly consumed by a light so glaring it seemed that she must have died in the crash too and the sudden bright was the Holy Father Himself calling her home. But the bright wasn't heaven-sent, it was from the SUV's one remaining headlight.

The SUV had recovered from the crash and was accelerating towards her in the left-hand lane. It had two curved bars extended vertically over its front bumper and she recognized those as being what Mason called "bull bars," for every one of North Bay's police vehicles were equipped with the same. So it must have been a police cruiser — of the "ghost" variety since it had no markings. But why it would be fleeing the scene of an accident — one that it had caused no less — wasn't so clear.

Hélène watched it race by before she turned back to the van, seeing the two blotches leaking blood down its windshield again. The sight was now compelling her with the same urgency she'd felt every time the paramedics had wheeled someone into the

ER, and that was enough to get her hand fumbling for the latch on the door. Pulling it in and pushing the door out, she eased her feet onto the pavement. Hearing the wail of sirens, like they were breeding out there in the dark, and feeling the stubble of rocks pressing into the soles of her feet. Looking down, she saw she was wearing only her slippers.

Oh my, she thought, alarmed even more than she was by the crash, *you can't go into town wearing your slippers!*

A sudden and incongruous exclamation, given that she was already in town and had spent the last fifteen minutes driving there, and one that only furthered her confusion. Looking up and peering into the dark, expecting to see her own house, for hadn't she just come out of it? Why else would she still be wearing her slippers? So certain was she that she had and yet the house across from her was a one-storey bungalow with white siding, as far removed from her own two-storey brick as the asphalt beneath her feet was from her gravel driveway.

She couldn't explain that and didn't have more than a moment to ponder on it anyway before a voice penetrated her daze, yelling out:

You cunt! You fuck!

Looking up, she saw a man walking up Maher, not more than twenty paces hence. He was wearing a neon-green windbreaker over a bare chest and carving a gash from his left breast to his navel with the claw end of a hammer as he lurched forward, every step taken like he had Jell-O in his knees in place of cartilage. Advancing in his raggedy wobble, blood gushing from his wound and draining down his belly, his jeans like they'd been dipped in it. Onward he came spewing his bile.

You cuntfuckingbitch!

Hélène cowering behind the truck's door, keeping it between them. But it wasn't she whom he was addressing, it was the cop.

She was now standing ten feet behind Hélène. Her sidearm was gripped in both outstretched hands. She was breathing in convulsive gasps as she sighted on the man, and the man seeming to take that as some form of challenge.

He was raging, Skullfucking time, you bitchfuckingcunt!, and pawing his foot at the ground, like a bull about to go into a full-on charge. Raising the hammer then over his head, he took that one step too many.

Bang!Bang! then: *Bang!*

The first two shots hit on either side of his chest and the last above his left eye, Hélène gasping as she watched the man collapse and a voice then calling out to her, Ma'am, you need to get inside!

Hélène too dazed to do anything but stare at the man lying dead not five feet away. A hand was touching her shoulder and she jerked around.

Ma'am, you need to get off the street! the policewoman yelled.

Hélène gaping back at her with quivering lip.

Do you live around here, ma'am?

The officer gave her shoulder a shake, as if Hélène had fallen asleep and she was trying to wake her up.

Ma'am, where do you live?

Scanning past the cop, Hélène searched for a familiar two-storey red brick farmhouse amongst the bungalows lining the street and was further befuddled by its absence.

Ma'am! We need to get you home. Where do you live?

I . . . Hélène started but the answer wasn't there.

Ma'am. Where. Do. You. Live!

Hélène conjured in her mind the old farmhouse and the barn and the windmill and that did her absolutely no good either but the desperate plea in the policewoman's voice, and more so in her eyes, was demanding she say at least something.

You know . . . she started again before faltering. To be honest . . . I . . . I . . . I'm really not quite sure.

W hat in the hell's going on? Ron asked.

      Fucked if I know, Dale replied, stepping out of the Jetta's driver's side door.

They'd pulled over at the McKeown quick-charge e-fueling station at the corner of Seymour Street and Franklin so the chief could make another pit stop. The power had gone out as far as the eye could see and two police cruisers were blocking Highway 11's southbound lanes just past the now-darkened traffic lights. A few seconds after Mason had scurried into the gas station's store one of them had pulled onto the shoulder to let a convoy of military vehicles through. They resembled tanks on wheels and each had a soldier standing in the turret, manning what must have been fifty-calibre machine guns. The last two were turning off onto Seymour Street.

Lighting a cigarette, Dale blew smoke in a dismissive billow as he watched the first tank-on-wheels swerve onto Franklin and accelerate past the line of cars waiting to get into the Tim Hortons drive-thru.

The second, meanwhile, continued straight. On this side of the highway, Seymour Street was only a block long and home to a couple of car dealerships, a city maintenance yard housing a ten-storey pyramid of road sand and the Holiday Inn, before dead-ending just this side of the Laurier Woods' northernmost boundary. The tank-on-wheels slowed as it approached the Chrysler lot and rolled to a stop altogether before it had reached the entrance to the city yard, the soldier in the turret pivoting with the machine gun, lining its sight on the dark expanse of woods beyond the Holiday Inn.

Well, something's going on, Ron said, lighting his own smoke.

Probably just another training exercise, Dale offered.

They'd both lived in town long enough to have grown used to seeing convoys of military personnel from the army base up by the airport snaking through the streets and others setting up blockades, cordoning off entire neighbourhoods and using the whole damned city, it sometimes seemed, as their own personal training ground.

It's always a training exercise, Dale added.

Well, they got to be training for something, don't they?

I told you what they's training for, Dale said, for he often had.

A cousin of his, Mike, had been in the infantry. He'd resigned his commission after four years, he'd never said why, though Dale was convinced he'd seen, or heard, something that had spooked him. Mike had since taken to living at his hunt camp outside of Kiosk, just north of Algonquin Park, eating only what he could catch, kill or grow and even spending his winters there. The last time Dale had gone to hunt moose with him, he'd asked Mike about the training exercises.

Hell's if I know, he'd answered, they don't tell infantry shit, and they tell privates even less.

But if you'd have to wager a guess? Dale had coaxed.

Then I guess I'd have to say they're training for The End.

The end of what?

The End period, full stop. As far as I can tell, it'll be coming along any day now.

When Dale had told Ron that story, Ron's first thought was that if he really was talking about The End, then an exclamation mark might have served him better than a period. In truth though, he'd thought Mike was just having Dale on. But he wasn't so sure now. He could hear a chorus of sirens and these were punctuated by a series of distant *Pop!*s. Those might just have been someone setting off a string of firecrackers except that they were immediately followed by a *rat-a-tat-tat* which couldn't have come from anything but an automatic weapon.

You can't park here!

The convenience store attendant was standing at the open door. He was a dark-skinned young man, probably Pakistani, for it was well known that a family from Pakistan owned all of the McKeown quick-charge stations in North Bay. He was wearing a blue medical mask, though those hadn't been mandatory for some years now, and glaring at them with pointed eyes, bristling at how Dale had pulled to a stop horizontally across three vertical spaces, including half of one reserved for the handicapped.

The man's proclamation had roused Whisper in the back seat. She was barking and snarling through the window glass as Ron answered back, We's on important police business!

He couldn't see the young man's mouth and so only had the narrow squint to his eyes to tell him what the attendant thought of that.

You still can't park here, he said.

Best take it up with the chief. He told us to wait right here. Then, seeing that did nothing to soften the young man's pointed glare: Well, ask him yourself, you don't believe me. You'll find him in your shitter.

The *Pop!s* and the *rat-a-tat-tats* were increasing in tenor and frequency and they were now accompanied by a less definitive pounding, a noise like a distant jackhammer pulverizing granite. Hearing that, the attendant ducked back into the store and Ron and Dale turned towards the fifty-calibre gun mounted in the turret of the tank-on-wheels a half-block down Seymour Street, studying its dormant machine gun with the idle curiosity of two kids poking at a rattlesnake run over by a car, trying to assess whether it might yet pose them any threat.

I-I-, Ron said, for he often stuttered when he was nervous. I think we ought to b-b-b . . . we ought to be heading home.

Dale, though, still didn't seem overly concerned and was just then retrieving the old Enfield rifle he always kept in his trunk, on the odd chance they might spot a deer or a moose on their drive back from town.

I was about thinking the same thing, he said, pulling the rifle's bolt handle, chambering a round. Well, what are you waiting for? Go fetch the chief.

Scurrying towards the store's door, Ron threw it open and bustled inside. As the door closed, Dale could plainly hear the attendant yelling, Hey, you can't smoke in here!

Ron must have paid that as much mind as he had the earlier warning. When he came back out thirty seconds later he was taking one last drag off his cigarette before pitching it into the dark.

Chief will be right out, Ron said, breathing hard and his face and shirt covered with such a profusion of sweat that it looked like he'd just gone swimming with his clothes on.

He damned well better be, Dale warned.

He was sighting down the Holiday Inn's parking lot through his rifle's night vision scope and Ron followed its declination towards the same. The lot had maybe a dozen vehicles in it. Most of their owners were likely staying there on government business since it was the closest hotel to The Pass, what everyone called the Passmore Transitional Housing Centre, named after the lake beside which it had been built two kilometres south of Seymour Street on Highway 11.

The parking lot was too far away and too dark to see much beyond that. But they could hear smashing glass and also what sounded like a woman's high-pitched scream sliced in half and then several more all at once, both men and women this time. These ended as abruptly as the first and then there was a quieter sound — a low murmuring punctuated by a growing cacophony of piercing shrieks rising in grim and savage mockery against the ones which had come before. It was almost bestial in nature and its mounting virulence had the hackles running up and down Ron's spine.

What the hell's going on over there? he asked, peering into the dark and still only seeing the swelling tide of people, even darker still.

You don't want to know.

Well I g-g-goddamned asked, didn't I!

His voice had risen a notch, escalating along with his rising panic, verging towards hysteria, as a sudden flash flared from the tank-on-wheels — a spotlight directed at the Holiday Inn's parking lot. A dozen heads bobbing above the cars were captured within its glare, the all of them snapping in perfect sync towards the source of its bright. One then broke away from the pack, and then a second, and then all of them were chasing after, stumbling in frantic flight towards Seymour Street with the delirious resolve of a flurry of moths hellbent on the flame.

They almost look like . . . Euphies!

A sudden thought erupting in his mind, punctuating his alarm, for he'd seen the footage of their so-called riots in China and all those Third World slums and refugee camps, along with everyone else. Watching them come, Ron's alarm veered towards outright terror and he looked back to the tank-on-wheels, seeking some sort of reassurance. The soldier in the turret had since sighted his gun on the parking lot too but if he felt any of Ron's mounting panic he made no sign, holding steady as if he wasn't willing to play his only trump card this early in the game.

Start the car.

This from Dale, who was holding his keys in one outstretched hand. And when Ron paused for only a second:

Start the goddamned car!

Ron snatched the keys and circled to the driver's side, opening the door and slipping into the seat, jamming the key into the ignition. Whisper, now in the passenger seat, gave his cheek a quick lick as Dale opened the door, ushering the dog into the back and slipping inside.

What about the chief? Ron asked.

But before Dale could answer, the old man's voice boomed through the convenience store's opening door.

Good news, boys! he exclaimed, though Ron found it hard to believe this night could proffer any but quite the opposite. She's heading back our way!

He was holding up his phone to the driver's side window. On its map Ron could clearly see a red dot rounding the corner on Franklin Street with its advancing proximity counting down in metres on the left side of the screen:

97, 93, 89 . . .

Mason oblivious to the gathering threat even then surging down Seymour and enthusing with the frenetic zeal of an

old-time sheriff who was just about to get the drop on a band of
murderous outlaws:

We'll cut her off at the Timmies!

H ey Mom, you still alive up there?

Jason was standing at the bottom of the stairs in the townhouse he shared with his mother in North Bay's east side Marshall Park neighbourhood, calling up towards the second floor. He then paused a moment, listening for signs that his mom was indeed still among the living.

It was how he often greeted her when coming home, ever since he'd graduated from high school nine months ago and had found work on a drywall and plaster crew for Grieg Construction, an outfit from down south which had been contracted to build the Sunset Towers, a low-rent housing complex that had been funded through the Northern Ontario Repopulation Act. Mostly he did it for his own sake, a bit of jocularity to temper the dread he always felt catching sight of her orthopedic cross-trainers sitting on the mat beside the door and the townhouse as quiet as a tomb. If his mom was still in bed, as she frequently was on her days off, he'd shortly hear the creak of metal from her bed frame followed by the pad of her feet shuffling into the hall.

Oh, I'm still alive all right, she'd most often reply, forcing a smile as she eased her way down the stairs, clutching at the handrail and wincing as if every step was causing her no end of grief. That is, if you'd call this living. Seems more like a slow death to me.

But this evening the creak of metal and the pad of footsteps were only followed by the click of the bathroom door shutting and he knew she still mustn't have been feeling well.

She'd been in bed when he left that morning at eight, asleep on her side with her face to the wall, both legs scissored beneath her and one cushioned on a memory foam pillow. It was how she'd always slept — if she managed to fall asleep at all — following the spinal cord injury she'd suffered at the Nipissing Manor long-term care facility, where she worked as a PSW. It was supposed to have been a temporary job, to pay the bills after she'd dropped out of nursing school some fifteen years earlier when Jason's dad had been killed, along with six others, by a semi truck ramming the barricades they'd set up on Highway 17 in solidarity with their fellow Land Defenders, hundreds of whom were then being rounded up by police all across the country. Five years ago she'd injured her back slipping on a blob of Vaseline one of her co-workers hadn't cleaned up in her floor's shower room. During her six months of disability she'd taken to supplementing the slow-release fentanyl patches she'd been prescribed — and which just barely dulled the pain enough for her to get out of bed in the morning — with the odd pill she bought from an ex-boyfriend for mornings when she'd awaken, or so she often said, feeling like her spine was made out of mismatched shards of broken glass.

Before then she'd only smoked weed, and only ever sparingly, and didn't like the way the pills made it feel like her whole body was encased in Styrofoam. But the six months of physio she was entitled to with her benefits hadn't done her much good and her doctor hadn't deemed the injury serious enough for her to qualify for surgery. After her disability ran out, the only way she could see fit to return to work was to take a pill in the morning and the only way she could fall asleep was to take another at night. Even that regimen left her with little relief for the long side of eight hours every day.

That she bought what she called her "meds" from Rhett Balmond didn't exactly set Jason's mind at ease. Even before Rhett had been fired from a city job for crashing a snowplow while stoned on meth, he'd been making a little on the side selling pills he got from his older brother, DB, a nickname the elder Balmond had earned as much because those were his initials as because he had the tattoo of a diamondback rattler coiled around his neck with its head rearing up onto his chin. DB had served three years after he'd been picked up in a raid on Clarence Boothe's farm, the police acting on an anonymous tip, or so they said, that it was Clarence who'd been responsible for selling the bad batch of "purple heroin" which, ten years ago, had killed thirty-seven people in North Bay over a twelve-hour period.

But when he'd raised his concerns, his mother had answered, That was DB and not Rhett and Rhett'd never sell me a pill from a bad batch. Besides, she'd then added when confronted by the dubious curl on her son's lips, it's better than the alternative.

The only alternative, in her mind, was to take a handful of pills and be done with the pain once and for all. So Jason had kept his tongue, combatting his worries about his mom overdosing by always keeping a supply of Narcan inhalers on hand and making sure he was always around when she was taking her pill, and also for a half-hour afterwards.

But that morning he'd found her asleep and since it was her day off he'd decided not to rouse her. He'd texted her a few times over the course of his morning, to check in, but hadn't received a response until he was eating his lunch.

I'm still here, she'd texted. *Just feeling a little under the weather. Could you pick me up some tea on your way home? ImmunoBoost, if they have it, Dreamland, if they don't.*

He'd got off the bus at the Metro on Lakeshore, a fifteen-minute walk from their townhouse complex on Booth Road, and had picked up a box of each along with a spinach lasagna in case, as he suspected, his mom had spent all day in bed. After he'd heard the rush of water from the upstairs shower he'd put it in the oven. He then prepped his mother's favourite cup with a bag of both ImmunoBoost and Dreamland and set the kettle on the stove.

While he waited for it to boil, he retreated to the couch in the adjoining living room and idled his time texting a joke to his step-father, Ron, as he often did when he'd heard a good'un at work.

He called Ron his stepfather, though really he was just another of his mother's old boyfriends. Him and his mom had only been together for six months, which was about the longest, she'd often lamented, she'd ever been able to put up with any man's foolishness. Jason had been twelve at the time and ever since Ron, who didn't have any children of his own, had treated him like a son, more so anyway than had any other man since Jason's real father had been killed when he was four. When he'd graduated from high school, Ron had asked him what he planned to do next.

I don't know, Jason had answered. But I sure am fuckin' well done with school, I'll tellya that.

Ron had started calling around trying to find him a job that very afternoon, treating it like it was a matter of life and death. And maybe it was, since being of age and not having a job in North Bay was just one step removed from ending up at The Pass. Finally one of Ron's teammates from when he'd played baseball had told him he could always use someone, as long as Jason had a strong back.

Ron had driven Jason to the Sunset Towers on his first day so he could introduce him to his former teammate, Craig, personally. Jason would later learn that his new boss was thirty-seven, but when they first met he'd looked like he could have been in his mid-twenties, owing to his baby face. He was on the short side of five-foot-six and lean, with a light fuzz of orange hair trimmed to the length of the scruff dirtying his chin. When they'd shaken hands to seal the deal Craig's grip had been so slight it was like shaking hands with a child, though Jason would shortly discover that Craig was about the strongest person he'd ever met.

His job interview consisted of only two questions:

You ever had a job before? Craig had asked.

I washed dishes for a couple of years at Cecil's, Jason replied, for he had.

If I call your boss there, what's he going to tell me about you?

That I was always on time and never missed a shift.

And that, as they say, was that.

His first couple of weeks on the job were a living misery, his shoulders and back ached so much from holding the sheets of drywall in place while one of the more senior members of his crew screwed them in. But he kept at it, bolstered by how Craig had quickly proven himself to be a more than gracious boss, buying everyone lunch on Fridays and giving him a two-dollar-an-hour raise after his first week, during which Jason had demonstrated he was a more than capable employee. Since then, he'd rotated between putting up drywall and plastering it and had spent the past couple of weeks subbing on a paint crew on Craig's recommendation, since it was always good to have something to fall back on.

Jason had been on the lanky side when he'd started. Where before that lank had been defined by skin and bone, his arms and

chest had since been transformed into such a sinewy muscula-
ture that most mornings it had him standing shirtless in front of
the bathroom mirror, revelling in his new physique as he tied his
shoulder-length hair into a ponytail. He'd even carved a little niche
for himself amongst the six guys on the crew, the same way as he
had amongst his classmates at school, which was by telling jokes.

He had a seemingly inexhaustible supply from the store he'd
collected over the years — mostly off the internet — and possessed
such a prodigious memory that once on a dare he'd recited over
thirty during lunch, rattling them off like he didn't have to think
anymore about it than he did taking a bite from his sandwich. By
the end, he'd had the whole crew convulsing on the ground, they
were laughing so hard, and he'd never received a better compli-
ment than when Craig had wrapped his arm around Jason's
shoulder and proclaimed, Goddammit, somebody get this boy a
microphone!

After that, a day rarely passed that someone from one of
the dozens of crews working on the Sunset Towers didn't tell
him a joke for his collection. To each, Jason listened with the
grim resolve of someone hearing bad news from a doctor and
answered every one with the same.

That's a good'un, he'd say, even if it wasn't.

The best of the bunch he'd text to Ron when he got home
from work.

He'd heard the one he was now typing into his phone from
an electrician named Connie, a petite Costa Rican woman who
was old enough to be his mom but who treated him more like
they were secret lovers, the way she winked at him. She'd told
him plenty of jokes before, and when she'd introduced herself to
Jason in advance of telling him that first one she'd confided that
she was an "Indian" too, from the Chorotega tribe, she'd said,
touching her hand to her heart so Jason knew it was a source of

pride. It also went a good way to explaining why the butt of her jokes were most often what she called "gringas."

This is what she'd told him during his afternoon break:

So this dimshit sixteen-year-old gringa asks her father if she can borrow the car. He replies that she can but only if she gives him a blowjob first. She doesn't really want to but then she's already late for cheerleading practice so she goes down on her hands and knees and starts gobbling away. (At this point in the telling Connie did a fair impression of what she must have looked like, holding her hand with her fingers curled in front of her mouth, stroking it back and forth, all the while staring at Jason with such unbridled lust that he'd felt a sudden twinge from down below.) After a second or two she suddenly pulls back in disgust (and in the telling Connie had followed suit). Jesus, Dad, she exclaimed, you taste like shit! Oh shoot, the father says in answer to that, I forgot, I already let your brother borrow the car a half-hour ago.

Chuckling to himself all over again, Jason pressed send and set his phone on the coffee table beside a Ziploc bag of Strawberry Cough. He fished a large bud from the latter, breaking it up into his grinder so he could roll himself a joint. Maybe he'd watch a little stand-up on *Comedy Now!* while he waited for the lasagna to be done.

He could hear the kettle whistling as he finished rolling the joint by wetting it in his mouth and sticking it behind his ear. He'd have to smoke it outside since his mom didn't allow smoking in the house, weed or otherwise, and on his way out to their back-yard, he slipped into the kitchen to pour his mom her tea.

Their backyard wasn't much beyond a span of fenced-in gravel the width of their unit and fifteen feet deep. At least theirs was one of the townhouses facing the fringe of trees along the outskirts of the several hundred hectares of provincially protected wetlands which cut Booth Road in half. In the summer, a maple tree provided their patio table and four chairs with shade for most of the day and his mother had enclosed these in a screened-in bug house so as to protect against the hordes of mosquitoes that spawned in the swamp earlier, it seemed to Jason, with every passing spring.

A few were hovering about his head and as he ducked through the enclosure's flaps he could feel one pricking at the back of his neck. He swatted at it, cursing, You little bugger!, though truth be told they'd never really bothered him that much. He had a natural immunity to their sting, which his mother said their People — the Ojibwe — had developed over the several thousand years they'd lived down south in Muskoka before the settler-peoples, and the diseases they'd brought with them, had reduced their once thriving culture to a few straggled bands of refugees fleeing north to escape the white man's blight.

Muskoka, she'd also told him, was the bastardization of the name of an Ojibwe Chief who went by Mesqua Ukie, which she'd said in their language meant *He who could not be turned back on the field of battle*. She'd often proclaimed that his name should stand as a rallying cry for Ojibwe People everywhere seeking redress for the endlessly broken promises made to them by the white man, though to Jason it seemed that such was really only a case of wishful thinking, considering the way things had turned out for his dad.

Settling into the nearest of the chairs, he lit the joint.

The unrelenting heat that had settled over the city for the past two weeks had sapped him of whatever energy he had left from work. He was looking forward to grabbing a cold shower and camping out in front of the TV, spending the evening basking in the blissfully cool reprieve provided by their unit's central air conditioning.

Best get at it then, he urged himself as he squeezed the cherry off the half-smoked joint between two fingers, saving the rest for later.

After the heat in the backyard, the air in their dining room felt positively frigid. The hairs on his arms were standing on end with the chill by the time he'd walked down the hall and was turning into the kitchen.

His mom was standing at the counter between the sink and the oven in front of a cutting board, a bag of romaine hearts, a tomato, a red onion and a carrot beside it, making a salad to go along with the lasagna. She was wearing her favourite pair of grey jammy pants and a black T-shirt with a wolf howling at the moon on it, both of which were two sizes too big for her and hung on her emaciated frame as they would have on a coat hanger on account of how much weight she'd lost since she'd started taking those pills. Her hair, which she'd always run a brush through before she'd even consider leaving her bedroom, was a dishevelled mess of sopping wet curls, hanging halfway down her back. She had the peeler in her hand and was staring down with a vacant gaze at the carrot, like all of sudden she'd forgotten what she was doing.

She'd been gapping out more and more of late, another side effect of her meds. Usually she snapped out of it without any prompting from him and Jason stepped to the fridge to grab one of the three bottles of salad dressing on the door's middle shelf. He was just reaching for the peppercorn ranch when his mother suddenly exclaimed, They're not going to get us this time!

She'd been muttering to herself quite a lot of late and Jason had found the best way to deal with that was to confront it head on.

Who, Mom? he asked, setting the salad dressing on the table. Who's not going to get us this time?

Most often when confronted in such a manner, his mother would shake her head and smile, answering, Just going crazy is all. Don't mind me.

And it looked like she was going to reply with the same this time too. She'd turned towards him and opened her mouth but all she could seem to manage was, Jason?

Yeah, it's me, Mom, Jason said, opening the cupboard to get a couple of plates. Who else would it be?

She didn't answer. When he turned back to her, she was holding the peeler pressed against her forearm, drawing its blade towards her elbow and a swath of skin an inch thick curling in its wake like wood from a planer.

Jesus, Mom! Jason gasped, rushing forward. What the hell are you doing?!

She didn't respond, nor give any sign she'd heard him, and he snatched the peeler from her hand, throwing it into the sink and grabbing the dish towel strung through the oven's handle. He folded the cloth in half and grabbed her wrists, turning her forearm towards him. Blood was bubbling from under the loose strip of skin and he wound the cloth in a tourniquet around her arm.

What the fuck were you thinking, Mom?

She still made no sign that she'd heard him and when he glanced up at her she was staring down at him with dead eyes, a shock almost as alarming as all that blood, for they'd always been so full of life.

Mom, what's the matter? What's going on?

Grabbing her by the shoulders, he gave her a shake, trying to snap her out of it, and her all the while staring at him through those dead eyes.

Mom, speak to me!

She opened her mouth as if she was finally going to answer him but instead of doing that she stuck out her tongue. She'd often do the same when he'd been sulking about something, tracking him down to his room or the backyard, standing there staring at him until he'd finally glance her way. Then she'd scrunch her face

72

and stick out her tongue at him, more like a younger sister might than a mom, as if such was her only defence against any and all bad moods he'd brought home with him from school.

Except she wasn't scrunching her face this time and her tongue was hanging limp between her lips instead of sticking straight out. Her teeth were then clamping down on it with the force of a guillotine, chomping it in two. So startled was Jason by the sight that he was helpless but to watch the severed end of the tongue falling past her chin and splatting on the floor, his mouth agape and his mom's body all of sudden shocked bolt upright. She began to shake in the throes of a seizure or like she'd just been zapped with an electrical charge. Her head was leaning back at a drastic angle and her eyes were rolling into their sockets and blood was spraying from her mouth in a frenzied splatter.

She looks just like a —

Shaking his head, trying to banish the thought.

No, it couldn't be. It just —

Stymied in any and all attempt to reason his way around it, what with his mother in the grips of such a violent seizure and her severed tongue lying so plainly on the floor.

What was it Mr. Edwards, his grade nine civics teacher had once said?

In the early stages of withdrawal they'll often self-harm. Sometimes they'll even bite off their own tongues.

He'd been talking about the Euphoral epidemic, as he regularly had until there'd been complaints from some of the parents that he was scaring his students. The school board had put a stop to what a rep from the parent council had called his "gratuitous fearmongering" after he'd shown a video in class shot by a drone in Beijing of a thousand people jittering in a palsy just like his mom was doing now. Mr. Edwards had called that stage two in their withdrawal and had advised the class that it usually lasted only a minute

73

or two. Stage three was a violent psychosis of such savagery that he'd said he couldn't in good conscience show footage of what that looked like to a bunch of minors, though most of them, Jason included, had already seen plenty of footage of that.

In the apology he'd made to the class shortly thereafter, as a condition of maintaining his employment, Mr. Edwards had been quick to assure his students that it was highly unlikely that the Euphoral epidemic would spread to Canada, since most experts were in full agreement that the drug's proliferation was orchestrated by authoritarian regimes looking for an excuse to cull their excess populations.

Canada is a ways from needing to do that just yet, he'd then quipped, trying to restore a little of his lost dignity.

But if that was the case, how then to explain what was happening to Jason's mom now?

He couldn't.

Except . . .

Except . . .

Those *Excepts* had a name and it was Rhett Balmond.

He's been feeding her pills for years . . .

But those were supposed to have been pain meds . . .

A notion disproved by what he'd just witnessed. If his mom really was in stage two of withdrawal, he'd have only a precious few moments before she was gripped by the violent psychosis. He knew from the footage he'd seen that she could even turn on him, her own child.

You need to call an ambulance!

A thought as sharp as a pinprick that had him spinning towards the living room. His phone was still sitting on the coffee table and that seeming a million miles away when measured against the thought of leaving his mom's side, if only for a second. It'd take the long side of a minute to get to the phone and dial, talk to an operator, and if she really was in stage two, a minute might as well be a lifetime.

You need to restrain her somehow, just in case . . .

The only rope he knew of was a coil of yellow nylon the unit's previous owner had left hanging from a nail in the basement. Glancing about the kitchen, thinking of what he might be able to find there, the answer came to him in a snap:

Saran wrap! he thought, an idea spurred at once from the memory of how, one Halloween, his mother had wrapped him up in the same.

He was twelve and he'd bought himself an Alfred E. Neuman mask from the Value Village beside the Metro. When he'd put it on, his mom had said, Oh, you're going as the guy from *Mad Magazine*. That's cool!

Her delight given added thrust in that it had been she who'd bought him a subscription to *Mad* for Christmas some years earlier. He'd been obsessed with it ever since, so it made sense that he'd want to go out dressed like that. Except such wasn't his intention at all.

No, he'd answered, pulling his black hoodie up over his head and taking out from the back of his pants the airsoft pistol Ron had given him for his birthday. I'm going as a school shooter.

A school shooter?

It was clear from her expression she wasn't overly keen on the idea.

School shooters are always white kids, ain't they? he'd answered, to which she'd scolded, You're not going out as a school shooter, I'll tellya that. Hey, I got an idea, why don't you go as leftovers instead.

Leftovers?

Sure. Close your eyes, I'll show you what I mean.

He'd protested that he was already late but his mom wouldn't be abated.

Just humour me, she'd said. You can do that for your mom, can't you? It won't take but a sec.

Finally, he'd relented and was more than a little peeved a few seconds later to discover his mother was winding Saran wrap around his torso and arms and legs, securing him so tight he couldn't move beyond a lurching stumble. All the while she was grinning like a fool, for it was from her that Jason had inherited his particular brand of humour.

Jason had been plenty pissed at the time, especially after she'd pried his gun from his hand and hidden it somewhere upstairs. He'd threatened to get her back, telling her he'd do the same to her while she was asleep, And then you'll see how funny it is!

He never had and the idea that he'd have to do so now was about as far removed from funny as his mother's severed tongue lying on the floor.

She was now thrashing about like a live fish in a red-hot frying pan and he pushed her up against the counter, securing her with one arm clamped around her arms and back, reaching for the third drawer down beside the sink. His mom only bought brand names when they were on special and all he could see in there was a box of the No Name plastic wrap wedged between the aluminum foil and the Ziploc freezer bags.

Thinking then how his mom always complained that the No Name was about as strong as tissue paper and that giving him pause. But only for a moment.

It would have to do.

M adness! Pure fucking madness!

Mason had been muttering it under his breath as a constant refrain the entire drive home. His head was spinning all the while at the memory of what he'd just seen, same as it had when he was sitting on the toilet only moments ago. In the all-encompassing dark of the store's bathroom it had seemed like he'd fallen into a vat of something warm and wet, sweating like he had a fever of a hundred and three, even as he knew it wasn't that.

Sons of bitches, he'd thought then, meaning Clete and Dale. *Those bastards hot-boxed ya!*

His phone then buzzed in his hand. When he looked down at it, a message had alighted on its screen: *Battery 15%. Connect to Charger.*

Swiping his thumb over it, the map of North Bay reappeared in its stead. The flashing red dot signifying his truck was moving north along Franklin Street, which meant it was heading his way. That finally enough to get him off the toilet.

Bursting through the store's front doors and calling out, Good news, boys! She's heading back our way! We'll cut her off at the Timmies!

The pound of what sounded like a jackhammer pummelling granite had turned him towards Seymour where a soldier standing in the turret of the LAV was unleashing its fifty-calibre machine gun on a mob of people coming down the street. Stunned beyond all recourse, he could barely process Dale's voice cutting through the relentless pound of the weapon, answering his previous declaration about cutting Hélène off at the Timmies.

You're on your own there, Chief!

The Jetta's tires squealed as it tore out of the parking lot, Mason never feeling so alone as he did watching after it. A second later he'd sighted on his truck turning into the Tim Hortons across the street.

What had happened after that was a blur.

Stumbling into the Timmies parking lot on legs that hadn't run for a decade, his knee joints feeling like they'd been wrapped in barbwire and his breaths coming in convulsive gasps. A Black woman in a North Bay Police Service uniform was just then stepping out of his truck's driver's side door and he felt doubly the injustice of Ron and Dale hot-boxing him. When he was a constable as young as her, he'd have never let anyone drive who smelled of weed like he must have stank now. Hell, he'd have impounded their car and if they'd protested he'd have hauled them off to the station, quipping when his cruiser had begun to smell as rank as they did, Whoo, I'm getting high just sitting here!

The officer was saying something into her radio, he couldn't hear what. Hélène was sitting catatonic in the passenger seat, not even looking his way when he'd exclaimed, Well thank god, you're safe!

A hasty thank-you to the officer, who didn't seem to glean to his condition nor recognize him, though he knew his photo was still up on the wall in the main lobby along with all the other ex-chiefs. The jackhammer's pummelling assault hadn't relented until he was spinning the steering wheel, angling the truck towards the parking lot's exit, and the last glimpse he caught of Seymour Street was of a half-dozen soldiers stalking towards the motley pile of crumpled forms sprawled over the asphalt, the red lasers on their rifles searching the bodies for any that might still be amongst the living.

Madness! he'd muttered for the first time as he turned onto Highway 11, heading south. Pure fucking madness!

He hadn't passed more than a glance at the stick-it note on the steering wheel until he was joining the line of cars this side of what looked to him to be a RIDE stop on Highway 11. That itself filling him with a sudden dread, thinking of how he must have reeked of weed smoke, though it was clear the police had more important things to worry about than a senior citizen driving under the influence. Another blockade, he could see, was set up beside the off ramp to Highway 17, this one by a LAV military transport parked over both lanes. He could further see that all the cars the police were letting through were turning off onto the 17. From there, most were taking the overpass back to the 11 and returning to the city in the northbound lanes. Only a scant few of them continued east.

Thinking, *Something must have happened down at The Pass.*

An idle thought washed under by the memory of what Clarence Boothe had declared only a few hours ago:

You all are going to rue the day you put me in prison!

If this really was his doing, then it's a good bet he'll be coming after you next. Likely before the night is through . . .

Mason gritting his teeth and answering himself back, *Well let him come. And won't he be in for one helluva surprise when he does.*

By that, he'd meant what he had locked up in the vault in his basement. But that seemed a world away from where he sat now, stuck in traffic. Tapping his fingers on the steering wheel, impatient, as he inched forward, waiting for the fifteen or so vehicles ahead of him to be waved on, his eyes had drifted down to the stick-it note.

This is what it read:

Dulcolax
553 Hardy Street
Purple Heroin
Goodbye!

It didn't take more than a glance to know exactly what Hélène had been up to, for hadn't she often mentioned the exact same address when she was working at the Serenity Hospice? The first time she'd brought it up had been only a few weeks after she'd started there. Upon learning she was the deputy police chief's wife, a nurse named Pat had asked her about it. Pat lived right across from the building in question and said she couldn't count the number of times she'd seen some druggie — her word — freaking out in front of it, screaming and yelling and threatening all manner of ill will towards its occupants, marching back and forth on the sidewalk, kicking over garbage cans and sometimes standing in the middle of the street itself, venting their ire at cars honking for them to get out of the way and generally making a right old nuisance of themselves. That night at dinner, Hélène had related to Mason how Pat told her how she'd asked her neighbours about the triplex and one of them had informed her that its three apartments were all occupied by drug dealers.

Apparently it's a one-stop shop, Hélène had added. You can buy crack on the bottom floor, crystal meth on the second and

Oxy on the third, that's what the neighbour told Pat. This was years ago and she said the cops know all about it, but refuse to do anything.

First I'm hearing about it, Mason had answered, though that was a far shot from the truth.

The truth was that he too had known about 553 Hardy Street for years. It was one of several dozen apartment buildings in the city owned by Bayview Properties, a property management company itself owned by Patrick Dawson, who was none other than Constable Bradly Dawson's older brother. It would be at another of Bayview's properties that, five years after Hélène had first asked him about the triplex, Officer Dawson would shoot that girl dead after he'd responded to a "wellness check" and, or so Dawson had sworn, she'd answered the door brandishing a steak knife. Until then Mason, along with every officer on the force, had considered it a courtesy that when something went down at any of Bayview's properties Constable Dawson would take the call, even if he was off duty.

But how to explain such a courtesy to Hélène without further complicating matters?

He couldn't and so had answered as he had, and Hélène had countered, Well someone in your department sure has.

She'd then related how Pat told her she'd often see two cruisers parked right in front of the building in the wee hours of the night. She said it was right strange because one of the cops would be sitting in his cruiser — it was always the same male officer — like he was just waiting there. After a few minutes — usually less than ten but sometimes as many as twenty — another officer would come out of the triplex and have a few words with the other officer then both of them would drive away. When Pat asked her neighbour about it, the neighbour had replied, As far I can tell, they're either dropping off or picking up.

Drugs, he meant, Hélène had clarified, though Mason had already got her point clear enough and also the inference that two of North Bay's finest were dealing on the side.

Still he'd answered, Well that's a load of horseshit!, even if he himself had ample reason by then to suspect that Constable Dawson, in the very least, might have been party to that, and maybe a whole lot worse.

Hélène must have detected a hint of something less than decisive in his response because she'd finished the conversation by stating unequivocally, Well the least you can do is look into it.

He'd answered that with a non-committal grunt but the truth was Bayview Properties was a thread he'd been unwilling to tug on. Patrick and Bradly Dawson's father was Donald Dawson, who'd been North Bay's mayor for almost a decade by then, and one of the worst-kept secrets in North Bay was that the mayor's own son was using said property management company to launder money for certain criminal elements of the highly organized variety. Pulling on that particular thread, Mason was pretty sure, would lead right back to the mayor himself.

Mayor Dawson and he had been friends since high school, when they'd played on the same Triple A hockey team. Mason was also a not-infrequent participant in the mayor's monthly poker game. Then there was the matter of how at one of those, fifteen years ago now, the mayor had told Mason he'd made the shortlist for the position of chief. The wink and the smile he'd proffered to go along with it had implied it was really a shortlist of one, and that had put a halt to any notion Mason might have had about launching an investigation into one of Donald's sons' properties.

Whenever Hélène asked him about it afterwards, which she did pretty near every week, Mason had answered, We're looking into it, don't you worry about that.

The last time she'd asked him had been the evening after his promotion had been made official. He'd answered with a variation of the same, and any doubts that she didn't believe him had been summarily dismissed by her rather curt admonishment, *Well I guess it's your police force now. If you're okay with your officers dealing drugs, then who am I to argue with The Chief?*

She'd punctuated her pronouncement by snatching up his plateful of shepherd's pie. She dumped it in the garbage and threw the plate in the sink hard enough to shatter it and for a week afterwards Mason had endured her cool silence, a paltry sacrifice, he told himself, for rounding off his career as North Bay's top cop.

Or so he'd thought then. He sure didn't think so anymore.

Some five years later, sixteen of the thirty-seven fatalities attributed to that bad batch of "purple heroin" were traced to none other than 553 Hardy Street. He'd gone a little crazy after that, there was no use denying it now. At the time, though, it had seemed like he was never seeing with more perfect clarity than when he'd looked at all those bodies in the refrigerator truck behind the hospital, eleven of the victims under the age of twenty and one of them on his own granddaughter's high school volleyball team, a girl of only fifteen. Three days later that clarity had ended with him beating Clarence Boothe half to death on his farm outside of Bonfield and then taking a sledgehammer to his motorbike. Except it wasn't all those bodies he was thinking of then, it was what Hélène had said to him all those years ago.

. . . *then who am I to argue with The Chief?*

The memory of that was forever entwined with the crash of the plate smashing in the sink. Hearing that again as he stared down at all those bodies, it felt as if something was breaking inside of him. The next three days were lost in the haze of his rage, all of which had amounted to little except the satisfaction he felt seeing Clarence Boothe, broken-toothed and bloody-lipped, locked in a cage. It was a paltry satisfaction at best and one that had lasted all of twelve hours before Inspector Montagne had come to free his undercover operative.

Throughout his investigation and Clarence's ensuing trial, Hélène had never once mentioned the triplex and he'd halfway convinced himself she'd forgotten all about it. Seeing the address now on the sticky note, he knew she hadn't, that it had been festering inside her all these years, like a sliver buried deep within her brain, finally pushed back to the surface by her increasing dementia.

She must have been going there to buy purple heroin, which was street slang for fentanyl. The *Goodbye!* left little doubt in his mind what she'd meant to do with it and he followed that thought through to its inevitable conclusion: how she'd hoped that he would come upon her in the truck a few minutes later, foam drooling past her distended tongue, her eyes open and lifeless, staring at him with one last castigating scowl. It was meant to be an act of pure spite, he was sure of it, for not giving her the whole bottle of anxiety pills like she'd asked.

Except her intel was long out of date: Bayview Properties had sold the triplex to a guard at The Pass shortly after Clarence was sentenced to fifteen years in prison. The guard had gutted it on his way to transforming it into a single dwelling, sealing off two of the entrance doors and covering its pebbled grey stucco with blue sheet metal. It was doubtful to the point of absurdity that he or anyone in his family would be selling drugs out of their living room. More than likely, Mason would have found Hélène standing out front, confused about where she was and how she'd ended up there. Or perhaps she'd have been in the guard's kitchen, drinking a cup of tea, while he or his wife called around, trying to find someone to come and pick her up.

Either way, it seemed she hadn't made it that far before she'd been intercepted by that constable. Whatever had happened to her before then he couldn't say either, only that it must have been something bad enough to penetrate her dementia-addled mind. There was absolutely no doubt about that from the way she was sitting catatonic in the passenger seat, her hands fidgeting in her lap and an expression of such entrenched despair on her face that it looked to have been carved in wax. The same damned expression she'd worn nine years ago on the way to the funeral home to attend the memorial service for their only ever grandchild, Kim, Jesse's daughter.

Kim had been sixteen when she'd died of an overdose a year, to the day, after Clarence Boothe had been sentenced. She'd passed lying on her back in the sand at the end of Marathon Beach, where she often ate or worked on her tan while she was on lunch break from school and needed a little "me time." They'd found a lethal combination of MDMA and fentanyl in her blood, which the coroner had taken to mean it had been a molly that had killed her. Even her best friend had admitted that Kim had liked to "tweak," though usually not alone and never, to her friend's knowledge, after that girl on her volleyball team had died.

Kim was just one of eight high school kids who'd died of an overdose since they'd put Clarence away. By all rights it should have been an open-and-shut case, just another tragedy which proved, if such still needed any more evidence, that no family was truly immune to the ravages of the opioid epidemic. And maybe it would have been that too if, when Mason had gone to view his granddaughter's remains, the coroner hadn't called his attention to something he'd found behind Kim's left ear.

Look at this, he'd said.

Dr. Watt had folded back Kim's ear and the mark Mason saw there gave him his fair share of suspicions. It appeared to be a small brown tattoo of a tree, about the size of a housefly, but which Dr. Watt informed him was actually made by a piece of heated metal.

Like a brand, you mean? Mason asked.

That's as good a word as any, Watt replied. And it was fresh too. Likely she'd got it only moments before she'd died.

He'd gone on to provide all the medical evidence one might need in a court of law to prove his point but Mason was no longer listening. Inspector Montagne had shown him a picture of the exact same brand while he was telling Mason about The Sons Of Adam, explaining that their members often branded people they considered their property.

So far, Montagne had added, we've only seen that sort of branding amongst the inmates in the province's correctional facilities but we expect, sooner or later, it'll make its way into the general population too.

Montagne had requested that if Mason ever saw such a brand to give him a heads-up, so they could track its spread. Kim's had been the only one he'd seen thus far but the last thought on his mind had been telling Montagne, or anyone for that matter, about finding it behind his granddaughter's ear. If someone made the connection between the brand and Clarence Boothe, he was certain it would get back to Hélène or Jesse and he couldn't bear having to face the thought that they'd end up blaming him for what had happened to Kim. On the pretence of it being evidence in an ongoing investigation, he'd asked Dr. Watt to keep it under wraps.

Ever since, Mason had shouldered the burden of that little secret all by his lonesome. There was no doubt in his mind that Clarence was sending him a message by way of the brand and the only comfort he could find to lift that weight even an ounce was in thoughts of revenge. How many nights had he spent lying awake, unable to sleep, thinking about Kim and contriving in his mind endless tortures he'd visit upon Clarence Boothe if ever he'd have the nerve to show his face in town again?

But that had been nine years ago.

Hearing the warning Clarence had made upon his release, his first thoughts hadn't been of revenge, but of his own safety.

At the time, it had seemed like he was talking directly to Mason. But it didn't seem that way so much anymore, the *You all* . . . now standing out in clear relief against the scene he'd just witnessed in North Bay.

But what exactly *had* happened there?

The easiest way to figure that out would have been to ask the officer standing in the middle of the left-hand lane, waving traffic through with a fluorescent orange baton. Mason was two cars away before he could see it was Donnelly, a semi-professional body builder and a black belt in Tae Kwon Do who'd joined the force three years after Mason had been made chief. It would have been hard for Donnelly not to recognize the man who'd hired him now driving past at a distance of five feet but if Donnelly did, he made no indication. Unless, that is, the way he pointedly turned his gaze away from Mason's truck as it passed by was indication in and of itself and Mason, rather acrimoniously, supposed that it probably was.

His was the only vehicle he could see which kept on the 17 after he'd crossed the overpass, heading east. Aside from two or three cars passing him in the oncoming lane, he had the highway to himself all the way home. He might as well have been sitting all by himself in the truck too, Hélène as quiet as a respirator, saying nothing, nor casting him a single glance, not even when, with no small amount of rancor, he tore her stick-it note from the steering wheel and tossed it out the window. In days not long past, such a brazen act of littering would have earned him her scorn. But still she kept her tongue and until Mason was pulling to a stop at the end of their driveway, he himself didn't utter a word aside from the odd, Madness!

Hélène —, he said after he turned off the ignition, having no real idea of what he might say next, only that he was trying to steer his tone towards a conciliatory note while he mustered the will to say something about that infernal bottle of pills Dr. Ballard had prescribed Hélène to ease her anxiety.

She didn't give him a moment to formulate whatever thoughts he had surrounding it and the instant the word was out of his mouth, she flung open the passenger door. She slammed it behind her on her way to stomping up their porch steps, the same as she'd done in years past whenever they'd argued about something on their way back from town. Then, Mason would watch his wife storming into the house, cursing her for being so unreasonable, and would sit stewing in the truck for a few moments longer while he contrived some outside chore that would keep him out of her way for at least the next couple of hours.

Tonight, though, he sat savouring the sight as a man in jail might have savoured the memory of even his worst day as a free man, waiting only until she'd slammed the front door behind her before easing himself out of the truck and shuffling in his weary plod towards the house and the reckoning he was certain awaited him therein.

The news was, in a word, apocalyptic.

Ron was sitting in his easy chair and Dale on the couch, the both of them too stunned by what they were seeing on their brand new LG holoscreen to so much as take a sip from the beers Dale had fetched for them from the fridge.

On screen now a drone was hovering fifteen feet off the ground above one of those tanks-on-wheels parked at the end of Laurier Avenue, the drone's spotlight and the tank's too scouring over the path leading into the conservation area beyond the train tracks. A hulking figure lurched into the bright, a giant man wearing full body army, all in black except for the *SECURITY* stencilled white across his breast, must have been a guard at The Pass. He was wearing a black tactical helmet that extended to just above his top lip and blood was pouring out of his mouth. As he came into the light, the security guard raised the military-style assault rifle in his hand only to be pulverized by the tank's fifty-calibre machine gun, and then Dale was flipping to the next feed.

Here a scene from The Pass itself:

The drone was maybe fifty feet directly above the compound and they could see the whole place was on fire. There were bodies — a hundred or more — strewn over the ground between the internment camp's dozen or so buildings. Soldiers were walking amongst them, firing rounds into the dead or the dying, it was impossible to tell. The drone feed then went all wonky, the image upheaved by a sudden gust and the drone righting itself, turning its camera on a military drone almost as big as a helicopter. It was black and unlit and firing a missile from one of its ports directly into the camera. A moment of static then and Dale cued the remote again.

Now an overhead shot from twenty feet above the Northgate Mall's parking lot. People were streaming out in a mad throng through the mall's doors, tripping over themselves and each other, the fallen and the otherwise infirm among them trampled underfoot by the wave of fleeing shoppers. Those who had managed to stay on their feet long enough to make it to the rows of vehicles were being set upon by a rampaging horde numbering a hundred or so. All of them were distinguished by orange jumpsuits and those informed Ron and Dale that they must have escaped from the Youth Correctional Prison a half-kilometre north of the mall on Trout Lake Road. The drone was skimming over the parking lot with such haste that it blurred the carnage into one vast and fathomless panorama of misery and woe punctuated by wailing screams of terror from the victims and the screams of the assailants themselves, those fierce and savage, almost bestial in tone.

It's just like in that movie, Ron said, finally finding the will to speak. You know, where everyone goes crazy and starts killing each other.

The Crazies.

No. But that was a good'un. The one I'm thinking of was a remake.

The Crazies was a remake.

It wasn't *The Crazies*. We just watched it six months ago. You know the one I'm talking about.

The Purge?

That's the one.

But *The Purge* wasn't a remake, it was a reboot.

A reboot? What's the difference?

A reboot is when they remake a series of something into a whole 'nother series.

But there was only one of *The Purge*.

So far. The ending left plenty of room for a bunch of sequels, didn't it?

That was true. The reboot had ended with the survivors fleeing a city on fire to face an uncertain future, a scenario ripe for any number of follow-ups. And what was happening on the holoscreen now certainly would have made a good scene for one of those.

A mall security guard was crouching behind a cedar shrub towards the rear of the parking lot. He was holding a taser clenched in his hand and glancing about feverishly. Catching sight of the drone hovering above him, he waved it off, whisper-shouting, Get out of here. Go on, goddammit, shoo! You're going to give me away!

But it already had.

A hand wielding a metal pipe flashed into view behind the security guard, striking him in the back of head. He slumped sideways and the drone pulled back to reveal that the person holding the pipe was a young man or woman, it was impossible to tell which. He/she/they were wearing an orange jumpsuit and his/her/their head was shaved to the skin, which is why he/she/they kind of looked like a guy, though there was something decidedly feminine about the convict's fine features and the rosy hue to what Ron finally decided were indeed a woman's lips. Her cheeks were blood-spattered and her eyes open wide with delirious zeal as she straddled one leg on either side of the security guard and raised the pipe again over her head with both hands.

But before she could bring it crashing down Dale had flipped to the next feed.

Here now a scene on North Bay's Main Street: the storefronts all smashed and half of the buildings on fire, thick plumes of black smoke blotting out the night sky and a North Bay Fire Services pumper truck parked over the two lanes. There was a firefighter operating a hose, though he wasn't directing it towards the nearest blaze but at a group of four or five people in the middle of the street, all of them being blasted backwards over the asphalt by the spray.

Really, though, Dale said after finally taking a sip from his beer, it's more like them Euphie Riots in China.

About halfway through the *Purge* reboot, he'd commented much the same, watching the rampaging hordes driven into a frenzy of violence and mayhem after, or so the policewoman who was one of the main characters had suspected, the city's supply of illegal narcotics had been contaminated by a drug called Boost. It was hard not to see a similarity between what was going on in the movie and the videos of the so-called Euphie Riots which, a decade previous, had begun pouring out of China and South America and Africa and pretty much everywhere in the world where mega-slums were threatening to overwhelm the more prosperous districts. In the film, it had all been part of a nefarious plot launched by the right-wing Founding Fathers to give them an excuse to clean out the ghettos, a none-too-subtle dig at the administration even now governing the United States, whose "Ten Point Plan for a Greater America" had provided much of the inspiration when the Ontario government had drafted NORA.

Maybe if you'd stop flipping, Ron snapped, we'd have a chance to find out. Just go to the d-damned announcer, see what she has to say.

Nellie Campbell had resided as a talking head hovering over the proceedings with her voice muted, and Dale directed the remote at her.

—amatic footage out of North Bay this evening, she was saying as her head and shoulders appeared, larger than life, before them.

A sudden flourish of lights then tracking over their living room walls through the front window.

Someone's pulling into the driveway, Ron said.

I got eyes, don't I?

Dale was already reaching for the rifle propped against the coffee table and for once it seemed to Ron like maybe that was justifiable, given the current state of things in North Bay.

We now go live to the scene with Stuart Campion, Nellie was saying from the TV. But Ron was no longer paying attention to her as he watched Dale stalk towards the window with the rifle guiding his way, hunched over with the predatory gait of a big-game hunter on the prowl.

Looks like Marnie's car, Dale said after he'd sneaked a peek through the drapes.

Marnie was one of Ron's ex-girlfriends. Her son Jason would often drop by their place when they'd lived in town but since they'd moved out to the country he texted often though he'd only visited them once.

Marnie? Ron asked, standing up, wincing against the pain spiking through his knee as he hobbled towards the window so he could take a peek himself.

What in the hell's she doing here?

M ason had flipped to the local station of the CTV News Network. It was the only network with an affiliate in town and as such was likely to have the most drones in play. They'd released a half-dozen over North Bay and Mason could see their feeds scrolling by in windows at the bottom of his old flat screen below announcer Nellie Campbell, the ex-hockey team captain.

Dramatic footage out of North Bay this evening, she was saying, but that would have to wait. The kettle he'd put on the stove was whistling and he turned away from the TV with Nellie's voice trailing after him.

We now go live to the scene with reporter Stuart Campion . . .

Mason had already put a couple of tea bags in the cup on the counter. He'd then added the powder from ten of the capsules in the bottle of diazepam he'd secreted in the cupboard over the fridge and as he poured water into the mug, the liquid turned a milky white with flecks the size of snowflakes bubbling to the surface. Carrying it over to the table, he stirred in a spoonful of honey, which was how Hélène preferred her tea. He kept on stirring until the white flecks had dissolved, all the while telling himself, *You ought to just make yourself one too.*

There were a dozen pills left. That should have been plenty to put him into an eternal sleep alongside his wife and as he gave the tea a couple extra stirs, his eyes drifted towards the bottle sitting on the counter.

Knowing your luck, he thought, *they'd kill you and not her and then she'd awake to find your body already growing stiff beside her in the bed.*

That wouldn't be fair to the old gal, he told himself. *Best make good and sure she's found her peace first.*

He punctuated that thought by tapping the spoon on the side of the cup, then carried it into the living room, skirting left into the hallway and catching only a brief glimpse at the TV. Stuart Campion was standing on the expansive wraparound porch of his house in North Bay's west end, speaking into a drone hovering a few feet away and looking more like a war correspondent taking heavy fire as he cowered behind the banister than a local broadcaster. It was an impression furthered by the sounds of gunfire and sirens in the distance and the hazy drift of smoke wafting around him.

We have yet to receive any clear indications from authorities as to what's happening in the city, he was saying as Mason reached the bathroom door, but a source within the North Bay Police Service has confirmed that it's part of a coordinated attack which first targeted the city's critical infrastructure, such as hydro and the communication systems . . .

Tilting his ear to the bathroom door's wood, Mason listened for signs that Hélène was still in there. He could hear the water running in the tub, which had seemed a little odd when he'd first noticed it a few minutes ago. Hélène only ever used the upstairs bathroom when she took a soak, since its jacuzzi tub was larger by almost double. He'd told himself that maybe she'd had to go pee and had got the idea for a bath while she was sitting on the toilet. In her confused state, it could have been she'd simply reached over and turned on the taps.

She hadn't answered when he'd knocked before, and when he delivered three tentative raps now she likewise made no reply.

Hélène? he offered, in the most conciliatory tone he could muster. I've brought you a cup of tea.

That didn't get him a response either and he raised his knuckle to knock again when he felt a sudden wetness at his feet. He was only wearing a pair of socks, having been too distracted earlier to fetch his slippers, and when he looked down at his feet, a steady stream of water from under the door was lapping at his toes.

Oh god, he thought, *she must have fallen asleep in the tub and drowned herself!*

This at complete odds with the fact that he was carrying a cup of tea with which he'd meant to accomplish much the same thing.

One of the things Dr. Ballard had advised him was to make sure he always had the key to every door in the house on hand in case Hélène ever locked herself in somewhere and then couldn't figure out how to get herself out. Ever since, Mason had carried those extra five keys on the retractable chain he wore on his belt and which he now reached for with his free hand. The downstairs bathroom key was the only one of the skeleton variety and it was easy enough to locate without any help from his eyes.

Hélène, he said, inserting it in the lock and turning, I'm coming in.

A small courtesy for different times perhaps, but one far too ingrained for him to ignore it now. Opening the door, he saw at once that the overflowing tub was empty and also that the window behind it was wide open.

Son of a bitch!

Turning with such haste towards the hall that the tea splashed over the rim of his cup, scalding the back of his hand and making him drop it. The cup shattered against the tiled floor and its contents were swept into the flood, the tea bags caught in the current and washed away along with the drugs. Stepping over the broken glass, heading for the door, Mason was halted by the sight of water funnelling through a heating vent. Spinning back around, he hastened to turn off the running taps then fled back into the hall, panicked by the thought of what Hélène might have got herself up to, or into, in the ten minutes since he'd last seen her.

The hallway ended at their side door, an entrance they rarely used. But it was the quickest way out now. In five spritely and sopping strides he was throwing it open and stepping out onto the concrete slab at the top of the four cement steps he'd poured himself almost forty years ago after Hélène had put her foot through one of the rotted wooden stairs, tearing a gash up her leg that had required twenty-three stitches.

He'd carried her to his truck with much the same urgency then as enlivened his steps coming down the stairs now. He was verging on an all-out run as he came around the side of the house, seeing his truck was still there and catching sight of the flicker of tail lights from the other side of the willows separating his property from the neighbours'.

Thinking then, *Maybe she's just gone to say hello to Jesse*, which is what she'd often done when she'd seen Clete and Dale returning home these past six months.

It seemed altogether unlikely though that she'd have crawled out the bathroom window to visit them. He'd come to the corner of the house and was scanning towards the road, not seeing anything there but hearing Clete's voice raised in alarm.

Goddammit, Whisper! he yelled. Get back here!

The dog appeared a moment later, slipping through the willows' drape on the near side of the truck. It paused briefly, looking towards the house and then raised its nose a notch to the wind. It must have got a whiff of something, for every other time it had got away from Clete or Dale it had made a beeline straight for Mason's porch steps, most likely drawn by the smell of whatever he or Hélène was cooking in the kitchen. This time, though, it set off towards the barn with the skulking prowl of a wolf catching scent of its prey, Mason watching after it and seeing a dim aura of light cast from the barn's open door.

That more alarming to him even than seeing the bathtub overflowing.

The driveway's hard-packed dirt and gravel underfoot gave way to a tractor path sprouting a median of grass and clover inside of two muddied tracks and he hurried along it. By the time Mason reached the corner of the barn, Whisper was standing in the column of pale yellow light projected through the open door, sniffing at a lump of something white on the ground, Mason couldn't tell exactly what. He could see, though, that it was the larger of the two doors that was open, rather than the wicket gate set inside it, and that tempered his dread a little.

Hélène only ever used the bigger door if she was bringing out their cows or goats or her mare, Peaches, and it had been years since they'd had any animals at all. Telling himself, *Maybe, she got it in mind to let the animals out to graze or take a ride on Peaches*. That seeming as unlikely as her climbing out the bathroom window to visit her dead son but, in the very least, it bolstered his courage enough to walk those last few steps.

When he'd come to within a few strides of the dog it swivelled its head, casting him an imploring glance. Apparently, it took his approach as a form of permission, for it then slipped into the barn, leaving behind what it had been sniffing at: one of Hélène's

Depends Fit-Flex under-briefs. The sight of it, engorged with urine and lying discarded on the ground, put a hitch in Mason's step as he came to the doorway, scanning down the aisle between the shadowed stalls as he did and seeing Hélène hanging by her neck at the end of a rope halfway down, her feet dangling mere inches off the floor.

One of her slippers had come off her feet. Whisper was licking at her bare toes and Mason charged forward, yelling, Get away from her! Goddammit, get the hell away from her!

The dog ignored him and when he reached it, he kicked out, catching it in the ribs, making it yelp and sending it in a startled scurry back towards the door.

The smell of excrement assaulted him as he peered up at his wife. A thin gruel of it was leaking down her leg and dripping off her toes — what the dog had really been licking at — and Mason helpless but to stand there peering up at her, feeling no great sense of loss or shock, as one might expect, but feeling a sharp pang in his chest nevertheless, knowing he wasn't there in her final moments to lend her what comfort he could. Feeling that pang doubly looking up at the listless droop to her head and the purple already clouding her face, imagining the sudden jerk of her body and the snap of her neck and hearing Clete calling out from the driveway, Whisper, where'd you get to? Whisper!

That only increasing his shame, knowing Clete was only a few feet from the barn and Whisper was standing just inside the door, whimpering again. Clete'd be coming in any second now and when he did, he'd see Hélène hanging from the rafters, an indignity beyond all imagining. Mason helpless to do anything about that either, helpless to do anything but wrap his arms around her waist, burying his face into her neck and crying out in vain mockery of his own sins,

Oh Hélène, what have you done!

They hadn't seen the chief all day.

You think he's d-dead too? Ron asked that evening while they sat on their patio, smoking cigarettes and drinking from tall cans of beer.

They'd got a call that morning from Graham, their supervisor at work, informing them that the Harvesters warehouse had burnt down during the riot, meaning they'd be out of a job for the foreseeable future. After registering for EI, Ron had taken the car over to the liquor store in Corbeil. He'd picked up two two-fours a piece — Kokanee for Dale and Old Style Pilsner for himself. Ever since, they'd been downing beers like prohibition was back on the books and they wanted to get a lifetime's worth of drinking in before there was none.

The memory of last night had become like a wedge between him and Dale, an unspoken misery that seemed to grow with every passing hour and each trying to deal with it in their own personal way, Dale with his rugged stoicism and Ron with quite the opposite. Overcome with tears whenever he thought about it or his glance so much as chanced upon Whisper, the sight of the dog leading him right back to the barn.

Coming upon her standing, whimpering, inside its open door and snapping the lead's clasp onto her collar's ring. Only then had he looked up and seen Hélène hanging from the rafters between the stalls, her husband clenching her body tight, crying out, Oh Hélène, what have you done!

He'd been too shocked to say anything and had left the old man to his grief, slipping quietly away and leading Whisper back towards their house. Thinking of how Hélène had always been so friendly every time she'd come over to give her dead son a jar of jam had ripened a tear at the corner of his eye. He was wiping at it with the back of his hand as he came through the willows and spotted Dale and Jason locked in a desperate embrace beside Marnie's Mazda. Jason's head was propped on Dale's shoulder. His body was bucking in great braying sobs and Dale was holding him tight with his arms wrapped around the young man at the height of his shoulder blades, the scene playing out between them close enough to what he'd just seen in the barn that it had checked Ron's step.

Whisper was pulling at the lead and barking and Dale had turned towards them. Tears streamed down his cheeks too and that'd told Ron that something even more horrible than an old woman hanging herself in a barn had happened to Jason, for in all the years Ron had known Dale he'd never once seen him cry.

Walking towards them, Ron spied a blotch of red leaking tendrils of what looked like blood down the Mazda's rear driver's side window.

Cutting the memory off right there with another sip of beer, unwilling to face again the sight of Marnie dead in the back seat of the car, her body bloodied and wrapped in cellophane and her face bloodied too, her mouth agape and revealing at first glance the stub-end of her severed tongue.

You know how the song goes, Dale was saying in answer to Ron's question, though it seemed like he'd asked it eons ago. Evil never dies. If that's true, that evil son of a bitch'll probably outlive us both.

They were married for over fifty years, you know, Ron offered in response.

So?

So how many stories you heard about an old couple married that long, one dies, the other dies right after.

And so what if he is dead? Except for giving me a chance to piss on his grave, I don't see what that has to do with me.

But Ron couldn't be quite so cavalier.

If he dies, his daughter'll sell the place, and where will that leave us? We'll b-be fucked.

Speak for yourself, I'll just go live with Mike up at the camp. He seems to be making out just fine.

Good for ff-ff-fucking you. But what about me? What about Jason and his friends?

Ron motioned with a sweep of his hand at the field behind their house and Dale's gaze drifted towards the community of a half-dozen tents which had sprung up there. Hard to so easily dismiss them. All of the tents were already linked by a maze of interconnected paths tramped down in the tall grass, with each of those leading to a communal firepit. Gathered around it was a group of eight young men and four young women, some sitting on lawn chairs or on stumps of firewood scavenged from the shed behind the house. All of their faces were lit by the glimmer of phones cradled in their hands and their expressions were frozen in abject terror, so it wasn't much of a leap for Ron and Dale to suppose they were watching the news. Three others were standing in restless agitation, biding their time feeding the fire with low hanging branches broken off from the trees at the far edge of the field.

The first four of the young men and two of the young women — friends of Jason's — had arrived in a van shortly after Ron's stepson. Two of the former were unmistakably Indigenous, both tall and lank — they looked like brothers maybe — and one was skinny and white with the dishevelled mop of blond hair and the casual slouch of a surfer-dude, the last maybe Pakistani and wearing a somewhat anomalous charcoal-grey suit jacket, collared shirt and tie over faded blue jeans. Of the young women, one was Black and skinny, the other white and plump, and both appeared to Ron as modern-day witches, dressed all in black and their equally dark hair sprouting matching bleached braids draped over their cheeks.

Jason had greeted their arrival with the deference of a classmate catching up with friends after spending a couple of hours in detention, shuffling from one foot to the next, his head downturned, and listening with something akin to genuine remorse while his friends filled him in on some grand adventure he'd missed out on. Ron and Dale were too far away to hear exactly what that might have been and the only indication that they were talking about what had happened in North Bay was when the surfer-dude had exclaimed, Shit's fucked up, I'll tellya that!

That sentiment found perfect expression in the way the seven youths nodded in silent pantomime, their own personal sorrows etched in the graven masks that had become their faces. Ron and Dale themselves had nodded along as the full weight of just how fucked-up shit was settled over them all with the terminal pronouncement of a funeral shroud.

After a few seconds the taller of the two Indigenous boys also said something neither Ron nor Dale could hear. Right afterwards Jason turned towards the house, approaching Ron and Dale with halting footsteps and wearing an expression of utmost reluctance, like something was further troubling his mind and he didn't know how to go about broaching whatever it was.

Is it okay if my friends camp out here for a while? he asked when he reached the patio, his eyes lowered and his gaze fastened to his feet such that he appeared to be counting the strands in the frayed end of one of his shoelaces. They ain't go nowhere else to go.

Ah, hell, Ron answered, the more the merrier I always say.

Only then did Jason look up, offering Ron a faint smile in which Ron couldn't help but see a glimmer of the boy's mother, for he'd often said that it was her smile's shining bright which had attracted him in the first place.

The mere thought of Marnie had been enough to bring a tear to his eye and he'd turned away, brushing it aside as if it was merely a piece of grit.

How they fixed for tents? Dale asked while Ron was otherwise distracted. I got a couple in the basement, if they're any use to ya.

That'd be great, Jason answered, genuinely relieved as he turned back to the van, mustering a rather lethargic jog on his way to telling his friends the good news.

While the others were setting up the tents in the field, the surfer-dude and the Pakistani had driven off again. They'd returned a half-hour later with several Foodland shopping bags stuffed with Doritos, hot dogs and buns, two jumbo bags of marshmallows, a couple of boxes of graham crackers and bars of milk chocolate. The two Indigenous boys had started the fire. As they and their friends roasted the wieners and made smores, they'd all carried on with such a frenetic exuberance, set to the propulsive beat of hip-hop blaring from a portable speaker, that Ron had come to suspect that they too were doing their best to forget about whatever personal miseries had brought them to the farm.

Others had begun to show up in dribs and drabs over the next twenty-four hours. With each new addition, the fire had seemed to grow exponentially such that they had a real rager going now. The flames were lapping at the encroaching dark at the height of almost ten feet.

Turning towards the field, Ron saw a sudden flourish of sparks erupting from the firepit. The slighter of the two Indigenous boys, who Ron had since learned was an Ojibwe named Darren, had just thrown a branch from what must have been spruce onto it. Its dried-out needles were set alight and then aloft, belching sparks from the flames and Darren dodging backwards, gazing upwards at the sight with the startled awe of a kid who'd just set off a bottle rocket in his backyard and was watching it zipping in a chaotic frenzy through a neighbour's window.

The embers were caught up by a slight breeze and pushed downwards by the same with the lazy drift of electrified snowflakes. The past winter had been the warmest on record. Its two months of, mostly, rain in January and February had given way to three months of what the news had taken to calling "drought-like conditions." The grass that had sprouted in the field during March was already reduced to dried-out husks by the beginning of April, perfect fodder for the blizzard of embers now wafting into it.

A torrent of smaller fires had alighted from its billow and Dale was already on his feet, charging across their lawn and hollering out, You're setting the whole damn field on fire!

Darren spun towards him with a look of a undisguised petulance, like Dale was just one more adult trying to get in the way of his fun, and Dale turned back to Ron.

Well don't just sit there, fetch the damned extinguisher!

Ron then also propelled into action. Hurrying into the house, he snatched the fire extinguisher from its holder beside the stove. Its shell was covered with a thick layer of dust-impregnated grease. Probably it had been there since the Lowrys had built the house for their son as a wedding present some twenty-five years ago and just as likely it was long past its expiration date. But its plastic tag was still unbroken, meaning it hadn't been used, and as Ron came back out he ripped the tag off and gave its lever a squeeze. A white mist sprayed from its nozzle. Encouraged by that, he hurried onwards, ignoring the pain in his knee as he cut into the path leading in a straight line from their backyard to the firepit.

Dale had picked up a spade shovel and was charging through the tall grass towards the sprouts of flame eking their way through the field to the east of the tent settlement. Jason was already there, dousing what flames he could with the ten-gallon water jug Dale used when he was hunting and which he'd gifted to the fledgling community so they wouldn't have to come to the house every time someone was thirsty. Darren and the others were all there too, stamping at the ground with their feet and Darren lashing out with a towel and every one of them treating it like it was a matter of life and death and it'd either be them or the flames.

From the infernal glow, the flames were clearly winning that battle.

Ron cut away from the main path, heading on an intercept course, wading into the tall grass in his limpity-hobble, pushing himself towards a run.

Dale had circled to the far side of the rapidly keening fires and was shovelling great clods of dirt at them in a mad frenzy. There was already a smouldering patch of blackened grass sweeping away from the firepit in a rough approximation of a baseball diamond. Ron came onto that, letting loose with the extinguisher, chasing its white spray over the fringe of fire creeping along the edge of the charred patch, waving the hose back and forth in short controlled bursts. He kept at it until the nozzle gave out one last sputtering puff. Only then did he look up, scanning along the perimeter of the charred area, about twice the size it was when he'd first started. He couldn't see any more flames. Tracing past Dale, who was heaving a couple more shovelfuls onto a smouldering patch for good measure, his gaze stopped at the group of young men and women who'd retreated back to the firepit.

The spruce bough had long since succumbed to its furnace and the fire had died down to about half its size as well. Within its diminished glow, the teens all gathered around Darren, watching with mirthful smirks as his girlfriend — a young Black woman named Annie — berated him, calling him *idiot* and *dipshit* and *fucktard*. With every insult she cuffed him upside the head or hammered at his chest with both hands and Darren took the punishment in silence with downcast eyes and a penitent frown as if he knew he deserved every single one of her slights or slaps.

You think it's fucking funny! she said, working towards her grand finale, though Darren hadn't made any sign he'd thought it was funny at all. You're a fucking moron. A total fucking shit stain. You fuck! I mean, look — look, look what you did to my fucking shoes!

The young woman gave him one last shove and stormed away, disappearing a few moments later into one of the tents with Darren trailing sullenly after her through a gauntlet of his peers. The other young men all patted him on the back and offered what appeared to be a series of gleeful warnings. The last, his older brother Eric, wrapped his arm around the other's shoulder and whispered something in his ear. It looked like he was giving his younger brother advice and Ron got a pretty clear sense of what that might have been from the way he finished by forking two fingers on either side of his mouth and sticking out his tongue in rapid undulations, making the universal sign for cunnilingus. Darren frowned in response, shrugging him aside even as he cast a long, reluctant look at the tent into which his girlfriend had just disappeared.

And that's where Ron left him, scanning over the field and sighting on Jason standing at the edge of their back lawn, peering at something on the ground just beyond the tall grass. He held the water jug in one hand, which told Ron he'd probably been going to the house to refill it before whatever he was staring at had stopped him up. Ron took a few steps in his direction before he realized what that was: the block of pink granite which served as a way-marker of sorts delineating the southeastern perimeter of their lawn.

Ron had chanced upon it just after they'd first moved in and wouldn't have paid it any undue concern if it hadn't been for the dog collar he'd found resting on its top. It was old and weathered and had obviously been there for years but he could just read the tag on it. *Spenser* it said and some time later he'd asked Hélène about it when she'd come over to give her dead son a jar of jam.

Oh, she'd answered as if she herself had been surprised she knew what he was talking about, you must mean my son's dog! That's where Jesse buried him.

The rock was eight inches tall, two feet long and six inches wide. It made sense to Ron that her son had used the slab of granite as a natural headstone, and also that Jason had seen a similar use for it.

With 911 not answering and, after what they'd seen in town, Ron and Dale figuring that wasn't likely to change any time soon, they'd finally decided they didn't have much choice but to bury Marnie themselves. Jason was covered with his mom's blood and while Ron ushered him inside to take a shower and put on a clean pair of clothes, Dale had started on the hole, choosing a location next to the woodshed on account of the patch of roses that grew wild there, thinking that was as good a spot as any. When he was done, Ron and him carried the body over to it with Jason trailing after them wearing a pair of Ron's swim shorts and a T-shirt, freshly showered and picking in rueful deliberation at the traces of blood he hadn't managed to scrub out from beneath his fingernails. None of them had said a word until they'd laid her to rest. Jason's friends had since returned from setting up their tents and the nine of them stood there staring down into the still-open grave, the body within concealed by the dark and all of them thankful for at least that.

You're going to want to say a few words.

It was Dale who'd broken the silence, setting his hand on Jason's shoulder, lending him his strength, and Jason shaking his head like it'd mean the end of the world if he had to so much as open his mouth.

So they'd covered her up without anyone saying anything and then Jason *had* spoken, asking only for a few moments alone, so he could say his goodbyes.

He'd spent the night lying beside her grave and both Ron and Dale had fallen asleep in their patio chairs, keeping a watch over him. They'd awoken to Whisper barking just as the first rays of light flickered through the trees towards the southeast, both aching from having slept in chairs as uncomfortable as theirs. It had taken only a moment before they saw Whisper was barking at Jason. He was using the shovel to dig out the perfectly rectangular block of pink granite from within the fringe of timothy grass encroaching on the yard but it quickly became clear that most of it was still hidden underground. Could have been the size of an iceberg for all the effort Jason had put into trying to dig it out over the next hour without ever gaining an inkling of its true depth.

Ron and Dale, in turns, had gone to lend him a hand but he'd shaken his head at them the same way he had when Dale had asked him to speak a few words. Thereafter, Ron and Dale consigned themselves to watching his progress, or rather his lack thereof, the two of them drinking beer and Ron huffing chutes and Dale taking puffs off his vape. Neither spoke a word except when Ron recounted the joke he'd discovered Jason had texted him a few hours ago and which he hadn't noticed until then.

Neither were much in a laughing mood but Dale, for his part, at least responded with a rather forced, That was a good'un.

They'd both then turned back to Jason, watching the boy in his desperate travail and Ron wiping maybe the hundredth tear from his cheek with the back of his hand. His throat was clogged with phlegm and when he spoke again it came out sounding like he was choking on the words.

It-it-it's g-g-gonna b-be the last j-j-joke he t-tells for a-a-a while, I b-b-be—

Consumed by grief at the thought — as if he couldn't imagine anything worse than Jason not being in the mood to tell jokes. Sobbing mercilessly, the tears turned his cheeks into a floodway. Snot drained in twin tentacles from each of his nostrils, his body bucking as he leaned over, putting his head in his hands, and Dale patted him on the back to offer what comfort he could before walking back into the house to fetch them each another beer.

With all the new arrivals, Jason must have abandoned the task of unearthing the headstone for his mom and had only stumbled upon the block of granite again while coming back to the house to fill up the water jug. As Ron set off towards him, Jason was kneeling beside the hole he'd cleared around the rock, pushing at it with all his might and, as far as Ron could see, not moving it so much as an inch.

Dale too had spied what he was up to and hustled towards him with the shovel. He got there ahead of Ron by fifty yards. As Ron approached, Dale was peering into the hole, scratching at the greying scruff on his chin and biting on his bottom lip, what he always did when he was deep in thought.

What we need is a pry bar, he said as Ron stepped up beside him. Get us some leverage. I think there's one in the basement.

As he hastened off towards the house, the sound of car wheels on the gravel road turned Ron back towards their driveway. Mason's truck was hurtling past at a fair clip.

So he ain't dead after all, Ron thought.

Dale too had stopped on the patio to watch it pass. As usual, he'd left his rifle propped against the front door's frame, remarking with his characteristic aloof as he did, Better keep this close, in case a Euphie wanders by, as if a Euphie wouldn't have posed more of a threat to them than a deer or a moose.

As Mason's truck hurtled past, habit had Dale's eyes drifting towards the gun. For a moment Ron thought he was planning to snatch it up, go through his usual pantomime of pointing it at the truck and uttering *Pow!* Instead, though, he hurried past the rifle without a second glance. Opening the door, he hastened inside on his way to fetching the pry bar and Ron turned back to Jason at the stone.

Eric and the surfer-dude, who Ron had learned was named Duane, had since joined him. Eric was mounting a frenzied attack on the dirt encasing the granite slab with the shovel while Duane was emptying the last few drops from the water container into his mouth on his way to refilling it at the house's exterior tap. These past two days hadn't given Ron much cause to rejoice. Between Mason being alive and Jason's friends so eager to help him in his trials at the unmoveable stone, it seemed fair cause to him indeed and he veered towards the patio, eager to sit and rest his aching knee, crack open an ice cold beer, maybe have a chute, the only ways he could think to celebrate such glad tidings.

T hose goddammed fucking idiots!

    Mason had been cursing under his breath ever since he'd spied the flickering orange through the kitchen window and had come out onto the porch to find they'd set the field on fire. He'd been eating a piece of toast lathered with Hélène's homemade corn relish and had stuffed the last couple of bites in his mouth as he'd rushed inside to grab the fire extinguisher from its holder beside the stove. He came back out ripping off the extinguisher's tag and setting down the steps, but when he'd come through the willows he'd seen Clete had already beat him to it. He was chasing after the orange glow snaking in talons through the tall grass — bursts of white mist spraying from the red cylinder in his hand — and Mason stood watching him for a few more moments, cursing under his breath, his ire inflamed not so much by their setting the field on fire as by the fire he'd just witnessed on TV.

He hadn't slept a wink the night before, the whole of that not much more than a blur of disjointed and increasingly desperate memories. Cutting Hélène down with the old scythe hanging beside the barn door. Her body dropping like a burlap sack filled with kindling. The crack of her elbow snapping backwards as it hit the ground, the dull thud of her skull striking the concrete. Rolling her body onto the old horse blanket that Hélène had draped over her mare's stall, a memorial of sorts for Peaches after she'd gone lame and Hélène'd had to put her down. Covering her up, unable to withstand the look of accusation imprinted on his wife's face and her dead eyes resolutely staring right through him. Standing over her, peering down at her body wrapped in the blanket, the bump it made so slight it might as well have merely contained her bones, he'd never felt more unsure in his life as to what he was supposed to do now that she was gone.

First off, he told himself, *you'll have to call Jill and then the funeral home to make arrangements for her burial.*

Recalling then that Hélène had always said she'd wanted her remains cremated and scattered around the matching pair of crabapple trees she'd planted to commemorate their first wedding anniversary. With the carnage he'd seen in town, and on the TV, it seemed likely it'd be weeks before North Bay's lone crematorium would be able to get to her. Hell, he'd probably have to wait that long just to get someone to come out and pick her up, meaning he'd likely end up having to drive her in himself. And for what? So she could end up stacked like cordwood in that refrigerated trailer at the health centre along with all the other bodies?

Better to just dig a hole behind the house, bury her there and get it over with.

He'd paused at the thought of what Jill might say about that, but only briefly.

Finally, he'd just said, Fuck it, and spent most of the night digging a grave on the far side of the two trees, just inside her pride and joy — the quarter acre flower garden she'd spent much of her married life cultivating in their backyard. Both trees were in full bloom and the flush of their bright pink blossoms scented the air with the sweetest nectar, an ever-present reminder of how Hélène had told him that she'd bought two of the trees because a single tree alone wouldn't produce any fruit — it needed to cross-pollinate with another of its kind.

And if that's not a perfect metaphor for a marriage, she'd added, though Mason had already got her point, then I don't know what is.

By the time he was five feet down, his heart was hammering with the toll of church bells calling him to his own funeral. Taking a breather and assuring himself, *It's deep enough, it'll have to do*, he heaved the shovel onto the lawn beside the hole and climbed out. Laying beside it on his back, panting like a sick dog, it had seemed like it'd be a miracle if he didn't have a heart attack before he saw her into the ground.

After he'd somehow summoned the strength to roll her in, he'd stood at the edge of the grave, looking down at her body and telling himself, *With what Clarence Boothe likely has planned for you, you might as well climb in after her, pull the dirt over both of ya, be done with the whole damned thing.*

The mere thought of Clarence Boothe had him gritting his teeth, knowing he'd never be able to rest in peace while that evil motherfucker was still drawing breath. Covering her up, he stood beside her plot for what seemed like hours, trying to think of what he might say in the way of a few parting words. But he couldn't think past the sight of her hanging there in the barn and how he'd forsaken her when she'd needed him most.

Thinking then of Jill, of what he might say to her.

Well, calling her and telling her that her mother was dead would be a start, anyway.

That was enough to get him stumbling off towards the house determined to ring his daughter without further delay. His phone was on the kitchen counter where he'd left it. Picking it up, the device buzzed at his touch so he knew he had a new message even before he'd swiped the screen. There was one unanswered call and three text messages, all of them from Jill.

The first of the latter was from 11:45 the night before and read, *Mom Dad, we're watching the news. Just wanted to make sure you're all right. Give us a call.*

The second from ten minutes later:

We can't believe what we're seeing. Please give us a call ASAP so we know you're okay.

The last simply:

!!!!!!!!!!!

Mason staring at the thread, imagining the panic overcoming Jill as she and her husband, Guy, watched the tragedy unfolding in North Bay. As he motioned to press the call button, his finger stalled at the thought that he had no idea how he could possibly explain what had happened there. His intent was further thwarted by the grandfather clock chiming from the dining room. Mason counted off five bells. The last one reminded him that it'd still be the middle of the night in Calgary, meaning he'd likely only get her voice mail.

No, it'd be better if you waited a few hours anyway.

The TV was still on in the living room. He sat down in his chair, too exhausted to climb the stairs to his bedroom and the bed seeming altogether too large and too empty and yet all too full of memories of Hélène lying there beside him.

Telling himself as he settled in, *It'd be good to get an update on what's happening in town anyway,* to give him a break from thinking anymore about her.

There was a commercial playing and he'd fallen asleep before the news announcer came back on. Hours later, he was awoken by his phone ringing from the kitchen coupled with the urgent need to pee and the traipse of light over his eyes, one final blaze lancing through the living room window from the sun setting behind the trees to the west.

Squinting against its fading bright as the phone ceased in its urgent clamour, he heard a familiar voice from the TV.

So if y'all know what's good for ya, it said, with increasing virulence, you'll leave us the fuck alone!

Startled bolt upright, certain it was none other than Clarence Boothe who was speaking. But the man who confronted him on the TV had a balaclava over his face and he didn't say another word to confirm whether he was Clarence or not.

The man had been sitting in a plastic green patio chair but was now standing and striding off screen. Behind his empty seat was a wall-sized map of Ontario, the kind that rolled down, like they'd used in school when Mason was a kid. A flame sprouted at the red dot demarcating North Bay and then two more sprouted at Ottawa and Toronto. Kingston, Barrie, Newmarket, Peterborough, Guelph, Kitchener-Waterloo, London, Hamilton, Windsor and Niagara Falls followed suit and then Timmins and Sudbury were on fire too, as were Thunder Bay and Sault Ste. Marie, the whole map then a seething mass of flames, burning itself into cinders from the inside out and Mason growing ever more certain watching the entire province go up that whatever had happened in North Bay must have happened everywhere else too.

The urge to pee was so great by then that it dispelled any notion he had of waiting around to confirm his suspicions. His arms and back ached from digging the grave and as he hurried into the hall there was a stabbing pain in his chest that felt too sharp simply to be his angina acting up. An inch of water was pooled on the bathroom floor and he forsook that for the still-open door at the end of the hall.

He peed off the back steps and when he'd come back into the living room, Nellie Campbell was saying, That was the scene last night in North Bay. Authorities are estimating that as many as five thousand people may have died in the riot and the ensuing fires . . .

He listened to both her and Stuart Campion recount the devastation for some time. They didn't mention anywhere else and, picking up the remote from the easy chair's armrest, he rewound the feed at triple speed until he saw the map on fire again. Rewinding it a few moments more, he pressed play when Nellie had reappeared.

She was saying: Two hours ago, a group calling themselves The Sons Of Adam posted a video online claiming responsibility for what authorities have now confirmed was Canada's first ever Euphie Riot. We go to that footage now.

The man Mason suspected was Clarence Boothe reappeared on screen. He was sitting in his chair and was flanked by two men as tall as professional basketball players, though their heavily muscled physiques more lent them the appearance of profes-sional wrestlers. They were standing in front of the map, the both of them bare-chested and their skin painted white as bone. The top of the screen cut off most of their heads and only their mouths and chins were visible. These were imprinted with skel-etal grins so they looked more like ghouls than men and if their mere presence hadn't been enough to tell Mason that The Sons had come out to the world in a big way, what the masked man was saying most surely did.

That was one helluva party we threw last night in North Bay, weren't it boys? he enthused and Mason knew at once that it was indeed Clarence Boothe, for hadn't he said much the same thing after Mason had slapped the cuffs on him during the arrest?

Spinning him around then, his eyes glaring hate, Mason had growled, You killed thirty-seven people three nights ago. You got anything to say about that?

Shoot, Clarence answered with his soon-to-be-all-too-familiar smirk, that must have been one helluva party. Sorry I missed it.

He'd been glancing around at the other police officers as he'd said it, seeking confirmation of his wit, the same way he was glancing backwards now at the two ghouls. Both responded much the same as Mason's fellow officers had — with expressions of grim malevolence — and Clarence looked back into the camera, shaking his head and *tsk tsk tsk*ing, before beginning again.

And to think, we's just getting started.

He spent the next few minutes spelling out real clear, in his words, what had happened in North Bay so there'd be no further misunderstandings. He started off by quoting a statistic concerning how many opioid addicts were living in Ontario alone. Over six million, he said, which amounted to a little under twenty percent of the population, the province having just crested the thirty million mark a few months previous.

Remarking then, That's a helluva lot of people you all have seen fit to discard like they were nothing better than human waste. Not so good for them — and for any of you's neither — but I tellya, it's been a real boon for us.

He went on to say that The Sons were responsible for ninety percent of all illicit drugs sold in Ontario and also that they'd spent the past few months introducing Euphoral into the mix. At present, he advised, over half of all opioid users in the province were now addicted to the drug.

The problem for all of you's, he continued with the calm assurance of a veteran high school history teacher talking about

Confederation, is that we's the only ones who know which half is which.

The moment he'd finished speaking, the two ghouls at his back stepped aside to reveal the wall-sized map of Ontario.

So if y'all know what's good for ya, the masked man concluded, leaning ever so slightly forward to increase his menace and also raising his voice a notch, you'll want to leave us the fuck alone!

He then stood, walking off the screen without another word, and the sight of North Bay's red dot going up in flames filled Mason himself with such a burning rage that it'd felt like he'd been set on fire too.

Seething with a hate so all-encompassing that it'd be another few minutes before he'd find his way out of it to look back at the TV. A panel of experts had convened to discuss what they'd just seen. One of them was a bearded, Middle Eastern–looking young man with a banner under his name — Samir Ganesh — labelling him a social sciences professor at Thunder Bay's Lakehead University.

It's the beginning of a civil war, pure and simple, he said. He went on to add that he himself had been warning of exactly that ever since the government had passed NORA, but Mason was no longer listening.

If it's a war they're after, he'd shouted at the TV, thrusting himself out of his chair, I'll give them a fucking war!

After he'd arrested Clarence, he'd taken home one of the C8 carbine assault rifles the North Bay Police Service had purchased for its tactical team in case any of Clarence's men were stewing with thoughts of revenge. He'd kept it a secret even from Hélène, storing it in the walk-in vault he'd built in the basement to house his prized collection of police ordnance, a veritable museum of both current and historical "intervention" technologies. A year later Clarence would take his revenge on Kim. Still, Mason had kept the gun, for reasons he wouldn't even admit to himself. But seeing Clarence and hearing what he'd said, there was no doubt in his mind as to why he had: he'd kept it to kill that son of a bitch and anyone else who got in his way.

The nine years since his granddaughter had died of an over-dose had tempered his anger some but seeing Clarence on the TV, it came roaring back. He'd gone downstairs to fetch the C8 rifle right then and there, intent on tracking that evil mother-fucker down that very night, filling him with holes or at least dying in the attempt.

He'd been stymied in this by a sudden weakness in his legs. It felt like they were about to buckle beneath him and he clutched at the stair's banister to keep himself upright. His head was spinning and his belly had taken to feeling like an emptied-out septic tank. Closing his eyes, taking a deep breath, trying to steady himself. Opening his eyes again, he'd sighted on the shelf at the bottom of the basement stairs.

It was where Hélène kept her store of preserves — jars full of jam and tomato sauce, pickled gherkins and candied yams, corn relish and red cabbage, applesauce and sliced beets. It had been a never-ending source of frustration for Jesse and Jill when they were growing up, having to make do over the winter with their mother's preserves instead of eating store-bought like, in Jill's words, every other normal family. But Hélène would not be deterred, refusing to even consider buying spaghetti sauce or pickles or anything else she could grow in her garden until the preserves were all gone. It had been a point of pride, and a great relief to her children, when she'd open the last of them, usually sometime in March, signalling that, in Jill's words again, they could finally join the rest of the civilized world.

Here it was already late April, though, and the shelf still held a dozen jars. All of them were coated with a thin layer of dust and the sight called into Mason's mind the memory of Hélène in the kitchen stewing up all those vegetables that September past. It was maybe the last time he'd truly seen her happy and he flinched at the memory of what she'd said after she'd lined up all of the jars on the table as she always did before carting them downstairs.

I don't know who in the hell you think is going to eat all that, Mason had chided, for it had been years since Hélène had gone to such an effort.

Hélène had beamed brightly back and said, It never hurts to plan ahead!

His plan to go after Clarence Boothe didn't amount to much beyond tracking him to whatever hole he was hiding in and bursting into that, gun a-blazing. All that would likely accomplish was getting himself shot and he got a sudden image of Clarence leering down at him, revelling in the blood bubbling out of his arch-nemesis's mouth and cracking wise.

Shoot, he might say in his adopted hillbilly twang, *and to think I was just comin' to look for* you!

Clarence raising his own gun then, wanting to put that final bullet into Mason's skull. Mason hearing the crack of its retort given over to a high-pitched whining noise — his tinnitus rearing full force.

He clutched the handrail harder still, feeling like he was going to puke, his legs wobbling ever-harder beneath him. Taking a deep breath, trying to bring himself back towards reason, his gaze again sought out the dozen or so jars on the shelf.

Truth was, he'd mainly sided with the kids, when it came right down to it. Before he'd begun to think that her going crazy stewing up all those vegetables last fall was actually her just going crazy period, he'd got it in mind that maybe she was doing it to spite him for some long-forgotten misdeed. There were plenty of those for sure, at least as many as the jars confronting him now. Standing there looking at all of them together, it had seemed like he was being forced to confront the catalogue of sins he'd committed against her and their kids.

He stood there for some time, the rage slowly draining out of him and replaced by a sinking sensation further hollowing out his gut. It could have been regret, or maybe it was just that he hadn't eaten anything since dinner last night and had shit all of that out in the meantime.

Hearing Hélène's voice again, another constant refrain she'd maintained whenever he'd tried to slip off to work without eating anything.

Boy, I sure do hope the bad guys are skipping breakfast too!

Forcing from his mind the delicately pleading grimace on her face as she'd say it but unable to contest her logic.

Drawing another breath and that giving him the will to take the last two steps into the basement. Walking to the shelf, he picked up the remaining jar of corn relish, the only one of her preserves which he truly did enjoy other than the jams, the last jar of which Hélène had given to Clete and Dale a week ago. He preferred to eat the corn relish smeared a half-inch thick on a piece of rye toast and, as he clomped back up the stairs, he tried to remember if they had any left in their bread box.

And there was Hélène's voice echoing in his ears, admonishing him again.

You know there's almost a half-cup of sugar in that, the voice said as she herself so often had, so if you're planning to eat the whole damned jar with dinner, you can bloody well skip your dessert!

C larence Boothe's farm was on Grand Desert Road, no more than a fifteen-minute drive from Mason's house on Voyer.

At present, Mason was driving past Paroisse Sainte-Bernadette, the red brick church located on Gagnon Street in Bonfield, a farming settlement smaller even than Corbeil. With its grandiose size and its ornate stained-glass eye peering out from beneath its towering steeple, the church's looming majesty had always seemed starkly out of place when measured against the town's few dozen houses, most of which were shabby clapboard bunga-lows amongst a scattering of sagging brick two-storeys covered with vinyl siding as a buffer against further decay.

But it hadn't been until he was driving past on his way to arrest Clarence Boothe ten years ago that his own ill-defined sentiments on the matter would find perfect expression by what then–Deputy Chief Brimsby, in the passenger seat, had commented upon seeing it for the first time.

There must be a helluva lot of sinners in Bonfield to warrant a church like this, he'd said, though his own disdain was likely as much a result of his being a devout Presbyterian as it was the building itself.

Well, I'll tellya one thing, Mason had answered with the conviction of the newly Born Again, there's going to be at least one less after today.

And here he was driving past it again on his way to see if that sinner had returned home to roost, growing ever more certain as the church faded in his rear-view that he was on a fool's errand at best. If Clarence really had been behind what had happened in North Bay and had even a lick of sense, he'd have put as much distance between himself and the scene of the crime as humanly possible.

Hell, after what he'd done, the moon shouldn't have been far enough away to escape what he had coming to him.

No, he won't be there, you can bank on that.

That thought had Mason projecting ahead to what he'd do when he found the place empty.

Burning his house to the fucking ground would be a good start.

And after that?

Disregarding the inconvenient truth that such a thing wouldn't be too likely either, given that the house in question was fashioned out of slabs of limestone eighteen inches thick, he answered himself, *Well, after that, I guess we'll just have to see.*

By the time he was turning off Bluesea Road onto Grand Desert a few minutes later, he'd at least begun to formulate something in the way of a rough idea of what that *we'll just have to see* might amount to.

David Balmond's younger brother, Rhett, was central in Mason's imaginings.

During his investigation into those thirty-seven overdose deaths, Mason had suspected that Rhett was even then dealing for his brother, though he'd never been able to prove it. The footage from Clarence Boothe's release from jail had made DB out to be The Sons Of Adam's VP in North Bay, which meant he'd likely be in the wind too. If anyone knew of their whereabouts, it'd have to be Rhett. As far as Mason could tell, he'd kept a pretty low profile since he'd been fired from the city a few years back for crashing a snowplow while stoned on meth. The only word Mason had heard of him at all was an article he'd read some months ago in *The Bay Today*, North Bay's online newspaper. The article had informed Mason that Rhett still lived in the house he'd built himself on Old Callander Road on the far side of the tracks from the Ontario Northland railyard and also that he'd been charged with shooting a deer out of season from his back porch.

The deer in question lived year-round in Laurier Woods and there'd been such an outcry from a legion of mostly elderly patrons of the conservation area that you'd have thought he'd killed one of their kin. But compared to the scenario Mason was toying with on the off chance he found Rhett at home, their anger would be a trifle next to the fury he was likely to unleash in Rhett's older brother.

The C8 rifle was propped beside him, its barrel resting against the Kevlar vest on the passenger seat with Mason's holstered Glock sitting on top. As he drove the five or so kilometres along Grand Desert — all that separated him from Clarence's compound — he imagined himself lying in wait in Rhett's backyard, sighting on the house's windows through the C8's scope, waiting for the younger Balmond to appear.

Maybe he'd be sitting in his living room watching TV, drinking a beer.

You could wait until he got up to take a leak and then slip in through the back door, hide in a dark corner so as to catch him unawares.

Imagining the look of startled bewilderment on Rhett's face as he settled back onto his couch and noticed the red laser from the C8's sight on his chest. Looking up and seeing Mason stepping out of the shadows, his confusion would turn into something else. In the best of all possible worlds, that'd be fear. But if he took after his brother at all, more than likely it'd be a grudging sort of bemuse finding himself confronted by an enfeebled old man, his initial alarm at having such a dangerous weapon pointed at him no doubt tempered by the way Mason's hands would be trembling on the rifle's stock, shaking with the infirmity of age as much as with his anger.

Hey there Chief, he might say, all casual-like, as if he thought Mason couldn't possibly pose him any more threat than had that deer. *What can I do ya fer?*

Maybe he'd go so far as to scrounge a cigarette from the pack on the coffee table, light it and lean back on the couch, puffing away with the satisfied air of an infant suckling on a teat.

Mason lowering the rifle an inch and pulling the trigger, deafened by the blast as the man's kneecap exploded in a geyser of blood and Rhett gasping in pain and shock. Spittle would be spraying out of his mouth as he choked out, *You fucking shot me!*

Mason charging forward, kicking aside the coffee table and ramming the muzzle of the gun up under Rhett's chin hard enough to shatter the other's teeth.

Where is he? he'd demand. *Your brother. Where the fuck is he?*

Fuck you! Rhett'd spit back, fighting through the pain. *I ain't telling you shit!*

I was hoping you'd say that.

Mason holding the rifle with one hand and slipping his Glock from its holster with the other, shoving the muzzle of that into Rhett's groin.

Wait! Rhett'd plead then. *I know where he is! I'll tell you! I will!*

Oh, I don't doubt that. But I'd prefer he came looking for me.

Imagining himself pulling the Glock's trigger, shooting that son of a bitch's manhood right out from under him.

Rhett buckling over, crying now like a baby who'd had the teat ripped from between his lips and pinched on his cheek besides, whimpering even as Mason quipped, *Be sure to give my best to your brother, now.*

Rhett screaming after him, *You're a dead man, you hear me. A fucking dead man!*

The whole scene playing out in his mind like in some movie about a renegade cop turned vigilante, even as he knew he could never do such a thing. Driven from his musing then by a sudden flash of red. Looking up through the windshield, he saw a sparkle of fireworks exploding in the night sky between the trees ahead.

The truck was cresting a rise in the road — a subtle incline before it pitched downwards into the valley where the Boothe family had owned a farm for as long as Hélène's had owned the one on Voyer. Switching off the headlights, he pulled the truck over to the side and craned forward in his seat, watching the night sky blossoming with glittering shards of greens and yellows and purples. White streamers trailed into those, their bright diffused behind a haze of smoke and their detonations muted too so it looked and sounded like he was watching the spectacle of it all from underwater, or through a thin sheet of ice.

And he did feel, right then, like he was encased in ice. The only things moving at all about him were his eyes as his gaze roved over the display of fireworks, knowing they meant something but not exactly what. Finally there was such a clamour of sound and fury that he knew it must have been the grand finale. It was capped off by one final sputtering tail of white sparks that barely made it above the trees before fizzling out. The *Bang!* which followed was as loud as a cannon blast and that told Mason its intent had been something more definitive than merely another flash of light.

A diffusion of smoke had dimmed the firmament of stars above. It was drifting over the trees surrounding the road, settling around the truck and its sulphurous tang leaking into the cab. From where he sat, Mason couldn't see anything of the house below aside from a subtle lightening of the haze where he knew it to be. Popping open the door, he eased out slowly, trying not to make a sound and startled in his caution by how loudly his boot heels crunched on the gravel.

While he stood listening for any sign that someone might have been guarding the forest against interlopers such as he, there arose the distinct strains of duelling fiddles. The first bleated with the fevered intensity of a virtuoso out to beat the devil and it was shortly answered as if by the devil himself. They were accompanied by such a frenetic clapping of hands and hoots and hollers that Mason had every reason to suspect there was a good old-fashioned hootenanny going on down in Clarence's compound, how he always thought of the Boothe family's farmstead, though in truth it more resembled an orchard than anything with such overtly military connotations.

When he'd first seen the place on the feed from the reconnaissance drone they'd sent in to scout the area in the hours leading up to the raid, Mason had been taken aback by just how picturesque it was. He'd thought that a degenerate dope peddler like Clarence Boothe would be living in some tarpaper hillbilly shack surrounded by an auto wrecker's worth of rusted-out vehicles and other assorted mechanical debris — old fridges, stoves and a litany of other appliances — the lot of it overseen by a pack of mangy dogs, a few of the more energetic ones chasing after a coterie of fatigue-wearing yokels doing donuts on their quads over the front lawn. But nothing could have been further from the truth and he'd been astounded beyond words catching sight of the two and a half storeys of limestone fashioned into an almost regal-looking plantation-style house nestled so idyllic amongst the several dozen apple trees framing the driveway.

The property had been bought at auction by a private holding company after it had been put up for sale as the proceeds of crime. In the meanwhile, Mason had driven by it a few times to see if anyone had ever gotten around to moving in. They hadn't and aside from boarding up every window in the house, the new owners had left it as it was, letting the property grow wild such that the last time he'd driven by, some two years ago, it had looked like the whole place was in the process of being reclaimed by the forest.

But if the fireworks and the music were any indication, someone must've moved back in. Considering the timing, it was a good bet that someone was none other than Clarence Boothe.

The idea that he'd be celebrating North Bay's misfortune so brazenly had the hair on the back of Mason's neck standing on end. Turning then back towards the truck's cab, his eyes fixed on the C8, he told himself that fortune favours the bold and the only advantage he'd ever have was the element of surprise, even if that wasn't exactly the truth. He had, after all, taken Hélène's advice about it never hurting to plan ahead to heart by loading the truck's bed with a fair sampling from his prized collection of police ordnance. This included his six-round riot gun alternately loaded with tear gas shells and concussion grenades, his latest stun gun and taser acquisitions, his sonic disruptor, and his prized tactical helmet equipped with its state-of-the-art audio- and vision-scape technology along with a self-activating gas mask / breathing apparatus.

From the sounds of the hoots and hollers coming from below, escalating at even pace with the increasingly frenetic duelling fiddles, he wagered that there were a dozen or more revellers in the compound.

And here you are with enough munitions to kill an entire army, he assured himself as he snatched the C8 from the passenger seat.

Best get to it then.

H is confidence lasted all of about thirty seconds.

Just remember, he reminded himself while he geared up at the truck's open tailgate, *there were only three men in the house when you raided it the last time. Even then you almost got yourself killed before getting your first glimpse of Clarence, and that was with nine men backing you up.*

Five of those — his so-called Beta Team — had taken up positions in the woods surrounding the property prior to the raid, along with Sergeant Purdy, who was operating the surveillance drone to guard against any surprises. On Purdy's signal — All clear! — Mason had led Alpha Team from their staging area in an old sandpit a half-klick down the road and never in all his time as a cop had he felt more of a rush than he had when swooping into the valley at the wheel of his Tahoe.

It was just past dawn and the whole property had been enveloped in an early-morning mist. He could barely see beyond the hood. After he'd swerved into the driveway his only means of gauging how close they were to the house was the apple trees flitting by in a blur. Mason had counted them off, trying to remember if there were ten or eleven parallel lines of those, knowing for certain only that the last of them wasn't more than ten paces from the house's front porch.

Accelerating through the mist, he'd lost all sense of time. It felt like he'd been driving through the haze for minutes rather than seconds — a result, he knew, of the adrenaline coursing through his veins, slowing time to a crawl even as he pushed the Tahoe faster still.

Passing the tenth tree in the row, Brimsby, in the passenger seat, had pleaded, Chief, Chief!

Brimsby was clutching at his shotgun with one hand and the other was pressed against the dash while the colour drained from his face, as if he suspected Mason's aim was to drive right up the house's front steps and into its living room.

Only after Mason had counted off the tenth apple tree emerging out of the mist did he slam on the brakes. The Tahoe had slid over the last few feet of the driveway's gravel, bucking as its bull bars struck the wooden porch steps and plowing through half of those before it finally wrenched to a stop. The house's limestone-grey, a mere ten feet away, had blended into the mist so it was impossible to see exactly where one began and the other ended. The bright of a light over its front door was shining like a miniature sun — paled and yellow — and Purdy's voice was yelling into his headset, We have movement in the trees! We have movement in the trees!

Mason throwing open the driver's-side door with Purdy screaming in his ear, This is the North Bay Police Service! Get on the ground! On the ground! Get on the fucking ground!

Hearing then a volley of shots from behind the house as he stepped out of the vehicle — three quick and controlled bursts that had him cursing himself for not leading Beta Team and missing out on all the action when he should have known Clarence, rat that he was, would try to flee out the back. Cueing his radio, about to ask for a status report, but not getting any further than, This is Alpha Team Lead—

The voice was sucked right out of him along with his breath by a low growl and the rake of nails on wood. Looking up, he saw a Doberman's snarling maw lancing through the mist as the dog charged, not five feet from where Mason was standing with one hand on his earpiece and his other on the butt of his holstered sidearm. He might as well have been standing there buck-ass naked, clutching at his limp manhood, for all the good it'd do him against the set of teeth lunging towards him.

The dog leapt off the porch before Mason even had a chance to blink and there was an ear-rending *Bang!* so loud it seemed to have swallowed the dog in its thunder. All of a sudden it was gone, evaporated into the mist, though he'd shortly learn it had actually been catapulted to a distance of some ten paces by the blast from Brimsby's shotgun. Mason's ears ringing from the percussion such that he'd lost his centre of gravity or he'd become one unto himself and the world was spinning around him.

Hearing then Purdy's distant voice calling to him from some far-off place, the words at first drowned under the high-pitched whining and then emerging in parcelled fragments, sorting themselves into a greater whole only in his recollection:

We got him, Chief. I repeat, we got that son of a bitch!

The elation he'd felt hearing those words had long since been washed under a tidal wave of regrets and anguish for what had happened to his granddaughter, though he wasn't thinking of her now so much as the memory of that dog's teeth lashing out of the mist, its deadly pincers aiming for his throat as it leapt.

*I*f it wasn't for Brimsby you'd likely have been dead and here you are still thinking you'll have a hope in hell of making it out alive all by your lonesome.

Conjuring in his mind then the image he'd manufactured of Clarence leering down at him, Mason lying on the ground, shot up and bloodied. Hearing Clarence cracking wise:

Shoot, and to think I was just comin' to look for you! Thanks for savin' me the trip.

Firming the image of Clarence's leering smile as he lowered the gun at Mason's head to take that one final shot, and that only further spurring thoughts of revenge, as if this killing had already happened and Mason was now but a vengeful ghost brought back to murder the man who'd murdered him. His anger surged with the gathering force of a funnel cloud darkening the horizon only to be pierced by the flare of headlights on his peripheral. Turning back to the road, holding his breath, he watched them accelerate towards him, thinking maybe it was someone else coming to join the party.

If it is and they catch you standing here . . .

The thought trailing off into irrelevancy as he watched the vehicle turn into the closest driveway, almost a kilometre down the road.

It was just someone returning home.

And that thought quite naturally leading to thoughts of his own home.

It might as well have become a mausoleum with Hélène in the ground and nothing but his own burial plot awaiting him, aside from the TV. That only serving to render, in all too immediate and vivid detail, a world spiralling towards a calamity worse even than befell North Bay. It could have been The End itself.

Hearing then another *Bang!* as loud as the last. Spinning around, he looked to the sky, thinking maybe it was a sign the fireworks were going to start all over again. The sky was as opaque as it was before so it must have just been someone firing off a gun. The only subsequent sounds he heard were the duelling fiddlers, whoops of joy and muted peals of laughter seemingly driving their bows to ever greater speeds. The revelry taking place below was at such odds with his own thoughts of home that his anger surged again.

Laugh it up boys, he thought reaching for his rifle, *cause you sure as hell won't be laughing when I get through with you.*

Meghan was dreaming about fireworks.

It was the time her parents had taken her and her brother down to a park off Toronto's Lake Shore Drive for the Canada Day celebrations. She had been six and Ben three. After taking two busses and a subway they'd arrived in the early afternoon with the intention of securing a spot next to the splashpad. In her mother's words, it was a better babysitter than any holoscreen, even if most of the responsibility for looking after Ben, as usual, had fallen to his older sister.

They'd spent hours shooting at each other with the water cannons, running through the spirals of metal pipe spraying them, at intervals, with a fine mist or jets of water that felt like liquified pinpricks on their skin, and standing under the giant bucket that tipped a tidal wave of water over a legion of shrieking kids every minute or so. Their mom laid out a lunch of ham-and-cheese sandwiches and chicken wings and store-bought potato salad and pizza buns on their picnic blanket but Ben and Meghan had been too busy in their frolic to eat more than a few handfuls of the jelly beans she'd brought for dessert.

Their father had brought his guitar and idly strummed acoustic serenades to his wife in between sips from the orange pop spiked with vodka both he and Meghan's mother had been drinking out of travel mugs all afternoon. By the time the fireworks had finally started, her mom was already passed out on the blanket, her head pillowed on the lush copper curls that both her daughter and son had inherited with several strands of her hair plastered to her chin by the drool leaking out of the corner of her mouth.

Ben had never seen fireworks before. As he stood peering up at the profusion of reds and greens, purples and blues blossoming above them, he'd clutched fearfully at his sister's hand, flinching increasingly towards abject terror every time he heard an especially loud *Bang!*

And that's where the dream began.

From a neighbour's stereo someone is crooning over an electric guitar about how he might as well go for a soda and that reminds Meghan of her own thirst. Her mouth is parched and her tongue is beginning to feel like the dead slug Ben found baking on the walkway's asphalt, her lips peeled and cracking from a day spent in the sun. Prying her hand from Ben's she tells him, I'm going to get us a pop. You stay right here.

Foraging in the lukewarm water at the bottom of her parents' cooler, she finds one can of grape — Ben's favourite — and one can of ginger ale, which isn't exactly her favourite but is better than nothing. She then turns back to where she's left Ben, not two strides away, but he's nowhere to be seen.

Where's Ben? she asks with mounting panic, looking to her dad.

He's since awoken her mom and is now propping her up with an arm clenched around her back. Her mom's eyelids are fighting to stay even halfway open and her head is lolling in a backwards wobble as if she's trying to keep the fireworks display within her ever-fluctuating field of vision.

It's beautiful, she slurs. So much beauty-ful!

Ben? her father answers with his characteristic nonchalance, as if his three-year-old son disappearing into a crowd of thousands was no cause for undue alarm. I thought you were supposed to be looking after him.

He was just here.

He's probably back at the splashpad. Well, what are you waiting for? Go and get him.

Encouraged by her father's cavalier response, she swivels her head towards the playground but her view is blocked by the throngs of people now standing up to catch a better view of the fireworks. Fighting her way through the crowd, every *Pop!* and *Bang!* increases her dread. The flashes of bright light from above and behind seem to freeze the expressions of wonder and awe on the people's faces such that they all appear to be wearing masks beaming with shimmering and plasticized delight. Their arms and legs are creating an ever-shifting maze of entanglements which, in her dream state, begin to make it feel like she'll be doomed to walk amongst them forevermore.

She's lost all sense of direction and can't tell if she is heading for the playground or away. Still, she pushes onward for what seems like an eternity. Finally she breaks free of the crowd and spots her brother standing under the giant bucket as it fills. His head is lowered and his eyes are closed and both of his hands are raised over his head with their fingers interlocked, waiting for the wave to come crashing down.

On that evening, she'd run to him, grabbing him by the arm and dragging him back to their parents' blanket. Ben all the while was pulling against her, as if she was dragging him towards his death, and screaming, Waddersplash! Waddersplash!, which is what he'd been calling the splashpad all day.

But in the dream she's just broken through the crowd and caught sight of her brother when suddenly the splashpad's lights all wink off, swallowing him into the dark. The *Pop!*s and the *Bang!*s have taken on an ominous note. They don't sound so much like fireworks anymore as they do gunfire, and there's a bleating red light infusing everything with its menace. It's accompanied by the mournful wail of a siren, growing louder. Suddenly, the crowd is swarming around her again. People are bumping and jostling against her in a frenzied panic shading towards outright hysteria, a thick and pungent mist engulfing them all.

Her eyes are stinging from tear gas and that tells her she isn't in the park anymore. It's nine years later — a mere two months ago — and she's at the Passmore Transitional Housing Centre on the night the food riot claimed the lives of both her parents and Ben too.

Feeling herself being carried helplessly along with the throngs fleeing the guards on the ground shooting at them with rubber bullets and the ones in the towers with live rounds. People are falling all around her and being trampled underfoot, the sting of tear gas in her eyes now feeling more like shards of broken glass. She's being pressed up against the yard's fence as she was then. She's gasping for breath and her face is mashed into the steel mesh. The bodies behind her are pulsing in rhythmic waves. All pressed together, it feels like they've become one great and terrible throbbing machine. A stabbing pain then in her rear end and that finally jarring her from the nightmare.

Coming to with her face mashed into couch cushions, her body was thrashing to a palsied beat at mercy to the man behind, on top and inside of her. One of his hands was clasped underneath her T-shirt at her breast so hard it felt like he was trying to rip it off and the stabbing pain had become so acute it felt like he was ramming the splintered end of a broom handle up her ass, though she knew it wasn't that.

The drugs her captors had been injecting her with had reduced her memory of the past two months to a fragmented muddle of jarring images and sensations. The former seemed ever more like a dozen puzzles jumbled up in the same bag, making it impossible to form a coherent picture out of any of it, and the latter were dulled and distant as if she'd died somewhere along the way and had been condemned to her own personal hell, which seemed mainly to consist of a never-ending parade of minor demons defiling her corpse.

Most of that had taken place in one of two upstairs bedrooms. Each was unfurnished except for a king-sized bed, one painted baby-blue with blotches of white, like clouds drifting through a serene sky, and the other pink and framed with a thin strip of wallpaper upon which pranced an assortment of laughing unicorns — what had once been children's rooms. In between the degradations inflicted upon her upstairs, she and another captive — of whom Meghan knew little except that she was a frightened little twelve-year-old girl named Jamie — had been consigned to the couch, in the main floor's living room, that her face was pressed into now. But she hadn't seen Jamie since the previous night, when she'd been carried upstairs by a new arrival — a man named Clarence, apparently their leader.

Or at least she thought it was last night. It had been dark anyway and it had since grown light and then dark again.

All she could see of the room was a thin wedge blurred by the tears in her eyes and the only thing she could make out with any clarity was the ever-present three-dimensional rendering of a house and a barn surrounded by a forest projected above an early-model desk-sized holo emitter stationed against the far wall.

When she and Jamie had first been sequestered on the couch — gagged and with their hands zip-tied behind their backs — the holoscreen had provided Meghan with the only clue as to where they might have ended up.

She'd seen enough movies to know that the five red dots hovering at intervals over the property were drones relaying, in real time, the footage the emitter used to create the three-dimensional image. The house, she could see, was palatial in size and had what appeared to be an apple orchard in its front yard. With her world otherwise reduced to the couch and the horrors visited upon her in the upstairs bedrooms, the several dozen trees blossoming in the orchard had come to seem to her like a vision of paradise itself.

On the second day after they'd planted her and Jamie on the couch, she'd spied what looked to be a little girl — no older than six — running through the trees on the holoscreen. She'd quickly crouched down in the tall grass sprouted around one of the trunks, which told Meghan she must have been playing a game of hide-and-go-seek. The man sitting at the holo emitter had taken an interest in her too and he'd zoomed in on her position, making the girl appear almost life-sized. A pair of legs had then stalked by, at a distance of no more than a few feet, and the screen zoomed back out to reveal a man Meghan had never seen before and whom she'd also never see again — maybe the girl's father. He was wearing a pair of khaki shorts and a blue T-shirt and peering left and right, making a big deal of not being able to see the girl though she would have been plainly visible to all but a blind man. As soon as he'd passed her by, the girl sprung from her hiding place and made a mad dash for the house, the man chasing after her, taking on the guise of a monster stalking after a fleeing maiden.

He'd caught up with her just as she came to the edge of the orchard. Hoisting her up in his arms, he'd tossed her into the air, and their joyful cavort had played out so close to where Meghan was sitting that she could hear the girl's wild shrieking laughter through the window at her back.

Doped out and stupefied on the couch, she'd become convinced in that moment that the scene playing out on the monitor wasn't being broadcast from the house's front yard but from within her own drug-addled imagination. For didn't the man — with his rockabilly flourish of muttonchop sideburns and hair like a crashing wave — look more than a little like her own father, who had often played such games with her? Watching the girl, who was maybe herself, and a man who could have been her father, it had seemed that something was trying to break through the surface of all the grief and misery, as if somewhere deep inside there still existed the fragile hope that she might yet preserve a little piece of herself no matter what ravages any man, or even demon, visited upon her.

As a balm against the pain and the anguish she felt being savaged by the man on top of her now, she again fixed her gaze upon the apple trees sprouting, it seemed, in mid-air on the holoscreen. A haze of smoke from the fireworks had settled over the orchard, consigning the trees to a murky oblivion, and she couldn't see much beyond the bursts of cascading light erupting in tandem with the fireworks lighting the room through the window.

Crying out in her despair and that amounting to no more than a stuttered gasp foundering in her throat, as dry and parched as it had been in her dream — a desperate and futile plea lost under the unrelenting cacophony of *Bang!*s and *Pop!*s punctuated by spiralling whistles and ecstatic whoops and hollers, what sounded like a crowd of a dozen or more cheering on the fireworks as they approached their grand finale. Whoever was on top of her seemed to have been spurred on to ever faster thrusts by their revelry and it felt, in that moment, that his intention was to split her in two.

Pressing her eyes shut, her mother's voice called out to her as if from beyond the grave.

Where there's life, there's hope, do you hear me? Where there's life, there's hope!

It was what her mom had said to her on the night their family had been evicted from their apartment in Toronto's east side Beaches neighbourhood. With nothing but the clothes on their backs, the four of them had just been escorted out of the building by six armed security guards. There was a plain white van waiting for them at the curb. Plenty of their neighbours had already been taken away in the same and Meghan had recoiled from the sight, knowing it was there to take them to the Don Valley Transitional Housing Centre. Even that momentary pause had been enough to earn her a violent push from behind, knocking her onto the sidewalk. Her mom had pulled free of the guard escorting her and had bent to Meghan, trying to pull her up.

I won't, Meghan protested, pulling back. I won't go there. I won't, I won't, I won't!

Her mother had dug her fingernails into Meghan's arm with the vehemence of an eagle's talons clutching at prey and when Meghan looked up at her, her mom's eyes were enflamed with such a fury that it startled Meghan more even than the sudden shock of pain, for her mother had never looked at her like that before.

Listen to me, she'd commanded, as if her daughter was simply being unreasonable and she herself hadn't heard the horror stories about what happened to people taken away in one of those white vans. Giving up is letting them win. Is that what you want? To let them win?

Meghan shaking her head and a strand of her hair becoming plastered to the tears on her cheek. Her mother's expression softened then and she reached out, wiping away the strand with a gentle caress.

We're still alive, do you hear me? And that's all that matters. Where there's life, there's hope. I want to hear you say it. Where there's li—

A black gloved hand then snatching at the back of her mom's hair, cutting her off mid-sentence and wrenching her away. Another hand reached for Meghan, grabbing her roughly by the arm and corralling her towards the back of the van. Meghan all the while forcing herself to utter through sobs, Where there's life, there's hope! Where there's life there's hope! Where there's life, there's hope!

It had since become her own personal mantra, the only way she had to rid herself of that memory and a hundred others even more grim, if but for a moment. She was whispering it again now in an endless refrain only to be wrenched from its sanctuary by an all-too-familiar voice calling out, Goddammit Rhett, I thought I told you to fetch another keg from the basement!

Seeing a pair of jean-clad legs striding into her field of vision. She knew they belonged to a man called DB and so it must have been his brother, Rhett, on top of her. Rhett's voice escalated towards climax as he answered, I'm getting to it. Just give me . . . one . . . more . . . ah . . . ah . . . aahhh!

A gushing throb then as he released. Rhett's hand relaxed on her breast shortly thereafter even as his full weight pressed down upon her with such gravity that it seemed like he was trying to smother her into the couch. Smelling the sour rot of his whiskey-breath against the tang of weed smoke impregnating the curls of his dirty blond hair, and feeling the prickles of his goatee on her cheek as he leaned lower still.

Thanks darlin', he enthused, planting a quick peck on the side her neck, I sure needed that.

After he'd hoisted himself out and off of her, Meghan felt a tug on her shirt that must have been him wiping himself on the tail of it as a sudden and definitive *Bang!* sounded louder than any of the others. It must have signalled the end of the fireworks. All she could hear thereafter as she lay panting through tears was the divergent strains of two fiddles duelling an urgent and perilous melody from the yard.

I think she's spent, Rhett was then saying with the casual air of a mechanic talking about a pair of spark plugs.

Well after you fetch that keg, DB offered, you can drive out to Duck's then, fetch us a couple more.

The mere mention of "Duck" was enough to make Meghan flinch against the memory of what that depraved hillbilly monster had done to her and the other girls she'd been locked up with in a cell in his basement.

But that's two hours there and back, Rhett whined in response. I'll miss out on the pig roast.

We'll save you some. And take Darcy with you too, give the boss a break.

Darcy? No fucking way. I swear to god, that fat fucker shit his pants three days ago and he still ain't wiped his ass. I ain't sitting with him in a van for two fucking hours, no fucking way!

You should have thought of that before you fucked that girl half to death. Well go on then, that keg ain't goin' to fetch itself. And mind you don't forget the dolly this time.

Hearing the petulant tromp of footsteps moving away and then the squeak of rusty wheels on hardwood growing louder as the man returned, Meghan went back to staring at the fuzzed-out orchard projected in front of the far wall. The little girl, if she ever existed at all, was nowhere to be seen. Neither, for that matter, was the one that she'd tried to preserve inside of her, smothered out of existence by the unrelenting abuse and the drugs. From what DB had said, there was little doubt in her mind that the little girl's fate — and Jamie's too — would shortly become her own, and she mouthed one last, Where there's life, there's hope, but it came out sounding like a lie.

DB was crouching at a hockey bag wedged into the corner on the far side of the holo emitter. When he stood again, he was holding two thick stacks of bills bound with elastic bands, one in each hand like he was weighing them against each other. It was the same thing he'd been doing the first time she'd seen him in Duck's dank and dingy cellar a few weeks after Jamie and her and four other girls orphaned by the food riot had been loaded into a van with the promise that a better life awaited them as pickers at the farm that supplied much of the fruits, vegetables and meat at The Pass.

Instead, they'd all been branded behind the left ear and then stripped naked before being locked up in the dark. They'd stayed that way until DB had bought her and Jamie. He'd given each a lone black T-shirt bearing the image of an apple tree cast against a diffusion of colours, such as might paint the sky at dusk, within a circular frame spelling out *Garden Valley Farms*, the same shirt she was wearing now. It had since become encrusted with semen and blood and sweat. Every stain and odour permeating it spoke to that broken promise, shattered ten or twelve times daily, and all of them together conspired to make her want for nothing more than to curl up and die, what she was trying her best to do now.

Hey, DB.

This from the man sitting in front of the holo screen.

His chair was of the wheeled variety owing to how he was missing both legs just below the pelvis. Everyone called him Sarge. For that reason Meghan suspected he'd lost his legs in the army and also that he'd lost a whole lot more than that since he was the only one of the dozen or so men staying at the house who hadn't taken a turn with her. He had ocular implants too — the low-rent variety which looked more like blacked-out welding goggles than eyes — so probably he'd been blinded in the explosion that had taken his legs and also his manhood. His right hand was cybernetic. As far as Meghan could tell, it was by means of this that he controlled the surveillance drones.

As he spoke his robot hand was twitching like it had developed a nervous disorder. This had the effect of causing the holo projection to zero in on a figure, hunched over and creeping down the hill in the forest to the west of the house. The man was wearing a suit much like the guards had worn at The Pass, except in place of *SECURITY* it had *POLICE* written in bold white letters over its breast, and cradling an assault weapon in both hands. The police, as far as Meghan knew, rarely travelled except in packs. That thought might have given her some hope of a possible rescue in the offing, or that she'd get shot in the crossfire and her ordeal would be over at last, had she not overheard Rhett's and DB's play-by-play commentary while they watched news footage of the carnage they and the rest of The Sons had wrought in North Bay.

Sitting on the couch between DB and Rhett in a drugged-out stupor, it had seemed at first like they were merely watching some horror film. The Balmond brothers, though, would quickly disabuse her of any notion that what she was seeing wasn't all too real.

Jesus fucking Christ, Rhett had exclaimed with genuine alarm as a drone hovering high above what must have been the downtown core revealed a city engulfed in flames, they're gonna send the fucking army after us for sure!

Don't you worry about the army, DB reassured him. I told you, we have contingencies in place.

Contingencies? You talking about those fucking drones? They might repel a fucking ground strike, if we catch them by surprise.

But what about if they launch a drone strike of their own. Hell, they could send one of them tactical nukes right through our front fucking door at the press of a button. You got a fucking contingency against that?

As a matter of fact, we do.

If the army didn't pose them any threat it seemed unlikely the police would either. For his part, Sarge didn't seem any more concerned about a possible assault than had DB.

Looks like we got a visitor, he said casually, as if it had been a stray dog who'd wandered on the property and not a cop.

DB stepped up beside him, peering up at the projection at the exact moment the officer seemed to have become aware that he was being watched. He also looked up, revealing his face to be old and grizzled and bearded in white curls.

Son of a bitch.

That who I think it is?

The one and only. He alone?

Far as I can tell. What do you want me to do? Drone attack?

Sarge's voice had risen in eager anticipation and he glanced, beseechingly, up at DB, only to have the other pat him, patronizingly, on the shoulder.

I think we're a ways from being there just yet. Besides, boss has something special planned for him.

I could at least incapacitate him.

What, and ruin all my fun? DB then reaching for a headset from the dozen hanging from a hook on the wall. Just keep me in the loop.

Number three tunnel should put you right behind him.

You don't have to tell me, DB scoffed, putting on the headset and walking towards the large grey metal locker beside the holo emitter. I was the one who fucking dug it.

What if he starts shooting before you get to him?

Then you can have at him.

DB had chosen two assault rifles and two pairs of night vision goggles from the locker and was already striding towards the door leading into the kitchen.

With a drone attack?

As long as you don't mind Clarence saving his little surprise for you.

So non-lethal?

I'd say. Well what are you waiting for, go on then, tell the boss the good news.

Sarge wheeled around, pushing himself towards the front door, and Meghan closed her eyes, making like she was passed out. She heard his wheels bumping over the threshold and a moment later felt a slobbery tongue lapping at her face. While plenty of the men had licked at her with their slobbery tongues, she knew this one belonged to the house's dog. It was a jet-black Cane Corso, a breed she'd never heard of before DB had made a point of correcting that twisted fat fuck Darcy with a cuff to the side of the head for the apparent sin of mistaking it for a mastiff.

On the day DB had brought her and Jamie to the house, he introduced the dog to them as Killer, adding, And if you don't want to find out how he got his name, then you'll want to make real sure you don't leave this couch without an escort.

The dog's one hundred and fifty pounds of pure muscle had made him appear sufficiently intimidating to her then. Killer, though, had since proven himself to be about the most skittish dog she'd ever met, which is why everyone other than DB called him Chickenshit. He was particularly averse to loud noises, like gunfire and people shouting. As far as Meghan could tell, the men at the house mostly occupied themselves with getting drunk and shooting off automatic rifles and yelling insults at each other.

As a result, Killer spent most of his days cowering on his mat behind the couch, whimpering and emitting tenuous growls if anyone got too close. The men, aside from DB, treated the dog like a running joke and Killer also seemed overly sensitive to their endless barbs, though more than likely that was because they were often punctuated by a declarative Boo!, apparently just so they could see him scurrying back to his mat with his tail between his legs.

But DB didn't think it was so funny.

She'd learned he'd bought the dog as a welcome-home gift for Clarence with the apparent aim of training Killer to live up to his name. Mostly this entailed beating Killer with the horse's crop he kept hitched to his belt or dragging him around by his scruff or starving him for days, trying to turn him mean. His training hadn't accomplished anything except give Killer just another reason to cower on his mat. Or, if DB was out of the room, to snuggle up on the couch with Meghan and Jamie, the only two people in the house who seemed to have any use for the dog at all. That didn't amount to much more than having something with which they could commiserate in their dismal fate and Killer rewarded their affections — their ear scratches and belly rubs and the little bits of food they saved for him from their own meagre allotment — the only way he could: with licks and tail wags or by merely lying with his head in their laps to offer them at least some form of comfort. And when Jamie went up with Clarence last night and only he returned, Killer mourned her absence by pacing back and forth, whining his confusion and casting Meghan furtive glances as if he couldn't understand how she could still be sitting there so calmly with such a gaping wide hole as Jamie had left on her side of the couch.

The dog had got so vehement in his distress that DB had finally chased him out the house's back door while yelling to someone in the yard, Mind you make that grave big enough for Chickenshit too. I'm about done with him!

It was the first time he'd called him by his nickname and his pronouncement was shortly followed by a loud *Bang!*

Meghan had thought for sure it was the last she'd ever see of the dog too. But a few seconds later he'd slunk, pulling tail, back into the living room on his way to curling up on his mat, whimpering, same as he always did when the men were shooting off their guns.

He must have been cowering back there during the fireworks, waiting for them to end and for DB to leave the room too before coming out so he could lick Meghan on the cheek, beseeching her for a little affection in return. But she didn't have the strength to play along and instead batted her loose hand outwards, striking the dog harder than she'd intended on the nose. Killer emitted a sudden yelp and scurried away, retreating to his mat and lying there whining in a mournful simper.

It sounded to Meghan like a desperate plea to an uncaring world, the same as she'd made so many times these past few months. She instantly felt bad that she'd struck him and made herself no better in his eyes than all the rest. Stretching out her arm, she dangled her hand over the couch's arm, wriggling her fingers and baiting the dog like a worm would a fish. She felt the cold and wet of his nose brushing against her knuckles. Even that sparse contact felt to her almost heaven-sent and she whispered the only assurance she had left to offer.

It's okay my sweet little Killer, she cooed, as much for her own sake as for the dog's, it'll all be over soon.

G oddamned fucking drones!
  Mason had activated the audio enhancement function on his helmet and had first heard it ten seconds ago — a whirring buzz growing louder like a deerfly zeroing in on his head. He'd set the helmet's visual acuity spectrum to both night vision and thermal and the drone now hovering just below the treetops directly in front of him appeared as a floating black hexagon surrounded by a dim yellow aura.

Cursing his hubris — *Well, what did you think? Clarence'd just you let walk right in and shoot him in the head?* — he turned his attention back to the house's porch. He suspected that Clarence was sitting on the rocking chair beside the front door, though he hadn't caught so much as a glimpse of him owing to the man standing in front of the chair with his back to Mason. He was as big as the ass end of an elephant and was wearing the same black leather cut with The Sons Of Adam's insignia as everyone else in view. His hands and prodigious arms were gesticulating wildly as if he was telling a story of some great import to whoever it was lounging in the rocking chair — must have been about an all-you-can-eat buffet, the way the man was carrying on. His outline was fuzzed by the thermal aura of orange surrounding him, as were the figures of the nine other men milling about the front yard. All of those were drinking heartily from plastic cups and stomping their feet in sync with the duelling fiddlers weaving amongst them.

Mason had just hunkered down behind a toppled birch tree so he could get a look-see at who, or what, stood between him and Clarence. As a precautionary measure, he'd set aside the C8 so he could retrieve the sonic disruptor from his belt. Its primary selling point was that it emitted a highly compressed sound wave that caused immediate disorientation, and sometimes blackouts, at a distance of fifteen metres, but Mason had brought it along mainly with its canine setting in mind. The ad copy had promised it would effectively deter any dog within a fifty-metre radius. While he couldn't see any within view, he wasn't taking any chances, not after what had happened with the Doberman Brimsby had shot.

If he did manage to snipe Clarence, as was his intent, he'd given himself even odds that he'd be able to make it back to his truck a few steps ahead of the posse that, no doubt, would be hot on his heels, but he'd never be able to outrun a Doberman. So he'd retrieved the sonic disruptor and was just setting it to canine deterrence when he heard the drone closing in.

It was a good bet, seeing it, that his goose was already cooked. A quick glance back at the porch proffered no evidence that word had been passed to Clarence about their unwelcome visitor in the woods. It could have been that whoever was monitoring the drones had slipped out to watch the fireworks, have a beer and listen to the fiddlers.

Maybe, Mason thought, *you still got the element of surprise on your side, but you'll have to act quick.*

Returning the disruptor to the clip on his belt, he picked up the C8 and set its barrel on the birch tree's trunk. He'd synced its scope to the helmet. The rifle's digital crosshairs appeared just off centre in his field of vision and he angled the rifle until they were dead set on the back patch of the man's leather vest. From this range a round from the C8 would go through any man, even one as fat as the ass end of an elephant, all that stood between him and, he hoped, Clarence Boothe.

His finger itching on the trigger, he saw a man in a wheelchair rolling out the front door. He was missing both legs and had ocular implants and in place of his right hand what appeared to be one of those cyber gloves, the same kind which Constable Purdy used to control his drones. It was a good bet that the man in the wheelchair was the one in charge of surveillance and had come to inform his boss of the threat in the woods, Mason feeling less like a "threat" with every passing second.

Telling himself, Fuck it!, he took a deep breath in advance of squeezing the C8's trigger, come what may, but was thwarted in this by the drone. It swooped to within five feet of him and barraged him with a strobing flicker of lights, the flashing bright reducing his visual acuity all at once to nil. The drone must have also had some form of sonic disruptor. Mason felt a sudden pressure in his ears and was at once overcome by a wave of nausea. It took but a split second before the helmet automatically compensated, producing a sensation not unlike his head had been vacuum-sealed and tinting his face shield so he could see again. It didn't do him much good, though, as the nausea had since sent him sprawling over the birch, spewing a bitter mush of corn relish and rye bread onto the forest floor beyond.

His head was spinning and there was a piercing whine in his ears that felt like his tinnitus had grown a set of fangs and was chewing on the inside of his head. The drone must have ceased in its sonic assault because after a moment he could hear again.

Hey there Chief! Clarence was yelling through a bullhorn. It's funny, I was just saying not five minutes ago I ought to send someone to track you down. I guess you saved me the trouble!

Looking up at the house, he saw Clarence standing on the porch beside the fat man. The bullhorn was pressed to his lips but it wasn't upon this that Mason's gaze had settled, it was on the sledgehammer sitting upright on the floor in front of him. It might as well have been the one Mason himself had used to trash Clarence's Harley those ten years ago, and the sight of it, as much as what Clarence had just said, told Mason that the ex-con must have been plotting his own form of revenge.

His free hand was resting casually on the handle's butt end and he was calling out again, Well come on down, Chief, join the party! You's missing out on all the fun!

Swallowing against the urge to puke again, Mason grasped for his rifle. It had fallen on the other side of the birch and he'd just got a hold of its strap when he heard another voice, this one coming from within the trees at his back and cautioning, Easy now there, old-timer.

Someone had snuck up behind him.

The goddamned tunnels! Mason cursed. *You forgot about the goddamned tunnels!*

After the raid, they'd found a network of them snaking through the ground under the woods. There were five in all and every one of them led to a hidden room in the house's basement. If he'd been thinking, he could have used those to get into the house. But it was too late to worry about that now.

Glancing back, he saw two red beams prying through the dark, one sighting on the middle of his forehead, the other on his cheek. Two men were approaching at a distance of fifteen paces, each holding him in their sights with matching AR-15 assault rifles slung low at their sides. Through his night vision he could clearly see they were the Balmond brothers. The elder was dressed the same as everyone else and also shaven of head, the younger with an anomalous mullet of dirty blond hair, wearing a pair of cut-off jean shorts and a brightly tie-dyed muscle shirt that looked like a neon hurricane swirling about his navel.

Stand up real slow now, DB in the lead coaxed. Hands where I can see 'em.

Mason did as he was told, raising his hands above his head and hearing Clarence's amplified voice again from below, You got 'im?

DB pressed his hand to the left side of his headset, answering back, Tell boss we got him all right. We'll be down presently.

Mason all the while watching the numbers on the top left side of his helmet's screen counting down:

3, 2, 1 . . .

He'd synced the sonic disruptor to his helmet and had activated its grenade function the moment DB had called out to him. The instant the countdown reached one the helmet's sound dampeners activated again. At the count of zero, both DB and Rhett immediately wobbled off balance, Rhett falling to his knees with his hands clutching at his ears, DB wincing against the pain and grabbing at the nearest tree to keep himself upright as he struggled to bring his rifle back to bear on Mason.

But he was too late by a split second.

Mason had already snatched both the taser and the stun gun from their holsters. He was pointing the latter at DB and pulling its trigger.

The twin electrified darts leapt from its muzzle, hitting DB in the chest. DB tilted sideways, shaking like a Euphie and collapsing to the ground. Rhett had rolled onto his back, bringing his own rifle to bear. Releasing the stun gun's trigger, Mason stepped over DB's still quivering body and jammed the taser right under Rhett's chin, shocking him with fifty thousand volts and snapping his head back same as if he'd been hit with a brick.

Slipping the taser back into his holster, he stood back up. Telling himself, *Maybe you still got the element of surprise on your side just yet*, he scoured the ground for his riot gun. It was sitting on top of his rucksack, just where he'd left it. As he snatched it up, Clarence was calling out, Oh, you's goin' to pay for that, Chief!

Aiming the riot gun's muzzle at a gap between the trees, Mason pulled the trigger even as he vaulted over the fallen birch with the sudden zeal of a much younger man. Bending low then and grabbing his rifle off the ground as the concussion grenade exploded below.

Giving himself over to gravity, he let the slope pull him downwards, his feet scrambling beneath him, trying to keep up, and his finger pulling the riot gun's trigger again and again and again. Two more explosions sounded between the faint *Poof!* of the three tear gas cannisters detonating amidst a mad caterwauling of screams and shouts punctuated by a chorus of rasping coughs and Clarence's voice booming out of the bullhorn trying to marshal his troops, Shoot that motherfucker! Goddamn it, shoot him!

Mason had reached the bottom of the hill. Clearing the treeline that separated the forest from the yard, he dropped the riot gun and levered the C8 upwards, grasping its handguard with his left hand while the index finger on his right reached for its trigger. He heard a few sporadic shots and the *Zzzzt! Zzzzt!* as the rounds passed him by or a *Thwunk!* as they struck a nearby tree. The tear gas had enveloped the entire yard between him and the house and from the trajectory of the bullets zipping around him no one seemed to be able to see him through the haze.

But with his thermal vision he could see them just fine.

Clarence was still standing on the porch. Within the thermal visual his face appeared as an undulating blur of orange shading towards red, so Mason couldn't tell exactly of his expression. There was a gaping black hole just above his chin and that gave Mason every indication that he'd caught him by surprise after all. A minor victory, perhaps, but one that had his lips curling into a malevolent grin as he sighted the C8 first on Clarence. Aiming dead centre at his chest, he fired off two rounds.

Clarence pitched backwards against the wall and the fat man, panic-struck, surged left only to run smack dab into the man in the wheelchair. The both of them went down in a tangle of sprawling arms. The fat man pitched down the stairs with the careening flop of a giant balloon filled with Jell-O and Mason sighted on him first, landing two shots in the crest on his back then taking aim on the legless man. He was clutching at his chair, trying to right it, and the shot struck him just above the ear. Swivelling his rifle towards the closest of the orange auras, Mason shot it too then turned to the next-closest and pulled the trigger again.

Feeling then the concussive pressure of a bullet hitting him just above the navel. The Kevlar vest took the brunt of its force and he felt another bullet glancing off the armour covering his arms. Another flash of white heat turned him towards the man — none other than Officer Dawson's brother Patrick. Patrick was shooting at him as a third bullet impacted on the vest right below Mason's heart, knocking him back a step.

He fired twice. The first shot struck Patrick in the neck and the second in the middle of his forehead, toppling him backwards. Tracking left then, shooting a man fleeing up the porch's stairs and another hurrying for the cover of the closest apple tree.

Striding onwards still, shooting with the same studied deliberation he'd honed during the yearly training exercises up at the army base which he'd made mandatory for every officer in his tactical unit. Killing without end and without remorse until every one of the orange auras lay crumpled on the ground, growing dimmer with every passing breath. His own were coming in laboured gasps by the time he was through and he took a moment inhaling deeply of the oxygen coursing through the helmet's breathing apparatus. The ever-present aching in his heart had become a sharply pulsing throb and the oxygen did nothing to relieve him of that. The pain had him bending over, the undeniable pull of gravity urging him, perhaps terminally, towards the ground.

He could hear someone coughing in ragged gasps. Fighting through the pain and the heaviness in his legs and chest, he pried himself back up and tracked it to the porch. He could see Clarence sitting with his back against the wall. The two bullet holes in his chest were weeping twin blotches of blood spreading over his shirt and his hand was groping feebly for the shaft of the sledgehammer lying beside him, as if it still might be of some use.

Forcing his legs forward, Mason came up the porch steps on leaden feet, thinking about something his father had often told him on their weekend hunting trips. A wounded animal could be even more dangerous, he'd warned, especially if it was cornered.

As long as Clarence was still drawing breath, he'd likely have a little bite in him yet and Mason was careful to keep his crosshairs pointing dead centre in the middle of the dying man's eyes, the both of them narrowed to black pits of seething hate, staring up at Mason. Clarence's mouth was twitching, no doubt in a vain attempt to spew whatever venom and bile he had left, and that amounting to nothing more than a red bubble bursting against his lips. His head lolled sideways and it was clear he was already dead but still Mason pressed the trigger, taking his own one final shot.

Clarence's head pitched back against the wall with a splatter of blood. Mason stood there watching a tendril of it leaking out from the hole between Boothe's eyes and in that moment it felt like the life was draining out of his body too.

He'd never felt so tired.

His knees were aching with the infirmity of age and the pulsing throb in his chest had become a stabbing pain, about what a serrated knife jammed into his breast might feel like. Slumping into the rocking chair, he sat there breathing hard and every breath like a clenched hand squeezing at his heart.

There was a half-empty forty-ouncer of Jack Daniel's sitting on the floor in front of the chair, what Clarence must have been drinking from. Hélène's father had been a violent drunk and as a result she wouldn't allow liquor in the house. Mason had never been much of a drinker anyway, so it didn't overly trouble him. The only time he ever imbibed was a glass of red wine at Christmas dinner and a beer or two when he was playing poker at the mayor's house, but he sure felt like having a stiff drink now. Craning over, wincing against the pain in his chest, he picked up the bottle. Unscrewing the cap, he took a hefty swig that felt like liquid fire in his throat, then took another. It turned into three, Mason gulping at the whiskey like it was the essence of life itself and that curdling in his belly, making him want to puke all over again.

Closing his eyes and thinking about DB and Rhett out there in the woods. Both his taser and stun gun were equipped with Axon Co.'s patented Bio-Shock, which induced a temporary paralysis that could last anywhere from ten to twenty minutes, which meant they'd be coming to any moment now. He'd left both their rifles beside them so they'd be armed when they did.

Fuck 'em, he muttered to himself. Let 'em come. I'll be waiting.

A sentiment entirely out of whack with just how heavy his eyes had become. Closing them and telling himself, *You close your eyes now, you ain't likely ever going to open them again.*

So what if you don't. Ain't nothing left for you back home. Dying here is as good a place as any.

That sentiment seeming to him a lie. If he did meet his end here, it wasn't likely he'd end up resting beside Hélène in their eternal slumber, like he'd always planned. As a balm against thinking any more about that, he conjured into his mind the memory of the first time he'd ever seen her — one last memory to bind them together for all eternity.

He was seventeen. He'd just finished two hours' worth of endurance drills with the Battalion, North Bay's Junior A hockey team, and he'd taken a seat in the stands to eat an Oh Henry! bar while he summoned the energy to make the drive back home. The rink had just been cleaned by the Zamboni and the moment the buzzer sounded, signalling to the next batch of skaters, a young woman wearing bright pink leotards had come darting out of the door leading to the change rooms. She was already moving at a fair clip and she'd hit the ice pushing her legs faster still. Three quick strides brought her to the first blue line and after taking two longer strides she leapt into the air with seemingly effortless grace, scissoring her legs beneath her at an even perpendicular to her body, and Mason was suddenly caught breathless watching her soar to what seemed an almost impossible height.

At the time no thoughts at all had penetrated his stupefied wonder at bearing witness to such a feat of poise and athleticism. But years later when he first told Jill, then six, the story of how he met her mother, he embellished it by adding, Watching your mother make that impossible leap, it immediately called to mind the image of a doe me and my father had once seen.

His father was a conservation officer, he'd explained. When Mason was twelve, a fire had burned through over ten thousand hectares just north of Timiskaming and he'd taken his son along with him to survey the damage. Either the wind had turned just as the fire had reached Highway 11 or the firefighters had made a last ditch, and ultimately successful, stand there, for on the eastern side of its two lanes the trees were all scorched into charcoal pillars but on the western side the forest had remained unscathed. Driving through a rock cut, nearing fifty feet tall on either side of the road, his father had spotted something on the shoulder and had pulled his truck over to get a closer look.

What he'd seen was a doe, lying dead at the base of the rock cut's westernmost cliff face. It was covered in flies and seething with maggots. Several of its rib bones were poking through its hide and its legs were sprawled like broken matchsticks beneath it.

At this point in the telling, Jill had exclaimed, Ew! That's gross.

It was pretty gross all right, Mason had agreed. And boy, did it ever reek too. Couldn't hardly get within ten feet of it without a gas mask.

Why would Mom remind you of a stinky old dead deer? Jill asked, quite within reason.

To which Mason asked her back:

Well how do you think the deer got there?

I don't know. Was it hit by a car?

That's exactly what I thought too — that it was just roadkill — but not my dad. He had an entirely different notion.

He was gazing up at the rock cut's easternmost summit and I followed his gaze to the same.

She must have tried to leap over the road to get away from the fire, my father explained. She almost made it too. Just imagine that.

The twelve-year-old Mason had, conjuring in his mind the image of the doe in mid-flight, soaring fifty feet above the chasm in a desperate, and ultimately futile, attempt to escape the flames.

And boy I tellya, I'd never felt such horror as I had imagining the deer falling short, if only by a few feet. That's why I thought of the deer when I saw your mother making her own impossible leap. The thought that she'd end up just like the deer drove me to my feet. My heart was pounding in my chest and I'd broken out in a sweat and I swear to god it felt like she was up there in the air for a minute rather than just a second. It seemed like she'd never come down.

But she did, right? Jill had asked, as if the proof wasn't sitting at the dinner table not five feet away.

Of course she did. She'd landed the jump like it hadn't meant more to her than, I don't know, you playing a game of hopscotch in the dirt. And I tellya, I'd never felt more relieved in my life watching her skating back towards the red line.

And that's when you fell in love with Mom?

Oh boy did I ever, he said, though that wasn't exactly the truth. Adding then: About as hard as that doe lying dead on the side of the road.

The truth was he had indeed felt something as a legion of much younger skaters swirled around his future wife, his own awe found perfect expression in their faces, every one of which was shading towards exultation. Though, if he was being honest with himself, it wasn't so much love as the primal sort of lust a hunter feels when he's just sighted on his prey.

It was a feeling that didn't last long.

The figure skating coach had come out to wrangle the kids. As they'd skated off to do their laps, Hélène — whose name he wouldn't get up the nerve to ask anyone for another three months — had turned towards Mason. He was standing dumb-struck with the half-eaten Oh Henry! bar sagging in his right hand and his tired legs withering further as she set her eyes upon him. Such a look of indignant ferocity in them that she didn't look so much like a deer anymore as she did a mama bear, warning him off her cubs.

She was angry at you? Jill asked when he'd reached that point in the telling.

Ah hell, it looked like she was fixing to tear me limb from limb.

Why was she so angry?

I guess you'll have to ask your mother about that.

She did and Hélène answered rather perfunctorily:

It was because he was a hockey player. And not just *a* hockey player, but the team's captain. And if there's anyone more, ahem, *arrogant* in this country than the captain of a Junior A hockey team, well I've never met 'em.

She punctuated that with a fair approximation of the first look she'd ever given her husband and, sitting in the rocking chair on Clarence Boothe's porch all those years later, Mason clung to the image of her piercing indignance — so wild and fierce. It had been such an indelible tether between them over their sixty years together that it felt, in that moment, even death wouldn't be able to sever it.

Drifting off into the eternal — never in his life longing for anything more than its comforting embrace — and then jarred back into wakefulness by someone shaking his arm.

Mister! a girl's voice was pleading. Mister, you got to get up! Please mister, wake up!

Its urgency pried through his drowse and he opened his eyes. There was a teenage girl peering down at him and that came as big a shock as any on a night already brimming with its fair share.

Where the hell'd you come from? he blurted out, without so much as thinking.

You got a car? the girl asked, sidestepping that.

A what?

A vehicle.

I got a truck.

Where is it?

It's uh, it's down the road a ways.

Hearing a dog bark then, one loud and definitive *Woof!* that had him turning towards the bottom of the porch steps. There was indeed a dog there, the size and relative shape of a mastiff. It barked once more and that seemed to impel the girl into action. She was striding away from Mason, pausing only briefly to grab at the handles of an old hockey duffel sitting at the top of the stairs. It was full to bursting and its weight seemed to be beyond her meagre strength. She didn't even bother trying to lift, instead dragging it — *Thump! Thump! Thump!* — down the steps and onto the gravelled driveway.

As far as Mason could tell she was naked except for a black T-shirt and was otherwise as wretched-looking a creature as he'd ever seen. Her hair was a matted tangle the colour of copper and her face was smeared with dirt and snot. She must have been crying not too long ago. There were lines carving streaks down her cheeks and he could see streaks darker still running down the inside of both her legs. They looked like blood.

Mason watching her dragging the bag up the driveway, thinking, *Those sick sons of bitches. What they must have done to her!*

Feeling his anger swelling again was enough to will himself towards his feet. He was feeling weak and more than a little drunk and couldn't manage to raise himself more than an inch off the chair before slumping back down. Taking a deep breath and it not so much feeling like a knife in his heart anymore as it did a sewing needle. Drawing some resolve from that, he planted both of his hands on the arm rest, summoning the strength to try again.

The girl had made it four strides into the yard, with the dog leading the way, and was now turning back to the porch. Seeing Mason still sitting there, she glared up at him with a scowl as fierce and wild as any his wife had ever mustered.

Goddammit, she fumed, don't just sit there! We've got to get the hell out of here!

D ale was ringing the old bell that ever since they'd moved in had been sitting on the window ledge in the kitchen, calling the campers to dinner.

Grubs on, boys and girls! he shouted. Come and get it!

Using his fifty-litre stewing pot, he'd cooked what was left in the freezer of the steaks from the moose he'd shot last January. To the diced meat he'd added a twenty-pound bag of potatoes, ten onions, two green peppers and a dozen carrots, and for the past hour those had been simmering on top of an old barbecue grill he'd propped on two cinderblocks over the firepit in their backyard.

Ron, meanwhile, had been helping Jason at what was now looking ever more to be a granite monolith. Thus far his help hadn't amounted to much more than standing beside the hole, watching the young man dig, and then, when the dirt gave way to a nest of smaller stones, taking the endless stream of tennis-ball-sized rocks Jason passed up to him and heaving them into the field.

By the time Dale was calling the campers to dinner, the hole had grown to four feet deep and six feet wide and when Jason leaned his weight into the chunk of granite it was now at least giving an inch, though not much more.

Jeez, Ron was saying as Dale tucked the bell's handle into his belt and unhitched the ladle he'd slung over the same, the thing looks to weigh a thousand pounds. We're gonna need Chief's tractor if we's gonna have a hope in hell of pulling it out.

Jason didn't seem to have anything to say to that. In place of an answer, he opted instead for a swig from the pop bottle Ron had filled with water for him.

The campers, meanwhile, were streaming in transient cliques of three and four across the field, heading towards the house. Eric, Darren and Duane were in the lead. Their haste was verging on an all-out mad dash as they hurried towards the promise of a full belly and they were grabbing at each other's shirts, trying to trip each other up. At the edge of the field, Darren tackled both Eric and Duane around the knees when it looked like one of them would take the race, and all three disappeared into the tall grass. Masood, who Ron had mistaken for being Pakistani but who he'd since learned was actually from Iran, was right behind them and so it was he who broke into the yard first, raising his hands in ironic mimicry of a gold medal winner.

What say we call that a night? Ron coaxed Jason while Dale ladled the stew into an assortment of bowls and mugs, several shelves' worth of which had come with the house. The rock'll still be here tomorrow.

Jason's only response was to toss aside the now empty bottle and crouch back down in the hole again. It was then that Ron saw the headlights coming down the road. His first thought was that it was another batch of Jason's friends — two more carloads had arrived in the meantime — and so he felt somewhat relieved when Mason's truck passed by their driveway and continued up the Lowrys'.

Chief's home, he said to no one in particular and then hustled off towards the willows, thinking now was as good a time as any to ask the chief about borrowing his tractor.

W hen he came through the closest willow's drape, the truck was rounding the far side of the house, slipping out of view.

It seemed a little odd, since he'd never seen the chief park back there, but that hardly slackened Ron's pace. He heard the truck's door slam shut while he was passing by the porch, the pain in his knee slowing him towards a fast walk.

Here, the chief was saying as Ron came to the lilac bush nestled in the alcove at the side of the mud room, let me give you a hand with that.

The idea that there was someone with the chief cautioned Ron's pace even more, for reasons he couldn't quite say except that in all the months he'd been living there he'd never seen anyone at the Lowrys' except the chief and Hélène. Inching ever so quietly forward, he peered through the purple lilac's fragrant blooms.

The truck was pulled to within a few feet of the house's back steps and the chief was hastening around the front of the vehicle from the driver's side. He was wearing an outfit all in black except for the white POLICE stencilled over its back and his chest, arms and legs were swollen to twice their size by the uniform's body armour. With his grizzled face and beard it lent him the appearance of an elderly football player, minus the helmet, suited up for one final game. That also seemed a bit strange to Ron but less so than the sight of the person he was talking to.

She was a scrawny little teenage girl with a mess of dishevelled orange curls and wearing only a black T-shirt, its hem draped to her knees. In the sparse light cast through the truck's open passenger door Ron could see that her cheeks were streaked with channels carved into the dirt plastered to her freckled skin, the long-dried tears remaking her face into some sort of map, one that from the look of her, seemed to chart the nether regions of hell itself. Tributaries of blood drained in crusted drips down her legs all the way to her ankles as if she'd just had a miscarriage. On second glance he could see a patchwork of bruises there too and also on her arms, their purpled haloes shading towards black.

A dog, looked to be a mastiff, stood at the top of the cement stairs behind her. It was wagging its tail and whimpering like Whisper always did when they were late in feeding her. The girl was standing bent over, on the lowest of the steps, clutching at the straps on an old hockey duffel, apparently trying to drag it up the stairs and failing miserably in that. Whatever was in the bag must have been sore heavy for when the chief grabbed his end of the shoulder strap he was barely able to raise it off the ground.

Jesus! Mason asked, looking up at the girl. What'd you say you got in here again? It's as heavy as a bag of bricks.

Ron thinking that was as good an excuse as any to step out from behind the lilac bush.

Heh-Hey there Chief, he said, walking towards them. You need a hand?

The girl froze stock-still at the sound of his voice and the dog let out a tremulous growl, its teeth parting its quivering jowls and its ears flattening against its head. Those combined were enough to stop Ron in his tracks. The chief was looking all of a sudden befuddled, glancing from the girl to the door behind her and then over at Ron, appearing ever so much like a prematurely aged teenager caught up in a bit of mischief by his father.

It's okay, he won't bite.

This from the girl. She'd since recovered and was looking up at the dog, her expression altogether uncertain, as if she wasn't entirely convinced she was telling the truth. The dog let out one last growl as if to prove her wrong and she scolded, Quiet, Killer!

Dutifully the dog ceased in its snarl and sat down, whimpering again.

Your dog's name is K-Killer? Ron asked starting forward. That's a funny name for a dog that don't bite.

Well I wasn't the one who named him, the girl said with such forthright petulance that it again stopped Ron in his tracks.

The chief, meanwhile, was scratching at the top of his head like he'd all of a sudden forgotten what he was doing. Ron was now close enough to see the two bullet holes in his armour, one just above his navel and one at his heart. The stub ends of the rounds were poking through the fabric and he could see another tear on his sleeve below his elbow, what might have been a bullet grazing his arm.

You all right there, Chief? he asked, not so much because he was worried that the chief had been shot but because the expression on his face was contorting into a mirror image of the confusion on Hélène's whenever she knocked at his door expecting to see her dead son and finding Ron there instead.

Oh, um, uh, the chief said, looking at the girl. Why don't you, uh, take the dog inside. We'll, uh, fetch the bag.

The girl looked down at the duffel like she'd have rather done anything but. Ron could now see that on the front of her shirt there was an apple tree cast against a sunset and encased in the words *Garden Valley Farms*. He'd seen the logo plenty of times before — mostly emblazoned on the back of any number of trailers being hauled by transport trucks up on Highway 17 — but there was something about seeing it on the girl's shirt that gave him sudden pause. It only took him a moment before he realized it was practically the same tree The Sons Of Adam wore as their crest. He hadn't made that connection before and now that he had, he knew it must have meant something, but not what.

Well go on then, the chief was saying to the girl. The door should be unlocked.

With grave reluctance she turned around. Walking up the steps and opening the door, she peered into the dark hallway beyond as if she was expecting any number of horrors awaiting her therein.

The dog had no such compunction. It bustled on past and that seemed to lend the girl a little courage, for she started forward too.

Bathroom's the second door on the left, the chief called to her as she slipped through the door. You can get yourself cleaned up in there.

The old man then turned back to Ron, who was staring right at him, his eyebrows curled into a question mark.

She's, uh, one of, uh, Hélène's nieces. Got herself into a little, uh, um, uh . . .

His voice trailed off into nothing as the click of a door turned him back to the hallway. It was followed by the scratch of nails on wood and the dog whining and the chief stood gazing in at the dog pawing and whimpering at the bathroom door, befuddled all over again.

It seemed to Ron that whatever he and the girl had been through was weighing heavily on him. Helping them with the bag was the only way he could see to ease their burden, if only a little, and he bent down, grabbing the bag's handles and hefting it in one mighty heave up and onto his shoulder.

There you are! Dale exclaimed as Ron stepped back through the willows.

He was washing out the stew pot with a garden hose on the far side of the patio. When Ron didn't answer he added, I saved you a mug of stew, but just barely. Boy, they sure are hungry. Like a pack of wild hyenas.

There was indeed a mug sitting at his place on the patio's table. It was dripping a tentacle of juice down its side and Ron got a sudden flash of that entirely different stream of brown he'd seen dribbling off of Hélène's foot when she was hanging from the rafters in the barn. The thought of that was enough to put him off eating for a week — and maybe forever — but he sat down in front of it nonetheless, eschewing the mug for his phone.

Swiping its screen, he typed "Garden Valley Farms" into its search window. The first hit was from the company's website and he scanned past it, looking for any indication that Garden Valley Farms was connected to The Sons Of Adam. He couldn't find any and settled for a feature article in *Maclean's* magazine from five years ago, the headline of which read, "Local Organic Farming Co-op Dreams Big."

While he scanned through the article he packed his chute with weed from his pill bottle, taking a huff before he was halfway through and then lighting a cigarette and reading the rest.

Garden Valley Farms, he learned, was a farming collective founded some ten years earlier with the aim of ensuring food security for Northern Ontario in an increasingly insecure world. It had started as a half-dozen greenhouses on a single property located just north of Algonquin Park and had grown to become the largest organic produce and livestock co-operative in the entire country, all while fulfilling the co-op's commitment to operating with a zero carbon footprint. It was heralded by environmentalists, agriculturalists and economists the country over as a model for creating a self-sustaining means of food production and its accomplishments were made all the more remarkable in that its farms were run almost entirely by ex-cons.

The rare exception was the Stokes family.

They'd started the original farm in 2030 and had been using it ever since to train their ever-increasing cadre of future farmers, all of whom were drawn from the province's correctional system. Tina Stokes, the co-chair of the collective's board of directors, was quoted as saying, "When my late husband, Jody, and I started Garden Valley Farms it was our dream that it would become a shining beacon to all which proved beyond a shadow of a doubt that only by lifting the lowest among us could we elevate everyone. And that's what Garden Valley Farms is really all about: giving people hope by showing that everyone has an integral role to play in harvesting a better future."

Not much to go on and so he typed in "Sons Of Adam." He read through an article published in the *Globe and Mail* two days ago and then clicked on his CTV news app, to see what it might have to say. "'Euphie Bombs' Terrorize Southern Ontario" was what the headline at the top of the screen read there. Seeking an explanation of what exactly a "Euphie Bomb" was, he scrolled down the screen only to be interrupted by someone asking him, Mind if I have a puff?

He looked up to see Darren, who'd wandered over and was wiping the last of the stew out of his mug with a finger. He was wearing only a black pair of jeans, having since taken off his shirt in deference to the heat, even then pushing towards thirty-five degrees.

How old are you? Ron asked, as he repacked the bowl with the ground-up bud.

I'll be sixteen in August.

So you're fifteen then.

Darren's face scrunched like he was having trouble with the math and Ron lit the weed with his Bic, drawing its silky smoke down into the plastic bag.

Ron himself had started smoking weed when he was eleven. He didn't have any regrets at all about that but, as he was running a little lean on the herb himself and the four plants of various strains he was growing in his basement wouldn't mature for another three weeks, he answered, Then it'll be a couple of years yet before you'll be smoking any of my weed. But you can have my stew if you're still hungry.

Boy, am I ever!

Snatching it up, Darren ran his finger along the drip of juice and licked it off as he wandered back towards Jason and his granite monolith. His brother Eric was already there. His face was buried in his square plastic bowl and his tongue was lapping at the last drops of his own stew even as he used his feet to shuffle one of the smaller rocks Jason had removed from his hole towards the edge of the field.

They're giving out seconds? Eric asked when he spied his brother drinking from a different mug. His eyes were already trailing back to the firepit, searching out the pot.

They were, Jason answered him. I got the last cup!

He held that up like a trophy and Eric lunged for it, grasping at his brother's outstretched arms and Darren dodging backwards, yelling, Hey, this one's mine! Not my fault you're too fucking slow.

Dale had since left the pot to soak and was just then stepping onto the patio. Unclipping his vape pen, he took a puff. Holding it in for a five count, he released the vapour in stuttered exhales through his nose while he surveyed the clusters of youth savouring a meal he'd cooked with the firm assurance of a feudal lord standing on a hilltop glorying in the industry taking place on the grounds of his manor below.

I th-think Chief's done something stupid, Ron said after he took another huff off his chute.

It wouldn't be the first time. Then, lighting a cigarette, Dale added: What, he tip over his tractor again, mowing the lawn?

I think he may have k-killed someone.

Killed someone?

Maybe even a b-bunch of people.

What makes you say that?

Ron was thinking of the bullet holes in the chief's suit and more so how when he was walking past the truck after the chief had ushered him out the house, he'd spotted the assault rifle in its bed. He'd picked it up, careful to keep his prints off the gun by using his shirt as a makeshift glove, and sniffed its barrel. Even now he still got a whiff of gunpowder every time he inhaled, which told him it must have been fired recently, and likely repeatedly as well. That seemed like his most conclusive evidence regarding the chief's supposed activities, so he started there.

The rifle I found in the back of his truck, for one, he said. I took a whiff off its muzzle. It had just been fired, there's no d-doubt about that.

So what? Could have been he was just out hunting.

It wasn't the kind of rifle you hunt with.

What kind was it?

The kind you shoot someone with.

Far as I know, you can shoot someone with pret' near any rifle.

This was an assault rifle.

He had an assault rifle?

A nasty-looking one too. Real nasty. The kind the army uses.

So who's he supposed to have shot with it?

H-how should I know?

You didn't ask him?

No, I didn't ask him.

Well go on then, nothing's stopping you from asking him now.

It was clear from his wry grin that Dale was just joking but Ron looked over at the Lowrys' house nonetheless. For a moment it seemed like he might be thinking about doing exactly that but it was something else he had on his mind.

If he was going to shoot someone, he said, I'd bet Clarence Boothe'd be at the top of his list.

Clarence Boothe? Who's that again?

The guy they's blaming for what happened in North Bay.

The one spiked all them drugs with Euphoral?

Yeah.

Dale thinking on that as he reached for his vape pen. He was just about to take a puff when something seemed to occur to him.

You don't think they spiked any of the shatter, do ya? he asked.

I think it was just the pills.

Well thank god for that.

Dale drew leisurely off the vaporizer and Ron took that as good a time as any to pack himself another bowl.

You know, Ron said while lighting the weed and drawing its smoke down into the bag, he just got out of jail yesterday.

Who?

Clarence Boothe. Taking his huff and exhaling. And who do you think put him away?

The chief.

So you have heard of him then?

I told you I didn't.

So how'd you know it was the chief put him away?

Why in the hell else would you bring him up?

Dale had him there and Ron thought on that a moment.

He's the same guy who killed Warren, he said at last.

Warren was a forklift driver at Harvesters and also a Cree from a reserve in Northern Quebec. He was a big fellow, huge really — six-foot-five and three hundred and fifty pounds — and wore his head shaven to a glossy sheen. Everyone at Harvesters called him Kingpin on account he'd dressed up as the cartoon villain one year for Halloween, though he was about as affable a fellow as anyone Ron or Dale were likely to ever meet.

Fentanyl killed Warren, far as I can recall, Dale said, trying not to think about him.

Sure but it was Clarence Boothe sold that bad batch. The same batch killed thirty-some-odd other people too.

Then I hope the chief did kill him. Serve that bastard right.

Except Clarence wasn't working alone. The way this guy was talking in the article I just read, sounded like he's got a whole d-damned army.

An army?

They's saying it's m-m-maybe the start of a civil war.

Ah hell, I wouldn't put much stock in that. They were saying the same thing about Indians not too long ago.

That was true. Some twenty years ago the federal government had deployed the RCMP in riot gear to quell peaceful protests over a pipeline on unceded First Nations land out west. The crackdown had escalated the scattered protests into a national "Defend the Land" movement. That had led to an uprising by Indigenous Peoples all across the country which had threatened, for a time, to become something more than mere civil disobedience. The government's response had been to declare these "Land Defenders" terrorists and thus give themselves free licence to round up anyone they claimed was aiding and abetting. Thousands of peaceful demonstrators were caught up, as if in a dragnet, while the leaders of the more militant groups had been hunted down, either shot on sight or simply disappeared. It was yet another sad and sorry chapter in the nation's history, made worse in that the government at the time had legislated reconciliation with Indigenous Peoples as a legally binding imperative, a startling level of hypocrisy which was often written large on protest signs, *Reconciliation Can't Happen If You're Pointing A Gun At Me* being one of the more popular variants of those.

The mainstream media had sided with the government, even though the majority of Canadians had sided with the protestors. As such, coverage of the uprising had been minimal at best. Most of Dale's information on the subject had come to him by way of his fellow inmates at the Central East Correctional Centre in Lindsay while he was serving six months for "resisting arrest" after then-Deputy Chief Lowry had pulled him over, Dale suspected, because his Ford Bronco sported a bumper sticker reading *This Land Is Our Land*, which had become one of the movement's rallying cries.

Dale had told Ron plenty of stories about his time at Central East and what he'd learned there, most of which had come by way of his cellmate, Murray. Murray was a co-founder of Native Pride, one of the first so-called terrorist organizations put on the government's "watchlist." He'd been apprehended using a snowmobile to sneak a sled load of baby formula behind the barricades on the Trans-Canada Highway, just north of Thunder Bay. With so many of his fellow "Land Defenders" also behind bars, he'd spent much of his time in prison reflecting on where he thought the movement might have gone wrong. The main conclusion he'd reached was that any such overt actions were doomed to fail from the start.

It's the 1970s all over again, Murray had opined to Dale who later related as much to Ron. What nobody seems to remember is that we came pretty close to an armed rebellion back then too. At the time, it seemed like the only way to get the government to stop stealing our kids and our land and start treating us like we were human beings instead of fucking vermin. And look where that got us. They practically criminalized an entire generation, just for standing up for our rights, and here we are still trapped in that same endlessly looping cycle. What we should have learned back then was that no amount of protest, or even armed resistance, is ever going to reverse five hundred years of genocide, not when there's so much as a nickel left for them to squeeze out of our land, much less the trillions of dollars still in the ground. It's only a matter of time before that particular house of cards collapses under the weight of its own hubris, and the rest of civilization along with it. As far as I can tell, that'll be happenin' any day now and if our Peoples are going to survive the fall we'd be better off layin' low, puttin' our energies into preparing ourselves, and our communities, instead of giving the fucking settlers just one more excuse to keep locking us all away.

Ron was now mulling over a rough précis of that, which is why it took him a few seconds to respond and also why he responded with, The difference is that Clarence and the rest of them Sons don't exactly seem in the mm-mood for lying low.

The rest of which Sons? Dale asked.

The Sons Of Adam.

Never heard of them.

That's what Boothe and his army are calling themselves.

The Sons Of Adam? What kind of name is that?

Hell if I know.

Well, what do you know then?

That's what I'm f-f-fucking tryin' to tell you!

Well, you're sure taking your sweet Mary time about it. That got Dale a pointed glare and he quickly added, Well, go on then.

Like I was saying, The Sons —

Of Adam.

Yeah, The Sons Of Adam. As I was —

Stupid name if you ask me.

Well, I weren't the one who come up with it, was I? Now —

They just ripped it off from *The Sons of Anarchy*.

The old TV show?

Now that was a good name.

And a good show too.

You don't have to tell me. The Sons Of Adam? That's a pussy name. Might as well have called themselves, I don't know, the fucking Sons Of Eugene or some shit.

Except there weren't no Eugene in the Bible.

What's that got to do with anything?

A guy in the article I read said that's where it's from. The Garden of Eden. You know, Adam and Eve.

You're talking about Cain and Abel?

Huh?

They were the real sons of Adam, weren't they?

Sure, everyone knows that.

So what do Cain and Abel have to do with this Clarence Boothe fella?

You got me.

Dale shaking his head.

Still a fucking pussy-assed name, if you ask me. Even if it is from the Bible.

You about done?

I'm getting there. Taking another puff off his vape pen. Now what was it you were trying to say again?

I was trying to say that The Sons Of Adam ain't exactly the type for lying low. One guy in the article was saying they'd done what they done to North Bay in revenge for Clarence Boothe being locked away for ten years. Imagine what they'd do if someone k-killed him.

Like the chief, you mean?

Who else?

What about the police? Or the army? They got as much reason to kill him as anyone.

The police and the army's been told to stand down. After what happened in North Bay, they's worried about inciting further rep-rep-reprisals.

Stand down? Like a détente? Dale asked.

No, it's a ceasefire.

That's what a détente is.

Then why didn't you just say so?

I'm boning up on my *Français*.

You can bone up on it all you like, come tomorrow it won't mean shit how much ff-fucking fransay you speak.

Remind me again what happens tomorrow.

The Sons'll be coming to get revenge on the chief for killing Clarence Boothe, like I fff-fucking toldya!

So you say.

So I say? Ain't you been listening to a fff-fucking word I said?!

He was getting himself worked up beyond all proportions. Spittle was flying out of his mouth and his eyes were bugging and Dale lit himself a smoke, trying to keep himself from egging him on any more than he already had.

Ah, you're just being paranoid, he said, on the first exhale. I told you already, you got to stop watching the news. It's giving you the fear. All we got is the *right* here and the *right* now. Pounding his finger on the table both times he said *right* to punctuate his point. And since I ain't seen no drones hovering around the property, I can't see how the news is going to do us any good.

It was just one article, Ron countered.

That's how they get ya. Like a goddamned worm on a hook.

Well how else was I supposed to find out about Garden Valley Farms, tell me that?

Garden Valley Farms? The produce company? What the hell do they have to do with anything?

That's what I was trying to find out.

You lost me.

It's what it said on the shirt she was wearing.

Who was wearing?

The girl Mason brought back with him.

He brought back a girl?

And she looked liked she'd been through hell, too. Chief said she was his niece.

But you don't think so.

On account of the bullet holes.

What bullet holes?

The chief was wearing a SWAT uniform. You know, the bulletproof kind. There were two bullets sticking out of it. One at his belly, one at his heart.

No shit?

No shit.

That finally gave Dale reason enough to pause. Taking a last drag off his smoke he dropped it into the coffee container on the table they used for butts and wiped his hand over his face, trying to digest all Ron had told him.

And you say these Sons are coming tomorrow.

Could be tomorrow, could be the day after, how the fff-fuck should I know? All I know is that when they do, they ain't likely to leave any witnesses. We'll all just be collateral damage. They'll come for the chief and kill us all too. So what are we gonna do about it?

Dale responded by reaching for the rifle leaning against his chair as if that'd do him any more good than speaking French against such savage killers as The Sons had proven themselves to be. But it wasn't thoughts of making some last, and likely futile, stand he had in mind.

Well I'll tellya one thing, he said, standing, *if* they are coming, they ain't gonna catch me on an empty belly, that's for damned sure.

There was a twinkle in his eyes to go along with the fragile crack of a smile eking at the corner of his lips when he said it and they told Ron he might as well have been whistling into the wind.

All righty now, Dale called out in a convivial holler to no one in particular, who wants to go bag a deer?

Darren and Eric were the only campers still in the yard, aside from Jason, who was still bent over in the hole under their watchful gaze. Both turned Dale's way but it was Darren who answered.

Hell yeah! he called, starting towards Dale. I'll go hunting with you. As long as you got another rifle.

Oh, I might have an extra lying around.

Making a big deal of glancing about the yard, checking his pockets, as if he was looking for a pair of keys and not his Enfield.

Oh shoot, he finally said, I must have left it in the car.

He was already making a beeline for his Jetta and Darren and Eric hurried after him, jostling each other with their elbows, jockeying for position.

I got first dibs, Darren called as he came to the vehicle.

You couldn't hit the moon if you was standing on it, Eric chided back.

Dale had slung his Remington over his shoulder and was just retrieving the Enfield from the Jetta's open trunk.

That's a load of horseshit, Darren countered. Then looking at Dale with the imploring eyes of a kid begging his mom for candy: I can shoot, honest I can.

And I can shoot better'n alls y'all.

This from Darren's girlfriend, Annie, who'd just come out from behind the shed. She was zipping up her jeans shorts so she must have been taking a pee. She'd since tied her hair into a ponytail and her eyes were outlined in mascara, a trickle of it dribbling down her face like a faux tear from the corner of one. Up close, she hardly looked to Dale older than fourteen.

Since when, Darren asked, as she approached with a swagger that seemed entirely too old for a girl as young as her.

Since I was six.

First I'm hearing about it, Darren scoffed.

That's cause you ain't never been in my bedroom. And you ain't never gonna neither.

Sticking her tongue out at Darren and then turning to Dale.

My daddy taught me. I even won a bunch of trophies at our gun club.

But have you ever hunted? Dale asked.

Sure, plenty of times.

Deer?

Mostly grouse since my, uh, my m-mom, she never could stomach the taste of game.

The way she'd stuttered over *my mom* gave Dale every indication that something horrible must have happened to her. Whatever that was, she didn't seem to want to think about it any more than she already had and quickly pushed on towards a memory of happier times.

One time I even killed two with one bullet, she bragged.

Dale stroked at the scruff on his chin, thinking on that, then offered, That must have been one helluva shot.

Mm-my daddy, she stuttered so Dale knew something horrible must have happened to him too, he-he said it was the luckiest damned shot he ever saw. He never did believe I was aiming for the both of them. But I was.

Annie had since planted her hands, resolute, on her hips and the pointed glare in her eyes served as a challenge to anyone who'd have dared contest her word.

Well there's a sure way to find out if she's telling the truth. This from Eric. Go on, Dale, give her the rifle.

Dale handed the Enfield over, saying, Be careful now, it's loaded.

Annie took it up, holding it crooked in one arm and checking the breech with her free hand. Seeing it was empty, she chambered a round and set the stock against her shoulder, sighting across the field.

She's got good form, no doubt there, Dale said, for it was the truth.

Go on then, Annie, Darren goaded. I bet you couldn't even hit the broadside of that shed.

I've always preferred a moving target, she said in response. Swinging the gun on a quick lateral, she sighted on Darren, right between the eyes. Go on then, what are you waiting for . . . Run!

Such willful malice in her tone that it made Darren flinch. His face blanched towards white and Eric nudged him with his elbow, goading, Yeah, Darren, what are you waiting for?

When Dale's uncle had taught him to shoot, the first thing he'd told him was to never point a gun, loaded or otherwise, at anyone. Good advice, for sure, and Dale thought maybe he should say something. Still, he sidled past the three as if a fourteen-year-old girl pointing a loaded rifle at her boyfriend concerned him as much as had Ron's dire warning.

Come on now, he said, his own tone shading towards utter jubilation, them deer ain't gonna shoot themselves!

Y ou okay in there?

Mason was leaning his ear to the bathroom door while he spoke, feeling no less a sense of dread than he had twenty-four hours ago, when he'd done the same while holding Hélène's cup of tea.

The girl, whose name he still hadn't learned, had been in there for almost an hour. He'd heard her running the bath after ushering Clete back out the side door. He'd been hovering close by ever since, venturing no further than the kitchen to eat through the jar of corn relish along with the last couple of slices of rye he'd found in the breadbox on the counter. After a few minutes she'd turned the water off and then all was quiet for a half-hour. He'd been called back to the door by the sound of her crying — a swelling tide of braying sobs that sounded like waves crashing against a rocky beach with her caught in their undertow, being swept out to sea.

The dog had been lying in front of the door the whole time. It started whimpering along with her and Mason had stood beside it in the hall, listening to her cry and telling himself it was a good thing, that it meant there was still something alive inside of her worth crying over. She'd cried herself out after ten minutes and then he hadn't heard a peep until five minutes ago when the rush of water *woosh*ing through the pipes under the kitchen floor told him she'd pulled the tub's plug.

It had reminded him that the only thing in the downstairs bathroom she'd have to dry herself off with was a small hand towel and he'd gone upstairs to fetch a regular-sized one from the linen closet. He was holding it under his arm now.

When she hadn't replied after a couple of seconds, he knocked again, offering, I brought you a towel.

He heard the squeak of skin shifting against the tub and then her voice — a fragile croak, no more than a whisper.

The door's unlocked, she said.

He reached for the knob and then paused, thinking how the downstairs tub didn't have a curtain, since it didn't have a shower. That'd mean if she was still sitting in the tub there'd be nothing between him and her.

I'll leave it in the hall for you, he said.

He was just bending down to set it on the floor and thinking that he should have also brought her Hélène's old bathrobe when the girl spoke again.

I need your help.

How's that? Mason asked, standing back up.

I threw up.

That's okay. I'll clean it up later, don't you worry about that.

I'm feeling dizzy. I-I don't think I can stand.

Mason taking a deep breath.

Okay, he finally said, I'm coming in.

Opening the door and slipping through, he averted his eyes but still caught a glimpse of the girl on his periphery nonetheless.

She was sitting hunched over in the tub, clutching at her knees, her hair wet, drooped over her face and plastered to her shoulder, the skin there red and raw as if she'd been dragged naked across rough cement. Her whole body was shivering with such violent tremors that it immediately called to mind a Euphie in stage two of withdrawal.

Oh please, lord no! Please, please no, oh lord! Oh please, lord no!

The voice in his head cycling in an endless refrain as Mason stared now uninhibited at the girl, the loop broken at last by a no less despairing thought:

If she was really in stage two it would have been better if you'd fetched your gun instead of the towel.

The dog had slipped past him. He was sniffing at a blob on the mat in front of the tub that didn't so much look like vomit as it did a wad of mucus — a thick and yellow viscous substance streaked with flecks of red. The girl's hand was then reaching out, stroking the dog's head in a clumsy caress, a gentle and loving act which no Euphie in stage two could ever likely manage.

Jarred from his stupor by this modicum of hope, Mason hurried forward, scolding the dog, Go on, shoo!

The dog let out a timid growl but still it slunk away, giving Mason a wide berth as he approached the tub, his eyes locked on the blob as much to avoid stepping in it as to avoid looking at the girl. Bending then, he folded the mat over the vomit and pulled it off to the side.

Here's your towel, he said, holding it out.

I can't, she replied. Please, I can't. I-I'm so cold.

Unfurling the towel and holding it out, keeping it between him and the girl as he bent over her, setting the towel over her back. Her hands clasped at it, cinching it under her chin, and Mason stood back up, peering down at the girl. She was shivering so hard it looked like she was about to fly all to pieces and he had no idea at all what he might do to ease her suffering.

On the truck ride home she'd seemed like she was holding it together pretty well, all things considered. Riding in the passenger seat with the dog lying between them, its tail slapping at Mason's leg and its head nuzzling in her lap, that bag of you-know-what wedged on the floor at her feet, her hand outstretched through the open window, her fingers grasping at the wind blowing through them, her hair tousled in the breeze and a sort of dreaminess about her eyes, she'd almost looked happy.

Mason telling himself, *She's going to be all right. Thank god, she's going to be all right.*

It had seemed a miracle at the time.

Not wanting to break the spell, he hadn't said anything until they were turning off Voyer and into his driveway. Then he'd only spoken to ask her if there was any family he should call to tell them she was all right.

My whole family's dead, she'd said so bluntly that it had robbed Mason of the will to speak again until he'd seen her trying to drag the duffel bag up the stairs.

Seeing her now, she looked to have shrunk to half her size and from the way she was trembling he knew what he'd also known then but had been afraid to admit: *She isn't all right at all. Hell, it'll be a damned miracle if she's all right ever again.*

He'd just spotted the familiar brown tree branded behind her ear and that recalled to him the one Dr. Watt had shown him on his granddaughter. Remembering how fragile and delicate Kim had looked stretched out on the table in the morgue, and here was a girl looking like even the lightest touch would shatter her clear to bits. Feeling then something on his cheek — it felt like an ant crawling on his skin. Wiping at it, he found it was a tear and that came as more of a shock than anything, for he couldn't remember the last time he'd cried.

It only served to reignite his rage.

Those evil motherfuckers! he thought. *If I could bring 'em all back from the dead, I'd skin every last one of them alive, those evil sons of bitches!*

His rage trickled out of him, staring down at the girl, and he hurried it along by telling himself, *No use thinking about that now. The only thing that matters a damn is the right here and the right now. The girl. She saved your life as much as you saved hers and there's no point wasting what little time you got left brooding on the past.*

Bending to the girl, he slipped one hand under her legs and set the other on her back.

Come on there little missy, he said, straining against her weight as he lifted her from the tub, let's get you off to bed.

Mason spent the rest of the night sitting in the kitchen chair he'd planted in the downstairs hallway across from his den, the one room he'd claimed all to his own.

When they'd first moved into the house, he'd worked his fair share of late shifts. Not wanting to wake Hélène when he returned home in the middle of the night, he'd stored a fold-up cot in its closet so he could sleep there. The last time he'd used it was during the week after he'd become chief. He'd come home from work on the first evening he was North Bay's top cop to find a comforter, a fitted sheet and his pillow sitting in the downstairs hallway. If the silence he'd endured the previous evening hadn't been enough to tell him Hélène was furious with him, those most certainly were.

He'd set the cot up while the girl was running her bath, using a queen-sized fitted sheet since he couldn't find any singles and placing two pillows and an old comforter on top of it. After he'd laid her down, setting her head on one of the pillows and snugging the blanket to her chin, he'd brewed her a cup of tea. From the way she was acting and from the track marks on her arms, he knew they'd been injecting her with some form of narcotic. From the way she was shivering, it was clear she was in withdrawal. Thinking maybe it would ease her suffering some, he added to the tea the powder from two of the diazepam gel caps Dr. Ballard had prescribed Hélène. She'd kicked off the blanket by the time he'd returned, though she was shivering now more than ever.

He'd brought her some of Hélène's clothes down too, but she'd spurned his efforts to help her get dressed. She was lying there stark naked and writhing in agony and the dog was lying beside her on the floor. It growled at Mason as he'd walked towards the cot, though in a lesser way, like it had lost any and all enmity it might have harboured against him and growling had simply become a habit it couldn't shake.

The girl had refused the tea, turning her back on him when he insisted and moaning, Leave me alone. Please, just leave me alone. Leave me the fuck alone!

Her mounting fervour had driven him out of the room and he'd fetched the chair from the kitchen, planting it in the hall so he could give her some space and yet still have a clear view of her through the open door. He'd fetched his Glock along with the chair and the whole time he sat there he held it in his lap, praying he wouldn't have to use it.

If it *was* Euphoral they'd been injecting her with, it'd take between eight and twelve hours from her last dose before she hit stage one in her withdrawal. The surest sign was self-harm and he had more than a few anxious moments because of that. In her sleepless wrestle, she clawed at her arms and sometimes her face, leaving deep gouges in her skin beading blood. Once at around the eight-hour mark she'd clutched at the budding mound of her adolescent breast with such fury that it looked like she was trying to tear it clean off and Mason was propelled to his feet, certain she was about to enter stage two any second.

With the violent rage that would follow in stage three, and which wouldn't end until she'd either gone into cardiac arrest or he intervened, he knew that if she had become addicted to Euphoral the only thing he could do for her was to shoot her — like she was no better than some rabid dog. He steadied his resolve by telling himself that'd be a kindness, though in that moment it felt to him that kindness itself was an antiquated notion as out of step with the modern world as was a landline phone. But shortly she'd settled into a fretful sleep and Mason had drawn the covers over her again before returning to his chair.

He must have dozed off because he was startled back into wakefulness sometime later by her crying out, Ben! Ben! Where are you? Ben! Ben!

She'd become tangled up in the blanket and was struggling to free herself with the panicked frenzy of someone caught in a riptide. He rushed to her side, setting the Glock on the den's desk and sitting down on the bed, tugging the blanket from out beneath her, freeing her trapped arms. She shocked awake at his touch, glaring up at him in sheer terror and gasping, I can't find him anywhere! He's gone. He's gone. He's gone!

Her hair had become slathered to her face and Mason wiped the strands delicately from her eyes with the pads of his fingers. Her skin was sticky to the touch and feverish. The fitted sheet had become soaked through with sweat and urine and there was a greenish-brown streak that must have been diarrhea overtop a tea-plate-sized blotch of red that made him think maybe it was her time of the month.

Not much he could do about that.

Even if he could root out one of Hélène's old tampons, there was no way in hell he was going to put it in for her. So he did the only thing he could. Taking up the towel he'd hung to dry on the back of his desk's chair, he set it over the mess on the sheet so she wouldn't have to lie in it and then went into the kitchen. He dumped a full rack of ice from the freezer into one of their stainless steel mixing bowls and then filled it half with water. She was calling out for Ben again when he returned with the ice water and the dishtowel that had been slung over the stove's handle.

Sitting beside her, he wet the towel and lay it across her forehead.

It's okay, he assured her, trying to bring her back to reason. We'll find him. We will. I promise. It's going to be okay. We'll find Ben, wherever he is. He can't have gone far. We'll find him. Don't you worry about that.

The girl's expression softened at the urgency in his voice and her eyelids drifted again towards sleep. How long he sat there beside her he couldn't say. It must have been hours though, for the room's dark slowly began to relent to the dawn. Mason bided his time rewetting the cloth and setting it over her head as the water in the bowl grew warm at even pace with the shadows retreating towards the room's four corners. Only when their fading dark had been vanquished entirely by the rising sun did he stand.

It must have been getting close to nine, meaning that the crucial twelve hours had passed.

If she was going to go all-out Euphie, Mason assured himself, *she'd have done it by now.*

Stretching against the crimp in his back and in his shoulders and the dog standing along with him, stretching out its back and yawning wide, looking up at Mason with pleading eyes like every dog he'd ever owned when they were begging for a scratch.

Mason obliged, kneeling and rubbing the dog behind the ears, telling it, You're a good dog, yes you are, you're a good dog, which was what he'd always cooed when doing the same to any of the five he'd owned over the years. The dog reciprocated by licking his cheek and Mason stood again, wiping at the slobber and driven towards the door by a sudden light-headedness and a queasy feeling in his belly, like it had become one vast and cavernous pit full of hungry snakes.

Well come on then, he said, motioning the dog to follow with a sweep of his hand, what say you and I fix ourselves some breakfast.

I s this some kind of joke?

Duane was standing in front of the back door, staring at the sign Ron had made out of a pizza box and taped to the window.

Bathroom Closed, it read in thick black marker.

If it is, I sure as heh-heh-heh-hell ain't the one laughing, Ron answered, for he sometimes stuttered merely for emphasis.

And that was the understatement of the year.

Just after two in the morning, he'd come up from trying unsuccessfully to fall asleep on the basement's La-Z-Boy recliner — where he always slept when it was as hot as it was last night — only to find the toilet off the kitchen plugged and overflowing and a thick soup of shit and puke covering most of the floor. It had taken him the long side of an hour to wipe it all up and he'd then spent almost half as long in the shower before he'd felt clean again.

Well I'm about ready to shit my pants, Duane pleaded, doing a little jig to prove his point, and Ron glanced up from the table, directing his gaze towards the spade he'd propped beside the door.

That's why I put out the shovel.

What am I supposed to do with that?

Shovels are for digging holes, ain't they?

You expect me to shit in a hole?

It's a damn sight better'n shitting all over my bathroom floor, I'll tellya what.

Duane didn't seem to have much to say to that.

Can I at least have some toilet paper? he asked.

We're fresh out, Ron answered, though he knew for a fact there was a full pack of a dozen rolls in the basement's laundry room.

Then how am I supposed to wipe my ass?

Far as I know, folks been shitting in the woods for thousands of years before they invented toilet paper. I'm sure you'll figure it out.

Duane gaping at Ron slack-jawed, as if he was joking and was waiting on the punchline.

I thought you said you were about to shit your pants, Ron offered him in return. I tellya, if you do, don't come around begging to use *my* washing machine.

That finally seemed to compel Duane into an admission of defeat. Snatching up the shovel, he tromped off towards the field and Ron called after him, Mind you bring it back in case anyone else has to take a shit too!

He really must have been in dire need to relieve himself. As soon as the teenager had breached the tall grass at the edge of the yard, he dropped his pants and squatted.

That was enough to get Ron on his feet.

You're supposed to dig the d-damned hole *before* you take a shit! he hollered but Duane made no sign he'd heard him.

Scanning away from him, his mood was further soured by the detritus of chip bags and empty liquor and beer bottles strewn about the yard and littering the field as far as the eye could see, and more so by the dozen people passed out on the lawn.

Ignorant little shits, Ron grumbled as he packed himself a bowl, his foul mood in no small way enhanced by the fact that he'd only managed three hours' sleep last night.

Around ten o'clock a caravan of some fifteen vehicles had converged on the property. When he'd first seen it, Ron was certain it was The Sons Of Adam come to seek their revenge on the chief for killing Clarence Boothe. So it was with more than a little relief that he'd watched from his patio chair as a legion of youth poured forth from the cars and trucks parked in front of his house, whooping and cat-calling to those in the field and the ones already there whooping and cat-calling back, Ron all the while thinking, *Now we're attracting the goddamned tourists!*

Still, he'd left them to their fun, keeping a close eye on the party from the patio, guarding as much against the likelihood of The Sons showing up and ending the party for good as he was against someone setting fire to the field again. They hadn't by one o'clock and, after almost falling asleep in his chair, he'd finally sloughed off to the basement telling himself, *Well if The Sons are coming, they can shoot me down there just as easily as they can on the patio.*

For the next hour he was kept awake by the non-stop clomp of footsteps above him as people stomped through the kitchen on their way to the bathroom. Finally, at just after two he'd got up and found the mess. He'd made the sign and locked the door and was back in bed by three-thirty but his simmering rage had kept him up until well after five.

He'd arisen twenty minutes ago and fifteen minutes later had come out to the patio with a fresh cup of coffee, his cigarettes, his pill bottle of weed and his chute. Neither the coffee nor a smoke nor two huffs off the pop bottle had done much to improve his mood, growing fouler by the minute as he scanned over the clutter of people and garbage strewn about the property. Finally it was too much for him to bear. After he'd smoked a second cigarette, he pried himself off the chair and grabbed the old broom they used to sweep the patio.

He came towards the maze of bodies yelling, Roll out! Come on now, the party's over. Roll out! Roll out! Roll out!

A few of the sleepers stirred, sitting up and blinking. There was none older than nineteen and they all wore embarrassed expressions as if Ron was their father and he'd just found them passed out on their own front lawn. But most of them couldn't be roused so easily and he walked through the maze, poking at them with the butt end of the broom and hollering a few more Roll Out!s for good measure.

A couple of his more virulent prods were answered with, What the fuck, man?, but mostly the revellers came to looking just like the others — shyly gathering themselves up and heading off into the field to look for lost friends or trickling back to their vehicles.

After all the sleepers in sight were on the move, he could still hear someone snoring. He tracked it to the granite monolith only to discover it was Jason. He'd fallen asleep in the hole and was sitting upright with his head resting against the rock at a dire angle. Ron was just bending down to nudge him awake with a gently prodding hand when the sharp report of a rifle's *Crack!* stood him back upright even as it turned him towards the field.

Oh geez, will you look at that!

Darren, Eric and Masood had emerged from the quad trail that led into the woods at the back of the property. They were dragging Dale's old hunting tarp, clutching at it with six hands between them and each and every one of those slung over their shoulders, their backs bent to the task of hauling a dead deer into the field.

Dale was in the rear, lifting the tail end of the tarp to keep the deer from sliding off and struggling to keep up with the teenagers' unrelenting pace. His rifle was slung over his shoulder so Ron guessed it must have been Annie who'd fired the shot. She was sitting on top of the deer, riding it with the majesty of a queen on parade. The butt of the Enfield was propped on her leg and the regal poise in her recline left no doubt in Ron's mind that she'd been the one who'd bagged the deer.

A crowd was already gathering.

Those who'd been milling about the encampment had come over to catch a glimpse and those who'd been asleep must have been roused by the shot. They were crawling out of their tents, blinking against the sun as Ron plunged into the field, hurrying towards its far side in his limpity-hobble.

Darren, Eric and Masood had stopped beside the firepit. Annie's friend, Kendra, was bowing in reverence before her, offering an enthusiastic, Milady, and holding out her hand like a royal valet would. Annie took it up and stepped off the tarp with an air of majesty that didn't seem entirely put on.

Ron was close enough now to see that Annie had two red warrior stripes on either cheek which she must have given herself in honour of the kill, for the index and middle fingers on her right hand were speckled with dried blood.

I can't believe you actually shot one, Kendra gushed with undisguised awe as Ron came within earshot.

No thanks to dimshit here, Annie replied slapping Darren hard with the back of her hand and Darren acting like he'd been mortally wounded, wincing and rubbing at his arm.

It's not my fault I had the shits, Darren countered. If you want to blame anyone, you ought to blame Dale. He's the one who made that stew.

You see, I'd just got it in my sights, Annie explained.

Snapping the rifle to her shoulder with military precision, she demonstrated that by sighting across the field as Ron ambled up beside Dale and caught his first sight of the deer. Its size and stunted antlers made it out to be a young male verging on adulthood and, as Annie continued, it was hard not to see in it a certain majesty as well.

Dawn was just breaking across the lake where we'd been camped out all night. Me and dimshit here were using a toppled oak tree as a blind — you know, hiding behind its upended roots. Dale and Eric and Masood, as far as I know, they'd gone off somewhere to jerk each other off —

Hey! This from Eric, his affrontery quickly quelled by Dale nudging him in the arm and teasing, I didn't see you complaining a few hours ago.

Dale chuckled along with the taunt even as Eric blushed against the mere insinuation.

Dimshit, as he already mentioned, had gone off to take a shit. He was gone for a half-hour so I figured he must have got lost, which hardly came as a surprise since he'd almost got lost twice already.

Well it was dark, weren't it, Darren protested. All those damned trees look the same in the dark.

Like I said, dawn had just broke so it was plenty light out —

Except when I left to take a shit it was dark and that's when I got lost.

Like I said, dawn had just broke so it was plenty light out. You'd have to have been blind to get lost especially since all you had to do was look for the lake, follow the shore right back to the fallen tree.

Annie casting a pointed glare at Darren as she spoke and that seeming enough to quell any further protests.

Anyway, she said, looking back through the rifle's sight, I'd just seen this buck stepping down towards the water. He was bending over to take a sip and I was aiming dead centre at his neck, about to take my shot. That's when I heard dimshit here calling out, Annie? Annie?

Her voice rose to a higher pitch as she called out her name, making Darren out to sound like some scared little girl.

That's bullshit, Darren spat. I didn't sound like no scared little girl. Fucking bullshit!

Annie? Annie? he was calling out. You better not have took off and left me in the woods! Like I hadn't been sitting in the exact same place for almost five hours.

I told you, I-I got turned around in the dark.

Regardless, Annie continued, letting that slide, the deer startled into a run. At that exact same moment I heard a shot which I figured was Dale. Except it missed so on second thought I figured it couldn't have been Dale and must have been Eric.

And I would've hit it too, Eric interjected, if brother fucktard here hadn't scared it off.

Luckily, Annie charged on, I prefer a moving target anyway.

Annie then swivelling the rifle, making as if she was tracking after the deer. Her aim roved about the group, past Eric and Masood and Duane and a dozen other faces peering back at her. A few of them flinched and others ducked low out of her sights as she searched out that one person in particular. Darren had since wised to her game. He was playing along by ducking low behind the crowd, peering out from behind their arms and over their shoulders, trying to stay out of her field of vision. And finally, failing at that, he made a fevered zig-zagging dash across the field in perfect imitation of a deer on the hoof with Annie tracking after him as calm as could be.

Crack!

The crowd startled at the rifle's shot and Darren's hand snapped to his neck as if he really had been shot even as he pitched to the ground in a sprawling caterwaul of legs and arms. Only when he'd disappeared into the tall grass did Annie look up from the rifle, the lines on her cheeks adding a certain gravity to her unmistakable delight.

And that, my friends, she beamed ecstatic, is all she wrote!

Y ou've got to drink something, Mason coaxed.

He was standing beside the cot with the cup of tea he'd rewarmed in the microwave after adding to it a spoonful of honey and the girl was staring past him through dead eyes, like she thought that maybe if she ignored him long enough he'd just go away.

But Mason wouldn't be abated.

I'm not leaving until you drink something, he said. Come on now, sit up. It'll make you feel better, I promise.

He reached down to take her by the arm and she shrugged him off with such vehemence that he was worried there'd be a repeat of the last time he'd tried to give her the tea. Much to his surprise, and to his alarm, she then cast off her blankets, exposing her naked adolescence with such brazen aplomb that it had Mason searching out the window, worried all of sudden that someone might be looking in and get the wrong idea.

The cot creaked beneath her so he knew she was sitting up and he shortly felt her hands groping for the mug. He released it and pivoted towards the desk, stepping to the chair where he'd hung Hélène's bathrobe. Picking it up, he turned back to her, holding it out like he had the towel, keeping her delicates well below his view. She had the mug clamped to her lips and there was a stream of brownish liquid draining over her chin, she was gulping it down so fast.

This was my wife's, he said, meaning the bathrobe. And I fetched you some clothes too. They're hanging on the hook in the bathroom. I also ran you another tub. I figured —

She'd finished the tea and the sharp rap of her setting it on the floor cut him off mid-sentence. Wiping her mouth and staring past him again with those dead eyes, she stood up, taking one first wobbling step, and Mason reached towards her, ready to catch her if she fell. She steadied herself on the corner of the desk and then pulled herself up straight-backed. A glimmer of defiance banished the vacant sheen in her eyes and she grit her teeth, taking another step. Mason himself edged forward, offering her the robe. She pivoted around that, passing him by with such forthright determination that he couldn't help but stare after her as she strode towards the door.

Her bare back was cross-thatched with dried-over scabs like the lashes from a whip that could just as likely have been made by fingernails. He got a sudden image of her screaming and thrashing against her attacker with the same sort of defiance as she'd just strode past the bathrobe, though probably, he conceded watching her turn into the hall and out of sight, she would have been too doped-out to manage anything more than a stifled groan.

While she was in the bathroom, Mason flipped the cot's mattress and changed the bedding. He stuffed the sheet, the pillow case and the comforter into a black garbage bag and set that out in the mud room. He then stood in the kitchen, appraising the cupboards, trying to think of what he had in there that the girl might be able to hold down.

He settled on Quaker Instant Oatmeal and filled the kettle and set it on the stove to heat up while he poured a healthy portion of the porridge into a bowl. He added to that a spoonful of brown sugar and a sprinkle of cinnamon, which was how he preferred it, but forswore the handful of raisins he'd have also added for banana slices, which was how Jill and Jesse had preferred theirs.

The dog — he still hadn't resigned himself to calling it Killer — had taken up residence on the couch. As he walked past, it stared over at him with guilty eyes, like it was used to being chased off the furniture. Hélène might have raised a protest — she never could abide one of his dogs on the couch. Mason didn't hold that particular qualm and sidled on past, his own gaze drawn to the duffel bag sitting beside his La-Z-Boy as he moved towards the hall.

When they'd raided Clarence's farm ten years ago, they'd found three similar duffels in one of the tunnels. Each had contained an even one million dollars. He figured probably this bag held about the same, though he hadn't got around to checking for sure. After he'd set the bowl of oatmeal on the desk beside the cot, he dragged the duffel into the den. He could hear the girl coughing and the faint splash of water. Mindful of how thin the wall was between the den and the bathroom, he unzipped the bag with the utmost care. Pulling back its flaps, he could see that the duffel was indeed stuffed with inch-thick stacks of bills, mostly twenties but a few fifties and bundles of hundreds too.

Zipping it back up, he dragged it to the cot. He pushed it underneath and stood back up, thinking that what he really ought to do was put it in the vault downstairs. But then it might appear to her that he was trying to steal her money, which wasn't his intent at all. Telling himself that if anyone had earned a million dollars it was her, he left it where it was. He could now hear the water draining from the tub and hurried out of the room. He'd made himself a fresh cup of instant coffee with the water left over from the tea. He was just adding a dollop of cream to it when he heard the bathroom door creaking open.

I left you some porridge on the desk, he called to the girl. Mind you eat it now. Be good to get something in your belly.

The only response he got was the den's door slamming shut with a definitive *Bang!* and he tried not to take it personally, reminding himself of all the times his own kids had answered him by slamming *their* bedroom doors.

Taking his coffee into the living room, he cued the remote, activating the TV with the aim of finding out whether there was any news yet about what he'd done to Clarence and his gang.

The prime minister's familiar youthful and goateed visage appeared onscreen in front of a podium at the top of the steps leading into Rideau Hall. He was flanked by the premier's bloated and pompous smirk and the solemn grimace of a heavily decorated man in uniform, a general of some sort.

— assure all Ontarians, and all Canadians, the PM was saying, that my government, in cooperation with the government of Ontario and the nation's military, are doing everything in their power to stop these unprovoked, and savage, attacks. If that means opening up a dialogue with terrorists then, yes, we are prepared to do just that.

Attacks, Mason thought, hearing what the PM said. *That must mean there was more than one.*

The steady stream of words scrolling beneath the prime minister seemed like the likeliest avenue for discovering what cities other than North Bay had been hit. Craning forward, he stepped to within a few feet of the screen so he could read what it said.

This is what it told him:

Footage of the so-called "Euphie Bombs" has been pouring in from dozens of incidents all across Ontario and the government is asking that anyone who is currently taking an illicit drug report to the closest screening centre for evaluation. For a list of those, and to find out more, please go to ctvnews.ca or click on the windows below.

Euphie Bombs? he thought. *What the hell are those?*

Using the remote, Mason clicked on the first of the windows below the scroll, enlarging the footage from a news drone to full screen.

It was hovering above a set of concrete steps in front of an official-looking building. The limestone pillars on either side suggested to Mason it belonged to the government, or was maybe the administrative building on some university campus. There was a woman in a red pantsuit kneeling at the top of the steps. She was clutching at the hair of another woman lying on the platform in front of her, pounding the other's face into cement, though by then it was already reduced to a bloody pulp. The high wail of sirens was zeroing in and the drone pulled back to reveal a police cruiser skidding to a halt on the sidewalk. As the driver flung the door open, he was already reaching for his sidearm and lining it on the attacker. She'd also spotted him and was now lurching down the stairs, her hands dripping blood and her mouth smeared with it as well. She hadn't made it more than two steps before a barrage of bullets ripped into her chest. As the woman toppled backwards, Mason flipped to the next feed.

It was from a residential street.

Two pre-teen boys had set up a skateboarding rail at the side of the road and were taking turns showing off their moves. At a house across the road, three down, there was a man wearing a hard hat and goggles. He was using a chainsaw to cut up a maple tree that had fallen onto the roof of a garage. A younger man dressed the same was feeding branches into the wood chipper parked at the curb and Mason stood there vacillating his gaze between the chainsaw, the chipper and the two boys, imagining any number of increasingly dire scenarios.

A flicker of movement from the centre of the screen drew his attention to a jogger running down the middle of the road, a half-block away. He was growing closer at an ever-accelerating pace. As he drew nigh, Mason could see he was dragging a small dog behind him on a leash, some sort of terrier. It was lying on its side and clearly dead. Probably his owner was in stage one or three of his withdrawal and Mason edged closer to the TV, terrified of what was about to happen to the two young skaters.

But it wasn't the skaters the Euphie was bound for, it was the wood chipper.

Swerving at a drastic angle the man leapt at the chipper's mouth, playing Superman with outstretched hands. A geyser spray of red spewed into the bin under the chipper's spout and Mason let out a relieved breath thinking, *I guess he must have been in stage one after all.*

The only one of the four other people who seemed to have seen it was the smaller of the two boys. He was uttering, Whoa!, in open mouthed horror, and that's where Mason left him.

The next feed was an overhead shot of a suburban backyard. It was teeming with twenty or so kids, all under the age of five and wearing party hats, and there was a clown/magician putting on a show on a stage towards the yard's rear under a banner that read, *Happy Fourth Birthday Abdul!*

Mason couldn't bear the thought of what might be about to happen there. He flipped to the next feed, and after he'd watched that, to the next and the next and the next. All revealed similar scenes of carnage. The sum total had his legs feeling again like putty and his stomach like someone had punched a fist right through it and was now clutching their fingers around his spine — the only thing keeping him on his feet. His shock and dismay were spiralling in a whirling dervish about his mind. Those finally congealed into one all-pervading thought ripe with implications even more catastrophic than anything he'd seen on screen.

Is this all happening because of me? Is that what these so-called Euphie Bombs are? Revenge for me killing Clarence and the others? What have I done? My god, what have I done!

Craning closer to the TV, he saw the caption on the scene playing out on screen bore yesterday's date along with the time: 11:22 a.m. That was almost ten hours before he'd shot Clarence so the so-called Euphie Bombs couldn't have been in retaliation.

That brought him halfway back to his senses. Pointing the cursor at the top right-hand corner of the screen, he clicked on *Breaking News*. A window opened up below it filled with headlines from the past twenty-four hours. Most were about the Euphie Bombs, the first of which he saw had been reported at 12:02 a.m. on April 23, which was yesterday. The only mention of Clarence was a feed titled *Boothe Bros. Sought In North Bay Euphie Attack*, but that was from fifteen hours ago.

He clicked on it anyway. It brought him to a clip from the footage shot by the drone at Collins Bay on the morning Clarence was released from jail, taken right after he'd made his fateful pronouncement. DB was just hopping on the back of a bike driven by a man wearing a Sudbury VP patch. A man bearing a president patch of the same was pulling up beside Clarence while the latter took a deep puff off what appeared to be a cigarillo from astride his customized Dyna Wide Glide. The camera zoomed in to reveal the former was indeed Virgil Boothe, apparently come out of hiding to welcome his brother back into the fold along with all the other Sons.

There was speculation at the time of his arrest that Virgil was involved with his younger brother's illicit activities. There was no corroborating evidence and Virgil had walked, or rather, he'd run, but to where was anyone's guess. As far as Mason knew, the last time anyone had seen hide nor hair of him was at his younger brother's sentencing hearing. After that he'd simply disappeared, or so everyone had thought. From what had happened, it was looking ever so much like that was just a case of wishful thinking. Somebody must have planned the Euphie attack in North Bay and Virgil was as likely a suspect as any.

The news announcer on the feed was providing a rough summary of the same. The image then froze with Clarence and Virgil smiling up at the camera like they were kings of the goddamned world and Mason's gaze zeroed in on the latter.

If Virgil had indeed spent the past ten years plotting vengeance for his brother being locked away, it wasn't much of a stretch to think of what he might do if someone killed Clarence outright.

Mason's addled thoughts tracked back to the night before, starting with the drone. Cursing it again, for it had surely been recording him in the moments before he went on his rampage and likely during it as well. And even if it hadn't, the Balmond brothers had seen him just fine. He'd left them lying unconscious in the woods and he cursed himself again for not going back and putting a bullet in each of their heads when he had the chance.

If he'd had his gun, he'd have shot both of the callously amused faces on the screen right between the eyes, but the only thing in his hand was the remote. His arm was already cocking back and throwing it at the two brothers still in freeze-frame. It struck dead centre between them, cracking the glass and causing the screen to go dark.

Motherfuckers!

It came out as a hoarse whisper through his laboured breaths and there was a high-pitched whine escalating in his head like a kettle on a hard boil, which was exactly what his brain felt like. A piercing pain then in his left eye, like someone had jammed a fork into it, and the world was spinning off its axis. He was reeling as if in a centrifuge and the light all of a sudden seemed to flee before him, like the sun itself had decided it couldn't be party to such madness — his and the world's — and had simply winked off in utter disgust.

Oh god, he thought, *now you're having a fucking stroke!*

The faint yet unmistakable report of someone shooting off a gun outside startled him back to reason. He was standing in the kitchen with no memory of how he'd got there. Both his hands were clutching at the back of his chair at the table and he was gasping in great mouthfuls of air. The muggy heat made it feel like he was trying to breathe underwater. It was an impression further enhanced by the speckles of dust swirling in eddies within a shaft of sunlight lancing through the curtained window above the sink.

Standing there, trying to find his breath and there not seeming to be enough air left in the entire world to fill even one of his lungs. Forcing himself to breathe in through his nose and out through his mouth, he tried to regain his composure while he stared over at the window in the mud room's door, expecting Virgil to appear any moment within its frame.

Who else would be firing off a gun?

He'd just managed to get his breathing under control when another sharp *Bang!* sounded, this one a trifle louder. It seemed to Mason then that it must have been Virgil calling him out. Swivelling towards the Glock he'd left sitting on the counter while he'd made the girl her oats, Mason lurched across the floor with the wearied slog of a man who'd just escaped from drowning only to find himself mired in a tangle of seaweed as he tried to claw his way back to shore.

Snatching up the Glock, the weight of it seemed to lend him its resolve. The strength was returning to his legs as he came onto the porch, the Glock upraised and his eyes scanning over the driveway, searching out Virgil and seeing no hint of movement at all except for the delicate rustle of the willow's leaves agitating in a slight breeze.

A cloud was drifting over the sun and its shadow was casting a darkening shroud over the yard. The rustling in the willows had turned vaguely ominous and the wobbling creak from the blades spinning on the old windmill behind the barn only added to the creeping sensation that forces of a most malevolent lilt were conspiring against him.

What are you waiting for, you sons of bitches! Here I am. Come and get me!

It came out sounding even to his own ears weak and feeble, like a child venting his torment at a world that seemed to have forgotten all about him and seeking confirmation that he existed at all by daring the world to do its worst, come what may. The world seeming to answer him with the faint strains of a merry and elusive laugh trickling along the breeze, taunting him in its fickle way for thinking he mattered enough for even that small consolation.

A figure then appeared within the willow's drape. Mason's eyes narrowed to a squint and he clutched his Glock tighter, peering through their feathered branches and detecting a familiar limpity-hobble, knowing then it was only Clete.

Hey there Chief! he called out, hustling onto the driveway. You got a moment?

His shirt was soaked in sweat and his face beaded with the same. The latter bore the exact expression it had when Clete had come over to tell him that their hot water heater had sprung a leak — his lips crimped and his brow furrowed, looking beleaguered, almost pained, and yet his eyes enlivened with a certain hopefulness. Now, as it had then, it called to Mason's mind the traveller Reverend Williams so often harped upon who'd been robbed and left to die on the road to Jericho and who, Williams had once argued, was the real hero of the story, rather than the Samaritan, for he'd never given up hope that the Lord could still reveal to him an act of mercy.

Clete's pace slowed as he came onto the driveway and then halted altogether ten paces from Mason.

You expecting t-t-trouble there, Ch-Chief?

Clete's eyes were pinned to the gun in Mason's hand so it wasn't much of a mystery as to what he was talking about. Mason side-stepped that by sticking the Glock in the back of his pants and countered with a question of his own.

That Dale I heard firing off his rifle?

His tone was a little harsher than he'd intended. It had Clete's expression blanching, like he'd been unjustly accused of some crime himself.

N-N-No, Clete responded. The only time D-Dale ever shoots his rifle is during hunting season and as far as I know that d-don't start for another few months.

Mason could tell he was lying and felt that familiar bristle of contempt, same as he always did when he knew a suspected perp was trying to deceive him during an interrogation.

Well someone was firing off a gun, he said.

It wah-wasn't Dale, I can promise you that.

One of the neighbours then, huh?

Mm-Must have been.

Sounded like it was coming from the field. You see anyone back there?

No.

Well if you do, you'll be sure to tell me right quick.

Will do.

I won't abide hunting on my property. Levelling then one last glare at Clete to make his point clear. Now what was it you wanted?

Clete gaped back at him like he had no idea what he was talking about.

You came over here for a reason, Mason prompted, didn't ya?

Oh, Clete said, as if he'd forgotten all about it. I wah-was wondering if we-we could b-borrow your tractor.

My tractor? he asked, with a dubious scowl. Whatya need ma tractor for?

To p-pull a stone out of the ground.

A stone you say?

His tone had lightened some, as if Clete had broached a subject near and dear to his heart. Point of fact, he had. Some of his fondest memories were of the hours him and Jesse had spent together digging rocks out of the field for Hélène's flower garden, the boy all of five or six at the time.

How big a stone we talkin' about? he asked, his tone now shading towards genuine curiosity.

A thousand pounds, give or take.

And you say it's in the ground?

We already dug it up. We just need to pull it out.

Well I don't know if my tractor could handle a thousand pounds. It's pretty much given up the ghost.

Clete was staring at him with eager eyes and Mason scratched in fretful contemplation at his beard.

Well, he said at last, I guess there's only one way to find out.

Ⓐ ll right now, we're going to want to take this nice and easy. Mason was sitting on the tractor, his body craned backwards, giving his final instructions to Jason, Ron and Dale, all of whom were standing behind the granite monolith.

Jason was in the middle with his hands tensing on the pry bar he'd lodged under the stone. Ron and Dale were on either side, holding at the ready the two four-by-fours Mason had scavenged from the pile of lumber left over from when he'd had to fix the barn after half its roof had been sheared off by a tornado.

He'd attached his snow chains to the tractor's tires, to give them a little more traction, and Dale had wrapped his tow chain around the base of the rock, looping it around twice to make sure it would hold. Mason had then sent Eric, Masood and Darren to his shed to fetch ten of the eight-foot lengths of birch he hadn't yet cut into firewood. He'd had them lay those out in front of the hole so that if and when the stone did move they could be used as rollers to avoid tearing up the lawn.

The boys had finished arranging them ten minutes ago and Mason had spent half of that standing in front of the rock, peering down into the hole, one hand scratching at his beard. His other was holding the dog collar he'd found discarded on the lawn. The way he was clutching at it — hard enough to turn his knuckles white — left little doubt in Ron's mind that it wasn't really the rock he was thinking about, but the dog which had been buried there, the bones of which Jason had unearthed and Ron had reburied in the field.

From the story Hélène had told Ron about that, though, it seemed just as likely he was thinking about his own son.

Three months ago, after Ron had asked about the dog collar, Hélène had gone on to tell him in her unabashed way about how, when they'd built the house for Jesse and his new wife, Jesse had brought his Staffordshire terrier to live with them. They'd let him out of the car and Spenser had taken a beeline for Chester, her husband's black lab, who'd just come over to greet them. In a fury, Spenser had attacked Chester. He'd latched onto the other dog's throat and Mason had waded into the fray, kicking at the pit bull and, when that didn't work, grabbing it by its collar, wrenching the dogs apart.

Chester was already as good as dead by then and Mason had slumped down beside it, setting the dog's head in his lap, stroking its fur as it panted its dying breath. Jesse's wife, Corrie, was squatting beside Spenser a few feet away, holding it by the collar with one hand and her other propped under the seven-month pregnancy bump bulging from beneath her light summer dress. The dog's maw was coated with blood and its tongue the same, lolling rather jovially out of its mouth, and when Hélène told Ron the story she'd said that, all in all, the dog looked like it couldn't have been happier with the way things had turned out.

Mason must have seen that look too, she'd gone on to relate. A dark cloud had descended over his face. There was murder in his eyes as he stood up and stormed back through the willows.

I knew he was going to fetch his gun and I also knew there was no way I could just let him shoot Jesse's dog. I turned back to Corrie, to tell her to get Spenser the hell out of there. And that's when I saw Jesse striding towards his wife clutching a clawhammer with the same look in his eyes as was in his father's only a moment ago.

I called out, Wait! but it was too late.

He was already swinging the blunt end of the hammer down on the dog's head, crushing its skull with one blow and causing Corrie to startle back, crying out in fright and horror, which was exactly what I felt too watching my son so casually kill his own pet.

Hélène had ended the story by saying, And things, I'm afraid to say, pretty much went downhill for Jesse after that.

Whether or not that was what was on the chief's mind, he'd been snapped out of his reverie by Darren shouting out, Hey guys, I found some rope in the shed!

He was hurrying towards the stone with a fifty-foot coil slung over his shoulder and added, If we tie it to the stone a bunch of us could help pull too.

They'd spent the next five minutes tying the rope around the rock. They'd left twenty feet on either end and ten of the young men along with Annie and Kendra had assumed their positions — six on either side of the tractor — with the grim resolve of a group of soldiers playing at a game of tug-of-war.

As soon as I give her the gas, Mason was now telling Jason, though his tractor was in fact electric, you'll want to heave on the pry bar with everything you've got. And Clete and Dale, as soon as that rock gives even a little, you'll want to jam them four-by-fours into the hole, wedge them underneath, to keep it from rolling back. And if it does start to roll back, he added, turning to Jason, you'll want to get clear, right quick. I seen a pry bar practically shear a man's face off one time when it snapped back on him.

He'd given Ron the same warning, fifteen minutes ago. The moment Mason had backed the tractor up to the hole, Jason had jammed the pry bar under the backside of the rock, such a look of fierce determination in his eyes that it had appeared like he was planning on giving it one last go alone.

Ron was trailing after the tractor, carrying Mason's tow chain, and Mason, slipping off the tractor's seat, had intercepted him.

That the boy lost his mother? Mason had asked, for Ron had already filled him in on some of the particulars.

That's Jason, yeah, Ron had answered.

Mason gave the young man a good hard looking-over and then shook his head.

Don't know if it's a good idea him manning the pry bar. That rock shifts, it'll snap the pry bar back like it was spring-loaded. I seen a man damn near lose his face the same way. Maybe it'd be better if you or Dale took his place.

You can ask him, Ron had said. Can't see how it's going to do much good, though.

Mason had appraised Jason again. Apparently he'd found no way around the young man's grim resolve for he'd then said, If we only had something we could stick under the rock so if it does shift . . . Scratching his beard thinking on that.

Shoot, he'd then said. I think I know just the thing!

He'd returned a few minutes later dragging two four-by-fours, one crooked under each arm, and hadn't been altogether pleased that Dale had taken it upon himself to wrap the chain around the rock in his absence.

He spent some time in the hole making sure it was indeed secure, Dale all the while scowling down at him like it was a personal affront, which maybe it was. Finally, Mason had conceded, Well it looks like it should hold.

It's the tractor I'm worried about, Dale said as Ron offered Mason his hand, helping him out the hole. It's a little long in the tooth. You sure it's going be able to handle the weight?

Oh she'll handle the weight all right, Mason had answered with a wry and secretive grin as if his tractor held some mystical properties only he was aware of. Don't you worry about that.

In the meantime, every last person from the settlement had gathered around. In the ten minutes since, those who couldn't find space on either end of the rope had arranged themselves into a horseshoe formation behind Jason, Dale and Ron. It was towards them Mason offered his final words.

All right now, he said, I want everybody who doesn't have a job to take one step back.

Dutifully the dozen or so youths took a rather exaggerated step back and Mason gave the rock one last long and solemn look before shifting the tractor into drive.

On the count of three now, he said then started: One . . .

Pausing there and fixing his gaze on the group of youths even then edging ever closer to the stone.

One, I said.

When that only resulted in a few ironic smiles, he raised his voice.

One . . .

Two, Ron called out, lending Mason his support.

Not bad, not bad. But I think we can do better. Come on now, give me everything you got. One . . .

Two!

Everyone in the crowd and everyone operating the ropes shouted it out along with Dale and Ron, the only exception being Jason. He was gritting his teeth so hard it looked to Ron like they might shatter and he set his hand on the other's shoulder offering his support while Mason enthused:

All right. All right. That's what I'm talking about. Now once more from the top.

One! everyone shouted again in unison, with real gusto this time.

Two!

Three . . .

M eghan had come into the kitchen looking for the garbage. She'd put on the pair of tan shorts and the T-shirt the old man had left her. The former was two sizes too big but had a tie string that held it up just fine. The latter was a plain aqua blue and made of a material so light and breezy that when she'd appraised herself in the bathroom mirror, the dark circles of her nipples stood out in clear relief. It was plainly meant to be worn with a bra but elsewise it was as comfortable as any shirt she'd ever worn. It also smelled faintly of lilac, which provided further relief from the bathrobe since that had smelled only of old woman.

She'd found the bowl of porridge on the desk beside her cot and was carrying it in one hand now. If there was one thing she couldn't abide, it was bananas. The mere thought of them was almost enough to make her feel sick, or rather sicker than she already felt, which was plenty enough without adding bananas to the mix. She'd come into the kitchen looking for the garbage to get rid of those. Killer had slipped off the couch and followed in after her. He nuzzled her hand as she scanned the kitchen, searching out the can and her gaze instead settling on a jar of honey on the table with a spoon stuck in it.

The old man had forgotten to give her one. It was the thought that she could root out the banana slices with the spoon which drew her across the kitchen, though it was the pill bottle sitting next to it that she picked up first. Diazepam, the label read, and she knew that was what the man must have dosed her tea with. She'd figured he must have dosed it with something, because halfway through the bath she'd felt a peculiar sensation oozing, it seemed, through her very veins. At first it had made her feel like she was melting into the water and shortly afterwards like whatever he dosed her with was seeping through her pores, hardening against her skin, encasing her in what felt like Styrofoam.

Feeling then a creeping sense of doom overcoming her, same as it had every time DB had given her a shot, knowing the sudden elation she felt would be short-lived and she'd be in for a particularly rough ride in but a few moments.

She assured herself that if the old man had any deviant plans for her, he'd have done it by now when, so far, he'd been right kind and gentle. Of course, when DB was giving her and Jamie a shot, he'd always been plenty kind and gentle too. Overwhelmed then by the memories of what him and the others had done to her while she was doped up. Their degradations were most often confined to the girl's room upstairs and the memory of those unicorns dancing in their merry frolic along the top edge of the wall reared in her mind, how they seemed to be laughing at her as those beasts satisfied their carnal lusts. Feeling then the weight of their bodies pressing down upon her again, and none heavier in her recollections than Darcy's. Sitting in the tub, suffocating under the catalogue of miseries he'd inflicted upon her, it felt like she was being smothered under that degenerate fat fuck all over again and his vile stench — like a three-day-old diaper doused with hot sauce — flared in her nostrils, choking the breath right out of her.

Where there's life, there's hope, she intoned in a stuttered whisper, trying to dislodge the memory. Where there's life, there's hope.

It came out sounding hollow and did nothing at all to relieve the heaviness pressing down upon her from, it felt, both without and within. Sinking back into the tub, she let its warmth wrap her in a soothing embrace. Then summoning whatever meagre resolve she had left, she bent it to the task of keeping her head underwater, willing herself to drown.

She hadn't managed to stay under for more than thirty seconds before the pain in her chest had forced her back to the surface, choking up water and slapping at its surface, cursing herself for being so weak.

Looking now at the bottle of diazepam, she told herself, *Swallowing a handful of pills'd be a damn sight easier than trying to drown yourself.*

Such a firm declaration in her mind that she was even then opening the bottle's childproof cap. There were a dozen or so pills left.

You can eat them with your porridge. Maybe it'll settle your stomach enough to keep them down.

But first she'd have to get rid of the bananas.

The garbage can was over by the door and Killer was sniffing at a metal bowl on the floor beside it.

I hope you like bananas, she said, stepping up behind the dog.

The dog responded by looking up questioningly with its head cocked to one side and its ears perked. Using the spoon, she plucked one of the banana slices from on top of the oatmeal and dropped it into the bowl. The dog sniffed at it then looked up at her questioningly again.

Well, I guess that makes two of us.

While she was spooning the rest of the slices into the garbage she caught sight of a flicker of movement through the window beside the door. Peering out, she saw it was the old man. He had two lengths of wood — beams of some sort — clutched under both armpits and was dragging them along the driveway. When he'd come even with the mud room, he turned towards the willow tree on the far side of the vehicle. After he'd disappeared within its foliage, she took the porridge back to the table and picked up the pill bottle, about to dump them in. Hearing then Ben's voice, calling out to her from some distant recess, and that staying her hand.

Bah, bah! he said.

It was from the day their mother had tried switching him from breast milk to solid food. She'd made him a bowl of instant porridge. He'd taken one spoonful and spit it out then reached both hands out for his mom saying, Bah, bah, which was how he always told her he was hungry.

You bit bah bah, their mom had answered. Bah bah is all sore. Now you get porridge. Come on now, open your mouth.

He'd clamped his lips shut and refused to take another bite. Meghan had just finished her own porridge and, in the brazenly precocious manner of a four-year-old, offered, I can get him to eat!

You're welcome to try, her mother had answered, relinquishing her chair.

Sitting in her mother's seat, Meghan had made a big play of pretending she was going to eat up all the porridge herself. After she'd taken two bites, Ben stretched out his hands to her, demanding, Bah, Bah!

You had your chance, Meghan countered. Now it's mine.

Ben let out a squawk that was about a half-decibel removed from a full-fledged scream and Meghan had finally relented.

Okay, okay. I'll let you have one spoonful but the rest is all mine.

In this way she'd got him to eat the whole bowl and also became the only person whom he'd let spoon-feed him.

You kill yourself, she thought, *there won't be anyone left to remember Ben at all. It'll be like he never existed. You eat those pills, you might as well be killing him all over again. Is that what you want?*

Shaking her head in answer to herself, she set the pill bottle down and picked up the spoon. She forced herself to eat every last bite of the porridge. By the time she was finished, Killer was at the door, whining to get out. She was almost too tired and weak to stand and steadied herself with a hand on the table as she started off towards him. The moment she opened the door, Killer slipped into the mud room and stood at its screen door, wagging his tail and looking back at her. She'd since been overcome with a dizzy spell and it took her a moment before she was able to manage those two last steps. The instant the door was open a crack, the dog pushed his way through and took off across the porch and down the steps with the urgency of a hound chasing a fox.

Swooning and clutching at the door frame for support, Meghan closed her eyes, waiting for a wave of nausea to pass.

Hearing then a chorus of voices raised in jubilant declaration.

Two!

Opening her eyes, she searched the driveway for Killer. Finding only the turd he'd left behind, she scanned past the pickup truck and caught sight of the dog's tail disappearing within the drape of one of the willow trees on the far side of the driveway.

Killer! she screamed, taking that first lurching step away from the door and onto the porch. Killer, get back here!

The voices were ringing out again before she'd even made it to the top of the stairs.

One! they were screaming even louder than before.

Two . . .

H ere now Ron and Dale come again to *Three!* with sanguine
hearts.

They'd just shouted it along with the rest when Whisper let
out a savage barking growl. Both looked over at the patio to see
her charging full bore towards the end of her lead and an instant
later being jerked right off her feet. So it was they missed, by only
a glance, the sight of the rock slipping out of the hole with the
ease of a canoe gliding across calm waters.

The four-by-fours in their hands sunk into the space left
behind. That brought them back to task but by then the granite
monolith was already lying on the bed of wooden rollers.

A rousing cheer went up from the crowd of onlookers.
To a one, they were gathering around Jason, patting him on
the back. In response, Jason was smiling in his shy way, which
seemed just short of a miracle to Ron. The people who'd been
working the ropes were giving each other high fives and fist

bumps and Eric had fetched a two-litre Coke bottle filled with water from somewhere and proceeded to douse Jason with it, as if they'd just won the Super Bowl or something. The property's water was drawn from an aquifer wedged between two sheets of granite, some one hundred and fifty feet below the ground. Even on the hottest day it came out as cool as a mountain spring. From the way Jason flinched against the cold, Eric must have just filled the bottle, and yet that only served to make the young man smile all the wider.

Seeing the sudden and unexpected joy blossoming on the young man's face had a tear ripen in the corner of Ron's eye. He was just wiping at it with the back of his hand when Dale exclaimed, Oh shit!

Looking up, Ron saw Whisper had slipped her collar and was racing across the yard towards the dog he'd seen the night before with the girl.

Jesus, Dale was cursing, setting off at a run, his haste a result of how, with the dire bent to her tail and the hackles running up her back, Whisper was looking like she was out for blood.

For its part the other dog was standing there wagging its tail with its ears upraised, looking more curious than anything, and Ron couldn't help but think back to the chief's dog Chester. Could have been he'd looked just the same before Jesse's dog had torn out its throat. Of course, the girl had called her dog Killer so maybe it was Whisper who'd be on the losing side of *that* fight.

Whisper! Dale was screaming as he came to the tractor. Whisper get back here!

He might as well have been trying to call off a rampaging bear for all the good it did him.

The chief, still sitting on the tractor, had seen her too. The harrowed droop to his jaw made it a good bet he was thinking about his and his son's dogs, same as Ron, the both of them watching with mortal dread as Whisper reached Killer. She went right for his neck with such a vicious snarl of gnashing teeth that it made Ron's heart feel like it was trying to lunge out of his mouth. Killer reacted by startling back up onto his hind legs, squealing like a pig being slaughtered as Whisper surged after him, growling such a fury that it seemed she was going in for the kill.

Goddammit Whisper, Dale was shouting, cut it out!

He didn't seem overly concerned, though. His fast jog had since relented into a quick walk and at the tenor of his voice Whisper ceased in her assault. She stood as still as a statue except for her raised hackles and her quivering jowls, curled back and exposing the sharp points of her canines, her eyes glaring, baleful, at the other dog. Killer meanwhile had retreated back to the girl. She was hugging him with one arm draped over his neck and the dog was eyeing Whisper with a series of nervous glances, his ears now sagged over his head and his tail drawn under his belly, looking downright penitent.

Oh god, Dale was saying as he approached. I'm sorry about that. She ain't used to other dogs. Did she hurt him at all?

He'd stopped a good five paces from the girl and could now see her face was as pale as a corpse's and the skin on her neck, arms and legs were riddled with a patchwork of bruises.

She must be the girl Ron was talking about.

A thought spawned as much because she'd come from the chief's property as because she did indeed look like she'd been through hell, and maybe hadn't yet departed its realm entirely.

Is he-he okay?

This from Ron, who was approaching from behind.

I think so, Dale answered. I don't see any blood anyway.

Sounded like he was being slaughtered, the way he was squealing.

That's because he's just a little chickenshit.

It was the girl who'd spoken and the two men turned towards her as if their heads had been pulled by the same tether.

Whisper, that's your dog's name? she asked.

It's my daughter's dog, Dale answered. But, yeah, that's her name.

You didn't mean him no harm, now did you Whisper?

The girl had turned to Whisper and a look had come into her eyes of almost gleeful abandon, as if she'd divined some deeper meaning in their dog attacking hers.

You were just showing him who's boss, she said, weren't you now, girl?

I don't see why we can't eat some of it now.

Eric was standing on the patio pleading with Dale as Ron slumped into his chair.

I done toldya, Dale countered, the meat's gotta cool down before we butcher it.

For that reason, he'd strung up the deer over the drain next to their washer and dryer, using the basement's portable air conditioner to make the laundry room into a de facto refrigerator.

Can't we just cut off a leg, Eric offered. We could cook it over an open fire like our ancestors.

Oh, it'll be a couple of days before we'll be cutting up any of that deer.

But I'm hungry now.

Last I heard, the Foodland in Corbeil still has plenty of food. As long as you got a bank card. Levelling then a pointed glare at the young man. You got a bank card?

Sure.

With money in it?

Yeah. I got money.

Well, there you go.

Eric started to slough off in defeat and Dale called after him, While you're at it, pick me up a bag of Lay's All Dressed and a two-litre bottle of Mountain Dew. Then teasing: And Ron'll take a bottle of diet ginger ale and a bag of plain rice cakes.

The h-hell I will! Ron shot back. I'll have a root beer, A&W if they got it, and Mug if they don't. And a bag of spicy corn chips.

You got all that?

What about money? Eric asked.

I thought you said you had a bank card, Dale answered.

You expect me to pay for it?

We'll call it rent.

Rent?

What, you never heard of rent? It's when someone who's living on someone else's prop—

I know what rent is.

Well then, what are you waitin' for?

Mason was just then driving by on the tractor heading for the driveway. Hitting the brakes, he called over, Did I hear someone mention something about the Foodland?

Young Eric here is making a run, Dale shouted back. You need him to pick you somethin' up?

Eric scowled at that, shaking his head, like he was being taken woeful advantage of.

Mason swivelled his head, his gaze sweeping over the field and the yard, making like he was counting heads.

Oh, a couple dozen steaks should do it, he said, turning back. And what about chicken? You like rotisserie chicken?

Sure, Eric answered.

Grab whatever they got of those. And cobs of corn. A couple bags' worth. Enough for everyone. And potato salad and coleslaw, a whole heap of it. Maybe grab a half-dozen cakes from the bakery, for dessert. And don't forget something to drink. I'm partial to ginger ale so make sure you grab a six-pack of that and anything else you can think of. A couple of bags of ice, maybe.

You want me to buy all that?

You're hungry ain't ya?

I can feel my stomach gnawing at itself, I'm so starved.

And I bet you ain't alone. Best wrangle a couple of your friends to help. I'll fetch you some money, meet you back here in, oh, five.

The tractor then lurched ahead, as if by its own volition. Mason exclaimed, Whoa there girl!, holding on for dear life like he was riding a rodeo bronc, and Ron watched after him with undisguised mirth as he reached for his chute.

God, he said, packing the bowl, you ever seen the chief so happy? He's like a damned kid at Christmas.

Dale opened his mouth to reply, likely with some caustic barb. Before he could, his phone buzzed and he reached over, checking the message.

It's Babygirl, he said. Shoot, I've been meaning to give her a call, tell her we're okay. Standing then and heading for the door. Give me a shout when the food's here.

Ron had taken his huff and answered on the exhale, Will do.

Lighting a cigarette a moment later, he sat back in his chair, scanning over the yard towards Jason. He was using a hook-bladed knife he'd found in the shed to scratch his mom's name into the base of the rock they'd planted, upside down, at the foot of her grave. It was five feet high and tapering to a point at its top, its form slightly curved to the right so that it looked kind of like the fossilized tooth of some giant prehistoric beast.

Just a few hours ago it seemed like we'd never get it out of the ground, Ron thought as he watched Jason scratching at the stone, *and yet there it is. And it weren't nothing neither. Probably could have managed even without the chief's tractor, the way everyone pulled together there at the end.* Taking a drag from his smoke and reconsidering. *But it was the tractor that gave you hope that such a thing might be possible, and it was that hope which pulled everyone together.*

Except it wasn't the tractor which had really given you hope, it was hearing Annie tell the story of how she'd shot the deer.

After hearing her account, he'd been overwhelmed by a sudden and irrepressible urge to do something himself, if only because Dale was acting so damned smug, like shooting that deer was part of some grand design when really the whole affair sounded to Ron like nothing more than just plain old dumb luck.

Walking back to the house and seeing Jason heaving another rock out of the hole — his fingernails broken and bleeding and his expression warped by an interminable despair — it had seemed like he was hell-bent on digging his own grave rather than unearthing a tombstone for his mom's. Ron had known he'd had to do something to help Jason out so he'd gone to ask about the tractor and that, as they say, was that.

Watching Jason etching his mom's name on the stone now, Ron was overcome with his own smug sense of self-satisfaction.

It was a feeling that didn't last long.

Whisper's chain rattled as it snaked across the porch. Looking up, Ron saw the girl approaching. Whisper came at her as if on the sly, nudging at one of her hands with her nose and then circling around behind her, following her onto the patio. Seeing the girl again up close, so pale and fragile, the dread Ron had felt seeing her the first time descended upon him like a dark cloud blotting out the feeling of hopefulness which had seemed so intractable only seconds ago.

Killer let out a disapproving bark, being left all to his lonesome, and Ron glanced over at him to distract himself from his sudden unease. It was a feeling wrought into a fever pitch by his own shame catching sight of the girl's budding adolescence prying through a shirt so thin and translucent she might as well have been wearing a clear plastic bag. Her dog was pacing back and forth at the edge of the willow tree where the girl had been sitting the whole time they'd been setting the stone in the ground. He'd been too afraid to come any closer to Whisper even after Dale had tied her back up and tightened her collar so she posed him about as much threat as the patio chair the girl was now slumping into.

Killer, Ron thought, *such a stupid name for a dog, especially for one as timid as him.*

What the girl had said to him last night came back to him with the force of a sucker punch to the gut:

Well I wasn't the one who named him.

It could very well have been Clarence Boothe himself who'd done that and it was a good bet he was also responsible for the girl's sorry state.

What he must have done to her . . .

A thought trailing off into an abyss and Ron picking up his chute to keep him from being swallowed into the gloom.

You mind if I have a puff? the girl asked as he packed the bowl.

He hadn't looked at her since she'd sat down and gave her the briefest of glances now, that only serving to remind him of how young she looked. She couldn't have been older than fourteen and smoking weed with a fourteen-year-old girl was a line he'd have never even considered crossing under any circumstances, even ones as grim as likely had led the girl to be sitting across from him now.

Th-that depends, Ron answered, trying to deflect. H-H-How old are you?

As old as the sun, that old enough for ya?

Her voice rang with such a matter-of-fact tone and she was fixing him with such a piercing glare of utter petulance that Ron wasn't able to muster anything in reply beyond, I-I-I'd say.

I just need a little something to take the edge off, the girl added while Ron lit the bowl, if you know what I mean?

It wasn't much of a mystery as to what edge she might have been talking about. The track marks dotting the inside of both of her elbow joints made the circle of bruises surrounding them look like someone had been using them for target practice.

I-I do, he replied, for want of anything better to say.

Drawing the smoke into the bag, he held out the pop bottle, figuring it wouldn't hurt her none. Hell, after what she'd been through, it might actually do her some good.

You'll want to go easy on it. It c-can b-be k-kinda harsh if you're not u-u-used t'it.

Snatching it up, she ignored the warning and took a long haul, sucking all the smoke in one mighty inhale like a seasoned chronic and then overcome at once by a violent coughing fit. It had her hacking up chunks of mucus and finer splatters that looked like blood spraying onto the table's top. Finally it relented into a few lesser coughs and she sagged back into the chair with a languor that told Ron the coughing fit had sapped whatever strength she had left right out of her. Wiping the back of her hand across her mouth, a faint trail of blood smeared over her knuckles.

That *was* harsh, she said and even those few words were enough to set her to coughing again.

I'll get you a glass of water, Ron offered and hurried off towards the house to fetch it without waiting for a reply.

When he came back she was slumped so far down in the chair she looked like a life-size rag doll someone had tossed there for safekeeping. The only thing alive at all about her were her eyes.

Jason was still scratching at the rock and she was staring over at him with such an intensely malevolent gaze that it had Ron wondering what he could have possibly done to earn her scorn.

Here's your water, he said, holding it out.

When she didn't reply he set it on the table and returned to his seat, reaching for a cigarette.

So who died, anyway? she asked, reaching for a smoke herself.

H-H-His mom.

Is that all? she said, sticking the cigarette in her mouth and lighting it with Ron's Bic. Such casual malice in her tone that it had Ron gaping at her in disbelief.

She took a drag off the cigarette and coughed again. She then ground the smoke out on the glass tabletop, as if she'd merely been using it for a prop, before tossing it into the coffee-can ashtray.

Thanks for the water, she said, pushing herself up, though she hadn't so much as taken a sip.

A-A-Anytime, he answered watching her walk towards Jason with the swagger of a much older woman, all the while thinking, *Boy that's one cold little girl.*

Killer met her halfway across the yard, his head swinging between her and Whisper, afraid to let the other dog too far from his sight.

Hey there you are, you little chickenshit, she taunted, swatting at his head and the dog ducking out of the way of the blow.

Coming to Jason kneeling at the rock, she circled around beside him, peering at what he was writing not so much with malicious intent anymore as with the mischievous air of a young sister bugging her brother while he was trying to do his homework.

She stood there watching him for a time with Ron watching her, growing ever more anxious that she might say something to shatter whatever good humour Jason had managed to reclaim. It was only when Jason was blowing the grit out of the *E* in his mother's first name that she finally did speak. Whatever she said Ron couldn't hear and he craned a little further forward, as if a couple of inches might make all the difference.

Jason, for his part, acted like he couldn't hear it either and took up an old toothbrush. He spit on it and then ran its bristles over the MARNIE he'd carved into the headstone. She responded to his indifference by stepping right up beside and swinging her hip at his shoulder, delivering him a body check hard enough to knock him over. Pushing himself back up onto his knees, Jason turned sharply towards her, scowling at her with his own undisguised malice.

Goddammit, Ron was thinking watching that, never feeling more like a father than he did right then, *just leave him alone! He's already been through enough without you needling him.*

Feeling a twinge of remorse from how caustic the words sounded in his head, knowing she'd probably been through a trial worse even than Jason's — more than any little girl should have had to have gone through, anyway. That still not seeming to justify her picking on Jason to lessen her own grief.

It would be only a second before he realized she was playing an entirely different game altogether.

I said, the girl proclaimed with such brazen aplomb that Ron had no difficulty hearing her this time, that's an awfully big stone you got there. You think might'n maybe I could put a few names on it too?

Dusk found Mason sitting in one of the patio's chairs, foraging with a toothpick for bits of steak lodged in his teeth as the sun's last rays painted the furrowed drift of clouds just over the treetops a hazy pink shading towards a deepening purple.

A crescent moon was hanging directly above him and the sky's first star had appeared below it, though really it was shining too bright to be a star at all. Probably it was just a satellite catching a last glint in its endless wander, though knowing that hardly diminished the tranquility that had descended upon him, gazing at a sight of such heavenly splendour.

You feel like a beer there, Chief?

It was Dale who'd spoken. He was holding two tall cans of Kokanee and a tall can of Old Style Pilsner as he kicked the house's door shut behind him.

A beer would be right nice, thanks.

Ah sure, why not? Dale said, setting a can of Kokanee on the table in front of Mason and a can of the other in front of

Clete's empty chair. Nothing better than a cold beer after a hard day's work.

Ain't that the truth.

Cracking his open, Mason took a sip.

Boy, that is cold.

Had 'em in the freezer.

That was thinking ahead.

Oh, I have my moments.

Dale cracked his own can and took a healthy sip as the gentle strum of a guitar turned them both towards the yard.

While Mason was grilling up the steaks on Dale's barbecue and the grill he'd hauled over from next door, Clete had started a fire in the ring of stones Jesse and Kim had scavenged from the field when the latter was all of three years old. Many of Mason's favourite memories from those days — a lifetime away — had been of them and him and Corrie and Hélène sitting around the campfire, roasting hot dogs and marshmallows. Later, Kim would often have camp-outs in the backyard with a dozen or so of her friends. Sometimes they'd be up well after midnight, laughing and carrying on in their youthful zeal, and Mason derived no small amount of pleasure seeing that it was being used again for the same purpose after sitting fallow for so many years.

After stocking the fire with a half-dozen logs from the wood-pile behind the shed, Clete had taken to roving amongst the thirty or so teens gathered in an ever-shifting circle around the pit with a black garbage bag, soliciting the dirtied Styrofoam plates and plastic utensils Eric and the others had picked up from the store along with the food. The teenagers responded by tipping him for his efforts with proffered puffs off the plenitude of vapes, bongs and joints being passed around. At one point, Eric had produced a giant Ziploc bag packed full of what Mason suspected was magic mushrooms. Clete had taken a pinch of those too, as had most of the teens, including the girl, whose name Mason still hadn't got around to asking.

He'd been keeping an eye on her ever since, worried that her mood might take a sudden downturn once the drugs kicked in. Ever since joining the circle an hour or so ago, she'd been sitting cross-legged on its far side, next to Jason. Killer's head lay in her lap and her hands were playing idly with one or the other of his ears. The orange flicker cast from the flames had enlivened her face such that it was almost possible to believe she was just another teenager having a good time with her friends even if, from what Mason had seen, she hadn't so much as smiled or opened her mouth since she'd sat down.

Duane had since produced a guitar and was playing a vaguely familiar and melancholy tune Mason couldn't quite place. It almost sounded like something he might have heard at church. On either side of him sat two girls — one a skinny Black girl named Annie and the other a plump white girl he was pretty sure was named Kendra. They were singing along in broken verses and laughing in joyful bursts every time they forgot the words.

Each was sitting between the legs of a guy. Annie was snugged up against the boy named Darren — a Native kid — and the other against a darker-skinned fellow whose name Mason had never caught, he looked vaguely Middle Eastern. Both boys were holding the girls around their waists. At intervals, Darren's hands would creep upwards only to be nudged back down whenever they got too close to Annie's breasts while the Middle Eastern boy's hands rested, unmoving, in Kendra's lap with her hands clamped over his so tight she seemed to be holding on for dear life. Only when Annie passed a lit joint her way did she release her hold, taking up the joint and having a puff, holding it out to the Middle Eastern fellow. He shook his head, waving it off, even as Clete reached over and grabbed it in his stead.

Your beer's getting warm! Dale yelled out as Clete passed the joint back to Kendra, laughing in ragged huffs at something she'd said.

That got Clete moving.

Circling the throng, he came towards the patio verging on an all-out run.

You put it in the freezer, like I toldya? he asked as he drew within a dozen or so paces, that apparently close enough to let his haste slacken.

Of course I did, Dale answered then quickly added, Don't know how cold it'll be now, though. It's been sitting on the table for fifteen minutes.

Ff-Ff-Fifteen minutes!

Or however long you've been cleaning up after the young'uns. Why didn't you just leave it in the ff-freezer until I was done?

Didn't think you'd take so long.

Shaking his head, Clete reached for the beer looking sour enough for someone to have shat on his chair. The moment his hand clenched the can his lips parted in a wide grin even as he shot a reprimanding glance at Dale.

You're lucky, is all I can say, he said, cracking the can and draining half of it in one fell swoop.

Mason had barely managed a sip of his own. He now took another, longer one, relishing the ice cold liquid draining down his throat and even more the company, for it had been years since he'd shared a cold beer with anyone. Clete was packing the bowl screwed into the top of his pop bottle with weed and when he had, he held it out to Mason.

Chute? he asked, as he had so many times before, though his tone was deprived entirely of the familiar mocking insolence that suggested he was just having a laugh at Mason's expense.

Oh, no, Mason replied with something approaching genuine conviviality. Thanks. I'm good with the beer.

Clete shrugged, lighting the bowl, and Mason turned back to the campfire, searching out the girl again.

She was looking over at Jason with a certain expectation, biting at her bottom lip, and the firelight dazzling in her eyes — positively smitten, that's how she looked.

The image of the girl shivering in the tub came back to him then. At the time he'd been overwhelmed with rage, thinking he'd have liked nothing better than to bring Clarence back to life so he could skin him toe to tongue. But the memory now only served to bolster his good mood, thinking how far she'd come in just a few short hours.

It seemed like another damned miracle that there'd still be a part of her left capable of looking like she did now. Reminding himself then that it wasn't really a miracle at all. Probably, she was just putting on an act like she had in the truck to give herself a reprieve, if only for a moment, from thinking about what those evil motherfuckers had done to her.

So distracted had he been by the day's activity that he hadn't passed a single thought towards Clarence and his goons nor how, at this very minute, Virgil and the Balmond brothers could very well be hatching plans of revenge.

It's more than likely you who'll be getting skinned alive, he thought now, *when they catch up with you. Hell, half The Sons Of Adam could be lurking out there right now, crouching in the dark, waiting for their chance.*

Such, though, was the feeling of utter calm that had descended upon him that whatever threat they might have posed seemed like a million miles away.

So what if they are? he thought. *Whatever they do to you, it was worth it, if only because you saved that girl. And you aren't ever likely to feel as good as you do right now anyway. Let 'em come, I say. Might as well die a happy man.*

Nodding contentedly to himself, he took another sip from his beer. It was growing warmer by the second and he took another, longer one that turned into three. The last ended with no more than a few drips left in the bottom of the can.

I notice you've been having trouble sleeping, Dale said as Mason set the empty can on the table.

It was true. It had been years since he'd got a full night's sleep. But Dale's question made it seem to Mason like Dale had been spying on him, and there was a certain gruffness in his voice when he answered, Why would you say that?

It's just, every night I see your house'll go dark at ten. At eleven, or shortly after, I'll see the kitchen light come back on. Then I'll often see you walking down the road. Figured you must be having trouble sleeping. You got achy joints, that it?

Boy did he ever.

Lying in bed most nights it felt like he might as well have been trying to sleep on cold cement rather than on their three-thousand-dollar Posturepedic mattress, the way he ached. Though that wasn't the real reason he'd get up most nights after waiting in bed for Hélène to fall asleep. The truth was that it was the only time he truly had to himself and he had come to relish his midnight strolls, same as he had the twenty-minute drive to North Bay when he was working.

What is it? Dale was then asking. Your shoulders? Your back?

Oh, it's a little of both.

Well this'll fix you right up.

He was holding out the vape pen.

Oh. No, I'm all right thanks.

It's pure Indica. One puff'll knock you right out.

Mason staring at the pen for a moment, actually considering it.

For years, Hélène herself had been trying to get him to use those CBD drops, more, she said, so *she* could get a good night's rest, the way he tossed and turned. He'd always demurred but then he'd never had two days like the ones he'd just had.

Dale must have gleaned that Mason was on the fence, for he then added, You won't feel nothing all night, I guarantee it.

I could use a good night's sleep, that's for sure, Mason conceded.

Well, a good night's sleep is just one puff away.

I guess it couldn't hurt.

That's the spirit.

Dale handed it over, explaining, Just hold the button down until you see the light turn green then you're good to go.

Taking up the pen, Mason did as instructed. He took a healthy drag, releasing the weed-infused steam in a steady stream through his nose as he'd done on the rare occasion when he'd had a puff off a joint when he was young, the last time when he was seventeen, since Hélène never could abide smokers, of weed or otherwise.

It tastes a little like blueberries, he said, handing the pen back to Dale.

That's what it's called. Blueberry Dream.

That right? I always did like blueberries.

The last word seeming to warp on his tongue, taking forever to get out. He could already detect a lightening in his head and sagged back in his chair. It felt all of a sudden like he was being watched but maybe that was just him being paranoid, which is what weed usually had done to him when he was a teen. Turning towards the firepit though, he saw that the girl was indeed looking at him.

She'd since crawled into Jason's lap. She was clasping his hands at her waist, apparently imitating the other girls. The young man behind *her* looked anything but comfortable with the arrangement and wore a rather pinched look on his face. Otherwise he seemed to be trying to ignore her all together, a daunting prospect at best especially since the frayed mat of her curls was brushing against his nose, causing him to wiggle it like a rabbit's.

The girl, meanwhile, couldn't have looked happier.

It seemed to Mason that she was just waiting for him to look her way. Now that he had, her eyes narrowed into the same slits of angry defiance they'd worn when she'd thrown back the blanket on the cot, exposing herself to him. Except this time her lips were upturned but the way she was smiling — as brazenly as she'd earlier frowned — hardly decreased the sudden and irrepressible dread overcoming him, he couldn't exactly say why.

His mouth was sticky and dry at the same time and he reached for his beer can as much to relieve himself of that as it was to keep his eyes from wandering back to her. There weren't more than a few drops left in it and while he slurped at those, Dale asked, You got the cotton mouth there, Chief?

When Mason looked up at him, the wry smile on Dale's face also appeared vaguely ominous, like he was mocking him, though his tone was more than congenial when he added, Blueberry Dream tends to do that. Let me fetch you a glass of water.

Clete too was smiling at him in an impish way. It also seemed altogether malevolent and only added to the creeping suspicion that helping Mason sleep was the last thing on Dale's mind when he'd offered him a puff.

Those sons of bitches, he thought. *They's just fucking with you like they did by hot-boxing you in the car!*

You-You okay there, Chief? Clete asked with what appeared to be genuine concern.

Just feeling a little dizzy is all.

The words seeming to sprout from his mouth without any help from his brain and doing nothing at all to capture the essence of how he truly felt, which was more like his head had become an empty chasm, vacant and hollow — the only way to explain why the words seemed to be echoing so resolutely in his ears.

Sh-Shatter'll do that to you, Clete offered. It's powerful stuff. Takes some getting used to.

A slight gust of wind was teasing at Mason's beard. Over the faint plucking of the guitar and the voices of the two girls singing another sad song, he could hear a delicate rustle coming from the willow trees and he turned towards them. The light over his porch was shining through their sinewy branches and in its flickering illume he could see the leaves were agitating against the breeze. Where before they'd always appeared to him as hair when tousled by the wind, now they looked more like they were being tugged along by the current of some gently flowing stream and it felt like he too was being carried along on the same current, being washed downstream, helpless but to let it carry him where it may.

A sharp rap almost as loud as a rifle's *Crack!* startled him from his languid drift and he spun around to see Dale had just set a glass of water on the tabletop.

There you go, Chief, he said, sitting back down and Mason gaping at the glass, suddenly worried that Dale had dosed it with something — just like Hélène had dosed his pudding. Wanting nothing more in that moment than to get the hell away from there, crawl into bed, fall asleep, even if the truth of the matter was that he'd never felt more wide awake than he did right then.

Dale had since lit a cigarette. When Mason next glanced his way, he was blowing smoke out of the side of his mouth and there was an unmistakable rancour in the way he was glaring at him, as there was in his voice when he'd finally summoned the will to speak again.

You know there, Chief, he said, I never did mention it, but we uhhh . . . we actually met one time before.

Sitting there in my chair, looking like he's king of the goddamned world. That smug son of a bitch!

What Dale was thinking as he set the glass of water on the table, hard enough to startle the chief.

Magnanimous, that's the word for it. Just because we used his tractor to pull the stone out of the ground and he paid for all that food.

Thinking then with the vitriol of some old gypsy, or a shaman, laying a curse, *Well you can't fool me, no sir. I know who you really are.*

Lighting a cigarette, he blew smoke in a dismissive billow out of the corner of his mouth and peered at the old man as if he meant to do him great harm, which wasn't far from the truth, even as he forced his tone towards congeniality when he spoke again.

You know, Chief, I never did mention it but we uhhh . . . we actually met one time before.

You don't say? the chief answered, Dale detecting a certain reticence in the way he cast him the most fleeting of glances and taking no small amount of satisfaction in that.

Oh, it'd be almost twenty years ago now, Dale continued. I was, uh, driving along the 17, which is why it seemed so strange to be pulled over by a North Bay cop since, as far as I know, it's the OPP who's responsible for patrolling that stretch of highway. Course, now I know you must have been heading home from work.

If I pulled you over, I must have had a good reason. Always did.

The reticence in the old man's eyes had succumbed to the familiar gruffness in his tone as if the mere insinuation that he might have pulled someone over for reasons entirely of his own had him bristling.

You said I'd performed a dangerous U-turn.

And did you?

Oh, I'd performed a U-turn all right. Can't see how it was too dangerous, though, since yours was the only other car in sight and that was a good half-klick down the highway, too far away for me to see it was a police cruiser anyway.

Mason clicking his tongue, thinking on that.

I don't recall ever giving anyone a ticket for doing a dangerous U-turn up the 17, he finally said.

Well maybe that's because you didn't charge me with performing a dangerous U-turn.

Well if I didn't charge you, then I must have let you off with a warning.

Such exactitude in his voice that Dale knew he truly mustn't have remembered, or elsewise had buried it so deep in his mind that he might as well have forgotten.

Oh you gave me a warning all right, Dale agreed. Now what was it you said? Scratching at his cheek with a conspicuously stiff middle finger. Oh right. You said, Keep struggling and maybe I take you to the morgue rather than the station. I was lying on the road at the time. My hands were zip-tied behind me and my face was mashed into the asphalt. You were kneeling on the back of my neck.

Mason's face had blanched and that lent Dale the impression that maybe he remembered the stop after all, though from the way the old man was shaking his head and gritting his teeth he didn't exactly seem apologetic.

I'd find out later you cracked a vertebrae. Dale pointing at the back of his neck, near the base of his skull. This one right here. Still feels like my neck's been put in a vice whenever it gets cold. And whenever I turn my head, I hear this clicking noise. He turned his head from side to side to demonstrate, sounding off as he did, *Click, click, click, click, click*. I tellya, it damn near drives me crazy.

Anyway, he continued, leaning forward and dropping his cigarette in the coffee can then plucking another from his pack as he settled back in his chair, I must have passed out because the next thing I know I'm waking up in the back of your cruiser. I was wedged in between the seats with my hands still tied behind my back so I couldn't get up. Plenty of Indigenous folk went missing in those days, or washed up on the shore of some river. Word on the street was that it was cops responsible for most of them so I figured you must have been driving me out into the bush somewhere. Maybe you thought I was dead and you were looking for a place to dispose of the body. Or maybe you were just going to toss me into the Mattawa River. Either way, I figured I wasn't long for this earth.

Ron was sitting there leaning forward in his chair, eating from his bag of corn chips like it was popcorn and he was watching a movie in which there was still some doubt as to Dale's eventual fate. A particularly loud crunch had Dale turning, irritated, towards him. Ron responded by chewing ever slower, trying not to make a sound as Dale lit his cigarette. He sat puffing at it with a contemplative air, as if he was still trying to make sense of that night himself.

It's funny the things that occur to you when you're facing certain death, as I thought I was, he finally offered. Now, I'd heard it said, like everyone else I guess, that at times like that your whole life flashes before your eyes. But that wasn't my experience. It wasn't my past I was thinking of but a possible future.

Taking a drag and tapping the ash off his cigarette against the arm of his chair, he asked, You ever go to the Dinner Bell diner there on the 17, at Bonfield?

Mason's gaze had since become fixed to the table and he seemed to be contemplating the flecks of ash scattered about it with the solemn deliberation of an astronomer studying a star chart.

Huh? he said looking up now as if he hadn't been listening to a word Dale had said even as the weary fret of lines cascading from the corners of his eyes and the crimp to his downturned lips seemed to suggest he'd heard every last word.

The Dinner Bell in Bonfield. Do you know it or not?

The Dinner Bell? Sure, I know it. Good burgers.

His voice was meek and cracked and came out on the quiet side of a whisper.

Best damn burgers in Ontario! Ron chimed in.

You don't have to tell me. That's why I always made it a habit of stopping there whenever I was heading to or from my hunt camp. Except it wasn't the burgers I was thinking of when I was wedged in the back of your cruiser, it was the waitress, a young woman by the name of, uh . . . Julie. I'd noticed her a few times before and I *know* she'd noticed me. She always gave me a big smile when I came in and would always stand around and chit-chat for a while when I was waiting on my order, even if it was busy and she probably had better things to do. She had sandy blonde hair that didn't entirely seem natural when measured against her skin. It was a shade darker than mine and she also had the tattoo of an eagle feather on her forearm. I figured she was at least part Native, which is maybe why she was always so friendly to me.

Now she weren't no beauty queen by any stretch. She was pretty enough sure, just not, you know, a knock-out. Except for her eyes. She had the strangest colour of eyes I ever seen. They were bluish green with flecks of gold in them and looking into her eyes always seemed to me like looking into a tropical ocean with, you know — raising his hand and scampering his fingers through the air to simulate — the sun dazzling over clear waters, the way they sparkled so. Gives me the chills to think of them even now. A man could lose himself in eyes like that and I guess maybe a few times I did because one time when she was handing me my bill she says to me, You keep looking at me like that, a gal might get the wrong idea.

And what idea's that? I asked.

That you're not just coming in for the burgers.

I'd had it in mind for some time to ask her out and I figured this was as good a time to broach the topic as any. I was opening my mouth to do just that but before I could the chef dinged the bell and called out, Order up! As she turned towards the kitchen, she swung out her hip, bumping me on the shoulder and casting me one of them — what are they called? You know, uh, one them, um uh — *come-hither looks*, that's what it was. She threw me one of those come-hither looks over her shoulder, real coy like.

I'd got to thinking that was a pretty good sign. I was planning on sticking around, to ask her out when she had a spare moment. But just then, don't you know it, a group of kayakers showed up. There was eight or nine of them and not a free table in the place. I'd finished eating a few minutes ago and the other waitress, a real sour old cow, was giving me the stink-eye for taking up a table for four and me all by my lonesome. So I dropped a twenty on a bill for thirteen dollars, which I figured couldn't do me any harm, and then skedaddled.

I knew Julie was a smoker and I had a couple cigarettes outside myself with a puff off my vape to brace my courage in between, hoping maybe she'd come outside on her break. In the meantime though, two RVs had pulled into the parking lot and eight people piled out of those. It was lookin' like she'd be busy for at least another hour and so finally I said, Fuck it, I'll catch her next time around.

I don't know if it was the puff of shatter or the fact that it had been six months since I'd been with a woman but on the drive back to North Bay I just couldn't get her out of my head. I kept seeing those eyes staring back at me. It was like they was offering the promise of paradise, and here I was heading the opposite direction. I must have contrived in my mind a hundred different ways I could have asked her out and by the time I'd come to the turnoff for Corbeil I'd convinced myself that I was a damned fool, and a coward on top, if I didn't turn around right then.

So I did, and the long and the short of that was I ended up in the back of your cruiser, certain you were going to bury me in a shallow grave or toss me in the Mattawa River. Of course, that's not how it played out, though the six months the judge sentenced me to for driving under the influence and resisting arrest did seem just this side of a death sentence at the time.

Pausing there, he took another cigarette from his pack and hazarded a glance at Mason while he lit it. The old man was sitting with his hands clasped on the table, one of his thumbs picking restlessly at a flap of skin peeling up from the other's nail, his face downturned as before. From the grave reluctance etched into the furrowed lines on his face he wasn't looking so much like an astronomer anymore as an astrologer who'd just seen death in the cards and was trying to figure out how to put a positive spin on it.

After I was released I spent a few years bumming around, picking up odd jobs wherever I could. Travelled all across the country, a helluva trip that, let me tellya. I ended up out in BC, planting trees. My boss spent the winter trapping fox and coyote in the Yukon and when he found out I was a hunter too, he invited me along. Did that for a couple of years and then my ma passed away. It was her funeral that finally brought me home. One of my cousins was working at Harvesters and said he could get me a job, if I planned on staying. He worked nine months a year and then spent three months on EI. That sounded like a pretty good deal to me so I told him, Ah hell, sign me up.

After work, a bunch of us would sometimes head over to Shooters, you know, for a pint. They had live music every Friday night, mostly country and western, which I never much cared for. Well one night there was this three-piece band playing blue-grass, which I usually liked even less than country. Probably that would have been reason enough for me to call it an early night, if it wasn't for their fiddle player. Never heard anyone make a fiddle talk like that in all my life. God, the way she could play. It was like my body had become a tuning fork, listening to her. Had me practically in tears the whole time. And there was something else about the woman too. She looked kind of familiar, though I couldn't say why. She was Native, I could tell that, but not much else except she had an eagle's feather tattooed on her arm. But it wasn't until the band had finished their set and she was walking past my table on the way to the bar, that I was able to put a name to the face.

Someone called out to her, Julie!, and when she turned towards whoever it was her face lit into a smile just like the ones she used to give me at the Dinner Bell. And if that still wasn't enough to tell me who she was, then the way her eyes seemed to sparkle in the overhead lights most certainly was.

As I say, she was going to the bar and since my own glass was empty, I figured I might as well join her. She'd already ordered and was fishing her wallet from her purse. I stepped up beside her and put a twenty down on the bar and says to her, A lady plays the fiddle like you should never have to pay for her own drinks. Do ya mind?

She looks over at me kind of cross like, as if she was used to men trying to pick her up in bars and resented nothing more.

Who says I'm a lady? she spat back, turning towards me and her eyes sparkling again with the same dazzle that had beguiled me all those years ago, which I figured was well worth the price of the drink all by itself.

She'd aged considerably since I saw her last. I knew from just looking at the lines carved into her face that she'd had some hard times and from the way she was looking at me, I knew most of those must have started and ended with men.

The bartender had returned with her drink, a shot of something dark on the rocks. He must've overheard what I'd said because he was looking from her to the twenty dollar bill and back again. She responded by putting her wallet back in her purse and so the bartender turned to me.

I'll have a double of whatever the lady's having, I told him, though truth be told I always prefer a beer over a highball.

There you are calling me a lady again, she said.

She'd turned around and was leaning against the bar, sipping at her glass, her gaze roving over the tables, as if she was looking for someone she was trying to avoid.

You keep calling me that, she added, a gal might get the wrong idea.

And what idea is that?

That you want something other than buying me a drink.

Just saying thank you is all. I never heard no one play the fiddle like that. Practically had me in tears the whole time.

That got me a crooked glance, as if she wanted to believe me but still had her doubts. She was opening her mouth to say something when the bartender returned with my drink and my change. Before he'd had a chance to set the latter down, I waved him off.

That's a generous tip, Julie said, giving me another glance, this one a shade warmer and it feeling like a little bit of heaven seeing that glint in her eyes so up close again.

Sure, why not?

Wait a second, she said. Don't I know you from some— The Dinner Bell! You used to come into the Dinner Bell, didn't ya?

Guilty, I said then added, I'm surprised you remember me.

Oh, I always remember the big tippers. Wasn't your name . . . Dale?

I was taking my first sip of what I gleaned was whiskey and answered by pointing a finger and cocking my thumb, signing a bullseye.

I'm Julie, she offered.

Oh, I remember.

At that she drank the rest of her whiskey in one fell swoop and set the empty glass on the bar.

Spot a lady another drink? she asked.

That depends, I said to her.

On what? she asked.

On whether you're okay with giving a guy the wrong idea.

That got me another smile and then she said, I'm starting to think maybe it's the right idea after all.

I'd find out later she was living up on the Atikameksheng reserve just south of Sudbury, which is where her people are from.

Her and the band were staying in the Voyager Motel, right behind the bar. After her last set, we ended up in her room. It had all the makings of a one-night stand, which is why I was so surprised some months later when she texted me to tell me her band had been booked back at Shooters. But that surprise was nothing compared to the one waiting for me when I showed up at the bar that Friday night in time to see her setting up on stage. It looked like she'd swallowed a damned bowling ball.

And that's how I'd found I was to be a father. Babygirl will be turning thirteen, come August.

Reaching for his phone, he swiped the screen and held it up, showing off a picture of his daughter kneeling beside Whisper, cradling the dog around the neck.

If you look real close, you can see she has her mother's eyes, though they're a shade brighter.

Mason craned forward to take a better look.

She's right pretty, he said, an eagerness to please adding a conciliatory lilt to his voice.

You don't have to tell me. And she'd be drop-dead gorgeous too if she hadn't inherited her father's nose.

Dale smiling at that as if he wouldn't have had it any other way. He then set the phone back on the table and took another smoke from his pack, tapping it on the glass idly as he said,

I'd find out later that when Julie was working at the Dinner Bell, she was actually engaged to the owner's son, which is how she'd come to work there for the summer. When I asked her why she was always flirting with me if she was engaged, she told me, For the tips of course. Then with a wink she said, Worked like a charm, now didn't it? I had to give her that. But that's beside the point. The point is, if I had made it back on that night, she'd have turned me down flat, no two ways about it. And I'd probably have just made a damned fool of myself on top.

Lighting the cigarette then, he puffed on it a few times, deep in contemplation, before starting again.

Now, I must've gone over that night at Shooters a hundred times in my mind, trying, you know, to make sense of how and why what had happened went down the way it did. And don't you know it, every time I think about it, the story leads me right back to that damned U-turn. If you hadn't pulled me over and saved me from making an ass of myself, she'd have said no and I doubt I'd have ever met Julie again. And even if I did I sure as hell wouldn't have had the nerve to buy her a drink which means she'd have never given me my Babygirl — there ain't no two ways around it. So I guess what I'm trying to say is that things couldn't have worked out better, for me at least.

Looking over then at Mason. The chief's head was still down-turned but his eyes — red and rheumy — were peering upwards at Dale, preening like a lifelong sinner's would at a priest after he'd made a deathbed confession and was waiting on his absolution.

And, ah hell, if it weren't for the damned *click, click, click*ing I hear every time I turn my head, Dale added since providing Mason with any sort of absolution was the last thing on his mind, I might even be inclined to say . . . Thank you.

Mason had been standing in front of what he'd come to think of as the memory stone for some time.

It was too dark to see more than a faint impression of the names etched upon its surface and yet that hardly diminished the awe he felt gazing upon them, for there must have been thirty or more now.

As far as he knew, the girl had been the first to add any names after Jason. He'd seen her scratching three into the rock when he'd returned with ten fifty-dollar bills from the girl's duffel. He'd given it to the boy named Eric and while he and his brother and two of their friends had set off in their van to fetch the grub, Mason had stood watching the girl working studiously at the rock. Jason all the while was standing beside her with an anxious apprehension, as if he wasn't entirely comfortable with her defacing his mom's tombstone.

When she was done, she handed the knife back to him and said something to Jason that Mason couldn't hear. Whatever it was, it had made Jason nod all solemn-like. He'd then propped the carving knife against the stone, an open invitation, maybe, to anyone else who had a name they wanted to add.

Afterwards, Jason had wandered over to join the others gathered around Ron, who was lighting the kindling he'd stacked in the firepit. The girl had trailed after him in perfect emulation of the dog following after her and Mason had gone to a take a look at what she'd written.

This was what he'd found:

MOM, DAD, BEN.

Ben was the name she'd called out when she was in the throes of her withdrawal and so that must have been her brother. Throughout what remained of the afternoon Mason had witnessed over a dozen youths also scratching out a name or two with the hook-bladed carving knife and the full weight of those struck him now.

Most of them must have lost someone too, he'd thought.

Such an indelible record of loss that it had a tear forming at the corner of his eye, contemplating how much grief they'd endured before coming to the farm.

Well, at least that means she's not alone in her grief, he told himself, wiping at his eye with the back of his hand, *whatever the future might hold for her, probably no different than what it holds for the rest of them.*

Sighing deep and long at that.

The world had obviously reached some sort of tipping point and after that only The Fall, into what he couldn't say. But if what had happened in North Bay was any indication, it wasn't likely to end with anything resembling a soft landing. Witnessing a Euphie Riot first-hand, it had seemed to him like pure fucking madness at the time. Yet watching it on the news later, it was hard not to view it as the logical extension of the unrelenting cycle of horrors beamed into his house day after day, hour after hour and, often, minute by minute — a tsunami of misery and despair starting halfway around the globe and the all of us standing here on the far shore like a bunch of fucking deer in the headlights, pretending to be mystified as the calamitous wave reared on our own horizon.

The same way you pretended Jesse shooting himself was some sort of mystery that defied any and all reason when you'd known all along things weren't going to end well for him either. You don't have to look any further than what he'd done to Spenser to have known that.

His gaze then drifting upwards and settling on the bone-shaped tag on the dog collar he'd strung over the top of the rock. He'd put it in his pocket after finding it discarded beside the granite monolith. It had seemed only natural that it should be returned to its rightful place, the same as it had seemed oddly fitting that when they'd set the stone at the foot of the grave, they'd planted it upside down. It was a sentiment lent no small amount of veracity by the way the world had suddenly seemed to have gone topsy-turvy while he was listening to Dale recount his story.

Such a wildly vacillating tumult of emotions that had over-come Mason in its telling. At first it had felt like he was being swallowed into the chasm that had become his head and was tumbling into an interminable darkness out of which he might never return. When Dale had shown him the picture of his daughter, who he'd said wouldn't even have been born if it wasn't for what Mason had done to him, he'd felt himself being lifted up again, flung out of the chasm and back into his chair. The night, all of sudden, had seemed as bright as day, lit as if by the twinkle in the girl's eyes — they really did seem to sparkle — and their dazzle shining ever the brighter because of how bleak the world had seemed to him just a moment ago.

Telling himself all the while that it was just the weed playing havoc with his equilibrium and that hardly stilling his mind as he'd listened to Dale winding towards his happy ending, though it had seemed like anything but to Mason. It wasn't so much that Dale's obvious intent had been to rub his face in the rough treatment he'd suffered at his hands, and more so under his knee. Mason had only a vague recollection of the actual incident, one amongst a plenitude of traffic stops involving "Indians" over the years. But he did remember all too clearly how it had seemed at the time that the country was verging on an all-out civil war and that it was primarily police officers who were forced to man the front lines as a bulwark against the nation sliding into further chaos. Or so he'd said practically every time he'd addressed his men before ushering them into the streets with the resolve of a battle-weary drill instructor sending conscripts off to war.

You'd only been doing what was necessary, he told himself now.

It was a turbulent time, at best. The whole damned country was splitting apart at the seams and nothing Dale — or a hundred others like him — could say would change that. Sure, he'd felt some shame being confronted by that particular incident and yes, he might have been a little excessive in his use of force, but then the same could well be said for those so-called "Land Defenders" too, let's not forget that.

Still, confronted with his own transgressions — first by finding Jesse's dead dog's collar tossed heedlessly aside by Jason and then even more so by what Dale had said — he couldn't shake the feeling that what he — and a legion of other cops — had done didn't really have anything at all to do with the greater good, not when measured against what he'd seen playing out in North Bay and then later on the news.

And neither had NORA, for that matter.

Thinking of all those campaign speeches he'd made in support of it alongside Vince Fanelli, the New Reform Party candidate for North Bay. Testifying with the fervour of a preacher sermonizing on the wages of sin that the world was at the precipice and that NORA was our only hope of pulling us back from the brink.

And look how that turned out.

All NORA had really done, he now saw, was give The Sons the means to push the world right over the edge, and here we were now in free fall. Only it wasn't the fall that killed you, it was the landing, meaning the worst was likely still yet to come. Recalling the map of Ontario they'd set on fire and trying to conceive of what he, or anyone, might have done to avert that, he heard Dale's voice swirling within the raging tempest of his mind.

I must've gone over that night a hundred times in my mind, he'd said, trying to make sense of how and why what had happened went down the way it did.

Hard not to hear an echo in that of what Hélène had said during one of the grief counselling sessions with Reverend Williams she'd dragged Mason to after Jesse had shot himself.

I just, she'd said, I just can't, I can't —

Shaking her head and then starting all over again.

I mean I've gone over it a hundred times and I just, I just, I mean — What did we do wrong? Can you explain that to me? I want someone to explain that to me. What the hell did we do wrong?!

Looking at the reverend with tears pouring down her cheeks, seeking absolution for whatever sin had brought them to this sorry impasse. The reverend, being of the United Church, had nothing to offer her beyond a few platitudes and a shoulder to cry on, which was more than Mason himself'd had to give.

Recalling then, as he had a thousand times, the crack of the rifle blast which had shocked him into wakefulness all those years ago. The time — 12:03 — was forever etched in his mind, twenty years in a patrol car having made checking the time into an unerring habit when the shit hit, the exact time being of the essence for when he'd later have to fill out his report.

Did you hear that? he'd asked Hélène, sitting up.

He might as well have been talking to himself since she wore earplugs at night, on account of how Mason snored. She hadn't heard the gunshot or Mason's question, had continued sleeping soundly, in fact, until Mason had returned to the room a mere thirteen minutes later — or so said the clock on the nightstand — to tell her that Jesse, their only son, had shot himself. Every moment in that intervening seven-hundred-fifty-odd seconds was imprinted in his mind with such clarity that it seemed to contain an entire lifetime within its meagre span.

Crawling out of bed and stubbing a pinky toe on the dresser as he made his way to the window, cursing the pain shooting pinpricks up his leg as he looked down at his driveway. Under a three-quarters moon Mason could plainly see Jesse's car parked in front of the house he'd once shared with his wife, Corrie, and their daughter, Kim. That is, until Kim had overdosed. Three months later Corrie had kicked Jesse out for reasons neither had ever confided in Mason or Hélène, leaving Mason to assume it was on account of Jesse's increasing reliance on alcohol and drugs to placate his grief. Corrie had then taken in another man, a fellow elementary school teacher and recent divorcee who, Corrie insisted to Hélène anyway, was only a friend in need of a place to stay and nothing more.

But Mason knew better.

Even then, he was inclined to take the odd midnight stroll. On his most recent, two days previous, he'd heard Corrie screaming, Oh god! Oh god, yes, yes, yes! Oh god, yes!

Such ecstasy in her cries that it had made Mason creep under cover of the closest willow, peering through its branches into what had once been his son's backyard and was now only his daughter-in-law's. What had been their bedroom window was open and was cast in a crimson hue, whether because Corrie had changed the drapes — which had always been green — or replaced the lightbulb in the overhead fixture with a red one, Mason couldn't tell. Listening to Corrie's cries rising towards climax, he'd been filled with an inconsolable anger.

That lying little bitch, he'd thought. *"Just friends" my ass. Fucking slut!*

Feeling a venomous bile coursing through his veins and that leading him back to a thought he'd had more than a few times over the past three months.

You ought to have chased her off the property after she kicked Jesse out and took up with another man, that lying bitch.

Standing there feeling like the bile had turned to lava and was threatening to burn him up from the inside out. Listening to her wailing like some ten-dollar hooker putting on a show for one of her regulars, waiting until she'd exhausted herself and then heading back to bed already knowing he wouldn't sleep a wink, not after hearing that.

In the years since, he'd convinced himself that he wasn't the only one listening to her on that night, that Jesse had also been hiding somewhere in the shadows. Maybe she'd known that too and what she was really doing was putting on a show for him, for in all the years they'd lived there together Mason had never heard such a vociferous display of passion coming from their bedroom.

How else to explain that it was only two nights later that Jesse returned and blew his head off in their backyard?

Coming through the willows after hearing the gunshot, he'd seen his son sprawled over the rock he'd used as a gravestone when he'd buried Spenser. His body was arched at an unnatural angle, his feet oddly bare, his toes pointing skywards. He'd known then exactly what had happened and yet still he'd started off at a run, crying out, Jesse, no. Please god, Jesse no!, as if words alone could have turned back the clock.

The shotgun was still wedged between his son's legs. Years of attending crime scenes had Mason tracking back in time, seeing Jesse sitting there on the ground, his back propped against the rock, the muzzle of the shotgun Mason himself had bought him for his sixteenth birthday crammed in his mouth, his finger reaching for the trigger. Flinching as he imagined the blast which had sheared the top of his son's head clean off, leaving his face below his eyebrows oddly intact, his eyes become two dark pits and his lips gaping wide, his teeth exposed and curiously unbloodied, their white glowing almost phosphorescent under the three-quarters full moon.

Confronted by Jesse's disembodied gape, Mason's grief had manifested as a living, breathing thing — a parasitic infestation that had seemingly attached itself to his spine and was snaking sinewy tentacles through his veins, wrapping themselves around his heart, squeezing the life out of him. That grief consumed then by a simmering rage and Mason wanting nothing more in that instant than to lash out at the world, knowing exactly where he'd begin.

Spinning towards the house and seeing the back door was open a crack. Corrie's face was peering out. Her skin's pallor was luminescent under the moon's harsh glare so he could clearly see her expression. Wrathful, that's what it was. A look of such scathing accusation that it had frozen him where he stood, seemed to freeze the very blood in his veins. The door closing and the click of the lock sounding afterwards reignited Mason's anger.

That fucking bitch! he'd fumed. *If it wasn't for her, Jesse'd still be alive. She might as well have pulled the trigger herself. She's a murderer, that's what she is. You ought to put a bullet in her fucking head for what she did to him, that lying fucking bitch!*

Thinking about his Glock, sticking it in her fucking mouth, blowing her fucking brains out, and her boyfriend's too.

That night he'd stormed back towards the house, hell-bent on fetching his gun. He'd got as far as the porch before his rage had been swept away by a tidal wave of grief and the weight of it had driven him, sobbing, to his knees.

The memory now buckling Mason's legs all over again.

Reaching out and steadying himself on the gravestone, breathing hard enough to have dragged it all the way over here himself, another image of Hélène arose, clear, into his mind. How she hadn't left her bed for three days after Jesse had shot himself and how she'd laid there clutching the stuffed dog that had come in the gift basket Hélène's fellow nurses had given her in celebration of the birth of her first-born. Hélène would come to call it Bobo and that would also be the first word Jesse ever spoke.

She must have sewed it back together and restuffed it a dozen times before he'd got too old to play with such things, both her and Jesse embroiled in an elaborate game of make-believe that spanned years, treating Bobo like it was a real dog such that Hélène would even use an empty syringe to pretend she was putting it to sleep before she stitched it back up. The last time she'd done so was when Jesse was ten and Mason, riled up from something that had happened at work — he could no longer remember what — had flown into a rage. He'd screamed at Jesse that he was too old to be sleeping with a stuffed animal anymore and then accused Hélène of filling the boy's head with nonsense. He'd finished his tirade by threatening to take the dog out back and burn it in their firepit, be done with such foolishness once and for all.

He never had, but Jesse had taken heed nonetheless. He must have, anyway, for Mason would never again see Bobo until Hélène was lying in bed after Jesse had blown his brains out, clutching at it so tight its eyes seemed about to pop. She must have saved it in the box of childhood treasures she'd made for Jesse and Jill on the pretence that she was saving the toys so that when her imagined grandkids came to visit they'd have something to play with too, except she'd never, in Mason's recollection, let Kim play with Bobo.

In later years, he'd come to realize she was simply using it as a prop in her efforts to banish the memory of what Jesse had done by retreating into the memory of the child he'd once been. But at the time Mason had been so wrapped up in his own tangled web of sorrow and rage that it had seemed to him more like she was clutching it out of spite rather than mourning, as if she was using it to teach him a lesson regarding his own shortcomings as a father — a merely symbolic act that told him in no uncertain terms that she blamed him for what their son had done, as if threatening to burn his son's prized stuffie some thirty-five years previous could account in any way, shape or form for the man he'd one day become.

Mason had spent the past nine years trying to find a way around blaming himself too, a futile effort which had only further isolated him from Hélène. Jesse's death became yet another sliver buried deep within her brain, pushed back to the surface by her increasing dementia, Mason now as certain as he had been of anything that Hélène hanging herself in the barn had been yet another act of spite — one final lesson for all time and one which, at long last, had left him absolutely no way around placing the blame for what she'd done on anyone but himself.

For if he'd just given her those damned pills like she'd asked . . .

But the prospect of living even a day without her had stayed his hand, not so much out of love but out of fear — the fear that when she was dead he'd never be able to kill himself and would be left all alone, forever doomed to wander the house and the property like some spectral manifestation of his former self that had become trapped in its own personal hell. And yet the only thing his refusal to cave to her wishes had really accomplished was to lead him to this moment — *right here, right now* — where he was feeling as disentombed as any ghost. Standing in front of a monument to his own transgressions, of the sins he'd passed down to his son and those forever intertwining them both in a solitude of regret, which had since been transformed into a beacon of solidarity — of hope — simply because they, a bunch of teenagers, had needed it to become so. Overwhelmed then with a desolation of loneliness such as he'd never in his life experienced, knowing that they'd lost what they had through no fault of their own while everything he'd lost could be — and must be — traced right back to his own hand.

Turning then towards the firepit with a roving gaze, seeking to temper his own solitude and finding only its reflection in the faces gathered there. Whatever hope they'd managed to preserve in the solidarity of their grief was faltering at even pace with the fire. Left unnourished, it was down to dying embers. Its own fate had become the fate of all those gathered around, the promise instilled in them by the day's activity now helpless against the gloom instilled in them by the encroaching night. Most of the faces now were all downcast and grim but a few were wide-eyed and darting about, plainly terrified, flinching at every sound and flicker or pop from the dying fire, as if the very dark itself was hiding all manner of horrors, lurking in the shadows, waiting to jump out and get them, likely a result of whatever they'd smoked or ingested.

And none of them looked more plainly terrified than the girl.

She was now clutching Jason's arms, holding on for dear life, her eyes fixed on the fading embers in the firepit with the desperate appeal of a ship's captain steering her boat towards a lighthouse's beacon in a dark and turbulent sea. Jason was also looking a little nervous, though from the way he was sitting rigid against her embrace, trying his best to ignore the girl who'd latched onto him, it was obvious to Mason that she was the primary cause of his angst.

Beside them, Kendra was weeping openly and her sobs seemed to best capture Mason's own mood. Except *she* wasn't standing off in the shadows, all by herself like *he* was. The Middle Eastern boy was still holding her tight and Annie was leaning over, giving her a kiss on the cheek and wiping the hair out of her eyes with a gentle caress. Kendra responded with a forced and fragile upturn of her lips, which had about as much in common with a smile as a wisp of smoke did with a raging inferno. It was ever on the point of succumbing again to her grief and Duane seemed to pick up on the cue. He was standing now, strumming a rather mournful chord on his guitar that perfectly captured the mood and also everyone's attention. Once they were all looking towards him, he let loose with a booming baritone which defied his tender age, drawing the first two words in the song out into a perfect expression of deep and intractable longing.

Well . . . I . . . wish I was in the land of cotton, Old times they are not forgotten, Look away, look away, look away . . . Dixie Land.

Such a strange song for him to be singing. And yet Mason couldn't help but feel a faint stirring in his chest, enough anyway to tell him he was still alive and happy for it. Such a powerful sensation that it hackled the hairs on his arms and made Mason feel, it did, like Duane was singing the song entirely for his sake as a balm against his beleaguered spirit. Hearing Duane strumming another solitary chord and his voice then rising again in its booming baritone, such that it sounded like he was dredging it up from the bottom of some long-dried river bed, its clay cracked and crumbling in a season of drought.

In Dixie Land where I was born, Early on one frosty morn, Look away, look away, look away . . . Dixie Land.

Taking a deep breath and holding it, every pair of eyes, including Mason's, glued to the young man, his head lowered and his body sagging as if he himself could hardly bear the weight of his desperate longing.

An interminable moment that ended with his fingers springing suddenly to life on the strings with the vigorous cavort of a swarm of bees and the guitar his hive, plucking honeyed notes from it with such zeal that it would have seemed more appropriate to a banjo than a guitar. The revelry in its tempo seemed to cast away that intractable longing in his voice, replacing it with a jaunty lilt that spoke to Mason not of someone waxing nostalgic for a distant past but longing for some equally distant future bright — the proverbial light at the end of a tunnel, both long and dark.

He was also now stomping his foot on the ground. He must have had a bell affixed to his ankle, for Mason could hear its jangling percussion pounding out the rhythm as he belted out, Away! Away! Away down south in Dixie!

Looking up from his guitar then and intoning again in his deep baritone, Sing along now, everybody!

Calling out then, Away! Away!, and leaning his ear towards the throng with dramatic flourish.

Away! Away!, a smattering of people called out with feeble croaks and Duane, spurred on by the lacklustre of their response, answered them with an even more boisterous:

Away down south in Dixie! Then: All righty then, again from the top!

A few more people joined in, including Kendra. She was mouthing along and wiping another tear from her eye, though this one seeming to sprout more from the raucous joy than from the imbedded sorrow. The Middle Eastern boy must have gained a little courage from the song too. He was bending to her neck, kissing her just beneath her ear. Annie responded to that by giving her friend a nudge with her elbow as she sang along with the others, none of whom were singing louder than the girl. She was swaying back and forth in Jason's arms in jubilant cavort and hollering out the refrain, louder even than Duane.

Then Ron and Dale were singing along as well as they bustled across the yard, their voices at once rising above the din and then being drowned under its sway.

Away! Away! Away down south in Dixie . . .

Duane's hand strummed a final climactic flourish that was greeted with hoots and hollers and a smattering of claps. The only person out of anyone who wasn't moving at all was Mason himself, as still as the memory stone itself except for his tears. They were washing in rivulets down his face and all at once it felt like they were washing away his sins, his breathing ragged and his chest swelling as if it could hardly contain the joy he suddenly felt.

And yet that joy was tinged with something else too — a feeling so outside of himself he couldn't quite place it. A kind of deep and intractable longing like at the beginning of the song, but that wasn't even the half of it.

It was . . .

But there was no accounting for how he felt in mere words.

Knowing only that he'd never in his life felt a deeper connection to anything than he had when listening to them sing that song, and also that it must have been exactly how Hélène had felt singing in the church choir, for she never looked more at peace than she did then.

Except . . . he thought. *Except . . .*

You weren't singing.

And that's why you feel the way you do now. Because you could have joined in and you didn't, same way you could have made a life for yourself outside of the force and yet you never bothered doing that either. Treating your own family like they weren't nothing but a constant source of irritation — a hindrance even — your own son an embarrassment — and look where that got ya.

A miasma of thoughts cycling through his mind as he scanned back towards Duane, never longing for anything more than for the young man to strike up another tune, telling himself that next time he'd be singing louder than anyone. But Duane was being led off into the field by a young woman wearing a tie-dyed summer dress with a bouquet's worth of flowers braided into her hair and was even then calling back over his shoulder, Don't y'all bother waiting up for me now, ya hear?

Stumbling then over some impediment — a rock or a clump of grass — and catching himself before he fell, his feet tripping over themselves trying to keep up with the girl pulling him harder still on a straight line for the closest tent. The whole circle was then breaking apart. Most of the teens were following after Duane and the girl, the lot of them in pairs too except for a group of four young males — the eldest of which couldn't have been older than thirteen. A fifth — Kendra's brother Davey — was hurrying after them with an upraised torch that he'd fashioned by tying a sock around the end of a stick. He was holding it up and proclaiming, Make way for the keeper of the flame! Make way!

Good idea, Davey, one of his friends offered in response. We can start our own fire!

Another remarking, It's too damned hot for a fire, if you ask me. What we ought to do is find somewhere to go swimming.

Shit yeah! It's been years since I took a night-swim. What about that lake where Annie shot the deer?

Fuck that. It's a half-hour's walk back through the bush and I ain't walking through the bush after dark, no fucking way . . .

Mason's gaze then returning to Jason and the girl. They were now standing and she was saying something through a yawn. It must have been goodnight, for after she was finished speaking Jason answered with a deferential sort of nod, like he couldn't have cared less. But when she turned her back on him, the young man stared after her with the same unease as he had watching her carve her family's names into the stone.

Mason was watching after her too, feeling no less a keen sense of concern. She seemed to be having some trouble keeping her balance. Her legs were moving in a wobbling meander, like the ground beneath them was shifting with each step, no doubt on account of the magic mushrooms she'd eaten.

She didn't seem to have spotted Mason at all, or at least was trying to pretend she hadn't, but Killer, trailing penitent after her, most surely had. He was casting Mason a series of clipped glances as he followed after the girl, stumbling in her lackadaisical traipse. She'd come to the closest willow and was fighting her way through its curtain with an all-too-dramatic flailing of arms — like she was battling her way through a nest of cobwebs rife with wolf spiders — so Mason knew she really must have been stoned out of her gourd.

And maybe the dog sensed it too.

He'd paused and was looking back at Mason, like he was seeking some sort of assurance or simply wanted him to come along too, and Mason harried him onwards with a sweep of his arm, urging, Well go on, then. Make sure she gets home safe. I'll be along in a moment.

The sound of his voice trailing off into the night and Dale's rising in its stead.

Well I don't know about you but I'm calling that a night!

He'd just reached the patio. Swiping his smokes and phone off the table, he called out, Come on Whisper, bedtime!

The dog was lying in a hole she'd dug to get a little relief from the heat and bounded out of that and into the house.

Ron then calling out, Goodnight Jason!

Hearing his name, Jason turned towards Ron with questioning eyes. He'd stepped over to the table where they'd laid out the feast, the same table Hélène had used when she took her preserves and whatever fresh vegetables she had left over to the farmers market held every Saturday in front of North Bay's heritage museum on Oak Street. The food had long since been ravished down to a few empty salad containers and the plates the cakes had come on. Jason was running his finger along the rim of one of the latter, getting himself a last taste of icing. Sticking his finger in his mouth, he waved at Ron with his other hand and Ron hollered,

The basement's good and cool if you want to sleep down there!

Thanks, Jason called back. I might just do that.

I'll leave the door open for ya. Make sure you lock it when you come in.

Jason gave him a thumbs-up and Ron followed Dale in through the door. Waiting until he'd shut it behind him, Jason then cast a rather imploring glance over at Mason. It was clear he still had some unfinished business to attend to at the rock and was idling his time at the table waiting for Mason to be done with his.

Mason obliged the young man, turning around and setting off towards the willows with the fervent stride of someone certain of his place in the world and yet, truth be told, right then he'd never been more uncertain of what exactly that might be.

As he stepped through the willow's drape, his belly gave out a hungry gurgle. That, at least, gave his mind a reprieve from thoughts of a less definite declination. The only thing he'd eaten since breakfast was a steak, a cob of corn and some potato salad. That had barely put a dint in his hunger but by the time he'd got it in mind to get himself a second helping, the food was all gone. He hadn't even managed to get himself a piece of the Boston cream cake they brought back with five others, Boston cream being his often-avowed favourite.

Coming out of the willow and onto his driveway he mused, *Boy, a piece of cake and a cold glass of milk sure would hit the spot right now*, and that leading him to mount a mental inventory of anything he might have in his cupboards to appease his sudden hankering after something sweet.

Chocolate chips maybe, left over from the last batch of cookies Hélène had made. Or he could open a jar of Hélène's candied yams, which had almost as much sugar in them as her corn relish. Still though, he'd never been much of a fan of those.

What I could really go for, he thought as he approached his porch, *is a stack of pancakes with maple syrup. I could use the chocolate chips. Butter melting all over them.*

He could practically see it dripping all over the plate against the aroma of fried sweet dough.

God, wouldn't that ever hit the spot!

The very thought had his mouth watering. As he mounted the steps he was trying to recall if they had any maple syrup before he remembered that he'd used the last of that just two days ago, when he'd eaten half a loaf of white bread dipping the slices in its sticky sweetness.

He'd have to pick some up at the Foodland tomorrow.

Telling himself then, *If you get up early enough you could buy a couple twenty-pound bags of flour along with it, make pancakes for everyone.*

That thought restored a little of the good humour he'd had watching the kids devouring the feast he'd bought for them just a few hours ago and, as Mason reached out to open the mud room's door, he clung to the sudden upswing in his mood by declaring, unequivocally,

By gum, I'm damn well gonna do it!

A thunderclap startled Ron awake just after eight the next morning.

He'd been having a nightmare in which he was walking in the back field amongst all the tents. The closest of them had suddenly burst into flames and then a second had too and a third and a fourth. Kids were stumbling out of them, drenched in fire, and then Ron, miraculously, had the fire extinguisher in his hand. He started forward, propelled by their screams, but his feet were trapped as if in quicksand. Looking down and seeing hands prying through fresh dug soil, grabbing at his legs. He was standing on Marnie's grave. The hands were clawing towards his knees and a face was emerging out of the dirt, Ron knowing it was Marnie and that he couldn't — he just couldn't — bear the sight of that again even as he couldn't summon the will to turn away. But when the face broke through the surface, Ron saw it wasn't Marnie's after all, but Clarence Boothe's.

Jarred then into wakefulness by the thunderclap. Hearing another a second later, realizing only then that it wasn't thunder at all, it was a rifle's *Crack!*

The Sons!, he thought sitting bolt upright. *It's The Sons of Adam come to kill the chief!*

A third sharp *Crack!* was enough to propel him out of bed. On his way to looking out the window, he grabbed the baseball bat leaning against his dresser, as if any piece of hardwood would do him a lick of good against a band of outlaws as heavily armed as The Sons were likely to be. The window afforded him a clear view across the backfield. Prying open its curtain, he stole a quick glance out. All he could see were the twenty or so tents ruffling in gusts from a stiff breeze. With the dream still so clear in his mind, he was half-expecting them to burst into flames. But then someone — Duane it looked like — was sticking his head out of one of the tents in the fore and he saw Dale too.

He was striding into the field with a black garbage bag unfurled in one hand and his rifle upraised in the other, almost like a torch. He was yelling something, Ron couldn't quite hear what, and then pressing the trigger. The rifle gave out another *Crack!*, and Ron turned away from the window, shaking his head and thinking Dale must have gone crazy.

W hat the hell's going on out here?

Ron had just come onto the patio to find a host of Styrofoam plates and chip bags and pop bottles blowing in their wayward drift over the yard and into the field, much as he had the previous morning. But he could see right away that it wasn't the kids who'd done it this time. The black garbage bag he himself had filled last night was sitting, torn open, in front of the upended food table, lying on its side. That had given him a pretty good idea of what had happened and yet still he'd called out what he had.

Dale had since handed the fresh plastic garbage bag to Duane. The teenager seemed to have taken some affront at that and stood glowering in bitter indignation after Dale tromping back towards the house. Behind him faces began to appear at the other tents, peering out of their opened flaps, as mystified by what had just happened as had been Ron.

We had a visitor last night, Dale said in answer to him as he broke into the yard.

A visitor?

A big old black bear.

You shoot it? Ron asked.

Bad luck to shoot a bear.

Well I heard you shooting something.

I was just scaring it off.

Reaching the patio, he paused, giving Ron a good looking-over.

It looks like it wasn't the only thing I scared.

Wh-What are talking about?

You look like you've seen a ghost. What, you think it was them Sons of Eugene come to exact their revenge on the chief or something?

He was grinning in his sly way and Ron knew making him think they were under attack had been his primary intent when he was firing off his rifle.

N-N-No.

Well you sure could have fooled me.

Dale sat down in his chair, plucking a cigarette from his pack and ignoring Ron shaking his head at him in rueful scorn. After a couple of seconds Ron grew weary of that and retreated inside to fetch his own smokes, his weed, his chute and his phone.

When he returned, Dale was still trying to light his cigarette. The swirling wind was thwarting his every effort and Ron cast his eyes skyward. There was a mass of grey clouds churning above them.

Feels almost like tornado weather, Dale offered after he'd finally managed to get his smoke lit.

A little early in the season for a tornado, Ron countered, though between the heady gusts of wind and the clouds and the dryness in the air, it did in fact feel just like that.

There was one down in Parry Sound just the other day, weren't there?

No, Ron said, packing his bowl, it was only a warning.

There weren't no tornadoes?

Just a few micro-bursts.

Well it sure feels like tornado weather to me.

Before Ron could add anything, he heard his phone buzz.

While he drew the weed smoke into the plastic bag, he leaned over, seeing it was a text from Val.

Val just texted, he said on his way to taking a huff.

Old Val, eh? What'd she want?

Ron was holding the smoke in and on the exhale, choked out, Well I ain't read it yet, have I?

Well what the fuck are you waitin' for?

Ron shaking his head again and reaching for the phone. He swiped the screen, bringing the message up.

Says she just got a call from the chief's daughter, he said after scanning through it. Says Jill's been trying to reach her folks for a couple of days now. She figures they forgot to charge their phone again and was wondering if I'd go over and tell them to give her a call. Jill, I guess she means. What should I write back?

I don't know. Dale rubbing his hand over his face, mulling it over. Tell her you'll pass the message along.

What about Hélène?

What about her?

Should I tell her Hélène's dead?

Best to let the chief give her the bad news.

Ron was more than content to do that and texted back, *We'll pass the message along*.

Speak of the devil and he shall appear, Dale said as Ron pressed send.

Sure enough, the chief's pickup was slowing to a stop at the foot of their driveway. The bed of his truck was packed with maybe twenty cages, each one holding a chicken. Their squabbling-squawk all but drowned out the old man's voice as he leaned out the window, shouting something over at them.

What? Ron called back, standing and bustling down the driveway so as to hear what the chief might have to say.

I said, Mason yelled back louder than before, how are you guys with pancakes?

Pancakes? Ron called back. Hell, I could always eat a stack or two of pancakes!

Then it's your lucky day!

He was grinning like some crazy fool and hitting the gas at the same time. The truck lurched forward and the chickens unleashed another fluster of startled clucks.

What was that he was saying about pancakes? Dale asked as Ron ambled back.

I don't know. I think he's fixing to make us all breakfast. You see all them chickens?

Is that what they were? I was wondering.

Ron smirking as he sat back down, for what else could they have possibly been?

Something's sure got into the chief, he said as he lit himself a smoke.

How's that?

It's like somebody's lit a fire under his ass. Ron then exhaling. It must have been that story you told him last night. It sure did shake him up.

Good.

You see how long he was staring at that rock?

Oh, round about sixty-three minutes, as far as I recall.

Ron took a drag of his smoke, thinking about what Dale had told the chief.

He'd heard Dale tell the story of how he'd ended up in the Central East Correctional Centre a half-dozen times but he'd never heard him tell it quite like that.

For one, he'd never mentioned Julie working at the Dinner Bell. As far as Ron knew the first time Dale had met her was at Shooters. Nor had he mentioned how he thought he'd end up buried in a shallow grave or dumped in the Mattawa river, though he always did blame that clicking in his neck on the chief for kneeling on him the way he had. And every other time he'd told the story, the main thrust of it was that he'd been carrying a vial of LSD when the chief pulled him over. He'd swallowed it and then shit it out the next morning when he was in a cell in the basement of the police station. He'd shared it with the three others locked down there with him and all of them had spent the whole day tripping. One of them, some elderly drug addict, had been screaming the whole time, Fan-fucking-tastic! They told me to get off the dope. They said it was going to kill me. Well, I say fuck 'em! This is fan-fucking-tastic!

The first time Ron had heard the story, just after they'd moved in together in town, he'd unleashed a riotous guffaw when Dale had proclaimed Fan-fucking-tastic! with the vigour of some carnival barker calling people to his booth. It was shading towards an uncontrollable giggle as Dale added, He was making such a ruckus the cops finally gagged his mouth and zip-tied his hands behind his back. But being tied up didn't seem to bother him none. In fact, I ain't never seen no one happier. He kept laughing with such unbridled hilarity for the rest of the night, I thought maybe it'd be the death of him.

And while he'd have loved to have heard Dale tell *that* story to the chief too, he had to admit the other version had struck a somewhat deeper chord.

How come you've never told me that story anyway? he asked, exhaling smoke and taking another drag.

It's because, Dale answered, I just made it up.

You just made it up?

Parts of it anyway.

Why'd you do that?

I don't know. I just kind of got into a groove and it started telling itself.

Must have been those mushrooms, Ron offered.

They were good, weren't they?

Fan-fucking-tastic!

That got a smile from Dale.

You can say that again. Have to see if Eric has any more.

Got to wait a week before you do 'shrooms again, else they won't do nothing.

Well, it never hurts to plan ahead.

Ron's phone buzzed again. Leaning over, he saw it was another text from Val.

All it said was *Thanks! Stay safe.*

Shoot, Ron said while he was answering her with a smiley-face emoji, I forgot to tell Chief to call his daughter.

Ain't nothing stopping ya now.

Ron had set his phone back down and was already standing.

I thought you were going to see the chief, Dale asked, watching Ron head for the house rather than the willows.

Well I'll need a fork and a plate, won't I?

A fork and a plate?

For the pancakes.

Pancakes? Dale asked as if he'd forgotten their earlier conversation.

I toldya already. Chief's making us all pancakes.

I'll believe that when I see it.

W-Well if he is, Ron said, pausing at the door to the house, I aim to be the first in line!

O h good, you're up.

    Mason had come into the kitchen carrying a twenty-pound sack of flour wedged under one arm, and in each hand one of two reusable shopping bags weighted with five pounds of butter, two dozen eggs, a four-litre jug of milk, a kilogram of frozen breakfast sausages and three bags each of chocolate chips and Skor bits. The girl was sitting at the table, staring balefully at a mug of what Mason assumed was instant coffee, since the jar of that was sitting capless on the counter next to the half-empty beaker of cream he bought from the farm next door.

    She must have had a shower or another bath. Her coppery curls hung limp in sopping wet ringlets over her light summer dress, the one Jill had bought Hélène for her birthday one year from the women's fashion store on North Bay's Main Street because, she'd said, its swirls of purple had reminded her of lilacs, her mom's favourite flower. It was one of three dresses Mason had left stacked and folded on the floor in front of the den's door the night before, along with two pairs of shorts, two T-shirts and a blouse, so she'd have some choice as to what to wear. He'd also left her three pairs of underwear and two so-called sport bras, which Hélène had always favoured over the other kind, even though they weren't too likely to fit, since Hélène's breasts were practically mountains compared to the girl's molehills. The girl hadn't bothered putting on either of those. She'd also left the dress's top button undone so the dress didn't conceal much more than the T-shirt he'd given her yesterday, which he'd realized only after seeing how it exposed her must have been one of the shirts Hélène only used for sleeping in, much to his later shame and regret.

The skin under her eyes was puffy and shading towards a deepening purple, in stark contrast to the pale white of her cheeks. She looked like she hadn't slept a wink the night before, maybe on account of the mushrooms, and when Mason had come in it looked like she was on the verge of falling asleep right there at the table.

Mason himself couldn't remember having slept better, so at least Dale had been right about that one thing. He'd awoken feeling like a man of fifty and ever since he'd been laying plans like a man younger still, one who had a future full of untold possibilities lying in store for him.

The girl didn't so much as look up at the sound of his voice and, trying to rouse her from her stupor, he enthused, I hope you like pancakes!

Still, she didn't answer him and Mason set the flour and the grocery bags on the counter then stepped to the corner cupboard where Hélène kept her baking supplies. On the drive back from the store, he'd realized he hadn't bought any baking soda and he'd been hoping ever since that there was some still there. He found a box sitting on the top shelf which was half-full. Satisfied that it would be plenty, he spent a moment debating whether he should bring in the rest of the groceries or start whipping up a batch of pancakes right off.

All that was left in the truck was the four-litre jug of maple syrup, a second bag of flour, the other box of sausages and the two heaping bags of toiletries he'd bought so the kids would at least have toothbrushes, toothpaste and sanitary pads. Figuring they could wait, he retrieved the biggest mixing bowl from the cupboard over the fridge. He set it on the counter then fetched the hand mixer from the drawer beside the stove.

He hadn't passed more than a cursory glance at the girl since he'd come in and did so now. She was still staring into her coffee as if it had done her some great wrong and it wasn't until Mason had measured six cups of flour into the mixing bowl and was reaching for the milk that he'd summoned the will to speak again.

You know, he said, looking back at her, I never did catch your name.

She responded by looking up at him. It seemed a little like progress, even though the quizzical expression on her face made it appear like he'd asked her something in a foreign language she couldn't quite understand. He didn't think she'd answer and was thus gratified when she did.

Meghan, she said, after a moment. My name's Meghan.

You look like a Meghan, Mason offered for want of anything better to say, and also because it struck him as pretty close to the truth.

My mom always said so too.

Well Meghan, I'm going to need your help, if you're up to it. It's going to be a busy day.

As if to prove his point, he'd barely finished speaking when there was a knock on the door.

Door's open, he called out, dumping the two cups of milk in the bowl and filling the measuring cup again.

Heh-Heh-Hey there Chief, Clete said, stepping into the kitchen.

He was carrying a metal camping plate tucked under his arm and had a fork in one hand. He was opening his mouth about to say something else when Mason cut him off.

Good morning to ya, Clete, he said then added: Can you do me a favour and fetch the rest of the groceries from the truck?

N-No problem.

Mason was mixing the batter and adding to it a half-bag each of the Skor bits and the chocolate chips when Clete returned.

Just the maple syrup, the sausages, the flour, the toothbrushes and whatnot and these plastic plates? Clete asked, lugging in the supplies.

Right, the plates. I forgot about them. I figured we'd save on the disposables by giving everyone their own.

That's a good idea. Where do you want 'em?

The table'll be fine.

What about the sausages?

What about 'em?

Well you aren't planning on eating them raw, are you?

That's a good point. Shoot, I should have started them before mixing up the pancakes.

You got a pan?

In the drawer under the stove.

Okay, I'll get 'em started.

Can you fetch the fry pan while you're at it?

Already got it, he answered, setting it on the stove. This your only frying pan?

No, we got a couple smaller ones in the cupboard beside the fridge.

There's also a waffle iron in here, Clete said, after he'd retrieved those. We could use that too.

Good thinking. What about an electric grill, you see one of those?

Nope.

Well, I know we got one. Hélène must have put it down in the basement. She always did complain it was too big for the kitchen.

That the door to the basement there?

He was looking at the door set in the wall leading into the hallway.

Yeah. But mind you get them sausages in the oven before you worry about that.

Will do.

As Mason ladled the first dollop of pancake batter into the butter simmering in the largest of the frying pans, he heard the door clicking shut. Glancing towards it, he saw the girl through the window, heading for the porch with her cup of coffee. Probably all the hustle and bustle had been too much for her delicate frame of mind.

Boy, don't that smell good already, Clete opined as he opened the first box of sausages and that brought Mason back to task.

Nothing better'n the smell of pancakes on an empty belly, he said adding another dollop to the pan.

You sure are right about that.

A half-hour later Mason walked amongst the campers gathered in his driveway hungrily devouring the pancakes, waffles and sausages on plates swimming with enough maple syrup to drown a rat. He was carrying a pan stacked high with more of the same, offering up seconds and taking no end of delight in how quickly they disposed of those too.

As far as he could tell, Dale was the only person who hadn't come over for breakfast. After they'd dished out servings to everyone, Mason had sent Clete next door with Dale's share while he'd cooked up what was left of the batter. He'd just doled out the last of the pancakes he'd made from that when he saw Clete coming back through the willows, eating off the metal camping plate that was meant for his housemate.

Dale skip off somewhere? Mason asked, sidling over to him, though he suspected otherwise. Dale had refused to eat any of the food he'd bought yesterday as well, instead cooking himself up a burger made of ground moose and liberally seasoned with onions, jalapenos and grated cheese.

Too many hormones in that store-bought meat, he'd offered by way of explanation when Mason had told him there'd be plenty of steak for him too. I prefer my meat organic.

Hearing the story he'd later told, Mason suspected that wasn't the only reason why he'd refused and also why he hadn't come over for breakfast.

He's never been much for pah-pancakes.

That so?

Made himself some eggs instead. Said to pass along his th-thanks for the offer, though.

Seemed unlikely, but Mason was in far too good a mood to let something as trivial as that put so much as a dent in it. Scanning then over the gathered youths. Most of the girls, excluding Meghan, were gathered around the chickens in the back of his truck and were feeding them pinches of pancake through the cages' wire. One must have got a nip of flesh, for Kendra was laughing and startling back. Holding her index finger up to the young Middle

Eastern–looking man — Mason couldn't remember his name — she smiled coyly as he took her hand gingerly in his, sucking at the bead of blood appearing on its tip, and Mason turned back to the porch. Meghan was sitting there in the wicker rocking chair with her eyes closed and her hands folded in her lap. She looked to have fallen asleep. She'd set her empty plate on the porch floor beside her. Killer was licking it clean. When his granddaughter, Kim, was young she'd often let his dog do the same whenever she came over for a meal and the recollection brought a smile to Mason's lips.

Jason was leaning against the porch in front of Meghan, picking idly at his own breakfast. All he managed so far was a few bites from his pancakes and one from his sausages. From the vacant sheen clouding his eyes, he also looked like he hadn't slept a wink the night before. The other young men were gathered in a loose horseshoe formation around him, finishing off their grub by licking their plates clean too.

Come on man, Duane goaded Jason, tell us one of your jokes.

Shoot yeah, Eric agreed. You remember how he told, like, thirty in the cafeteria that one time at lunch. Almost shit myself, I was laughing so hard.

If Jason heard either of them he made no sign. He continued staring dazedly down at his plate and Duane nudged him with his elbow, trying to rouse him from his stupor.

Come on man, tell us one of your jokes.

Say, how you fixed for freezer space? Mason asked, turning back to Clete.

Far as I know, we got plenty of room in the freezer in the basement. Why?

Got a side of beef coming later this week. Ordered it from Shane Brady when I bought the chickens.

Shane Brady was the owner of the farm which bordered the property's easternmost field. It was his father, Denis, who'd sold them a dozen chickens and two Jersey cows when Hélène was pregnant with Jesse and had got it in mind to get back into farming. After Kim had overdosed and Jesse had shot himself, Hélène had lost interest in keeping cows and chickens of their own and Mason had taken to buying their eggs, milk, cream and a fair share of their meat from the Bradys. It was why he'd stopped by there on the way back from the Foodland, though he had another idea in mind entirely when he'd tracked Shane to the barn.

Unlike his father, who was about the most gregarious person Mason had ever met, Shane had been a morose child who'd since grown into an increasingly dour middle-aged man. Mason had attributed this to him having been born with a club foot. He'd had a half-dozen operations on it over the years but still walked with a limp. That had grown more pronounced with every passing year, as had his surly demeanour. He had three older brothers who'd all been star hockey players in high school and who'd then gone on to university — two to become doctors and one an engineer — so that probably hadn't improved his disposition much either. He treated his infirmity, and later the farm itself, as an unwanted cross he was forced to bear and how he'd ever convinced such a spritely and congenial woman as Emma Dufresne to marry him was beyond any attempt at reason.

They'd barely passed more than four words in all the years Mason had been dropping by. When Mason let himself into the barn, Shane had looked up from detaching the milking tubes from one of the fifty or so cows confined to their stalls, squinting against the light and glowering at the intrusion.

If you're looking for eggs, you'll have to talk to the missus, he said gruffly, as if he'd never seen the man who was walking towards him now.

Already have, Mason answered. I was hoping to talk with you about something else.

He'd laid out his plan with an exactitude that suggested it was a lifelong dream and not something he'd hatched only that morning. Shane's only son, Andrew, had since wandered over. He was seventeen and six-foot-four and towered over his father's stout five-foot-eight. He was a good-looking boy, with his mother's strawberry-blonde hair and her ruddy cheeks. Last Mason had heard, he was also a starting defenceman on the Battalion's Senior A hockey team, which is to say that he seemed to have taken after his uncles, though his disposition he owed all to his father. While Mason made his pitch, the both of them listened with the disapproving scowl of a devout atheist who'd had his dinner interrupted by a pair of Jehovah's Witnesses knocking at his door.

When Mason finished, Shane had shaken his head dismissively before delivering his verdict.

I'm not much in the habit of selling off ma stock, he said, turning his back on Mason and picking up the milking machine from the floor.

I understand that, I truly do, Mason countered, following the farmer to the next cow in line. That's why I'm prepared to let you name your price.

It'd be more'n you can afford, I'll tellya that.

Mason recalling now with some satisfaction the look on that miserable old coot's face when Shane had named his price and without so much as a blink, Mason had stuck out his hand to seal the deal while enthusing, So long as you don't mind cash!

Is that where you got the chickens? Clete was asking now. I was wondering.

I got some cows coming tomorrow too.

Cows?

Which reminds me. We got to get that fence fixed before they arrive.

Fence?

And I figured while we were doing that, we could get some of the kids to clean out the barn. Maybe get a few others to start tilling the vegetable garden. Mason nodding to himself, firming the plan in his mind. It's going to be a busy day all right. I guess we ought to get —

I told you, I don't feel like telling a fucking joke!

Jason's voice rose in angry declaration, cutting Mason off, and every one of the youths, and Mason and Clete too, swivelled their heads towards him.

His animosity was directed at Duane, who was now shaking his head, his eyes lowered.

Sorry man, I didn't mean —

You think there's anything funny about what's going on?

No, I —

You think a fucking joke is going to make everything all better?

I didn't —

A fucking joke. Yeah, I'll tell you a fucking joke! You, Duane. You're the fucking joke! Fucking head up your ass, as usual!

He didn't mean —

This from Eric as he reached out to set a comforting hand on Jason's arm. But Jason was clearly losing it.

Get your fucking hands off me! he shouted, flinching away.

Jay—

Don't you fucking Jay me!

He'd clenched his free hand at his side and the way his eyes had narrowed to squints told Mason he was one breath away from taking a swing at Eric. A terrible silence descended over the crowd, except for the stuttered clucks from the chickens and the dog's simpering whine from the porch. He'd since nuzzled his head into Meghan's lap. Both he and the girl were casting nervous glances at Jason, as was everyone else in the yard, and that only seemed to inflame the young man's rage. His whole body was shaking now, as if he could hardly contain it.

Kendra sniffled, looking like she was about to cry, and Masood drew her close, holding her in a tenuous embrace.

Mason himself stunned into silence by the outburst, feeling the good humour draining right out of him and thinking, *They're starting to crack. I guess it was only a matter of time.*

Clete alone seemed to have divined some way out. He was striding forward banging his fork on his metal camping plate, calling everyone to attention and hollering out,

All right, gather round, gather round! We got a busy day ahead of us and I need everyone to listen up real close!

There you are!

Jason was sitting, brooding, on the bench in the flower garden behind the chief's house. His plate of mostly uneaten food sat propped on his lap but the shame he felt over how he'd yelled at his friends had sucked whatever appetite he'd had right out of him. He had about as much stomach for company as he did for pancakes and sausages, especially when it came to her. The moment he heard the girl Mason had called Meghan shouting over at him from between the two apple trees, he could feel his hackles rising.

Her dog, as always, traipsed along behind her in its shy way. She'd called it Killer, which seemed a damned strange name for a dog as skittish as that, but in the very least it gave Jason something to look at instead of her. Watching as the dog startled at a grass-hopper flittering out of its way, dodging right like it had meant to do the dog some great harm and casting a ripple of suspicious glances about the yard, which it seemed to believe was filled with all manner of untold dangers lying in ambush.

I've been looking everywhere for you, Meghan said as she sidled up to Jason.

When he didn't respond, she plucked up one of the sausages from his plate and took a bite, chewing on it while she surveyed the garden.

Boy, it sure is nice back here, she offered, the uplift to her voice making it seem like some kind of an olive branch.

Jason wasn't much in the mood for that either but it was hard to argue with what she'd said. The garden was like something out of one of those magazines his mom often brought home from the long-term care centre after she'd cleaned out the room of some old lady who'd died. They had names like *Better Homes and Gardens* and *Birds & Blooms* and she'd accumulated about two dozen of them in the cupboard under their bathroom's sink. Whenever she was on the toilet she'd sit drawing up no end of plans for how she might enliven their own meagre backyard, none of which had amounted to more than a couple of butterfly bushes and a bleeding heart in planter boxes. Jason himself had spent a fair share of his time on the shitter idly flipping through the pages but, truth be told, nothing he'd seen in any of the magazines held a candle to the natural splendour of flowers and shrubs, trees and brightly coloured bushes surrounding him now.

The whole of it was outlined with rocks about the same size as the ones lining the firepit. They numbered in the hundreds and were arranged in a circle about thirty feet in diameter, unbroken except for the gap between the two apple trees that had led him into the garden and a horseshoe of flat limestone slabs enclosing a solar-powered water fountain on the opposite side of the clearing from the bench. The fountain was two-tiered and burbling with the soothing melody of a late-summer creek.

A robin washed itself in the topmost pool and a squirrel sat on its haunches chewing on an acorn on the bottom tier. Chickadees and warblers and orioles and cardinals and a host of other birds he couldn't name flitted about the branches of the lilacs and magnolias and crabapple trees, sounding off each in their own way against the frolic of chipmunks. Those nattered back at the winged interlopers with urgent protests and there was a steady whine of cicadas and the hum also of bumble- and honeybees drinking at the foliage's sweet nectar, the scent of which was so profound it lent an easy comparison to the heady waft coming from the perfume counter at the Shoppers Drug Mart in town.

Sitting there for the past half-hour, it had been hard to cling onto the anger he'd felt. It had shortly relented into the ever-sharpening pang of shame for how he'd treated Duane and Eric, who'd never been anything but the best of friends to him. His gaze had wandered to what was unmistakably a fresh dug grave in the space just inside the two crabapple trees and he'd found himself sliding into a deepening sorrow, thinking about his mother's grave and what had happened to her.

Recurring thoughts of how her dreams of having a garden just like this had amounted to jack squat had his anger simmering all over again until finally it was back at a full boil, making him want to smash and stomp every damned plant in the garden to tatters. For why should someone else be blessed with such abundance and she with so little? A hummingbird was hovering in front of the delicate bells dangling from one of four bleeding hearts at the foot of the fountain and he'd got it in mind that that'd be as good a place to start as any when the girl had called out to him moments ago.

Glancing up and seeing her sauntering into the garden, smiling like some wanton simp, or maybe a siren, trying to lure him towards his doom, had only further enflamed Jason's ire. She was wearing a summer dress with purple swirls that reminded him of the lilac bushes blooming throughout the expansive garden. That might have made him feel a little less uncomfortable than that shirt she was wearing yesterday except she'd left the top button undone so it didn't conceal any more than had the other. Whatever game she was playing at was still a mystery, made no less inscrutable by the way she was always smiling in some half-baked attempt at putting on a brave face.

And Jason was certain it was a game, and one he'd likely be on the losing side of, especially since she couldn't have been much older than fourteen with him almost twenty now.

When he was in school, he'd known plenty of girls just like she appeared to be — girls who had the misfortune of being born both pretty and poor and were thus prime targets for all manner of predators, both related and otherwise. Girls who'd been abused from the time they'd been in diapers, their lives become one vast gaping wound which they'd try to cauterize, perhaps paradoxically, with sex, and that, more often than not, only tearing open the wound even more. Or so his mother had opined about Cate Willowby, his first real girlfriend, whom Jason had broken up with in the ninth grade after he'd found out she was screwing half the senior boys' basketball team behind his back.

You can't blame yourself, his mom had then added by way of commiseration. She was fucked up beyond all repair long before you showed up.

For some reason, it was girls like Cate who seemed to gravitate towards him. While he'd had a little fun with more than a few, he'd learned that the price of all that fun was far too high for his taste — the cost measured in the broken pane of glass in his bedroom window when Cate threw a rock through it the night after she'd seen him talking to Sherrie Taylor at his locker, the door of that smeared with dog shit not a month later by, he

300

suspected, Sherrie herself because he'd been ghosting her. And then there were all the flat tires on his bike, eight in three years. The last of those had finally been enough and in his senior year he'd forsworn girls altogether for a bottle of hand lotion and his laptop, figuring he could manage well enough on his own.

But there was no doubt in his mind that Meghan was crazier than Cate and Sherrie and a half-dozen others all rolled into one. Watching her saunter towards him had him cursing himself for letting her crawl into his lap the night before.

What the fuck were you thinking? he admonished himself now, for it seemed to have emboldened her beyond all propriety.

How else to explain her nudging his back with her toe the entire time she was sitting behind him in that wicker chair while he leaned against the porch, like some grade-schooler playing footsies. No wonder he'd lost it with Duane and Eric. And here she was again trying to entice him into her madness.

Jason gritting his teeth at the very thought while she surveyed the garden. Popping the rest of the sausage in her mouth, she licked her lips, glancing at him sideways and smiling wider still, seeing that he was looking up at her.

I told Mason you'd help me with the dishes, she said. And when he answered by looking away, she added, It'll take your mind off things.

That about as patently absurd a statement as he'd ever heard. Shaking his head and looking back at the butterfly bush, he clung to his anger by imagining himself again tearing it out by the roots, kicking over the fountain and then laying waste to the whole damn garden.

It would serve it fucking right!

Feeling then the girl's hand on his arm, clenching it tight, and the girl pulling at it, trying to drag him to his feet. Jason jerked his arm back and Meghan clutched it tighter, digging her pincer-like nails into his flesh. That was enough, at last, to get him to look her way again, glaring at her with an unconcealed hate.

Ain't no use sitting around brooding all day, she urged, meeting his glare with the same look of brazen defiance she'd worn when she'd interrupted him carving his mother's name in the stone. And when that didn't get him to move even an inch, she dug her nails into his arm hard enough that Jason could feel them raking against bone. Her eyes then narrowed into the dire squint of some woodland beast — a wolf or maybe a bear — who'd fixed her prey in her sights and was just then zeroing in for the kill.

Come on now, she said, though it came out sounding more like a snarl. You wouldn't want to make me a liar, now . . . would ya?

G awd, what a mess!
      Jason was just closing the door behind them, sneaking a peek as he did so at Duane and Eric. Each was hefting a chicken cage from the back of the chief's truck. He let his gaze linger, hoping one or both would turn his way so he could give them a nod to tell them that there were no hard feelings, but neither did.

You wash and I'll dry, Meghan said cheerfully and he turned towards the kitchen, taking in the enormity of the task ahead.

Dirty dishes were stacked on every available surface and the floor was riddled with dirty shoeprints tracked through blotches of pancake batter and splatters of syrup so that it looked like a herd of sneaker-wearing buffalo had stampeded through the room just moments before.

You need gloves? she asked when he'd been standing there for a couple of breaths.

She was holding up a pair of yellow rubber ones, the same kind his mom used when she did dishes. He shook his head.

All right then, let's get at 'er. Them dishes ain't gonna wash themselves.

He'd filled up the dish rack with clean plates before she spoke again.

She'd cleared the counter on the far side of the dish rack before wiping it down with a rag so she'd have somewhere to put the dried dishes. She was now standing straddle-legged over the vent in the floor beside the fridge, delighting in the stream of cold billowing up her dress from the central air, all the while emitting subtle moans that were verging far too close to the wanton variety for his comfort.

Boy, don't that feel good, she offered when she'd caught him looking. I'd sure hate to be stuck outside in this heat.

Giving him a wink that had his gaze scurrying back to the sink.

It felt like I was melting in my chair, she said. And here it is only ten o'clock. It sure is going to be a hot one today. Good thing I volunteered us for the dishes.

An idle bit of chit-chat to pass the time and Jason about as inclined towards that as he would have been to drink a glass of the scummy water filling the sink.

As he reached for another plate, it was hard not to feel his mother's presence. She'd often sat at their kitchen table watching him do the dinner dishes while she drank a cup of decaf and it took every ounce of his will not to glance backwards, as he'd often done then. How many times had he scowled at her when he'd caught her gazing with the pride of a mother whose son had just graduated from medical school, or some such thing, and wasn't simply washing a couple plates and whatever pots she'd used cooking dinner, the same as he had every damned night since he could reach the sink. Scowling back at her not because of how foolish, even simple, she looked but because it was merely the role he played in the pantomime they'd contrived between them ever since — in his mind anyway — he'd grown too old for hugs and sloppy kisses on the cheek, and scowling with ironic disdain had become his only means of expressing his love. His mother playing along, sticking her tongue out and Jason more often than not answering her with a playful smirk on the way to warning, You better watch it, someone's liable to cut that off!

Trying then not to think about how his mother had bit off her own tongue and what had come after. Failing miserably in that, the world all of a sudden seemed to grow dark around him. Looking up through the window, seeing a charcoal-grey cloud swallowing the sun and it feeling like he'd been swallowed into its gloom too.

The sun peeked out through a crack a moment later and that made him feel worse yet. It seemed to him an illusion as fragile as the girl's act, her moans sounding desperate and forced — like something she'd seen in some stupid rom-com on TV and here they were stuck in a living horror show where any amount of good humour was bound to be answered only by an equal amount of grief.

And that thought leading quite naturally to another.

Him and his mother watching scary movies together on the couch. His mother professed that those were her favourite, though Jason was convinced it was just a ploy to get him to watch TV with her, since she said she couldn't bear to watch them alone. Every jump scare caused her to clutch at his arm, her nails digging into his flesh almost as hard as Meghan's had in the garden, and she'd bury her head into his shoulder during the particularly gory scenes like some timid teenage girl might with her boyfriend at the cinema. One time when she was doing that, he'd seen Eric and Duane's playful smirks appear at the living room's window, which is how they often announced their presence before knocking at the door. On that night, they never had.

Although they'd also never mentioned what they'd seen, Jason had been mortified at the thought of what him and his mom must have looked like and it was the last time he'd ever watched a horror movie with her.

Such a despondency of vaguely articulated thoughts congealing into a mounting sense of utter despair that when the sun dipped again below the cloud it seemed like it might never reappear again.

Startled then from his delirium by a sharp stab at his side and that spinning him towards the girl. She was holding a fork clenched in one hand — apparently what she'd stabbed him with — and looking as fierce and wild as one of those Amazonian women he'd once seen in a movie facing off against a man who'd dared trespass upon her domain.

I said, she was saying, though he hadn't heard her speak a word, what is it you got against jokes anyway?

The tone of her voice was as determined as her glare yet her lips were contorted into a pained crimp, and that spoke to Jason of something else entirely. In that moment it seemed her whole world was hanging in the balance, with Jason's answer the only thing left that might tip the scales in her favour.

How to answer such a desperate plea?

He couldn't and turned back to the sink without saying a word. Fishing a ladle from its murky water, he used the scouring pad on the back of the sponge to mount an attack on the pancake batter hardened into cement on its handle.

I know a joke, the girl said as he set the ladle in the dish rack and then reached into the sink to pull the plug, figuring the water was already dirty enough and that he ought to start the next stack of plates afresh.

It seemed unlikely that anything he said would deter her. So again he said nothing and, in the moment of silence that followed, he was hoping maybe she'd got the point.

She hadn't.

Lashing out, she stabbed him in the ribs with the fork again. The sharp pain was double this time and also accompanied by a *Pop!* like a needle puncturing bubble wrap, though he knew it was the fork's tines going through both his shirt and his skin.

What the fuck? he yelled jumping back. Are you fucking crazy?!

It works better if you're looking at me, the girl replied all casual, like she hadn't just stabbed him hard enough to draw blood and his hand wasn't even then quivering at his side, about to slap the stupid right out of her.

So you want to hear it or not?

Jason gritting his teeth as he lifted his shirt, dabbing at his skin and feeling its viscous ooze, telling himself that if he had any sense he'd get the hell out of there while the gettin' was good. Stymied in this by the fork clenched in her hand hard enough to blanch her knuckles white in stark contrast to the gently imploring entreaty in her eyes, as if her whole world would fall apart if he so much as blinked at her the wrong way.

Well go on then, he offered, less as a peace offering than as an expression of utter defeat. What are you waiting for?

That got him a smile tinged with genuine relief and she opened her mouth, letting it hang there for a moment as if she'd forgotten how to begin.

So . . . she said, then cleared her throat. So . . . A lady walks into a bar —

Smacking the flat of her palm then against her forehead and exclaiming Ow! as she whipped her head back, as if the bar she was talking about was of the steel variety.

Not three days ago he would have responded to her feeble attempt at humour with, That's a good'un, all right, as he often had at work, even when it wasn't. But that seemed a lifetime away, or rather, it seemed a different life altogether. Instead, he responded by gritting his teeth a little harder to suppress the sliver of a smile even then forming on his lips, further concealing it by stepping back to the empty sink and pushing in the plug, readying it for the next stack of dishes.

It's funny, huh? she asked.

Then when he didn't respond:

It was my little brother who told it to me.

It came out sounding almost like an involuntary spasm, as if she hadn't wanted to speak of her brother but was being compelled by forces beyond her control — her voice a trifle too loud and sharp and startling Jason as would have a beaver slapping its tail on the water as he walked along the marsh behind their apartment.

One of his classmates told it to him when we were at The Pass, she continued, her tone at first quivering like ripples of water left in the beaver's wake. You know, the Passmore Transitional Housing Centre. You heard of it, right?

Jason nodded, all solemn. His mother had often railed against the Transitional Housing Centres, calling them "rape factories" and arguing that they were simply an extension of the prison system since, statistically speaking, Indigenous People were seven times more likely to end up there than a person who was white. That Meghan was about the whitest person he'd ever met didn't in any way diminish the resurgence of the shame he'd felt earlier thinking about how he'd treated Eric and Duane.

It's no wonder she's gone crazy, after what she must have gone through at The Pass . . .

A thought that had him thinking back to the names she'd written on the stone. Three to his one. The last was Ben, which must have been the brother she was talking about.

That's right, Ben, she was then saying.

For a moment it seemed like she'd been reading his mind until he realized he must have muttered the name aloud.

You must miss him, Jason offered, covering for his own involuntary spasm. It came out sounding forced and awkward, as his voice often did when he was talking to some girl at a party, or at school, after he'd sworn off the opposite sex altogether.

Of course, I miss him, she answered gruffly, like she'd lost all patience with anyone stating the obvious. He was my little brother, after all.

Her voice had softened a touch and when Jason glanced her way again she was staring out the window over the sink. Her eyes had taken on a glassy sheen. It recalled to Jason the image of innumerable old ladies he'd heard recounting stories of better days during the family picnics his mom dragged him to every year at the long-term care centre, and that telling him Meghan was talking more for her own benefit than his.

And what I miss most about him is hearing his laugh. It was like a cool summer's breeze, if you know what I mean?

He did, for his mother's often struck him as roughly the same.

I tellya, nothing could get that boy down. It was like he had his own little sun inside of him and when . . . and when he died it was like the light was snuffed right out of the whole wide world.

It was exactly how Jason felt about his mother and hearing her say it out loud about her brother had a shiver running down his spine. Listening then in dread silence — one hand clutching a plate and his other the sponge, unable to move or, it seemed, even breathe — as Meghan continued.

It happened during a food riot at The Pass, the second one since we'd been transferred there four months before . . .

Recounting then a story of such unrelenting misery and woe that, with every new detail, his own grief seemed to grow paler in comparison.

Telling him how, after her parents and Ben had burned to death in their dorm, she'd been freed from The Pass with the promise that a better life awaited her at a place called Garden Valley Farms and how that had turned out to be one of the nether regions of hell. Hearing her tell of being stripped naked and languishing in a cold cellar for weeks on end. Jason flinching at the mere mention of such a thing, wishing he was anywhere but here listening to her even as it seemed that the world had shrunk to the size of the kitchen and there was nowhere left for him to flee. The girl prattling on, unabashed, speaking in her whimsical way, like some schoolgirl talking about a favourite TV show and not the living nightmare that had become her life.

This degenerate hillbilly fuck named Duck would come into the cellar at night, she was saying now. He'd be naked too and wearing a hat with a flashlight on it, you know like the miners do. He'd stand over one or another of us, jerking himself off . . .

On and on she talked unbidden, every new depravity feeling like a handful of dirt shoved into Jason's mouth, choking the breath out of him. Hearing how she and an even younger girl — Jamie — were bought by a man with a snake tattoo on his chin as a present for another man to celebrate his release from jail, and how he'd confined them to a couch in the living room of some secluded farmhouse. Finally, when she spoke of how she hadn't been there for more than a minute before some disgusting fat fuck named Darcy had pried her legs apart and plunged his fingers into her sex just so he could have a taste, it was too much for Jason to bear. He'd have happily told a thousand jokes if only she'd stop talking. Except his mouth was parched beyond all capacity for speech and his head was reeling like he had a miniature tornado inside his skull which was liable to suck anything he might be able to say into its vortex.

Still he couldn't, he just couldn't, he couldn't listen to another word.

As he so often did during class, or on the bus, when he felt the all-too-familiar dread creeping up on him, he sought refuge in the vast catalogue of jokes he'd collected over the years. They were all jumbled in his mind now as if they'd been rent apart by the cyclone swirling inside his head — a whirling debris of set-ups and punchlines and every one of the latter soured with the memory of his mom's reaction when he'd first told them to her — her lips curled into a bemused frown as often as upraised into a smile, a startled chuckle if she hadn't gotten it right away, the unhinged exuberance of her laughter the rarest gift of all, though it hardly seemed that way now. It was channelling through his brain in distorted reverberations, like the spectral manifestation of a long-dead joy he'd never feel again, and he knew right then he'd go mad if he had to hear its echoing refrain for another solitary moment.

Spared in this by a voice rising out of the bedlam — his mother's, it sounded like, calling out to him from beyond the grave.

Thanks darling, she was saying, I sure needed that!

It's what she'd often said to him after he'd given her a neck rub on the mornings she'd come downstairs complaining that it hurt almost as bad as her back. It only took him a moment to realize that it wasn't his mom's voice after all, it was Meghan's.

Can you imagine someone saying that to a sixteen-year-old girl he'd just raped in the ass? she was asking now.

Jason startled as much by that as he had been by the fork in the ribs and swivelling his head towards her. She was looking at him with such cavalier disbelief that at first he thought he must have misheard her, or that she was talking about someone other than herself.

She wasn't.

Right then, I would have liked nothing better than to have crawled into a hole and died, be done with this whole damned miserable excuse for a life.

Jason feeling his head nodding all by itself. It was how he'd felt when they'd set his mom in her grave, him wishing the whole time he could have laid down beside her and have Ron and Dale bury him too. The brazen defiance was then flaring in her eyes again — wild and fierce. Yet, where before it had made her look even crazier than she already did, in that moment she'd never looked more sane.

But like my momma always told me, she said, where there's life, there's hope. Well I'm still alive and they's all dead. Whatever they did to me, it'll never change that.

Her eyes then narrowing to slits of seething hate and her tone become a perfect expression of a woman all-too-often scorned.

So I say fuck 'em. I say . . . Fuck 'em all!

The sun was fading behind the trees in the south as Ron slumped into his chair at the patio table with a plate of Dale's homemade shepherd's pie, the first time he'd sat down practically all day except for when he was driving the tractor.

Him and the chief and ten of the youths had spent the morning, and a good part of the afternoon, fixing the fence which had been ripped up by one of the tornadoes that had so devastated the region last fall.

It was a day Ron remembered all too well.

While he and Dale hid out in the basement, one of the three funnel clouds which had touched down within North Bay's city limits had torn off the entire second floor of the house they were renting on John Street. All the while the madly howling winds sounded almost alive and it felt like at any moment some preternatural beast would snatch them into the swirling abyss of its rampaging maw.

The chief had a similar story to tell, of him and Hélène cowering in the vault in *their* basement. It was soundproof so they were at least spared the tornado's bestial roar, which had so tormented Ron and Dale. The Lowrys were also lucky in that the only real damage the one which had struck their property had done was shear the roof off their barn and uproot the ash tree in the field where their cows used to seek shelter from the heat, before carving a hundred-metre-wide and three-hundred-metre-long path of destruction through the woods behind their pasture — a mere pittance compared to the havoc its kin had wrought in the city, where the damages had been in the millions and the official death toll one hundred and twenty-four, the youngest victim only three weeks old.

The chief had hired someone to fix the barn, more so it seemed for appearance's sake since it hadn't been used for almost a decade, but had left the rest as it was. The span of fence wire which had been torn free was tangled up in the tops of the trees at the end of the still-gaping wound carved through the forest. While the chief and Ron were cutting it down and disentangling it, the youths had taken turns digging holes with the chief's hand auger while the others foraged through the carnage of splintered tree trunks for any logs they might be able to use as posts.

Meanwhile, Mason had assigned another team to clean out the chicken coop and barn, and a third to start work on the vegetable garden, tilling the soil and removing any rocks which had wormed their way to the surface over the winter. Mason planned to start planting the very next day. He'd placed an order for twelve family-sized pizzas from the deli counter at the Foodland when he was buying supplies for the pancakes and Dale had even offered to pick them up himself. Dale must have been laying a few plans of his own, for he'd come back with a couple bags of mostly vegetables. After lunch he'd conscripted his group of hunters, with the addition of Kendra, who hadn't left Masood's side all day, to help him cut up the deer and grind enough of the meat so he could make a whack of his mother's "famous" shepherd's pie for dinner.

Everyone else, it appeared, had already eaten their share. Someone — likely Dale or one of his crew — had fetched the sprinkler head from the windowsill in the laundry room and hooked it up to the hose in the backyard. It was of the impact variety, the kind they used on golf courses. A good many of the youths were frolicking in its ice cold spray as a balm against the heat, laughing and shrieking like kids at a water park when the high-pressure stream tracked their way. Eric and Darren had also found the two Super Soaker water guns that were hanging in the shed. They were using them to wage war against each other and anyone else who came within their sights, their expressions as solemn as soldiers and their countenance lent extra gravitas by the low, throbbing beat of the gangster rap pouring out of a portable speaker.

Those who'd had their fill of the sprinkler were gathered around the firepit, though no one had got around to lighting it yet. The girl, who the chief had since told Ron was named Meghan, was the only one standing amongst them. Jason and Annie and Kendra and Masood and Duane and Brittany — the girl with the flowers in her hair — were all staring up at her intently as she smacked her forehead hard with her hand. She exclaimed Ow! at the same time, snapping her head back and her legs wobbling beneath her as if she'd just run into a low hanging beam.

Okay, she said slumping down into the empty space beside Jason and giving him a nudge, your turn.

Ron hadn't heard his stepson speak a word since his outburst, not even after he and Meghan had come out to help with the fence when they'd finished the dishes. From the pained look on his face it didn't appear he was quite ready to break his silence just yet.

Come on, Meghan coaxed, I told you my joke, now you tell us one of yours.

Ron's hand stalled in mortal dread with his first forkful of shepherd's pie halfway to his mouth, remembering how Jason had reacted the last time someone had asked him to tell a joke.

Maybe this'll help, Duane said, when Jason didn't respond.

He was holding up an unlit joint that seemed to Ron more in the nature of an olive branch. Jason seemed willing at least to accept that. He craned forward, taking it up and wetting it, before putting it in his mouth and touching a flame to its end with his Zippo.

A couple of puffs seemed to do the trick. After he'd passed it back to Duane he began to speak in a murmur, too low for Ron to hear. It looked like he was indeed telling a joke, and from the way he kept glancing in a reticent, almost penitent, manner at Duane and Eric it was clear he was doing so mainly for their benefit. When he was done, the boys all responded with deep chortles while the girls all frowned and Meghan went so far as to slap at Jason's arm with a gently admonishing hand, chastising him further by declaiming, Ew, that's gross!

Could have been he'd told the same joke as the last one he'd texted Ron. That one was pretty gross, for sure. Reading that, Ron had been certain it'd be the last joke Jason would tell for the foreseeable future — and maybe ever. But here it was only three nights later and he'd already reclaimed at least that fragment of his former self.

Maybe she's good for him after all, he thought taking that first bite of the shepherd's pie.

It seemed, anyway, to bode well for Jason's future prospects, and maybe for the rest of the kids too. Ron took no small amount of comfort in that and yet it still wasn't enough to dislodge the lingering unease which had been dogging him these past three days.

He couldn't shake the feeling that something terrible was brewing on the horizon and that Dale's *right here and right now* couldn't possibly amount to anything more than a momentary calm before another shit storm hit. It was a pervading sense of doom exacerbated by the nightmare he'd had that morning and also by something the chief had reminded him of while they were working.

Recalling that, he googled "Euphie Bombs" on his phone in between his next two forkfuls of the shepherd's pie. Watching the feeds as he ate, and reading through the various commentaries, confirmed everything the chief had said and a few things besides. The foremost among those was that the number of "Euphie Bombs" had been steadily decreasing over the past twelve hours. This proffered some hope that the worst might be over, though there was some concern amongst the authorities regarding a rather startling new development.

One hundred and fifty-two "incidents" had been reported province-wide. The majority of these appeared to have sprung from Euphoral but the last sixteen were now confirmed to have involved people who, in one commentator's words, had "with willful and malicious intent self-detonated." These appeared to have been targeted "attacks," as each had begun in the bathrooms or parking garages of various government buildings in either Ottawa or Toronto and all had occurred within a half-hour span. Every one of these so-called "Suicide Euphies" were males between the ages of sixteen and twenty and each had taken the additional measure of Super Gluing all manner of sharply bladed implements to both hands, apparently to render maximum carnage. They were also found to have had the same brand of a tree behind their left ears and this had led an inspector with the RCMP to speculate that they were operating on behalf of The Sons Of Adam. He further went on to say that his special task force was looking into any ties The Sons might have with an organic food company, since twelve of the sixteen had been employees of Garden Valley Farms.

Learning that was an Aha! moment for Ron and it also had him searching Meghan out in the yard, for he'd noticed while she was helping out with the fence that she had the very same brand behind her ear. She'd since managed to procure one of the Super Soakers and so had Annie. They were chasing Darren around the yard, blasting him with the spray and encouraged in their efforts by a female rapper yelling out from the speaker, You give 'em hell, girl. You give 'em hell. You give 'em, you give 'em . . . You give 'em hell, girl!

Darren was ducking and dodging like he was trying to avoid a swarm of hornets while Killer circled them all on a wide perimeter, barking his own encouragement. Out of breath, Darren turned towards them, holding his hands up and pleading, I surrender, I-I surrender!

For a moment, it looked like the two young women might actually accept it. But then they unleashed their twin streams directly at his face anyway. Darren snapped backwards, going down like a man shot, and the girls gave each other a high five as they swaggered back towards the firepit swinging their hips in a most exaggerated manner to the hip hop's propulsive beat.

It was a far sight removed from how she'd acted the first time Ron had seen her and gave him absolutely no indication that she was going to go full Euphie anytime soon.

Probably, Ron mused, *The Sons were grooming her for something other than becoming a "Suicide Euphie." And besides, she's a girl, when all of those have been boys.*

And yet that was a no less unsettling thought and one that had him immediately scanning over the field of tents. There were more than fifteen in all now. The bulk of them were clustered around the firepit, same as would a group of pioneer settlers seeking safety in numbers against any manner of wild beasts. Only four of their owners had eschewed the comfort of close proximity by setting up their tents on the outskirts in rough approximation of the points of a compass. Two were neon red and the others a brightly coloured orange and it had seemed kind of strange to Ron that they'd have chosen spots so far away from each other since he'd seen all of their owners arrive together that afternoon.

After finishing the fence and checking in on the other two crews, the chief had got it in mind to have a go at the upended ash tree, telling Ron it was never too early to get started on the winter wood. Ron had helped him by lugging the eighteen-inch lengths he'd cut from the uprooted tree to the trailer the chief had attached to his tractor. He'd dropped off his first load in the chief's woodshed and then skirted into his own yard to refill his two-litre pop bottle with water and to grab himself a quick chute and a smoke. That's when he'd seen the four young men coming up the driveway. They were all wearing black T-shirts and black jeans and their heads were all shaved to within a millimetre of their scalps.

They were lugging green army-style knapsacks slung over their backs with rolled-up tents hanging below on straps. The youngest of them appeared to be around sixteen and the oldest twenty, with the others ranging somewhere in between. All were pale of face and walked with the shambling plod of a group of refugees traversing a desert. When they'd caught sight of Ron looking back at them, they'd come to a halt and stood gaping at him as if he were an oasis appearing between two sand dunes and they weren't quite sure whether it was real or not.

You all coming from North Bay? Ron called out, walking towards them.

The four exchanged nervous glances and the eldest took a step forward.

This the Lowry farm? he asked in place of an answer.

The one and only.

A friend told us we could stay here for a while.

Yeah, and who's that?

Jacob Shulman.

Ron scratching his head, trying to think if he knew anyone by that name and coming up blank.

I don't know any Jacob Shulman. But you're welcome to stay as long as you like. You just missed out on pizza for lunch but there'll be shepherd's pie for dinner. And when that only resulted in four pairs of blank eyes staring back, he added: In the meantime, you can p-pitch your tents in the field yonder, with all the rest.

He'd then gone inside to fill up his water bottle and take a leak. When he'd come out they were setting up their tents around the perimeter of the others. At the time he hadn't thought much about it. Learning what he had, it all of a sudden seemed altogether far too conspicuous. Of course, could have been Dale was right and it was simply what he'd read in the news giving him the fear all over again.

Telling himself now, *You're probably just being paranoid*, he took up another forkful of shepherd's pie.

He hadn't seen the four new arrivals all afternoon and turned his attention to the group of six youngest teens, who'd retreated back to the field and had lit a raging bonfire on the ashes of their last. Over the hip hop blaring from the yard, Ron could just hear the faint pound of heavy metal from their portable speaker and one of the youths seemed to be trying to get some kind of a mosh pit going. From his long hair and almost skeletal frame Ron assumed it was Kendra's little brother, Davey. He was stomping around the firepit, thrashing his head about and imploring his friends to join in. None of them seemed much in the mood, probably because they were too tired and sore from the day's labour, and rebuffed his enticements with weary shakes of their heads or by lying down on the ground, plumb tuckered out.

He couldn't see any of the new arrivals there and let his gaze wander back to the closest tent, which sat in the middle of the burnt-out patch of field. It was one of the red ones and was lit from within by what must have been a lantern, or a flashlight, hanging from its ceiling. Its rosy glow fostered an immediate comparison to the sky above, the cloud-streaked firmament shading towards a deepening crimson as the sun faded beyond the ever-darkening clouds massing just above the treeline.

He'd been staring at the tent for some time when he heard the door open at his back. He turned to see Dale coming out of the house, cracking the tab on a tall can of Kokanee.

I thought we were out of beer, Ron said, his disquiet momentarily assuaged by his thirst.

I picked up a can when I was fetching the pizzas.

Well, what about me?

Oh, you wanted a beer, did ya? If I'd known, I'd have grabbed you one too.

Ron gaping at him as Dale sat down. Dale's expression went all wonky as if someone had put something on his chair and he exclaimed, What the hell! As he stood back up, Ron shook his head, already knowing what game he was playing at, and Dale carried it to its inevitable conclusion by reaching into his back pocket.

Oh, shoot, here's the problem, he said, pulling out a can of Old Style Pilsner and setting it down in front of Ron. Ron immediately cracked the tab and took a hearty sip.

You just get the two? he asked, already thinking of how good a second would taste, especially after a day like the one he'd just had.

Now when in the hell have you ever known me to get just two beers?

Ron took another slurp of his, this time draining half the can.

You put a couple more in the freezer? he asked, picking up the fork from his plate.

I did.

You better 'ave.

Taking another bite of the shepherd's pie then and Dale asking, How is it?

It's good. Really good. It's got a little spice to her too.

That's the Frank's RedHot. My mom's secret ingredient. Gives it a little tang.

Well it sure is good.

I saved a plate for the chief. Where's he at?

Still cutting up that tree, Ron answered through a mouthful. He could hear the faint whine of the chainsaw above the duelling strains of hip hop and heavy metal.

Ron had just brought his third load of logs to the woodshed when he'd heard Dale ringing the bell for dinner. When he got back to the tree, he'd told the chief about the grub being done and Mason had told him to go ahead, he wanted to get as much of the tree cut up as he could while he still had the light. Ron had stuck around for another fifteen minutes, worried about leaving the chief chainsawing all alone. It was only when the chainsaw's battery had run out that he'd finally made it back to the patio.

The chief had said he'd be along shortly but he must have found a spare battery and had gone right back to it.

I swear he's gone crazy, Ron said.

That wouldn't be too far a trip for the chief, Dale answered, taking a puff off his vape.

Says he's got a whole herd of cows coming tomorrow.

Cows? What the hell's he need with cows?

Says it never hurts to plan ahead.

Plan ahead? Plan ahead for what?

He didn't say.

Ron took a couple more bites, washing each down with a sip from his beer, before he spoke again.

I figure maybe he's just trying to keep his mind off The Sons, he said.

The Sons? Funny you should bring them up. I was just thinking about 'em only a moment ago.

Thinking what? Ron asked, wondering if Dale had been listening to the news while he was cutting up the deer and had maybe got around to thinking along similar lines as he had.

I was thinking, Dale said, that if the chief was already dead, they'd have no reason to bother with us. I was thinking we could make it look like an accident. You know, cut his leg off with that chainsaw of his and nobody'd be the wiser. Then we could cut his head off too maybe, hang it on the mailbox so if The Sons do show up —

You're having me on, Ron scolded, cutting him off, even though Dale had never sounded more serious.

What? Seems like a reasonable plan to me.

You ain't killing the chief.

Who said anything about me? I already cut up the deer. If anyone cuts up the chief, it ought to be you.

Well I ain't killing the chief either.

Suit yourself. But when The Sons show up and kill us all, that'll be on you.

But Ron couldn't take the matter so lightly, not after what he'd just read.

He was down to the grease on his plate. As he wiped the last of that up with his finger, he glanced to where Dale would usually have propped his rifle beside the door when he was sitting outside. It wasn't there.

Where're your rifles at? he asked.

Dale looked around, as if maybe he'd forgotten, then replied: Must have left 'em downstairs in the laundry room.

Well they ain't going to do us any good down there.

Why, you planning on shooting some cows?

Ron had stood and was already moving towards the door.

Do me a favour, he said, turning back, keep on eye on those four new tents until I get back.

What new tents?

The two reds and the two orange ones over there on the outskirts.

What am I supposed to be keeping an eye out for?

Euphies.

Euphies? His crooked head and scathing eyes as he peered over at him told Ron all he needed to know about his thoughts on them. Now why the fuck would I be looking out for Euphies?

Ron was opening the door and turned back about to answer when he felt Whisper brushing against his legs — the dog slipping past and darting into the yard.

Oh shit. Whisper!

Habit had him setting after her but Dale had spotted her racing past and was already lunging out of his chair, yelling, Whisper! Goddammit, Whisper, get back here!

She was charging full bore towards Killer, who was lifting his hind leg at the memory stone, peeing in a steady stream against the rock. Jason had seen him too. He'd just set up a quarter log on the full one they used for a chopping block and was hurrying towards him with the splitting axe in his hand, shouting, Get the hell away from there! Goddammit, cut it out!

Killer responded by dodging away from the stone as if Jason had taken a swipe at him with the axe, though he'd never got within five feet. And that's when the dog saw Whisper bearing down on him, her ears flattened and her hair bristling. Killer seemed to have learned something from their last encounter. He plopped right down on the grass in submissive recline with his head lying on the ground between his outstretched paws, whimpering what sounded like a plea for mercy. Whisper didn't seem to be in the mood for that and let out a vicious snarl. It looked like she was about to tackle the other again, but a couple of feet from the prone dog, she skidded to a halt and stood there glowering over Killer, never looking more like a wolf than she did right then.

Oh knock it off, you big old bully, Dale chastised as he approached.

At the sound of his voice Whisper dodged away, scampering five paces hence and turning back, pouncing on the ground, barking at Dale, begging for a game of catch-me-if-you-can.

She just wants to join the party, don't ya girl?

It was Meghan who'd spoken. She was walking past pumping at the Super Soaker in her hand as she approached the memory stone, maybe intending to clean off her dog's mark.

Can't you let her off the lead for a little while, she added when Dale didn't respond beyond shaking his head and scowling at Whisper. She'll behave, I know she will.

Dale opened his mouth, about to explain that it wasn't her behaviour he was worried about, but her taking off, when he caught a sudden flicker of movement on his periphery. Turning to the field, he tracked the flicker to one of the tents Ron had asked him to keep an eye on. It was the red one on the western-most side. It was lit from within, as were the other three, and it was twitching and shaking, almost like a miniature tornado was forming inside.

A sudden dread washed over him, recalling what Ron had said only moments ago about keeping an eye out for Euphies. He'd been certain Ron was just being paranoid again. But watching the tent shimmy and shake it now began to seem to him it didn't look so much like it had a tornado inside as it did a malevolent force thrashing to get out even as he was thinking,

No, it couldn't be a Euphie. It just, it just couldn't possibly be . . .

E w, that's gross!
       Meghan slapped him with a lightly admonishing hand
as she said it and there was nothing in her voice to suggest she'd
been overly offended by the joke. But the moment after she'd
spoken Jason felt the piercing, and decidedly spiteful, grate of a
fingernail raking across the skin under his shirt, at level with his
navel, and he knew he'd struck a nerve.

He hadn't meant to.

He'd simply told *that* joke because he knew Eric and Duane
hadn't heard it yet and was using it as a bit of a peace offering to
make up for laying into them so savagely.

Flinching against her rebuke and that recalling to him the
horror story she'd told him earlier, the shame he'd felt yelling at
Eric and Duane returned double. More so than even the shock
of the nail digging into his flesh, it had him startling to his feet.

Duane and Eric were looking over at him with a dire and
intractable dismay, as if they thought telling the joke had been

too much for him to bear and he was set to explode at any moment.

I-I was thinking of getting a fire going, Jason said to cover. He was already turning towards the chopping block to start on some kindling.

Killer had followed him over and had then wandered past on the way to pissing on his mom's gravestone. Seeing that had enraged him beyond all reason and he'd come within less than a breath of lashing out at the dog with the axe in his hand. Really, though, he was only angry at himself, for being so stupid as to tell that joke when he could have told a hundred others instead.

Seeing Whisper tearing after her dog, his belly had knotted with a terrible fright as if Whisper was just acting out the malice he himself felt when really all she was doing was what came natural to her. His sense of relief then when she hadn't attacked Killer had folded into a deepening sense of guilt as the girl walked past pumping at the Super Soaker. She ignored him altogether and, even though that was exactly what he'd been wishing for these past two days, it somehow felt worse than her stabbing him with a fork or her nail.

While she used the squirt gun to spray down the rock where her dog had left his mark, he returned his attention to the log he'd set on the chopping block, happy to have something to do to take his mind off things, if only for a moment.

He was just raising the axe to take his first swipe when Dale, not ten feet away, gasped, Oh Jesus!

He was breaking into the field at an all-out run and Whisper was chasing along behind him, nipping at his heels as she often did in play, though that seemed to be the last thing on Dale's mind. He was drawing the hunting knife from his belt as he ran and Jason tracked past him, trying to figure out what had irked him so. As far as he could divine, Dale was moving in a straight line for a lone tent on the westernmost side of the encampment. It was thrashing with a violent palsy and whoever was inside was slashing at its canvas with what appeared to be two blades blurring in their rampage with the speed of a blender set to mince.

Davey had seen it too.

He'd broken off from the gang gathered at the bonfire. He appeared to be peeing into the tall grass not ten feet on this side of the red tent and was gaping over at it as the blades reduced its canvas to tatters. The sight didn't seem to have registered in his mind as anything beyond a mild curiosity and he continued relieving himself unabated even as Dale screamed out, Davey, get the hell away from there!

The person inside at last thrashed his way through the gashes in the front of the tent and stumbled out of the hole and into the field. He was naked aside from what appeared to be a loincloth and his skin was painted a stark white, his mouth outlined in black with a skeleton's grin so at first glance he looked more ghoul than man. He was clutching what appeared to be paring knives in both hands and, as he surged through the hole in the tent, Jason's own sudden fright was provided perfect expression by Kendra's voice raised in alarm.

Oh Jesus! she gasped. Davey run!

The bonfire, though, seemed to be a more alluring target than someone taking a piss in the shadows. Letting loose a hiss like a rabid cat, the ghoul set off towards it in a crazed scurry, his body hunched over, almost ape-like, and his bladed hands swinging in drastic arcs in front of him.

The other five youths had seen it too and were already making a mad dash for the yard. The ghoul must have spotted them and he suddenly took a hard left, angling away from the bonfire on an intercept course. Every one of the five was wailing a terrible chorus of despair over the unrelenting pound of death metal and the ghoul's almost bestial roar as he bore down on them.

Dale was charging after him screaming out, Leave them alone you son of a bitch!, and that about as much a deterrent as the timothy grass slapping harmlessly against the Euphie's legs.

Those gathered in the yard, and Jason too, emitted a collective gasp, watching the slowest of the five teens stumble into a sprawl. His hair was almost as long as Davey's and he had a similarly lank frame, honed over years at the skatepark, the same as the rest of his friends'. He'd also been on the fence crew and so Jason had learned his name was Matty. The boy seemed to be reeling in slow motion, his hands pinwheeling in front of him and his legs scrambling feverishly trying to keep him upright, but it was no use. He landed face first, disappearing into a patch of tall grass. Dale gasped a futile exhortation — Oh god no, oh please god no! — that might as well have sprung from Jason's own heart watching the boy's head pop back into view as the ghoul flailed towards him with the menace of some demon moose on the rut.

He wasn't more than five paces behind him now, to Dale's fifteen. The boy had made it back on his feet and was surging forward, though he seemed to be moving as if in a dream — his legs pounding at the turf, moving altogether too slow to avoid the inevitable, and his mouth unleashing a protracted and panicked wail. A feeling of such unrelenting terror overcame Jason in that moment that it froze him in his fright, unable to turn his head or avert his eyes, or even breathe.

The ghoul never looking more like an undead fiend as he did when he zeroed in on Matty. His chin and lips were dripping blood, his eyes were black beads of utter desolation and the blades in his hands were flaring above his head, about to strike. In that instant Matty seemed to have accepted his fate, though he was far from resigned to it. His own eyes were opened wide in a last desperate clutch at life, as if they were trying to absorb the whole of the world in a fraction of a second. Or could have been they were searching out one final connection with another living thing to say his short span on earth had amounted to something beyond the terror that had become his all, his everything, and finding exactly this in the thirty pairs of eyes peering back into his, every one of those filled with the same desperate plea to a merciful god as was Jason's.

A feeling of stark despair crashed up against the futility of hope welling in Jason's chest and in that moment — no longer than the flutter of a hummingbird's wing — he knew beyond knowing that the fate of the world itself would be determined by what happened next. It felt like the very future itself hung in the balance — *right here and right now* — such that the sun might have gone down for the last time, never to reappear again, if he and all the others were condemned to watch this boy being slashed into ribbons before their very eyes.

A feeling then of such connection as he'd never felt with another person, much less with thirty, and that making this moment feel even more terrible than his worst moment ever — watching his mother thrashing about on the kitchen floor wrapped up in cellophane and him, all alone, powerless but to watch as the only person he'd ever loved, and maybe ever would, became a monstrous creation slobbering a bloody drool and glowering at him through eyes consumed by such malice that he knew she'd have as soon ripped out his throat with her teeth as take another breath.

The ghoul was within arm's reach of Matty and the blades in his hands were upraised with the dire bent of an eagle's talons about to snatch up its prey. The oxygen seemed to have been sucked from the very air as the ghoul lashed out, the intractably perilous future being made in this moment then spiralling into some nether region with such force that it seemed never to have existed except as a fleeting thought, of no more consequence than a pea skipping off a fork and rolling across the floor.

A set of teeth lunged out of the tall grass like the field itself had spawned them in answer to his plea and a feeling of weightlessness overcame Jason. Watching Whisper's teeth latching onto the ghoul's downward slashing wrist, it did indeed feel like there must have been a merciful god watching over them all and he'd sent the dog in answer to Jason's and all the others' prayers. The bite deflected the Euphie's blow and the blade merely glanced off of Matty's shoulder, knocking him off balance but not off his feet. Those seemed to have gained thrust from the pain and carried Matty out of reach of the ghoul's other madly flailing hand. The blade in its grip veered from its intended target and struck instead the dog in the neck, stabbing it with the pulsing thrusts of a sewing machine and Whisper never letting go of his wrist even when it was clear to all that she was already dead.

Too many things then happening at once to form any coherence beyond the sudden and overwhelming relief Jason felt seeing Matty stumbling into the yard. A trickle of red sprouted from beneath his short sleeve's black, draining along his arm, and tears streamed down his cheeks as he staggered out of the tall grass and onto the short, his body heaving against a sob breaking with such force that it buckled his legs so again he looked like he was about to fall. Kendra rushed towards him and caught him before he could, wrapping him in a tight embrace and letting him cry into her chest even as her eyes were searching out her brother, still lost to her, somewhere on the far side of the field.

Not twenty yards away, the ghoul was bent over the dog, his uninjured hand hacking in a frenzy of stabs at Whisper lying on the ground, the other hand hanging limp at the end of his wrist. It was held on by mere threads and yet was still clutching the knife as if enmity alone was holding it fast. Dale, not five paces away, charged at him, hell-bent for revenge and cursing, Motherfucker!, as he raised his own knife above his head.

Thwarted in his revenge by a resounding *Crack!*

It might as well have heralded a lightning bolt striking the ghoul between the eyes for the way his neck snapped back, toppling his body into the field's dark after it. Jason sneaking the briefest of glances towards Annie, standing at the fore of the group, the Enfield's stock at her shoulder and a spiral of smoke draining from its barrel, the enmity written in her own eyes making it clear that she'd had her own run-in with a Euphie in North Bay. Could have been it had killed her whole family.

A voice then crying out, Guys! Guys!

Jason swivelled to see Davey charging towards him, half the field still between him and the yard.

What he was yelling about suddenly became clear to all: both the southern and easternmost tents were twitching in the same frenzy as had the westernmost one before. Only Dale hadn't seemed to notice. He was kneeling at where Whisper had fallen, his hand set on her head, and such was the quiet that had descended upon the yard that his voice rang out loud and clear.

You did good, Whisper, he was offering as alms for the dead. You did so good. Yes, you did.

D ale, get back here! There's still three tents left!
     Ron was holding the .303 as he called out and looking plenty nervous about it too, for he'd never been one much for hunting himself. At the sound of his voice, Dale jerked his head around, glancing over at the tent on his left. The sight of it twitching was enough to get him to his feet. He took a last look

down at Whisper, reluctant to leave her, before turning on his heels, his stride quickly hastening towards a run.

I th-thought I t-told you to wah-watch out for Euphies, Ron stuttered as Dale reached the yard and Ron tossed him the .303.

While Dale cocked a bullet into the chamber, he didn't seem to have anything to say about that. His roving gaze passed over the shaking tent in the south and settled on Annie.

I'll take the high, he said to her, you take the low.

Annie nodded grim-faced and swivelled on a quick pivot towards her assigned target. At that very moment an orange tent, not twenty paces hence, gave out a sudden shudder and Killer responded to it with a growl.

Ever since Whisper had attacked the Euphie, Killer had been standing at full alert. His tail had become a flag post at his rear and his fur was bristling all along his spine as Meghan knelt beside him with her arms interlocked around his neck, clutching him tight, not willing to let her dog so willingly embrace the fate which had befallen the other.

Killer, No! she was commanding as Ron's voice raised itself in alarm at the latest threat.

Dale — he said before he was cut off by the same.

I see it.

Boy, we sure could use another rifle, Darren offered, stepping up beside Dale.

Don't you worry, Dale answered, sighting on the southern-most tent through his scope, two'll be plenty enough.

While they spoke, Jason's eyes had never departed from the closest shaking tent. Its spastic contortions immediately called to mind again the image of his mother flopping about on the kitchen floor, in stage two of her withdrawal. Then he'd been too terrified to do anything but stand frozen over her. The lights had suddenly winked off, pitching the apartment into a darkness so complete that he might as well have been blinded by the sight, his vision returning only when he'd flung open the front door to find Eric and Duane standing there, the both of their faces framed, terror-struck, in the light from the torches on their phones. It was a fear that had never really left him. Gaping at the shaking tent, frozen again in his fright, he knew it was a fear that would follow him to his dying day unless he did something drastic.

There ain't no way around fear.

What his mother had told him after she'd brought home a flyer she'd plucked off the notice board at the grocery store advertising *Amateur Comedy Night!* at Shooters, the country-and-western bar off Algonquin Street. He'd balked at her suggestion that he try out his act, which really wasn't anything more than a bunch of jokes he'd stolen from his favourite comedians along with a few asides, and his mother had countered, I know you're afraid of getting up in front of a bunch of strangers. I would be too. But I also know this, there ain't no way around fear. You want to conquer it, you gotta confront it head on.

He'd taken her advice and that had turned into the best night of his life. Seeking comfort now in the memory of standing in the spotlight, hearing the scattered applause dying down, taking a deep breath and launching into his routine. He took a breath now, even deeper, and yet here he stood, still too afraid to move, or barely even breathe.

Killer was barking and growling with a menace he'd never heard before. When Jason looked over at where Meghan was trying to hold the dog back, Killer was wriggling against her embrace and looking like he'd tear free at any moment. If he did, he'd likely meet the same fate as Whisper had and where would Meghan be then?

She was even then looking back at him, her eyes again pleading as they had in the kitchen, though without her earlier resolve. The hope was already draining from her eyes and yet she was fighting to keep a hold of it, same as she was the dog. Killer was surging forward, dragging her a few steps ahead. Her fingers had come unlocked and as she clutched at the folds of skin on the dog's neck, Jason saw her for what she truly was: nothing but a scared little girl clinging to the last vestiges of a sanity which seemingly had no place in a world such as theirs.

A strident and altogether unexpected sensation then washed over Jason, chasing away his fear.

It was almost like the feeling he'd had a moment ago when it seemed like the future had hung in the balance. But where that had manifested as an all-consuming dread, this time he was filled with the opposite. He knew in that moment that ever since he'd first set eyes on her, everything that had happened had really only been about the two of them, three if you counted the dog. An image of her face flashed in his mind, supplanting the stark terror on it now — that look of willful defiance, so wild and fierce, that had punctuated what she'd said in the kitchen.

Catching a glimpse then of her future: Meghan lying on the ground, cradling her dead dog and him standing behind her, no idea at all of what he ought to do or say to relieve her grief.

No! A voice in his head screaming. I won't let that happen! I won't! I won't! I won't!

He was already lifting the axe in both hands over his head and striding into the field. Hearing then another voice echoing in his head — hers — so that when he spoke again it was as if their two voices had become one.

Fuck 'em, he said, fuck 'em all!

Mason heard the unmistakable *Crack!* of a rifle just as he was hanging the chainsaw on its hook in the shed.

The last time he'd heard the same, he'd been thinking about Virgil Boothe and the Balmond brothers coming to exact their revenge. Such a fright it had given him that it seemed to have channelled down through the days, startling him all over again.

Then it had just been Dale shooting off his rifle and likely it was him doing the same again now. He felt that familiar ire rising from his gut but he was feeling altogether too satisfied with the day's activity for it to sour his mood beyond a minor pang of irritation. It had felt good beyond memory seeing how everyone had pitched in. It was the kind of day which he'd hoped would never end and it was the insatiable desire to preserve that feeling which had compelled him to saw up the ash, even if it was just him and Ron by then.

That had been a mistake, there was no doubt in his mind about that now. Or rather, there was no doubt in his back and his shoulders and his knees. The former ached like someone had been using it as a pincushion and both the latter like their joints had been filled with rusty nails. While he'd trundled back from the field with the chainsaw, he'd been thinking he'd need another puff off Dale's vape if he wanted to sleep at all that night and also hoping against hope that Dale had saved him a piece of the shepherd's pie.

It was a personal favourite and he himself used to make it weekly from his mother's recipe when the kids were still at home. He'd rarely made it just for himself and Hélène and, stepping through the willows, whatever umbrage he'd felt upon hearing the rifle's *Crack!* was thus well placated by the thought that a plate of it would sure hit the spot right now. But what had really bolstered his mood was the promise of resuming his burgeoning fellowship with Ron and Dale while he ate. They really were pretty decent guys after all, they'd proved that beyond even the shadow of a doubt over the past few days. Stunned then beyond all recourse as he came into the yard and set eyes upon the scene playing out there.

The entire gang — thirty or more in all — were huddled at the edge of the field, their bodies pressed so tight together that it immediately called to mind the image of a herd under siege by a pack of wolves with the elders all grouped around the outside, protecting their young. Dale and Annie were at the fore, each sighting through the scopes on their rifles, Dale's lined on a red tent at the far south side of the field and Annie's on a matching one towards the far east. Both tents were lit from within and thrashing with a life all their own as was the closest — an orange one — less than twenty paces inside the tall grass. The only other sign of movement at all was Jason striding forward into the field, raising an axe over his head.

Two *Crack!s* then in quick succession — Annie and Dale firing off their rifles. They might as well have been starter pistols for the way they set Mason off into the yard, hollering out, What in the hell's going on over here!

Ron, apparently, was the only one who'd heard him, the only person anyway who turned Mason's way. He'd been standing beside Dale lowering his hands from over his ears as a buffer against the gunshot and was hurrying towards Mason now.

It's Euphies! he exclaimed as he cleared the edge of the group.

Euphies?

They's su-su-sssuicide Euphies!

Mason's gaze searched out the field again, trying to make any sense out of that. The two red tents which Annie and Dale had been aiming at were lying on their sides, upended when whomever they'd shot had toppled over. Jason had reached the orange tent and was hacking down at the person inside with a torrent of vicious swings of the axe.

Oh lord, no!

A sudden thought that came out sounding less like a prayer than a curse and given added exclamation by the spiralling *ticka-ticka-ticka-ticka* sounding from behind, almost like a rattlesnake shaking its tail. Ron had heard it too and both he and Mason spun in unison towards the driveway from whence it hailed.

Five figures were standing there.

Their faces were enshrouded in shadow from the gathering dusk and the darker shade cast by the closest willow's drape. Mason couldn't see much about them except the two figures standing on either side of the three in the middle appeared to be near-giants. They were verging on seven feet tall and had shaven heads and each was holding an upraised stick in one of his hands. Mason hadn't formed more than a vague impression that he'd seen such hulking beasts somewhere before when a flame blossomed from the top of what Mason now saw weren't sticks at all, but two of those holo torches. They looked just like the real thing.

The illumination radiating from each washed in reddish-orange flickers over the giants' bare chests, both painted white and their faces painted white too, except for the skeleton imprints of graven smiles etched over their mouths and chins. And yet Mason's fright at seeing such fearsome creatures didn't hold a candle to what he felt seeing Virgil Boothe and the Balmond brothers standing between them.

Rhett had shaved off his long blond locks since Mason had last seen him so the three might as well have been triplets. He was wearing a submachine gun of the Scorpion variety slung low at his belly, with his hands resting idly on its stock and barrel. His brother DB was holding a child's spinny toy in his hand — apparently what had made the rattlesnake's shake, though it might as well have come from the diamondback inked around his neck, its head rearing up on his chin, about to strike. He was even then flipping his wrist, releasing another *ticka-ticka-ticka-ticka* and that remaking the pins in Mason's back into coffin nails being hammered into his spine. But they were a mild discomfort compared to the crushing weight he felt pressing down upon him seeing the sledgehammer propped on Virgil's shoulder, and the eager and malicious squint in the elder Boothe's eyes provided Mason with a clear and resounding glimpse into his own future in which, no doubt, they'd be using it on him.

How long he stood there staring at them, he couldn't say. It might as well have been a lifetime with Mason none too eager to reach the end of that and The Sons seemingly quite content to let the suspense build towards a climax all on its own.

Or perhaps they were simply waiting for an audience.

Mason could already hear the pad of thirty-odd pairs of feet approaching from behind. How Mason wanted to turn and steal a final look at all of them, to bask in the solidarity of their fellowship one last time. But the certitude that he'd condemned them to his own fate kept his eyes fixed, resolute, on the sledgehammer.

Ron and Dale had ambled to a stop beside Mason, on his right, and Jason was on his left, holding the axe ready at his side, its blade dripping blood along its sharp edge. Meghan was beside him and Killer standing a few feet in front of her, held fast by a chain looped around his neck — the same one which Dale had used to tie Whisper up in the yard. The dog was snarling a warning about as far removed from his usual timid growl as a chipmunk's natter was from a lion's roar and it was punctuated by a rifle cocking.

That enough at last to get Mason to turn his head, if only an inch. It was Annie who'd chambered a round in the old Enfield, the weapon of choice for Canadian soldiers for much of the country's history. She was standing beside Meghan and it indeed looked like she was readying for war.

Oh, she said with a mirthful smirk, I'd sure love to shoot me another skinhead.

Such intensity in her gaze that Mason knew, right then, that she'd lost someone dear during the Euphie Riot in North Bay and also that she'd learned enough about what had happened there to know it was these five men standing in front of her who were directly to blame.

Mason at once feeling an upswelling of pride in her resolve and of the others surrounding him. He hadn't experienced such an overwhelming show of support since Mayor Dawson had pinned the chief's badge to his uniform and his entire police force had responded with a single voice, all cheering for him.

But then they'd all hung him out to dry, simply because he'd done the right thing. In the intervening years, his whole world had seemed to shrink with every passing month until finally it was reduced to just him and Hélène, their house become a mausoleum occupied by a pair of bickering ghosts and the property one vast cemetery, his only hope for any peace at all being the grave he should have dug beside his wife's when he'd had the chance.

The image of Hélène hanging from that rope in the barn coming back to him with such resolution that he felt himself swooning even as his own voice was echoing in his head — *Oh Hélène, what have you done!* — like she'd been to blame when it had been his doing all along. His own crimes, of omission and conceit, laid bare before him now in such a multitude that he knew he'd been running from them these past ten years, and never more so than when he was standing still.

His daughter's voice, dredged up from some distant and oft-neglected past, then imparting its will. Just one more thing he'd tried to forget.

I don't know why you just don't leave him.

He'd overheard her say it during the meagre two days she'd allotted for her brother's funeral, the first time she'd returned from Calgary with her husband, Guy, since she'd moved there fifteen years before. She hadn't said more than a couple words to Mason the whole time and her silence had made it plain that she blamed him for Jesse shooting himself. He'd got the sense that there was something else on her mind too and when he'd seen her following Hélène out to the barn on the morning she was set to leave, he'd snuck up on its far side so he could eavesdrop on their conversation.

It had felt like a stab in the chest, hearing their daughter say what she had, but that had been a trifle compared to the betrayal he felt hearing how his wife had answered her.

What, she'd said, and let him win? I'd just as soon dig my own grave with a teaspoon.

Her voice had carried the whimsical tone of a mother dismissing her daughter after she'd said something patently ridiculous and in the intervening years that had made it easy for Mason to disregard what Hélène had said. He saw the truth in it now. Their marriage really had been a battle of wills and he didn't have to think past the memory of Hélène hanging from the rafters to know she'd finally, and terminally, got the better of him. And when he should have heeded that one final lesson, what had he done? He might as well have been pissing on her grave, going off half-cocked, consumed with revenge like he had, as if killing Clarence Boothe might have set things to right and the measure of how wrong he'd been about that standing, right now, in front of him.

And yet, and yet . . .

If he hadn't done what he had, Meghan would be dead by now, or worse. She'd given him a reason to live and he'd done some good, at last, with the life he had left — the gang of thirty or so rallying behind him being more than ample proof of that. A paltry consideration, perhaps, with her death again — and theirs — seemingly so close at hand.

His gaze had returned to the sledgehammer propped over Virgil's shoulder but where before he'd seen in it only a future brimming with pain and suffering, he began to glean from it a little hope at last.

If The Sons had wanted to kill them all, they'd have done so by now.

No, they've come for you and you alone.

The Euphies they'd sent in as their advance guard had merely been a warning that if he didn't surrender himself of his own accord, there'd be more than hell to pay. They were telling him, without the need for any words, that they held all the power — maybe they always had — and that the only agency they'd left him at all was the choice to admit it or face the consequences. The notion that anything but acquiescence would result in another bloodbath was at last enough to break the impasse that had kept him frozen where he was.

His legs were moving forward in a herky-jerk lurch as if his body was being operated by remote control. He hadn't made two steps when he felt Ron's hand on his shoulder, holding him back. Turning to his neighbour and seeing such a mournful look in the man's eyes that it spoke to him as much of the possible future he'd lost as had finding Jesse's dead dog's collar. There was also a trace of panic on his face, found perfect expression in the tremble to his lips just now opening as if about to ask a question.

It's okay, Mason cut him off, trying to placate the other's sorrow and his fear. It's me they want. They ain't gonna bother with you. But you'll have to let me go. There ain't no other way.

Ron opened his mouth, maybe in protest, but Mason didn't give him the chance to do that either. Spinning back around, he shrugged off Ron's hand. As he walked away, the herky-jerk lurching of his first few steps evened out into the steady stride of a man who'd finally found his one true calling, even if surrendering to a bunch of vermin like The Sons went against everything he'd ever believed in.

The vindictive smile blossoming on Virgil's lips only spurred him in his resolve. His pace never slackening and yet it feeling like he was moving in slow motion so the few seconds it took him to reach the five men eagerly awaiting him in the driveway seemed to stretch into the eternal, as if the universe itself couldn't stand to watch such a horror and was prolonging the moment as long as it could.

DB and Rhett were parting ways to let him through. The moment he had, DB slung his arms around Mason's shoulders, giving him a squeeze.

Boy, he said with the exuberance of a man greeting a long-lost brother instead of a mortal enemy, ain't you a sight for sore eyes. We's goin' to have so much fuuun . . .

Within the light cast by the torches, the driveway beyond appeared to be encased in a shadow seemingly without end. It was beckoning Mason towards a future no less dim, merely another road to hell paved with his good intentions, and as he passed from the light into the dark, all too complete, Hélène's voice was echoing in his head all over again.

Well don't act so surprised, she was admonishing with startled chagrin, an all-too-common refrain. *Didn't your mama ever teach ya, you can only ever reap what you have sown?*

HELENE AND MASON,
TOGETHER AGAIN

R on was standing a few feet back from the memory stone, appraising what he'd written and thinking it was pretty fitting when Dale, as he so often did, raised his voice, trying to prove him wrong.

I'd imagine, he said, they's ain't together quite yet.

Well they's both dead, ain't they?

Oh I doubt that. I mean, you heard what that one Son said, didn't ya?

Ron had but didn't feel the need to speak, or even think, about it now.

Dale, though, seemed to be revelling in it.

I imagine they'll be keeping the chief alive for some time, torturing him and whatnot. Hell, they'll probably keep him alive for at least another week.

He was smiling in his cavalier way, as if thinking things couldn't have worked out better. Even Ron had to admit he was probably right, for the time being anyway.

You think we've seen the last of them? Ron asked, thinking about that. The Sons, I mean.

Oh, I'd imagine they've got bigger fish to fry than little ol' us.

A comforting sentiment that didn't do much to ease the lump Ron felt building in his throat looking again upon the chief's name etched in stone next to his wife's. Originally, he'd thought about scratching CHIEF but the moment he'd touched the hook-bladed knife to the rock he'd known it'd have to be MASON. So that's what he'd etched. Gazing upon it now, the name reminded him of something else.

You know, he never did know my real name, he said with such solemnity that it sounded like he couldn't have imagined anything worse. Then pushing past the lump with his voice cracking: He was always calling me Clee-Clee-Cleee—

By then the lump was threatening to turn into something else and Ron clamped his mouth, fighting against the urge to cry for he'd promised himself that he'd never shed a single tear, not for the chief.

All right, Dale was then saying, give me that knife. I'll see if I can't find a spot somewhere for Whisper.

After The Sons had left with the chief, Dale had carried the dog back from the field and everyone had gathered round to give her one final pat. Matty, the boy she'd saved, was the last. After he hugged Whisper around the neck and kissed the side of her snout, he'd asked Dale if it was all right if he kept her collar.

Tears were streaming down Dale's cheeks, as much out of

sorrow as joy for how everyone had rallied around his daughter's dog, and his voice cracked when he replied, I think she'd have liked that just fine.

Matty strung it around his own neck and after that there was only the matter of where they might lay her to rest. It was Jason who'd suggested they bury her beside his mom.

She always did want a dog, he'd explained, but the co-op didn't allow it. Nice to think at least one of her wishes might finally come true.

So Dale had dug a hole beside Marnie's and while he was covering Whisper up, Meghan had let out a yawn so wide it seemed to have been put on.

Well, I don't know 'bout y'all, but I'm 'bout ready fer bed.

Turning towards the willows, she made to set off for the chief's house. Practically everyone else was looking towards the tents in the field with doleful expressions and she seemed to have gleaned their reluctance about spending another night out there, after what had happened.

There's plenty of room in the house, she'd said turning back, if anyone wants to join me.

Her tone was enlivened with such alacrity that in that moment she sounded just like any teenage girl might have inviting her friends over for a party while her parents were out, though while she spoke her eyes were fixed resolutely on Jason and there was no doubt in Ron's mind that she was really only speaking to him.

Regardless, the entire troupe had marched off towards the willows with her in the lead and Killer on one side and Jason on the other. She'd wrapped her arm around his back and was leaning her head into his side and the image of Jason reciprocating by wrapping his own arm around her and giving her shoulder an affectionate squeeze had been plenty to send Ron off to his own bed with a smile upon his face.

He hadn't heard a peep from next door since he'd awoken a half-hour ago but he could hear the first stirrings of life now — a door slamming shut followed by Killer letting out a brazen *Woof!*

What he was barking at became immediately clear. A jack-rabbit was even then bounding out from within the willows, weaving in a zig-zagging hop into the yard with the dog chasing after it in eager pursuit and Meghan's voice ringing out, Killer, get back here!

The rabbit shortly disappeared into the tall grass on the far side of the shed. Killer chased it right to the fringe and held up there, reluctant to go any further. He was peering past the timothy grass, flinching as a grasshopper flittered past his nose and letting out another *Woof!* to tell it what he thought of that.

Killer, get over here!

Meghan stood on just this side of the willows, looking as much like a woman scorned as Ron had ever seen. Killer responded by turning tail and slinking towards her, all the while casting Ron a series of furtive glances as he made his way across the lawn, pleading, it seemed, for some sort of a reprieve.

You keep running off, Meghan said as she strung Whisper's old lead around his neck, I'm going to have to tie you up. Oh yes I will.

Looking up then, seeming to catch her first glimpse of Ron looking at her.

If you's interested, she called out, affecting the lilt of a country girl born and bred, we's fixing to whip up a whole mess of pancakes.

Pancakes! This from Dale, now stepping up beside Ron. Boy, I sure do love pancakes!

And there'll be scrambled eggs too, fresh from the hens.

Turning back to the willows then, she beckoned them to follow with a sweep of her hand.

Y'alls are more'n welcome to join us.

C ows!
   Ron and Dale were leaning against the open tailgate on the chief's truck, finishing their breakfast, when Darren shouted it out.

Looking down the driveway they could see a whole herd of them coming up the road their way. The neighbour's son, wearing a cowboy hat and riding a horse, was corralling them from behind and everyone gathered in front of the chief's house was watching them advance with ever-widening eyes. Killer was barking up a storm on the end of the chain Meghan had tied to a porch rail and otherwise Jason was the only one who seemed to have anything to say about them.

I'll get the gate! he called out, turning towards the barn with Ron watching after him, as proud as any father for how quickly the young lad had taken charge.

I guess she likes cowboys even more than Indians, Eric was then saying to Darren with the mirthful reproach of an older brother revelling in his younger's latest folly.

They were both leaning on the side of the truck and Darren was staring forlorn over at Annie, leaning against the porch, for the way she was gazing with such unbridled longing at the young man in the saddle.

But it wasn't him she was looking at after all.

Oh, Annie crooned, I just got to get me a horse!

At that, Meghan standing beside her, set off with a virulent stride, calling out, Hey mister, how much you want for that horse?

The young cowboy responded by sneering down at her and calling back, Oh this horse, she ain't for sale.

You wanna bet!

From the look of willful defiance on her face, that would have been a fool's wager at best. She'd come to the rider and was following along beside him, apparently haggling over a price. The cows had reached the gate leading into the back pasture when the cowboy pushed his hat back on his head with dramatic flair, shaking his head as if insulted by her offer.

Well shoot, girl, he admonished, expressing quite the opposite, you could buy four horses for that!

Ron watched the scene unfold thinking about the bag of money he'd helped move on the night Meghan had arrived and her apparent generosity with it went a good way to easing his mind regarding any and all possible futures in store for the lot of them.

What the hell are we supposed to do with a bunch of cows? Dale then scoffed.

Ron responded by turning to the group trailing after the herd and hollering out, Anybody know anything about cows?

Masood, walking in the rear with one hand in the back pocket of Kendra's jeans and her hand in the back pocket of his, swivelled his head around and shouted back, My uncle had goats!

Your uncle, you say. Where was this?

A village in Kurdistan.

Ron pondered on that a moment and then called back:

They milk goats there in Kurdistan?

Yah, Masood answered back with undeniable pride.

All right then, you're in charge of the cows!

It appeared nothing could have made Masood happier. His lips curled into a smile that was in danger of swallowing his whole face and he grabbed at Kendra's hand, pulling her with quickening steps after the receding herd and yelling out, Ron said I'm in charge of the cows!

That was quick thinking, Dale said, giving Ron a nudge with his arm.

I do have my moments.

It seemed cause enough for celebration and his thoughts were already drifting towards his chute.

A few short moments later he was sitting in his chair on the patio, reaching for the two-litre pop bottle with its bottom cut out. Dale was sitting across from him, holding his ear to his phone, and saying, Hey there Babygirl. I'm afraid I have some bad news . . .

Sitting there huffing a chute and smoking a cigarette, he listened to Dale tell his daughter about what had happened to Whisper. By the end of it, both of them were crying as much from pride at what she'd done as from her loss.

How'd she take it? Ron asked after Dale had signed off with his usual, You be sure to mind your mother, now ya hear?

She was pretty upset, Dale answered, rubbing his hand over his face, to wipe away the remaining wetness on his cheeks. But she's already planning for the next. As luck would have it, her friend's dog just had pups, said they's just giving 'em away.

It ain't a husky, is it?

Oh god, I sure hope not. Be nice to have a dog you don't need to chain up, for once.

You're telling me.

Both of them then lighting a smoke thinking on that and Dale remembering something on his first exhale.

You ever tell the chief his daughter called Val? he asked and Ron's expression blanched.

Oh shoot, he said. I forgot.

It seemed a small thing really but it had that old dread creeping up into his belly, thinking it was the least he could have done.

Well you know how these things go, Dale answered with his characteristic aloof. There's always bound to be a few loose ends. Then because he knew Ron all too well, he added: I wouldn't beat yourself up too much over it.

Sensible advice, for sure, but still Ron was reaching for his phone, thinking he ought to at least text Val, to give her the bad news.

He'd been staring at the screen for a few seconds, trying to figure out what he might write, and was given a short reprieve in his deliberations by Jason stepping through the willows.

He had such a look of dire concern on his face that it had Ron wondering to himself, *Oh lord, what's happened now?*

Andrew says we're in need of a whole heap of supplies, if we want to keep a dozen cows, Jason said stepping onto the patio. Buckets and feed and milking machines, whatnot. Said we can get most of it at the feed store in Mattawa. Thought maybe I could take the chief's truck?

The latter came out sounding like a question but before Ron could answer with, Say that's a good idea, Dale beat him to the punch.

I don't know if that's a good idea, he countered. Best not to draw any undue attention to ourselves. Better if you take Eric's van.

Jason nodded all solemn at that and Ron chimed in, I'll go with ya.

I'd appreciate it.

Give me a few minutes?

Whenever you're ready.

Turning then back towards the willow, Jason strode off with a confidence in his gait that was at stark odds with the awkward shuffle he usually ambled about with. Just one more thing to celebrate and Ron was already reaching for his chute to do just that.

You planning on paying for all those supplies yourself? Dale asked while Ron packed the bowl.

Won't need to, Ron answered. Meghan brought a duffel bag full of money with her.

A duffel bag full of money?

Must have stole it from The Sons.

You don't say.

How do you think the chief bought all them cows?

Boy, that girl, she sure is full of surprises, ain't she?

You can say that again.

Dale was stretching his arms above his head high enough that his shoulders cracked.

Well, it's looking to be another busy day, he said. I guess we should get back to it.

Ron was even then lighting the herb and drawing its silky smoke down into the bag.

A chute to start things off right, he said, offering it first to Dale, as he so often did.

Truth be told, Dale would much rather have had a hit off his vape but he knew how much the other liked sharing a puff and it seemed a minor concession, especially for a friend like Ron. He was already leaning forward with his hand outstretched and enthusing with genuine ardor,

Ah hell . . . Don't mind if I do!

With Special Thanks To

Ron, for the idea
Dale, for the stories
Whisper, for the chase
Jason, for the comedy
&
Jill, Guy, Eric, Duane, Val, Murray, Mike
Samir, Craig, Masood, Darren, Kendra
&
Jacob Shulman

And To

Denis, Barry, John and everyone else at Conspiracy of 3
Craig Beattie, Kyle Richardson & Rob Jackson
Les Edgerton, J. Todd Scott, David Swinson,
Waub Rice, Wayne Grady, Lawrence Scanlan
Nicholas Ruddock, Stephen Henighan, Dietrich Kalteis,
Rebecca Kramer, Graeme McGaw, Matthew Del Papa
&
CW, for a little bit of "Dixie"

To All The Fine Folks at ECW
Jack David, Emily Schultz, David Caron, Peter Norman,
Michel Vrana, Samantha Chin, Claire Pokorchak, David Marsh
Thanks will never be enough

To Tiphaine Girault, at the Canada Council for the Arts
Who proved it is possible

&
To Tanja, Anyk, Kai & Drake
For the journey

This book is also available as a Global Certified Accessible™ (GCA) ebook. ECW Press's ebooks are screen reader friendly and are built to meet the needs of those who are unable to read standard print due to blindness, low vision, dyslexia, or a physical disability.

At ECW Press, we want you to enjoy our books in whatever format you like. If you've bought a print copy just send an email to ebook@ecwpress.com and include:

Get the ebook free!*
*proof of purchase required

- the book title
- the name of the store where you purchased it
- a screenshot or picture of your order/receipt number and your name
- your preference of file type: PDF (for desktop reading), ePub (for a phone/tablet, Kobo, or Nook), mobi (for Kindle)

A real person will respond to your email with your ebook attached. Please note this offer is only for copies bought for personal use and does not apply to school or library copies.

Thank you for supporting an independently owned Canadian publisher with your purchase!